Assessment
SPECIAL

A Novel by

Marvin J. Nodiff

Community Associations Press
Alexandria, VA

Special Assessment is a work of fiction. The events, characters, and places are imaginary. Any similarities between this story and reality are entirely coincidental.

ISBN: 0-944715-67-2
Special Assessment
All rights reserved.
Copyright 2002 by Community Associations Press, a division of Community Associations Institute.
No part of this publication may be reproduced in whole or in part without the express, written consent of the publisher.

Community Associations Press, 225 Reinekers Lane, Suite 300, Alexandria, VA 22314.

Printed in the United States of America

To order additional copies of this product, please write to the publisher at the address above or call (703) 548-8600. You can also order online at *www.caionline.org/bookstore.cfm*.

Library of Congress Cataloging-in-Publication Data
Nodiff, Marvin J.
  Special assessment : a novel / by Marvin J. Nodiff.
    p. cm.
  ISBN 0-944715-67-2
  I. Title.
  PS3614.O37 S64 2002
  813'.6—dc21
                                         2002002538

I WANT TO THANK all the people who encouraged and helped with this novel. First, this novel would not have been possible without the intriguing individuals I have encountered over the years. For your unwitting contributions to my learning and the background for this story, I am grateful.

Linda and Monica, my wife and stepdaughter, respectively, you have my deep appreciation for always being supportive and serving as a sounding board against which I could bounce bizarre ideas. For Rose Beckham, my assistant, many thanks for your loyalty and patience as this work evolved over four years. Thanks to Cissy Lacks who edited my work with honesty and trust. Last, I am grateful to Debra Lewin for her keen eye for polishing my writing and to Community Associations Press for believing in *Special Assessment* and supporting its publication.

Marvin J. Nodiff
January 2002

Author's Note

"Nothing so needs reforming as other people's habits."
—Mark Twain

AMERICANS ARE IN LOVE with the exercise of democracy. But, like any worthy love affair, it requires high maintenance and has its moments of doubt, disappointment, and great pain.

Special Assessment explores our love affair with democracy at its most intimate level, the community association, where elected leaders are largely untrained, unpaid, and unpredictable. Life in the association is a curious mixture of volatility and apathy, of common interest and self-interest, of noble aspirations and hidden agendas. This story is a work of fiction and fun although the reader may find a nugget of truth here and there.

1

Wearing latex gloves at the keyboard was a tedious affair. He was not a proficient typist, but word processing was not a skill he would need tonight. All that counted tonight was his keen knowledge of computers as he hacked his way into the sophisticated software.

The glow from the monitor reflected like a veil of gauze on his face, casting murky shadows that disguised his features, yet even the shadows revealed a man deeply absorbed in his work. Hunched over the keyboard, right hand scooting and clicking the mouse, he patiently and meticulously called up the financial ledgers of one account after another.

Other than the light from the computer monitor, the offices of Preferred Site Management—or just PSM, as it was usually called—were totally dark. And they were totally quiet, except for the muted tap-tapping of the keyboard and the soft hum and gurgling of the fifty-gallon aquarium in the lobby. With the air conditioning turned off for the night, the offices were hot and stuffy, and he was sweating uncomfortably. A few more files, and he would be finished.

He had been to PSM's office many times before, although never at night and never when all the staff were gone. During his frequent visits, the owners of PSM, Mac and Michelle, had come to rely on him for information technology. He knew that the owners also used other technicians, but he had applied his clever knack for engaging conversation to foster a growing friendship with the receptionist, Jennifer Hiscock, trying hard to develop a special relationship. Jenni was a bit older than he, probably in her late thirties, he guessed, divorced and good looking, although she fretted needlessly about carrying a few extra pounds. She found him an attractive alternative to working the phones, which were incessantly ringing. Between phone calls Jenni would carry on a nonstop dialogue with him. She liked him, and told him more than once, "We have the sort of bond that only kindred spirits could forge."

Jenni was a great storyteller. She had the rare ability to tell long, multi-layered stories, full of rich embellishment and colorful description, despite being interrupted countless times by the phone. Yet, she would never lose her place in the narration, which caused him to wonder whether this was an acquired skill or a natural gift. They compared disaster stories about their respective divorces, new movies, the best rib joints in town, her beau-of-the-month club, and all the crank and cranky calls that came in to PSM. Four years after her divorce, she was still recounting horror stories about her ex-husband, unaffectionately referred to as "the shit."

He wouldn't need to expend much of his charm to engage Jenni in a relationship. She was an extrovert, unabashedly talkative, and refreshingly candid. She'd probably reveal her bra size, if he were bold enough to inquire.

On one recent visit, he stood in front of the huge aquarium for a long time studying the tropical fish. Jenni read his interest as an invitation to start another marathon monologue and wheeled from behind her desk, revealing the shortest of skirts and a pair of shapely, well-tanned legs. She stood next to the tank, pointing as if it were an exhibit, posing as if she were a model for the latest women's summer wear. She described the rare tropical fish and how the tank operated. He couldn't help but admire the ebb and flow of her breasts as she demonstrated how the twin pumps worked.

Some Sunday he should take Jenni to the zoo's aquarium in Forest Park, followed by lunch at Le Café des Arts at the art museum. We could see the great white shark, he thought, and then dine on crepes Newburg or sautéed salmon, with fresh endive, washed down by a decent pinot. It would be a no-pressure, no-big-deal date. But, it would have to wait until he had some real money.

It wasn't nearly as hard as he had thought to get into the offices after hours. He knew from his frequent visits that PSM was protected by a state-of-the-art alarm, installed at the same time they had upgraded the accounting software system last year. The sophisticated new system had email links with clients, electronic bank transfers, and automatic "real time" updating. All the bells and whistles. The upgrades only made his task easier, except for the new security measures.

The control panel for the new security system was located in the interior corridor, not visible from the reception area. Jenni confirmed this. "At the same time as we got the new computers," she had told him, "PSM installed a new security system, with motion detectors throughout the suite and contacts on the front and rear doors, and all windows, that would activate unless you entered the code within thirty seconds. We barely have enough petty cash on hand to get carry-out at Freddy's, but we have an alarm system that would be the envy of Fort Knox." Freddy's was the all-night coffee shop at the end of the strip mall.

All he needed was the code to disarm the system, and this proved to be surprisingly easy. Early one morning he waited outside for Jenni to arrive. Then, he walked around with Jenni and distracted her with mindless conversation while she opened the office. As she entered the code in the numeric control panel, he peeked over her shoulder and memorized the seven magic numbers.

He knew that once he got into the offices it was out of the question to turn on the lights or even use a flashlight. Yet, he didn't want to trip over a chair mat or any wiring that ran across the floor, or disturb even a leaf on the ficus tree that had overgrown the lobby and was threatening to push the ceiling tiles into the second floor. So, he had prepared a scale drawing of PSM's offices, a work of art, indeed, depicting the location and dimension of every piece of furniture, file cabinet, and pencil holder. Four colors were used to make the drawing fit his special needs: red for furniture to avoid, green for computers (*and money*, he thought), yellow for the corridors and passageways he would use, and black for everything else. He had studied the drawing twice a day until he could reconstruct the entire layout from memory. Some of his friends called him anal, but he preferred to say, "when meaning matters, I get down to detail."

Still, other problems had confronted him, like the deadbolt lock in the front door. To assist him, he had looked up Vincent "the Bug" Buggieri, who, with his younger and dimmer brother, Ernie, practiced a variety of vocations. The brothers Buggieri referred to themselves as versatile capital venturers who had given new definition to the term "opportunistic." Months ago he had helped them on their tax concerns, suggesting a variety of creative techniques to play hide-the-ball with the IRS to protect the brothers' outrageous cash-producing transactions.

The brothers Buggieri went to tax sales like some people go to yard sales. They had made a science—and a killing—out of buying remnant properties at back-tax sales, then "selling" them back to the original owner. Among their more notorious acquisitions was the swimming pool of an upscale condominium complex in the fashionable west end, and the parking lot of an apartment across from Forest Park. The residents soon learned of their situation when they were charged exorbitant fees to use the amenities they previously thought they owned. In a city that had more than its share of legends in the gray underbelly of society, it was difficult for minor players to gain much notoriety. Yet, the brothers Buggieri achieved such legendary status when they bought a long forgotten ten-foot wide strip of land for a grand total of $257.78 in back taxes and late fees. Then they sent a certified notice to the owner, a global chemical operation, ordering the company off the Buggieris' property. Of course, the company wasn't about to budge because this narrow strip ran directly under the middle of their plant. The company's staff attorneys, dressed in their nine hundred dollar suits, stormed into the Buggieris' grungy office, alternately huffing, bluffing, and hurling allegations wrapped in Latin phrases, seasoned with threats of costly legal action. At the end of the day, however, the fancy attorneys settled the matter with a briefcase filled with cash, grateful to hold the robbery to one hundred thousand dollars.

The tax concern facing the brothers Buggieri was that their new Cadillacs, the cases of Pinch, box seats at the Dome, and other favors to various city officials, couldn't be written off against the modest office in the backroom of a storefront on South Broadway. Vinnie Buggieri invited him to a meeting. After a leisurely dinner of cavatelli and two bottles of Ricasoli chianti with Vinnie and Ernie at Pisano's on the Hill, he drew up a plan for a legitimate business.

The brothers Buggieri quietly renovated the storefront and opened a used furniture shop, with no advertising and only a dozen or so assorted armoires, desks, and tables. They would boast that their LaSalle Antique Trading Company could locate any specialty piece requested by a preferred customer. At the same time, a select collection of phantom antiques moved invisibly through the store, leaving nothing more than a paper trail. While not financially successful by any CPA's definition, the LaSalle Antique Trading Company allowed the Buggieris to recycle old furniture and dirty money at the same time. It was then that Vinnie the Bug began calling his friend the Consultant. It was a term bestowed with honor and endearment.

The brothers Buggieri loved their new business arrangements and remembered the Consultant last Christmas with a case of Chianti Classico Riserva. But, he had no doubt they knew the consulting was strictly on a barter basis, and that they owed him an appropriate, unnamed favor. Helping him at PSM was a payback they would gladly accommodate.

Vinnie the Bug paid a visit to PSM's offices and discreetly checked out the hardware on the front door. Afterward, he immediately purchased an identical deadbolt lock. Professor Bug then conducted an advanced course in the fine art of lock picking for only one student. The final exam was to perform a clean pick, blindfolded, in under ten seconds.

No one was quite sure how Vinnie the Bug had earned his nickname. Acquaintances assumed it was merely shorthand for Buggieri. Some of his childhood friends insisted the moniker came from his stature—an oversized head on top of a rotund belly, separated by a thin neck. His contemporaries, however, who insisted on anonymity, contended it derived from his special expertise in the applied electronic sciences. Among his other skills, the Bug was a self-taught electronics expert, with subspecialties in surveillance devices and telecommunications systems. Vinnie could have been licensed if he ever wanted to go legit, but for a certain question on the application that asked whether the applicant had any felony convictions.

Coaxing the entry code from Jenni and learning how to pick a lock from Vinnie were comparatively easy. The centerpiece of his scheme was highly confidential, and the Consultant was careful not to share it with anyone, even Vinnie. As is often the case for those who daily search for ways to penetrate software programs, the Consultant, somewhat by accident, had discovered a security gap in the software of Master Bookkeeper, a popular program used for financial management and administration. It was the software program of choice for millions of computer users, including PSM.

He had devoted himself to finding a way to transfer electronic data, or edata, as he called it. After months of tinkering with the Master Bookkeeper software, he had discovered that the key to gaining access was to inject a special program into the user's web browser. It would hide there, unnoticed, until the user initiated a banking transaction. Then it would pad noiselessly around the user's software on its tiny cyber feet until it found Master Bookkeeper, where it would take over at the controls of the host software and await further instructions.

The fruits of all his detailed plans were now glowing on the computer monitor, and he allowed himself a moment to applaud his own genius. *A clever or malicious little program*, he thought. *Malicious or clever?* He couldn't decide which he liked better.

He forced himself to concentrate on reviewing the last few files. It had taken almost three hours, but he had scrolled through all of PSM's accounts. He studied the dollar amounts spread across the screen in neat columns, headed by the designated account numbers. A wide smile parted his lips.

PSM was well respected for its expertise and track record in the field of managing community associations. Their reputation had yielded an impressive portfolio of association clients. The Consultant's research on the Internet, where he had located data on a nationwide basis, had indicated that large community associations—mostly upscale condominium associations and large mixed-use planned communities—had *huge* sums of money, *real* money, squirreled away in what the industry called "reserve funds." It was the kind of money that would propel an instant change in lifestyle, the kind of money that only the lottery, or a bank robbery, or the death of a rich uncle would produce in a person's lifetime.

Now, at the PSM offices, conveniently pre-assembled under the electronic roof of a single computer system, was the mother sow of all piggy banks. He was so elated, so ecstatic, that his fingers trembled and jiggled on the keyboard. It was beyond his fondest expectations, his wildest wet dreams of wealth, to find several associations with over half a million dollars each. Yet, there they were—the dollar signs, digits, and decimals that comprised the American vocabulary of wealth, winking and blinking back at him in the soft glow of the monitor, and reflecting on his pale cheeks and in his green eyes. This cash cow was ready to be milked.

The Consultant didn't want to leave any indication of his visit, so he decided against printing hard copies of the accounts. Instead, he jotted all the account numbers in his pocket-sized memo book. He filled the first page, and turned now to the second page. In a parallel column was the amount of reserve funds in each of the accounts. He added the amounts on the first page and carried the total onto the second page, and continued down the column. The total was over five million dollars. *Not a bad night's work, indeed.*

He pulled a disk from his shirt pocket and fondled it lovingly. *Clever or grossly malicious? Malicious or merely clever?* He kissed it gently and whispered, "With the power and authority vested in me as your humble master, I hereby christen thee 'Special Assessment.' Now, sleep well, my darling little applet, I'll be in touch soon." Then he inserted the disk and clicked Enter to launch the program.

The next time that PSM used Master Bookkeeper for a bank transfer, the applet would signal the Consultant's computer. He could go home and monitor PSM's activities. But first, he would need a special bank account.

He clicked out of the individual accounts, and returned to the screen saver. *Done, finished, mission accomplished!*

He squinted at his watch and saw that it was four o'clock in the morning. He stretched his arms above his head, then stood and carefully restored the chair, keyboard, and mouse to the exact positions in which he had found them. Gingerly, he touched and felt his way through the offices until he reached the lobby, where he paused to do a final review of his mental checklist. All programs on the computer had been closed, and the monitor returned to the screen saver. He hadn't turned on any lights, so there was none to turn off. He patted his shirt pocket to make sure he had the applet disk and his memo pad. He reminded himself to lock the deadbolt when he left. *What else?* There was nothing else that he could think of. Yet, something nagged him. *What am I forgetting?*

He was stretched tight with tension, and nothing else came to mind. His face and clothes were soaked with sweat. He was eager to leave.

From inside the lobby, he peered cautiously through the blinds into the shadowy parking lot. No sight of any security patrols. No cars driving around. It was early Monday morning, and the sun would be rising in an hour or so. It would be another steamy July day in St. Louis.

He was exhausted, hot, and sweaty—yet, ecstatic and wild with anticipation and excitement. *Clever or malicious? Malicious or clever?* He quietly walked outside, locked the deadbolt, and slipped unseen into the shadows of the parking lot.

2

"There are over two hundred thirty thousand community associations in the United States today, compared to ten thousand in 1970. Nearly one out of every six Americans lives in some form of common interest community governed by a community association," the female speaker paused for effect to let the numbers be absorbed by the huge audience seated in the ballroom. "Even so, in America, we know more about building houses than building communities.

"All of us in the industry face the problem of unruly, obstreperous owners. Some of these disruptive owners are like children, constantly challenging the authority of their parent figure, the governing boards. Others just want to be recognized. To meet these challenges, we must foster a more reasonable approach to governance, and put community first. Thank you very much." Flashing an engaging smile, Angela Laclede brushed aside a wisp of wavy chestnut hair and reached for the glass of water next to the podium. Instantly, hands in the audience began bobbing above heads, seeking recognition by the keynote speaker, an attorney whose expertise and successful practice were in community association law.

It was ten-thirty Monday morning in London, the opening session of the Global Conference on Community

Associations. The ballroom of the hotel was brimming with managers, attorneys, accountants, insurers, bankers, association leaders, and a wide variety of consultants and other professionals involved in the industry who were eager to bring their expertise to the exploding market of Europe.

The exhibit hall featured dozens of booths, where companies promoted every niche of the marketplace for condominiums, planned communities, and cooperatives—from computer bookkeeping software for assessments and do-it-yourself packages for reserves, to insurance, security systems, the newest methods for termite control, and materials for nonskid pool decks.

"*Da*, Natasha?" said Angela, acknowledging the manager from Russia seated in the second row. Natasha Semenkov, a stunningly beautiful woman with high cheekbones, coal-black hair and dark eyes to match, stood at her seat. "Miss Laclede," she began through an interpreter, "our housing is so old, the plumbing and everything is constantly breaking down, and we can't possibly keep up with the maintenance problems. What do we tell our members who now own their homes for the first time in their lives?"

Angela considered the question carefully and thought about how she could respond in simple words to make it easier to translate. "Like your situation in Moscow, we also have plenty of older housing in the States," she began with deliberation, organizing her thoughts. Angela had that rare combination of experience, knowledge, and a disciplined mind that allowed her to create mental outlines of multiple concepts.

"There are four main points to pursue, Natasha," Angela said, warming up to the issues. "First, you must make sure the governing documents are clear. Each owner must know what he or she is responsible for. Second, you must train the owners on how to maintain their property.

Third, for the long term, you should start building reserves. In the States, our associations have a combined total of eighteen billion dollars in reserves. We collect over twenty-four billion dollars in assessments annually. If our assets were combined into a single business, we would lead the Fortune 500. Last, you should seek partnerships with American developers to build new and affordable housing in Russia."

"*Spaciba, mil grazie, merci,* thank you very much. *Das vidanya, ciao, abiento* and *ta-ta,* everybody, and enjoy the rest of the conference," Angela said, exhausting most of her foreign vocabulary in one fractured phrase. She removed the lapel microphone from her blue business suit and waved as she strode off the platform. Everyone applauded with appreciation.

Angela hoped no one would trap her with more questions as she walked briskly toward the mahogany paneled coffee shop of the historic Black's Hotel. Her body still hadn't recovered from the sleepless, nonstop flight from St. Louis to London. She glanced at her watch and realized she should be asleep. It was still four-thirty in the morning on her biological clock. Next trip, she thought, there must be a stopover, but where? Iceland? She sat alone and ordered a cappuccino. Studying the conference brochure, she confirmed that her presence wouldn't be required at any of the sessions, and the evening reception was optional.

Angela Laclede made an adequate, if not spectacular, living through her law practice. It was mostly grind-it-out, hourly work. Her days were full of demands for instant answers to complex legal questions, which invariably were presented on the phone by community managers, many of whom seemed to reject the concept of a calendar as an unnecessary inconvenience that simply added another time-consuming burden onto their busy day. They predictably called an hour before the monthly board meeting, with a typical introduction, "I know this is a dumb question, but I'm sure it has a simple answer, and it will just take a minute, so the board wanted me to ask…" It was almost as bad as the bar exam, where law school grads with sweaty pits were called on to respond to sixty questions on constitutional law in sixty minutes.

Her evenings were full of board and association meetings that were always too long. But, no client was too far away to be served. Grateful that she didn't live in a community association herself, Angela often wondered why some people ran, and actually campaigned, for a seat on their board. The position seemed like such a thankless job, a combination of owning a small business, sitting on a city council, and being a judge and a police officer, all rolled into one. But, the politician's hat fit best. Board members, regardless of their backgrounds, soon became skilled at dodging and weaving, evading tough decisions, and leaving assessment increases to the next board.

Most of practicing community association law was not about the law. It was about people. In particular, board members who served as unpaid, untrained volunteers whose motivations ranged from taking a turn at respectable civic duty to an unblemished grab for power. Requests for assistance from board members encompassed everything from the noble to the nefarious, often embroiling the unwary attorney in bitter internal board battles or a bloody coup d'etat aimed at deposing perceived enemies and casting them into ostracism within the community or hurtling them into exile. Some dethroned leaders couldn't endure the humiliation. They usually elected to leave the community, vowing they would never again get involved in association politics. Angela wrote the dean at her old alma mater, St. Pius University School of Law, to suggest that classes in psychology and group dynamics be added to the curriculum.

St. Pius was a private Jesuit school reputed as a hardworking, blue-collar law school that was not distinguished for producing legal scholars. When Angela graduated, she had faced a difficult challenge in finding a position. The overworked expression around the law school was that A students made good law professors, B students made good judges, and C students made successful practitioners. Angela resigned herself to the last category.

Angela found that there were five law school grads competing for each job opening. She had no connections that could open doors in the large law firms—the only places that recruited and advertised for entry-level positions. It took nine months of groveling, but she finally landed an associate position with the general counsel of a large builder-developer. After only two years she grew weary of handholding disgruntled homebuyers, applying gloss over shoddy workmanship, and apologizing for hollow warranties.

She promised herself that she would never again prepare a resume or interview for a job. With more determination than money, she opened a one-woman law office in a loft building in Midtown in the theater and arts district of Grand Centre. And there was room to expand, since she was the sole occupant of the entire fourth floor of the converted warehouse. The lofts on the lower floors were occupied by young artists who could live and create their art in the same space. They were fun to be around, but were not a good source of referrals.

In launching her new practice, Angela mailed notices to a list of associations she obtained from the assessor's office in the city and each of the suburban counties. A tiny trickle of calls started, and she avoided starving that first year.

She read every book and article on community association law and every leading case from across the country. Angela was successful because she outworked, overprepared, and outsmarted her opponents. Some opposing attorneys failed because they approached legal issues in community association law from a simplistic view, only to be overwhelmed and outflanked by the complexities and nuances commanded by Angela. Other opponents simply lost their way in the noxious swamps of this specialty.

Angela Laclede was generally well respected in the legal community for her thoroughness in working up a case, although she was quietly despised by a loosely-knit group of developer attorneys who thought she was too serious and vengeful, and called her Angry Angie behind her back. They would sit and strain for a new defense in each case, as if their steady diet of developer stew, simmering unattended in ancient boilerplate language, had rendered them mentally constipated. In fact, they hadn't passed an original legal thought in the last ten years. Angela rarely missed an opportunity to give them a legal enema.

She gradually gained unique stature around the courthouse in the narrow niche of community association law. When the judges saw her in the courtroom, they knew she had a condo or planned community case and that she would be prepared with the law. Her signature in the courthouse was a blue and white lapel button that read, I SPEAK CONDO.

Street smart and not always polite, Angela was pleased with what she had accomplished, but she never rested, always looking for a new challenge and a higher plateau. After a few years she added an associate, Joshua Fyler, to share the litigation work, and he became a junior partner. Joshua was thirty-two, a graduate of a highly respected private law school in Chicago. He didn't have Angela's street instincts, but he was hard as an anvil beneath a calm exterior and loved to be on his feet in the courtroom.

Angela and Joshua complemented each other. She could stir the jury's passion. He was coldly objective. She worked like a jackhammer. He was a slow-turning drill. She sold the sizzle. He was the steak.

The Law Offices of Angela Laclede continued to grow, adding two law students and paralegal staff. She plowed her profits into the latest computers, Internet and CD ROMs, and modems to link her home with the office and her legal assistant, B.J. Page. The practice gradually grew over the years and now counted over four hundred community association clients throughout the city and surrounding counties and as far south as the Arkansas border.

She pushed the staff relentlessly, and they both loved and feared Angela the Great. But, she pushed herself harder than anyone else. Building her practice with satisfied clients was Angela Laclede's way of having fun, a substitute benefit for a love life that was remarkably unsuccessful. Angela lacked a significant other, a continuing irritant that had reached the point where any sort of fling with a member of the opposite sex would be welcome.

Sipping her cappuccino and reviewing the brochure again, Angela wondered if she should attend the breakout session on privatization in Eastern Europe. These sessions always had great shoptalk, and maybe she could make a contact or two. Yet, she was too fatigued from the long flight to sit through the sessions, and the rush of adrenalin that had boosted her through the speech had dissipated. This day must be balanced by something that combined the absence of stress with instant gratification. And, something worthy, like bolstering the British economy.

When Philip Palmer suddenly appeared at her table, she knew she had found her diversion. Although she hadn't seen Philip in six months, they chatted as if they had just left each other a few hours before. He whispered an invitation in

Angela's ear, and soon both were strolling down the mosaic floors, past the marble columns, and through the revolving door of the hotel. The July London air was refreshingly clear and cool. A few blocks down Cromwell, past the majestic Victoria and Albert Museum—the V&A, as Londoners fondly called it—then a few more blocks up Brompton Road to the undisputed crown palace of consumerism: Harrod's.

"Angela, I haven't seen you since San Francisco," Philip said. "You look fantastic! How have you been?" They were out of sight of the hotel now. Angela took Philip's compliment as an invitation to slip her arm in his. Arm in arm, they looked like any other European couple strolling along a boulevard.

At the mere mention of San Francisco, Angela flashed back to the first night she had spent with Philip, six months ago. He was so good. It was so good. She wondered how all that lust had been ignited. *Was it the way he looked into my eyes during that incredible dinner? How did we start with shoptalk and end with fantastic lovemaking?*

The suppressed, romantic voice inside her had argued that the experience was the beginning of a potential relationship, but her logical side contended that it was merely a lusty, temporary yet refreshing "stress release" for her. She refused to analyze the memory any further, but, almost as an involuntary reflex, hugged Philip's arm as they crossed Brompton. The blaring horn of the black taxi startled her, and she wondered if she could ever learn to look to her right before stepping into a British crosswalk.

"Philip, I was really hoping to see you at the conference, but I figured that you'd probably not be here, because it's so far away and all" *And*, she could have added, *because you think San Francisco was just a meaningless one-night fling, and I haven't heard a word from you since.*

Philip listened attentively, easily hearing between the lines, sensing Angela's insecurity percolating to the surface. "To the contrary," he countered in a soothing tone, "I decided to attend for the usual reasons of business networking, but mostly because I knew you would be here. You were featured prominently in the registration brochure. By the way, your speech was excellent. Now, I hope that's settled. Tell me, how are you?"

"Philip, I'm doing well and doing good. Both, I'm pleased to say. And you?"

"I've been busy as hell. How's Sean doing?"

"Sean?" Angela asked.

"Yeah, Sean Eastgate. He's a software whiz from your hometown. I met him at the conference in San Francisco. He takes care of the systems at Preferred Site Management, and I just figured that you knew him because you work for so many of PSM's clients."

"His name isn't ringing any bells."

"No big deal. And how's your practice doing, Angela?"

Angela tightened her grip on Philip's arm. "You know, Phil," her words measured, "there are three things I can't figure out in this business." She looked up at his face to make sure he was paying close attention. "First, why is there such lack of interest among the owners in community associations? It's like intense apathy. Second," she paused, her face scrunched up, signaling that a weighty contradiction was about to be explored, "given that there is great apathy, why do some people fight like dogs to get on the board?"

He glanced down at Angela with questioning eyebrows, but knew better than to interrupt in the middle of her multiple points. "And, what's number three?"

"Third," she continued, "You're a manager, Phil, so you deal with these people all the time in Boston. Tell me, why do owners only get involved when there's a crisis, like the time you had to enforce the restriction against flagpoles, only to find out that the issue was the American flag, and that half of the owners were in the VFW?"

"Look, Angela, it's purely a matter of human nature. There are two types of people in the world," said Philip, playing her number-the-points game. Proud of his two-prong attack, he stopped in the middle of the sidewalk for emphasis. "First, you have all those selfish farts who think their home is their castle and all the land around is their fiefdom. Then, you have all the arrogant assholes who just hate regulation," he said, his arms stretched wide to encompass the world of farts and assholes. "Anyway, it's really good to see you again."

They stood facing each other, oblivious to the throng of businessmen and shoppers scurrying past and circling to avoid them. Philip gently brushed a strand of hair from her forehead and parked it behind one ear. He bent slightly and kissed her on the forehead.

"Oh, Phil, I've missed you so *much*," Angela whispered, and hugged him closely. He returned the embrace, his arms easily enclosing her slender waist.

"Are you sure you're not just a little randy?"

Their lips met in a warm, moist kiss. A passionate kiss. For Angela, it was a perfect kiss.

3

The gavel banged three times on the podium. "The July meeting of the board of directors is now called to order at..."—the board president paused to glance at the watch on his thick wrist—"exactly 7:05 p.m.," the strong, deep voice bellowed. His burly hand still wrapped around the gavel, the president used it as a pointer to coax the other directors to their seats at the table. They reluctantly seated themselves for the regular monthly board meeting, heads bowed, pretending to review the night's agenda, avoiding eye contact.

The most upscale residential sites in the entire St. Louis metropolitan area were the rugged hillsides of West County, where the visual clutter and congestion of fast food restaurants and strip malls gave way to peaceful winding country roads and Geese Crossing signs. And the most preferred address among the wealthy elite was Estrella Cove Condominium.

The Cove was a not a particularly large development as planned communities went, consisting of only three hundred condominium units. The developer had completed construction and sold out the final phase last year. He advertised them as luxury town homes, but to characterize these as *luxurious* was to classify the Rolls Royce as a *mere car*.

Although the units started at a modest base price of half a million dollars, the well-dressed sales people were skilled at enticing the buyer into a complimentary consultation with a team of creative architects and trendy interior designers. In less time than it took to read the four-color brochure the overwhelmed and outmaneuvered buyer would be ordering Italian marble for the foyer, burl walnut paneling for the study, leaded glass for the living room, a fireplace with glazed tile in the master bedroom, a hot tub in the expanded deck, a bidet with antique brass hardware in the master bath, and a few other details, options, and upgrades that only the ridiculously wealthy could not live without. These buyers could easily afford such amenities, but justified their decisions by the rhetorical question, "oh, what's another ten thousand dollars here and there?"

And, for an undisturbed view of one of the three azure-blue recreational lakes (actually, they were required by the local sewer district to provide storm water retention basins) that dotted the community, the buyer could ante up an additional fifty thousand dollars as a "preferred site premium," which entered the Cove's unique lexicon as the notorious PSP. After all the dotted lines were signed, the average price of a unit in the Cove hovered around a wallet-shattering, ego-inflating one million dollars.

In 1914, long before walled and gated communities became so popular among America's real estate developers, Robert Frost raised the question in his poem, *Mending Wall*,

Before I built a wall I'd ask to know
What I was walling in or walling out.

There was little doubt at the Cove. To keep out common criminals, solicitors, the financially challenged, and other undesirables, the Cove was surrounded by thick, six-foot high brick walls, camouflaged on the exterior by burning bushes. Eight-foot-high wrought iron gates, with the Cove's sculptured logo (a star over a symbolic body of water) emblazoned in the center, guarded both of the entrance driveways. Residents were issued passes and were required to display them to the attendants at the gatehouse located at each entrance. Others could gain entrance only if they had an appointment with a resident or were on the approved list kept by the attendants. The prestigious list of regulars included a select line of upscale hairdressers, masseurs, and even dog groomers, but hardly a pizza delivery driver.

The walls and gates of the Cove echoed a trend in the country since the 1980's in which real estate developers and community builders sought to meet the growing demand for this lifestyle. Outsiders considered the Cove as an exclusive fortress for the elite, designed and intended to foster the separation and withdrawal of its residents from the surrounding community. Local government officials feared that the social, political, and economic fabric of their jurisdictions would be Balkanized by gated communities.

As of 1996, an estimated eight million Americans lived in gated communities, half a million in California alone. Some homeowners liked gated communities because they provided separation for leisure activities, such as golf and other recreation amenities as well as country clubs. For others, the walls and gates symbolized the prestige of residing in an exclusive enclave for the wealthy.

But the most basic purpose was personal safety. The residents of the Cove, not unlike other homeowners who happened to live in more urban or transitional neighborhoods, sought security from the fear of crime. Some gated communities had experienced a significant reduction in crime, and property values had appreciated more rapidly than elsewhere.

Whether gated communities represented escapism or the creation of new neighborhoods was undecided. And, whether crime, like termites, would simply migrate and infest nearby neighborhoods, was also uncertain.

The residents of the Cove loved their quiet lifestyle and their sense of having their own community, at least in their own fashion. The vast majority of them dutifully paid assessments to the association for using the many private amenities like the clubhouse and recreation facilities and for the many public functions like maintaining the streets and the retention basins—all performed by the association.

Yet, there was an undercurrent of dissatisfaction within the Cove as more owners questioned why they paid their condo assessments, yet also paid property taxes to the county, even though public services were not performed within the Cove. This double taxation resulted in a handsome windfall for the county, which the government quietly pocketed.

The Cove clubhouse was located high on a ridge near the center of the development between the largest lake to the north and the swimming pool and tennis courts on the south. Beyond the recreation facilities was the eighteen-hole, pro-am golf course, designed by one of the top money golfers as her signature course. A huge cedar deck, which stepped down to a stone patio, was located outside the south glass exposure of the clubhouse and was the favorite site for gala evening parties and receptions. Two hot tubs beckoned many a weary soul after a long day of golf or tennis.

Inside the clubhouse, a lodge-sized stone fireplace was situated at one end, next to assorted arrangements of overstuffed armchairs and couches. Game tables for cards, chess, and checkers overlooked the pool. Residents could admire the lake through the spacious windows that framed the formal dining room at the opposite end of the clubhouse. In the fall the vivid colors of the oaks, maple, and hickory on the far hillsides reflected on the lake, but now they were scorched and parched by the relentless July heat.

In the center of the clubhouse were administrative offices including a station where Bruce Miles, the concierge, fussed over the residents and pampered them with services befitting their inflated self-images. Everything from dog-walking and house-sitting to making reservations at plush restaurants and renting videos from the Cove's extensive collection that was provided as another outlet for Blockbuster.

Bruce was attentive, always ready with a compliment, as with his consideration of Edith Lindholm, who was greeted one morning by Bruce's cheerful, excited voice at the concierge desk, "My, don't you look stunning in that lavender jumper, dear—simply ravishing! It's definitely you." Such coddling was vintage Bruce.

Beyond the offices were the Cove Bistro and Café and the Cove Business Center. The business center provided the opportunity for semi-retired business tycoons to use computers, log onto the Internet to track their investment portfolios, and discretely order flowers for their secretaries or mistresses, or both. The business center was also the brain of the Cove's Intranet, a system of fiber optics that provided all the residents with community information—everything from board minutes to notices of association and committee meetings, social events, chat rooms, and electronic forms for reserving tee times.

The clubhouse, indeed, was the hub of the Cove. Most of the men were newly or semi-retired, in good health, with little to do, and all day to do it. They would end their morning power walks with coffee at the Café, which had been dubbed the Cove Information Center, where they would read the morning paper, swap lies about fortunes made and lost, and argue about the trades they would make to bolster the Cardinals' erratic pitching staff.

The next wave would be the women, arriving in mid-morning at the game tables where they would tell horror stories of PSP one-up-manship between hands of mahjong and bridge, and exchange the latest Cove gossip with Bruce.

All things considered, the paradigm of Norman Rockwell's American neighborhood, with its wide front porches and white picket fences, was shattered by the community living experience at Estrella Cove.

Presiding over this gated enclave of the self-indulgent, the fabulously affluent, and the shamelessly powerful, was William Curtis Carlton, a bull and a bully of a man with an iron fist in a velvet glove, whose ambition was equaled only by his utter contempt for losing in business or in any other of life's endeavors.

Curtis had retired modestly from Carlton Wholesale Plumbing Supply, a company in the warehouse district near the Mississippi River levee that his grandfather and father had built up over fifty years. Unlike most of his neighbors in the Cove, Curtis, by almost any yardstick, was far from rich. His condo was heavily mortgaged with a second from the developer that greased the purchase with a cash down payment of only five percent. Perhaps it was merely coincidental that all the water lines, waste stacks, specialty faucets, tubs, and toilets used in the development originated at the humble warehouse of Carlton Wholesale Plumbing Supply.

But, William Curtis Carlton was also a man of great finesse. His favorite game was currying favors with local and state politicians, pouring plumbing money through a pipeline of generous contributions. During elections he was fond of telling his favorite candidates he was just a faucet voter. Unwise was the politician who failed to give Curtis special attention, for the contribution pipeline would soon dry up.

His tireless schmoozing with the politicos ultimately paid dividends that almost satisfied his ego, which was even more ample than his waistline. Curtis found himself on the Planning and Zoning Commission and later was appointed to head a blue-ribbon task force to create a vision for future development of the West County corridor, where he would team up with his old buddy and aficionado of fine plumbing products, none other than the developer of Estrella Cove.

The Cove had over five hundred residents, all of whom were automatically members of the Estrella Cove Residents' Association, a mouthful of a name that was usually reduced to an acronym that sounded like a southern shade of yellow—ECRA. For most of them, paying the monthly assessment of one thousand dollars per unit was their only exposure to ECRA. Like public elections, voter turnout at the annual meeting reflected widespread apathy, registering less than one third, unless a special assessment was on the agenda or free drinks were promised. That was the norm until Curtis flexed his considerable political gut.

The board consisted of nine directors, one owner elected from each of the eight phases (or wards, as Curtis preferred to call them) and the ninth elected at large from the entire community. The advantage of the at-large director's seat was that he or she would automatically be president of ECRA for a term of three years.

Teased by years of seducing politicians but never personally having the pleasure, Curtis hungered for the limelight himself. His campaign for the coveted at-large seat would have shamed the city's most skilled ward healers. His advisory council consisted of the campaign managers who had successfully masterminded last year's races for mayor and state legislator. They were given little choice by their bosses but to plot Curtis' campaign strategy. Gratis.

Residents for Carlton was born and the names of a dozen owners, who were alternately bludgeoned and caressed, appeared on his campaign literature. Slick brochures soon found their way into the expensive brass mailboxes of the Cove. Curtis borrowed the foot soldiers of his political pals to flood the Cove with door hangers.

Yard signs—prohibited by ECRA's restrictions—shot up everywhere overnight like dandelions, even in the common grounds in front of the clubhouse. Curtis kept a careful list of the owners who removed any yard sign. After the election, their pool and tennis passes would be mysteriously misplaced until a campaign contribution was discretely sent and received.

The editor of the *Cove Tattler* was Edith Lindholm of the lavender jumper. Widowed for several years, she volunteered for several civic organizations. Mrs. Lindholm was proud of the *Tattler*'s bi-monthly collection of hearsay and notices, published under her personal motto of Your Source for Honest Gossip. When Curtis vaguely threatened that she could lose her position as chair of the newsletter committee because of a parking violation, she gasped in astonishment. "But, Mr. Carlton," she had pleaded, "surely you can't blame me! My son had just come to visit, and he didn't know a reserved space from a visitor's space."

The next issue of the *Tattler* featured a glowing editorial endorsing Curtis' candidacy, characterizing him as "Bushesque" in stature and intellect. "Leaders like William Curtis Carlton are not born every day," she wrote. *Thank God*, she might have added.

Of course, in a private residential community association such as ECRA, voting rights were based on unit ownership—one vote per unit—regardless of the number of adults who lived there. Constitutional guarantees of one person, one vote had yet to reach these private communities. Thus, the cunning candidate had only to buttonhole the dominant voice of the household, which, at the Cove, Curtis assumed would be the man of the house. Curtis had little use for women outside the kitchen or the bedroom, and most certainly not in the boardroom of business or the backroom of politics. Accordingly, he found the Cove's voting system—where womens' right to vote was largely a myth—very much to his liking.

Which is not to say that the campaign trail was always easy. Knocking on Gus Pataglia's door one Sunday afternoon, Curtis was curtly rebuffed when the owner told him, "I never vote. It just encourages 'em." Curtis had a remarkable memory and took tedious notes and made detailed to-do lists, particularly of people and instances that required corrective action. After the election, Mr. Pataglia was ordered to remove the satellite dish from his balcony.

Curtis was the sort of man who blew his nose and then inspected the contents of his handkerchief. Although he had assembled some of the best local political minds for his kitchen cabinet, he ignored or rejected their advice when it was related to the platform and content of his campaign. He preferred to handcraft his own message to the people. After all, he fashioned himself as just one of the common folks, unique only for being thrust forward by circumstances beyond his control. The quest for leadership was his calling, he was merely the voice of the people. It was the owners who dictated policy, he was merely their scribe. He would speak to the people directly. He would speak to them heart-to-heart. In plain words.

Thus deluded by an overabundance of narcissist self-interest and bloated self-confidence, Curtis fashioned himself as histrionic and worked hard to articulate his central theme, defining himself and his sense of place in history. He outlined his vision of what the Cove should be. He developed the foundation of what would become his standard stump speech.

What is the Cove? More than anything else, the Cove is our *community*, the place we call home. And what makes the Cove a good community is that we're all the *same*. Some voices call for diversity, but I say to you that diversity is a recipe for disaster because it breeds differences, discontentment, and disagreement. If elected, I would foster community by casting aside the voices of diversity and, in their place, continue to build the Cove upon what has made it great today—our shared values and our common interests. Our *sameness*.

It was a message that struck an uneasy chord in the Cove. Most residents nodded silently in agreement when they heard his message. They just didn't want to talk about it.

Beneath the thin veneer of Curtis' image as the people's choice, he was a grand master at sound bites and sloganeering, as reflected in the primitive simplicity of his campaign literature and yard signs: "Elect Curtis Carlton. Keep Low Assessments." He could have pledged to abolish capital gains for the obnoxiously wealthy, and he wouldn't have attracted more support.

He had built a powerful political machine. Two weeks before the election, Curtis' troops were contacting residents to see who would be out of town on Election Day and were hustling proxies from them. Upon discovering that several residents had signed proxy votes for his opponent, Curtis visited these residents personally, shamelessly cajoling and threatening them until they revoked their proxies and filed new forms.

On Election Day, his phone bank and get-out-the-vote vans were dragging residents out of their homes and hauling them down to the clubhouse. "On Election Day," Curtis was fond of telling his supporters, "I'd rather have a million votes than a million dollars." Bruce speculated in hushed tones with the skeptics at the Cove Information Center that Curtis probably would have both when it was all over.

No one had seen such a full-court campaign, a rich mixture of bribes and badgering. The result was a record turnout of seventy-five percent of all the owners. Two thirds voted by proxy, and no one dared challenge their ballots.

4

"The first item on the agenda is the manager's report," Curtis announced, turning to his left as he did so. "Miss Gratiot, would you give us a summary of your written report? We have a full agenda tonight, so please be brief. And, I thought Miss McPherson would join us for this meeting, but I see that she's not here."

Michelle Gratiot, 31, and Lindsay "Mac" McPherson, 35, were co-owners and partners in Preferred Site Management, the company that provided management services for ECRA. Curtis relied on them as his personal staff to make sure all the administrative details were handled to his satisfaction and, of course, to his total credit. At five-foot-six, Michelle was athletically built, with the long muscles and lean body of a swimmer. She had long, dark, wavy hair and black eyes, with an olive complexion that glowed like the warm natural beauty of southern France. Although Michelle's expertise was in marketing, she handled many of the important accounts at PSM because of her people skills. As Mac's protégé in the management field, Michelle learned to always be overprepared in order to overcome the implicit bias against women in a ruthless business world dominated by men.

Michelle's linen suit jacket was draped over the back of her chair in resignation to the hot weather. As she stood to begin her presentation, she tugged gently at the bottom of her blouse to make sure it wasn't gapping. "Lindsay McPherson sends her regrets. It seems at the last minute, she, ah, was detained at the office," Michelle said to the board members, but her eyes were downcast, concentrating on the file.

"The monthly financials are all laid out for you in the spreadsheets behind the agenda," Michelle continued. "They reflect the Moores' delinquency which, as you know, has continued for over a year because of their pending divorce, and both of them refuse to pay until a dissolution settlement is reached. The Cove's attorney, Angela Laclede, is threatening both parties that ECRA will foreclose on the lien in order to force their hand. Finally, at the bottom of the statement, you can see that reserves have grown to approximately eight hundred thousand dollars, but we caution the board that this figure is only about seventy percent of our target."

Michelle turned to retrieve some papers from the table. "Also, we received a letter from the county sheriff. It seems the guard at station two, or I should say the 'attendant,' " she corrected herself, "refused to allow a process server to enter. We understand that the process server was serving papers in a domestic matter involving one of the owners." Handing copies to the board members, Michelle tried to sound as matter-of-fact as possible, "The sheriff warns that if it happens again, he'll have the guard arrested for obstruction of justice."

Curtis' ruddy complexion was turning the color of his red hair while he removed his reading glasses. He directed his glare at Michelle, boring into her eyes.

Don't shoot the messenger, she prayed silently.

"Well, that's just absurd," Curtis growled. "I don't know where Sheriff Yale is getting that nonsense. This is a private community, and we have the right to protect our residents. I'll have a little talk with Norty and set him straight. And, to think that we just got him re-elected," Curtis snorted, putting his reading glasses back on his bulbous nose and looking down to scribble a note in his binder. The room was silent. After a moment, Curtis looked around the table, glaring at the board members through slits of eyes. "Does anyone have any questions on the manager's report?" His intimidating gaze dared the other board members to depart from his script or lengthen the meeting by some insipid remark that hadn't been cleared with him before the meeting.

All eyes were fixed downward, hoping the agenda would supply a safe harbor from Curtis' turbulent gusts. "Yes, I have one question on the reserves line item," Allen Russell ventured tepidly.

Russell was down-sized several years ago as comptroller of a pharmaceutical conglomerate headquartered in a huge high-tech research park in suburban St. Louis, although he always referred to it as "early retirement." Somewhat of a self-contradiction, Russell was a small, mousy man who chose the mundane world of accounting and finance as the battlefield that would define his life. His driving personal passion, however, was to design a secret computer program that would beat the house at the Riverboat Belle Casino and make him conspicuously wealthy. As yet, however, Russell was conspicuously unsuccessful, leading to rumors of embarrassing gambling debts that were mounting in geometric proportions.

But no one doubted Russell's sharp mind, particularly himself. He just had a hard time channeling it in the right direction. Several years ago, he resigned from the school district board, immodestly proclaiming himself to be overqualified for the position. Leaders of the teachers' union, at their own news conference, gave his statement a C for composition and grammar, but awarded an A for reaching the correct conclusion.

"As the association treasurer," Russell continued, "I must inquire into how the reserve funds are being maintained. In short, where are they invested and what's our yield?" His eyes were pleading with Michelle, hoping she would have a comforting response.

Michelle had barely opened her mouth when Curtis quickly stared her down and said brusquely, "Look, Russell, we have several projects on the drawing boards for the rest of the year, so I directed PSM to keep the funds in liquid accounts. Now then, there being no further questions, we'll move on to the next item," he said, adding a sneer to dismiss Russell.

The meeting labored down the agenda, covering reports of rules violations and maintenance requests. Mrs. Donovan filed her third complaint that Mr. Eichelberger was spotted on his deck again with his high-powered night binoculars aimed at her bedroom window. There was a complaint from Mrs. Lindell that her roses still hadn't been mulched. "This would adversely affect the quality of my little buds," she said.

And so on until nine o'clock when Curtis abruptly interjected, "It's good to see that the day lilies and the reserves are both growing so nicely." With that pronouncement, he pounded the gavel sharply on the conference table and declared the meeting adjourned.

The Cove, in its fashion, was governed for another month.

5

As the board members filed out of the conference room, Curtis turned to Michelle and said, "Can you stay for a minute? I need to go over a few things with you. Let's go into my office."

"Of course," Michelle said, wondering what she was agreeing to. "Oh, by the way, Mr. Carlton," she said as they walked out of the conference room and into Curtis' office, "I didn't think the entire board needed to know this, but Mac was tied up at the office because it looks like someone might have broken in last night, but we can't find anything missing."

Curtis stopped at his expensive entertainment system and inserted a compact disk of Handel's *Messiah*. He sat down and motioned to Michelle to take one of the guest chairs.

"All of our office files appear in proper order," Michelle continued.

Glory to God in the highest...came from the stereo speakers.

"Ah, Mr. Carlton," Michelle said, "The *Messiah* was written for Easter and is usually heard at Christmas. I'm just curious, why are you playing it in the middle of summer?"

"The *Messiah*? I love it." Curtis was waving his arms, conducting the orchestra. "I just love rich and powerful music, don't you? Now then, you were telling me about your files."

"Right. Our files didn't appear to be disturbed. But, in any event, the police were quite thorough, and their investigation took a long time. Mac couldn't possibly leave the office to attend the board meeting." Michelle nervously looked up at Curtis, trying to read his reaction.

Which didn't take long. Curtis aimed an unblinking glare at Michelle. His jaw was set, his face turning crimson. He rose slowly and spread his right hand on the desk to support his considerable torso as he leaned into Michelle's face. She could see the veins in his temples pulsating. "You girls better get your act together," his voice raspy. "If you can't secure your little operation, how can you expect to take care of ours? I'm sure there are other management companies, you know, eager for our business."

King of Kings, and Lord of Lords. . . .

Curtis paused, still looking at Michelle, and realized by her face that he had reacted too strongly. His breathing slowly came under control. "I don't understand," he said, "if there's nothing gone, if everything appears in order, how do you know the office was broken into?"

"The police aren't releasing that information," she said, ignoring his glare. It wasn't exactly a lie, but she hoped it would deflect his question. She didn't want to admit that the electronic security system had been compromised.

He sat down again, exhaling a long sigh and spreading his beefy hands on the desk. "Look, Michelle, it's too bad about that incident at your office, and if there's anything I can do, anyone I can call, please let me know. I know a few people in this town, I can push a few buttons, and maybe we can get the investigation on a fast track. But, as for my little job here, I was just elected, and I'm still finding my way around." He paused and looked Michelle in the face.

"Now then, you seem to be a bright and competent young woman." His gaze lowered with metric precision to examine her bosom. "I think we'll get along just fine," he added with a barely disguised smirk.

Michelle tried to look up at Curtis. She unconsciously fidgeted with the top button of her blouse, digesting his words, regretting that she had mentioned the incident at the office. Her eyes turned toward the door, carefully measuring the distance, plotting a quick if not graceful exit.

"What I really wanted to tell you," Curtis continued, "is that we need to install major landscaping behind building number seven. I've got the landscaping contractor's proposal here, which I've signed. Now, please give this your highest priority," Curtis said, as he handed the paper to her. *She didn't need to know about the generous contribution he received from Tony Schneider, who owned #703.*

"I'll start the planning process first thing in the morning," Michelle said, picking up her briefcase and taking a first step toward the door.

"Hold on a second, pretty lady," Curtis called out. To Michelle, the phrase "pretty lady" grated like fingernails on a blackboard. "I'm not finished with you—there are a few other items," he went on. "I've got an employment issue. That Brucie, the concierge, he's history. He makes me uncomfortable. I don't think our people want his kind in a respectable place like the Cove."

"You want me to terminate Bruce? He's been the concierge from the beginning, and his job performance has been excellent." Michelle was stunned. "We haven't heard a single complaint. He has good reviews in his file. What has he done to merit…?"

Curtis raised his hand like a meat cleaver, brutally hacking off her next words. "Young lady, that's quite enough. You better remember that I'm the president of this association and that you're my hired manager. And Bruce, he's my un-hired concierge." Curtis' glare bore down on her. Michelle turned away, biting her lower lip. She didn't know whether to bow, salute, or kick him in the groin.

"Last, I want you to know you did a great job fixing up my office." She looked up and could see that Curtis was smiling again. *Is the storm over?* Michelle wondered.

After last month's meeting Curtis had given her a floor plan and "a list of a few things we need here." She had looked down the list and was stunned to realize that Curtis wanted to create an executive office for himself, containing roughly three hundred square feet in an oval shape. The drawing showed that the office would have a large, oval Oriental rug with the logo of the Cove in the center. The office would feature an antique walnut desk "not less than six feet long" with matching credenza, a leather executive chair, a phone and fax, a computer and copier, a coffee machine, a stereo system, and other office items. Stapled to the shopping list was a card from the LaSalle Antique Trading Company on the city's south side and a handwritten note, "Walnut desk, ask for Vinnie or Ernie Buggieri."

Michelle could only stammer as she gathered her thoughts, her eyes unable to release from the list. "Shouldn't the board approve all this?" I mean, these plans would cut the coffee shop in half and cost a lot of money."

"Michelle, while I'm the president," Curtis had responded in his most soothing tone of voice, "the buck starts here. I am the president, and I'm responsible for all this," he had told her, gesturing with his arms as though encircling the entire condominium. "The president needs a little place to do his job. And I need a computer linked to PSM so that I can monitor our finances on a daily basis. I can't keep schlepping down to your offices every week to get the latest data. Now, there's plenty of money in the president's fund. I know you'll get on it right away."

For He shall reign forever and ever. Halleluyah....

THE ACCOUNT THAT WAS euphemistically called the "president's fund" was the ever-thirsty brain child borne of Curtis' raw ambition, and it should have served as the first red flag of his insatiable quest for power. Rather than include a line item in the budget to handle contingencies and midstream fiscal surprises, which would have been prudent fiscal planning but would have violated his electoral pledge of "no new assessments," Curtis simply cut all maintenance expenses in the budget by six percent. Describing this as a modest surcharge to create a contingency fund, Curtis ram-rodded the maneuver through an unwary board at the first meeting. The money was nowhere to be found as a separate line item in the budget and, of course, was actually diverted into a separate and secret account in another bank, which he referred to privately as the president's fund.

After making sure Michelle had understood every item on the list of furniture and equipment, Curtis had stressed, "And don't forget the cell phone and my business cards." For emphasis, he had pointed a stubby finger at the papers in Michelle's hand.

When all was done, Michelle had indeed worked a minor miracle, getting the contractors to work overtime and finish the project within two weeks of that initial meeting. Now, Michelle could look around the office and admire the results of her hard work. "Yes, it did turn out rather well, and I appreciate your compliment. Thank you, Mr. Carlton," she said with a forced smile, her mind unable to shake thoughts of the impending disaster with Bruce.

She hurried to the door, but stopped when she heard Curtis calling after her, "Oh, too bad Mac couldn't be here tonight. Tell her I said hello. Anyway, you're a helluva lot better looking. Don't tell her that, heh, heh. I'm sure you and I will get along just fine," he repeated with a slimy grin.

Nice tits, he sighed to himself as he watched Michelle walk out the door.

Michelle walked slowly through the clubhouse, heading vaguely in the direction of the front doors. She was biting her lower lip, fighting back tears. Her mind was replaying the conversation with Curtis, when a man's voice called from behind her.

"Hey, lady, got time for a drink?"

She turned around to see Bruce.

"Don't you ever go home?" Michelle tried to transform her face into a welcome expression as she wiped away tears with the back of her hand. She managed a faint smile. "What a pleasant surprise."

"Well, I was getting ready to go home, although I hate to leave, and you just walked by, looking as if you had just lost your best friend. My dear girl, such a worried expression does not belong on such a beautiful face! That's not the Michelle I know. Let's have a glass of wine over in the lounge. We can dip into my private stock."

She could hardly refuse. Bruce was so observant. He was a kind and thoughtful person, but it was obvious he had no idea that Curtis was about to fire him.

"I think you'll simply love this cabernet sauvignon," Bruce announced as he joined Michelle at a small table. They were alone in the lounge. Bruce removed the glass chimney and lit the candle in the center of the table. He sat the bottle of red wine and two glasses on the table, uncorked the bottle, and poured half a glass for each.

"This is a '94 Carmenet cab from Sonoma County. It's called 'dynamite cabernet' because, according to the label, the mountainsides where the vineyards grow were so steep and rugged that they had to be blasted with dynamite." Bruce and Michelle swirled, sniffed, and sipped the California cab and nodded to each other with silent acknowledgment of its soft and supple taste.

"So now, Michelle," Bruce said quietly, "What's got you down?" Bruce had a full head of curly light brown hair and a neatly-trimmed beard, which gave his face a look of distinction. "You can tell Bruce, I'm your friend," he added.

Somehow, Bruce's little compliment comforted her. If anyone else had said those words, she would have been on guard. But, Michelle and Mac had hired Bruce for this position. It was their first major management decision for the Cove and, Michelle reflected, was one of their best.

God, I can't tell Bruce that Curtis decreed his firing. Not now, not here. "Bruce, it's just that I have such a terrible feeling of inadequacy whenever I'm trying to deal with Curtis," Michelle looked at the wine as she avoided a direct response to his inquiry. "I don't know if it's because I'm a woman, or…or what? Does he treat everyone like they merely exist for his convenience?"

"Did you take philosophy in college? Curtis reminds me of a quote from St. Bonaventure. 'He's like a monkey: the higher he climbs, the more you see of his behind.'"

Bruce chuckled softly in appreciation of his own humor and continued. "Curtis is a lot like Machiavelli, but more subtle and complex. He doesn't care if the residents love him, he'd rather they respect and fear him than anything else. The damned irony is that they love it—they love being treated that way. Curtis is one of those people who will sweet-talk his peers when he wants something. The rest of us are treated like peons, as expendable as a stopcock in one of his toilets. On the surface, the man appears to have no social skills, but he's capable of being very manipulative. A warning to the wise—dealing with him is like trying to catch a falling sword. He can hurt you and do it so fast you won't even know it happened."

"Yet, Bruce, you really seem to enjoy working here."

"Well, the guy just crowned himself King of the Cove. You know me, Michelle. You know that I truly love this job. My fantasy—and I don't use the term as if it's something frivolous or whimsical—is to run a resort hotel, and this job comes pretty close. I attend to the urges of our residents, regardless of how trivial the request may seem. They're treated like cherished guests. Moreover, who do you think keeps this place humming so efficiently? You won't see it on any formal organization chart, but that's part of my job. I'm the only one here with any training and experience in the hospitality business, which is what we do here, so I look after the chefs and kitchen staff, the valets, the landscapers who keep the flower beds around the clubhouse, all the furnishings and floral arrangements inside, the cleaning staff—the whole thing, inside and out."

Michelle listened intently, but she didn't need to be reminded of the fundamental role that Bruce played in keeping the Cove operating at a high level of quality. She realized how absurd it would be to fire him and that she wasn't capable of doing it. "Are you having any problems with Curtis?"

"Curtis has given me more than a few hard glances. You know the piercing glare he can throw at people. He hardly ever says anything to me, and I'm not sure why. I get along with just about everybody here. But, you know, he and I are fundamentally different. I love to help people, to make them feel good. He loves to exploit them, to make them feel inferior. Whatever he said to you, try not to take it personally."

Michelle looked into Bruce's face, and tears welled up in her eyes again. She had to turn her face. *It's so wrong to fire this selfless, caring person. I'll go back to Curtis and try to change his mind. In a few days.*

"I didn't mean to touch a nerve, Michelle, but if you must cry, let it all out. Tell me what's bothering you. That always helps."

"Your words are so kind. I'm touched by your thoughtfulness."

"Do all your communities have egomaniac, psychodictators like Curtis?"

"You know what they say. 'In America, anyone can be elected president—that's the risk of living in a democracy.' Curtis is not exactly what I had in mind when Mac and I started PSM."

You and Mac should be proud of what you have accomplished with PSM, and you're always looking for ways to improve your business. You know, I've been working on some exciting improvements for our internal management here at the Cove, which I'd love to talk to you about next time you're out here. And, on a personal note, if you don't mind, my girlfriend and I broke it off a few months ago, and I'm ready to meet some new women. Preferably someone my own age, not the blue hairs who live here. So, if you know of an emotionally stable woman in her thirties, who loves the wonders of life, and who wouldn't mind going out with a hospitality nut, let me know."

Michelle's mind clicked through her directory. "I'll check it out, Bruce. You have my promise." *There's no way I can allow Curtis to fire Bruce. Curtis has got to realize that he won't look so good when the place doesn't run right. Maybe I could persuade Bruce to apologize for whatever, kiss Curtis' ring, and all will be forgiven.*

6

After asking endless, repetitive, mind-numbing questions, the county police finally became bored and mercifully exited PSM's office. They said they had to "tackle their paperwork."

Mac McPherson was exhausted from the lengthy and unproductive ordeal. She leaned back in her chair and rested her feet on the desk. Jenni, the receptionist, sat across the desk in one of the client chairs. In the other chair was Michelle, who had returned late from her meeting at the Cove. It was Monday, almost midnight. Now that the police and staff were gone, PSM's offices were suddenly tomblike.

"This has been a helluva night," Mac said with exasperation as she returned from the kitchen. She popped the caps off three Bud longnecks and handed bottles to the other women. Reaching for the polished cherry humidor on her desk, Mac said, "Anybody want one of these?" She displayed a panatela from the handsome wood case. Jenni and Michelle declined. "Well, then, excuse me while I indulge myself. To paraphrase W.C. Fields, 'A man is only a man, but a good cigar is a smoke.' "

"Over five years in this business," Mac sighed, blowing a plume of blue smoke at the overhead light fixture, "and we've never been robbed. Or is it burgled? It feels like I've been personally invaded. So, what do you guys think? What's going on here?" Her head was tilted back against the chair, and she spoke vaguely at the ceiling.

Lindsay "Mac" McPherson had just turned thirty-five and was the opposite of Michelle in almost every way. She had the body of a fire hydrant—short, stubby, and built for utility. She wore her light brown hair short. Her glasses were too large for her face, making her look like the nameless, ageless, never-smiling woman in Mary Engelbreit's greeting cards. Tonight she wore slacks and a golf shirt with the PSM signature on the left breast pocket. Even though PSM bought several of the handsome cotton shirts for each of the staff and Mac was never without hers, Michelle hardly ever wore the shirt. Not since William Curtis Carlton walked up to her one night at the Cove clubhouse, spent more time than necessary to examine the logo and said, "So, what do you call the other one?"

Despite only two years of college, Mac had rapidly taught herself the details of property maintenance. Out of necessity she became an expert in roofs, sill plates, trusses, siding, concrete, asphalt, and landscaping. Her first job was in apartment management, well before the concept of community management emerged as a distinct field of specialization. She became familiar with the contractors and vendors, learning who could be trusted to show up and do the job right the first time at a reasonable rate with a good warranty and adequate insurance.

She learned from engineers, architects, and geotechnical experts about problems like structural settlement, hydrostatic pressure, delamination, deflection, and others that visited her properties like silent plagues.

Soon promoted to the position of senior manager, Mac had been responsible for over thirty large apartment complexes. She earned the only professional certification available at that time, proudly referring to herself as a certified property manager and using the CPM after her name. She developed more efficient and effective systems for maintaining rent rolls, maintenance expenses, insurance, and other financial and administrative information.

But, after eight years, Mac realized that she was having the same experience a hundred times a week, instead of having new and different experiences. Her learning curve was flat. And, as she described it, she became weary of working her butt off so someone else could make a lot of money. She was working harder and harder and enjoying it less and less.

It was in the midst of this crisis of "thrashing about," as she referred to it, that Mac attended an industry seminar on future trends. A young woman, barely out of graduate school, presented an insightful paper on changes in the residential market. Mac stayed afterward to meet the speaker, Michelle Gratiot. The two women shared a commitment to their similar professions that carried an initial conversation into friendship. They exchanged war stories about their jobs, men and failed relationships, and their current disenchantment and dreams with their professional careers in St. Louis.

Mac couldn't avoid noticing the changes in the market. It was just as Michelle had described. Increasing numbers of condominium and planned communities were being built, and there was a corresponding decline in new apartment developments. Existing rental stock was being converted to condo. Mac's market—rentals—was flattening. She started a new file folder, and filled it with articles she clipped about the exploding condo market in the metropolitan area.

During lunch one day, she and Michelle discussed a recent newspaper article that quoted statistics from a new group called the Organization of Community Associations, or OCA. That afternoon Mac tracked down a phone number for OCA, and soon she was speaking a new vocabulary of "common-interest communities" and their "community associations." She and Michelle were excited to discover the network and resources of OCA. After a few meetings, the two women knew they were ready to launch a management business together.

They prepared a business plan and arranged for start-up financing through the Women's Business Network. Six months later they leased a small office in a suburban strip mall and announced formation of Preferred Site Management, "specializing in professional management of condominium and subdivision communities." Mac McPherson and Michelle Gratiot never worked harder in their professional lives. And they never looked back.

"We've got to figure out this burglary," Mac said. She took another long drag on her cigar. "Can you imagine the impact on our business if this becomes public?" A long pause followed. "Our clients will leave us in a stampede, no doubt. Now, is there anything we've missed, anything else we can tell the police?" Mac asked.

"It's just like I told the police," Jenni said. "I always set the alarm before I leave at night. It's part of my ritual. I'm almost positive that I set it Friday night." Mentally, she retraced her footsteps.

"But, isn't it possible you could have been distracted as you were getting ready to leave?" Mac looked at Jenni. "A last-minute phone call or visitor? I mean, isn't it possible you didn't set the alarm?"

Jenni defensively folded her arms across her chest. "Mac, you're making me feel like I'm being cross examined on the witness stand, and it's making me very uncomfortable. Isn't it also possible that someone else came in over the weekend, and they're too embarrassed to admit that they forget to set the alarm?"

Michelle was making some notes in her day planner. "Nobody's blaming you, Jenni," she said, putting a hand on Jenni's shoulder. "The only fact we know for sure is that when you opened the office this morning the alarm wasn't on. So, let's look at the scenarios. One, you forgot to set the alarm, in which case maybe there was a break-in, but probably there wasn't because that would be too much of a coincidence."

Michelle took a sip of her Bud, wiped her mouth indelicately with the back of her hand, and checked her notes. "The second scenario is that you did set the alarm. If so, why wasn't the alarm on this morning when you opened up?" Michelle asked, looking at Jenni. "Not a power outage—we have battery backup. Someone broke in, and they knew how to disarm the system. But, he forgot to reset it. Or, maybe it was a she."

"But, assuming the second scenario," Mac thought aloud, nervously rubbing her forehead, "What's the motive?" The overhead lights reflected off Mac's glasses, masking her eyes. "The petty cash, and it really is petty, is still locked in Jenni's desk. All the client files are here. None of the keys is gone—they're all in the safe, which wasn't touched. Hell, let's face it—we don't have a clue."

"And, neither do the police," Michelle said. "They couldn't find any forced entry, so they figure whoever it was must have had a key. They couldn't find any fingerprints except ours."

Jenni's face was resting in her hands. "The police must think we're dizzy broads," she said. "Or, that it was an inside job. Either way, this is not fun."

The three women looked at each other and then sucked on their beers in silence.

7

"*Bonjour*, B.J.! *Comment ça va, mon amie?*"

"Angela? You wouldn't be speaking French unless you found a good restaurant in London," B.J. Page responded. "Or, no, don't tell me—you're in France?" B.J. was the chief paralegal at the Law Offices of Angela Laclede.

"*Oui, mon cher,* but of course. I am in Paris, the City of Light!" Angela held the phone tightly to her ear as she sat on the hotel bed. She looked over the tops of the bright yellow marigolds on the windowsill and opened the double windows to admire the scene below—the street was bustling with students from the nearby Sorbonne. A light breeze played with her hair. "It's absolutely perfect here in Paris—lovers embracing, everybody sitting around sidewalk cafes getting their espresso fix, and eating *jambons* and fresh baguettes. And the weather is *tres fantastique*."

"Well, I'm glad to hear that," B.J. said with a husky voice that sounded like it was being filtered through gravel. B.J. Page had worked for Angela for almost five years. "You couldn't have picked a better time to be gone. It's so hot here we ran out of cold water. How come you're in Paris when you're supposed to be in London?"

"It was really a spur-of-the-moment thing. So unlike me, right? It's Tuesday and my part of the conference is done. I took the train from London, you know, that high-speed train called the Eurostar, and practically flew through the Chunnel. We got to Paris in only three hours. Already been to *La Tour Eiffel*, and I loved it. Oh! I don't want to forget to give you the hotel phone number here." Angela read the eight-digit number on the phone and gave B.J. the international prefix for France—thirty three.

"Um, Angela, you said 'we' got to Paris. Who are you traveling with, or do you expect me to believe that you went to the City of Light alone?"

"I'm shocked, B.J. You know the DADT policy—don't ask, don't tell."

"You'll tell, sooner or later. How's the language barrier?"

"Overstated," said Angela. "I never thought that two years of college French would be useful, but it's coming back. If you make a reasonable attempt to speak French, they're really very nice to you. You can't let the first surly waiter make you feel bad." Angela paused to break off a piece of baguette and to cut off a slice of Port Salut cheese. "Unfortunately, you see a lot of obnoxious American tourists here who are so ignorant. They demand that the French speak English and then get angry and start yelling when the French refuse."

"Where are you staying?"

"At this small hotel, with a cranky old elevator, in the Latin quarter, right on La Place de la Sorbonne. It's next to the university and circled by cafes and lime trees, and the entire plaza is teeming with students. There was a huge student demonstration here in 1968 that turned bloody and lasted two days. Four hundred people were injured. I just read about it."

"Did you rent a car, or what?"

"Drive in Paris? Are you *folle*? Crazy? People here ignore stoplights, use the sidewalk as part of the street, and drive with their horns. You should see the circle at the Place Charles de Gaulle, you know, where L'Arc de Triomphe is located. Twelve streets converge on that circle, and it's full of homicidal maniacs in a race that makes the Indy 500 look like a soapbox derby. Rent a car? *Bonne chance*. Good luck."

Angela placed the cheese on her piece of baguette and popped the snack into her mouth. Chewing as she talked, she continued, "Walking is the best way to see Paris, but you really have to watch where you're going—I read in *Access Paris* that one third of Parisians have dogs, and 'the average pedestrian sets foot in canine droppings every 286th step.' I can confirm these facts from personal experience. And, try to get a taxi going the same direction as you are: *tant pis*. Too bad."

"Listen, Angela," interrupted B.J., "I hate to be the bearer of bad news from the office, but Mac McPherson called at five o'clock Monday afternoon, our time. Since it was very late where you are, I didn't want to bother you. She wants you to call her anytime day or night. Some unspecified emergency. Needs to talk to you ASAP. And when Mac says that, it's usually something serious."

"I'm occupied for a while," Angela said, winking at Philip who was lying in bed. "But the laptop's plugged in, electric adaptor and all, so please call Mac and ask her to email all the gory details. I'll get back to her right after I read her message. *D'accord*—okay?"

"Angela? Don't hang up. I need to tell you one or two little things quickly. Michelle attended the meeting with the Cove board Monday night, and you won't believe what that overweight slime ball dictator did now, besides trying to get into Michelle's pants. Anyway, the Cove was slapped with a TRO. The full caption on the lawsuit is, Application for Temporary Restraining Order, Preliminary Injunction, and Permanent Injunction."

"You always save the best for last, *mon cher*. Give me the details."

B.J. summarized the pleadings for Angela.

Angela thought for a minute then said, "OK, here's what we'll do. First, I know Joshua is preparing for another trial, but this is urgent, and he'll need to review the pleadings. If it's a TRO, he should get on it right away while I'm gone. And I fully intend to stay gone. At least for a week, maybe two. Second, Joshua should call both the client and Michelle, summarize the facts and prepare an initial strategy, and email it to me. Third, scan the petition and email it, ASAP. I'll be waiting for it. *Merci. Au revoir.*"

Angela hung up the phone and stared at it for a moment. When she looked up at Philip, the twinkle in her eye had returned. She pulled her pajama top over her head and jumped into the bed.

8

"Look folks," Joshua said, referring to his calendar, "unless there's another continuance, we're scheduled to go to trial in four short weeks with Judge Margaret Aberdeen. The reason I asked you all to come down here is that all settlement discussions with Dunwoody have failed, and we need to prepare for trial. We need to review our testimony, prepare for depositions, and prepare our exhibits." Joshua was standing at the head of the conference table, files and black three-ring binders spread out in front of him. A poster-sized aerial photograph of "The Vineyard Townhomes" community was perched on the easel.

Joshua was just under six feet tall, with short, sandy hair and a trim, athletic body that he kept in good condition with a year-round routine of ice hockey and basketball. He studied each of the three board members sitting around the table and then looked at Michelle Gratiot, the manager of the Vineyard, who had arrived late from a site inspection with a plumber. She had carried a hacksaw and a frustrated expression with her into the conference room. As Michelle slid the hacksaw under her chair, Joshua made a mental note not to provoke her.

The Law Offices of Angela Laclede provided legal representation for many of the two dozen community associations in PSM's portfolio. While he had talked with Michelle on the phone countless times relating to minor occurrences and requests for legal opinions, Joshua hadn't had the opportunity to work with her on litigation until this occasion, the second lawsuit filed by J. Thomas Dunwoody against the Vineyard Townhomes Association.

The Vineyard was a small residential development consisting of ninety six townhomes, situated in row house buildings of three to five units each. Although the townhome originally sold for under eighty thousand dollars, it was clear that the developer had greater aspirations when the Vineyard was on the drawing boards.

The developer, Richard "Dick" Kamper, had a weakness for spending his considerable profits on travel, seeking new inspiration and vision to substitute for his poor taste and feeble imagination. He visited California for new architectural concepts and toured Europe for new themes.

After one trip to southern California, he started an upscale development in South County called California Hills, which his glossy brochures promoted as "California Living at Midwestern Prices." The brochures should have read, "California Style in Midwestern Weather." The developer bought the plans from a Los Angeles architectural firm and transplanted them to St. Louis without modifications. The fashionable style was a stunning and appealing departure from more conservative designs of the area. A feature story with color photos that ran in the real estate section of the Sunday St. Louis *Post-Dispatch* was a windfall of free advertising. Sales were brisk, and Dick Kamper was ecstatic.

However, few buyers in the community of California Hills stopped long enough to notice the absence of gutters. With far greater rainfall in St. Louis, and no gutters to catch it, the rain cascaded off the roofs in sheets. The siding was stained and rotting in less than two years and surface water gushed into the lower levels, ruining many a carpet. Signs appeared in windows and in front of the townhomes imploring prospective buyers to DICK KAMPER BEFORE HE DICKS YOU.

The Yuppie owners at California Hills retained Angela Laclede to prosecute a massive construction defects case on a contingent fee basis. In her closing argument, Angela recalled the words of Frank Lloyd Wright, "'A physician can bury his mistakes, but the architect can only advise his clients to plant vines.' But, at California Hills," she concluded, "the owners couldn't even plant vines to fix the damages. They are victims of a sophisticated developer who padded his profits by cutting corners." A jury of shocked homeowners awarded $565,000 to the association. News of the verdict cascaded through the courthouse like a heavy rain at California Hills.

The Vineyard reflected Kamper's infatuation with France, where his limited imagination was smitten by the chateaus of the wine region. A certain false smugness, a faux pas of pretentiousness permeated the development. Simple-looking townhomes of cheap quality faced streets with names that suffered from affluenza, like Pauillac and St. Emilion. Buyers, who could barely afford the townhomes, couldn't pronounce the names of the streets they were built on. The gap between the lofty marketing of the community and the lowly character of the dwellings led the residents to wonder whether Dick Kamper had lost his mind, or simply lost the drawings of the French chateaus he visited.

If California Hills embodied the perfect Yuppie community, then the Vineyard was the perfect working class community. And, if the Yuppies of California Hills sued Kamper to correct an injustice, then the blue-collar residents of the Vineyard sued each other merely to engage in combat. Whether due to the failure of the developer's expectations or to its location in conservative South County, the Vineyard had become known among realtors as the most litigious residential development per capita in the entire metropolitan area. Some crazy lawsuit or another was always crawling at a snail's pace through the overburdened judicial system, pitting neighbor against neighbor, eroding all good feelings, stigmatizing the small community, and chilling resales more than if a repeat sexual offender lived there.

The most recent lawsuit was produced by the twisted and paranoid genius of a unit owner named J. Thomas Dunwoody, who lived on St. Emilion. Some people go through life absorbing and coping with unthinkable injustices. Others engage in trench warfare over the slightest personal inconvenience. Dunwoody anointed himself as the spiritual advisor and head cheerleader for the trench combat group.

A small, wirery man in his early fifties, Dunwoody lived alone, having chased off three wives at last count. How he managed to meet three women was a mystery. Dunwoody carried the sour expression of perennial indigestion. His face was the color of a snake's belly, his mouth curved downward into the scowl of a perpetually hapless man. A line of shiny scar tissue ran from the left corner of his mouth down his chin, a badge from a bar room brawl or a domestic disturbance with one of his wives. It made him look like he was in a state of constant drooling, as if he could lick stamps without using his tongue. With no visible source of income, a trio of former wives thirsting for maintenance payments, and his preference for wearing short shorts, Dunwoody was an item of constant speculation among the residents of the Vineyard. He simply scoffed, sneered, and drooled at them whenever the subject of his personal life arose.

9

Dunwoody's first suit against the Vineyard Townhomes Association had come without warning when the board was served at its monthly meeting. He alleged that the board failed to enforce a restriction against commercial use of homes because one of his neighbors—known to despise Dunwoody—conducted a telemarketing consulting business in his townhome. The suit sought fifty thousand dollars in unspecified damages plus diminished value of Dunwoody's home.

Word of the lawsuit spread quickly among the neighbors. Some of the owners supported Dunwoody, believing that rigid enforcement of all the restrictions was the only barricade between having a stable, attractive community and becoming the type of unkempt neighborhood they had recently fled. His small band of supporters, with their guerilla mentality for community living, had been nicknamed Dunwoody's Commandos. The vast majority of sane owners simply shook their heads over the home-office dispute and muttered, "let's be reasonable" and "who cares?"

Dunwoody certainly didn't care about legal fees. He represented himself, *pro se*. The association's insurer, impressed with the courthouse gossip about the

California Hills litigation, retained Angela Laclede's firm to defend the association, with Joshua as lead counsel.

Dunwoody prepared his case like a man possessed. He wanted every piece of evidence in the right place, every word of testimony from his witnesses to be scripted. Every step of the trial would be predicted and predictable. Compared to J. Thomas Dunwoody, Mr. Murphy of Murphy's Law was an optimist.

At trial, Dunwoody displayed several photographs to his first witness, Joe Compton, who was the ill-fated delivery driver employed by Metro Office Supply. The photos showed Compton, clad in the blue uniform of Metro Office, maneuvering a hand truck containing two boxes of paper up the driveway to one of the townhomes. Dunwoody had taken the pictures himself, lying on the ground, hidden under the shrubs.

Now, as he turned with theatrical flair to Compton, pointing to the photos and flashing a drooling grin, Dunwoody said, "These photographs are sort of a worms-eye view taken in front of the subject townhome." A somber Compton admitted, "Yeah, that's one of our trucks." While poor Compton resisted offering any unnecessary assistance on the witness stand, he could not avoid testifying that he had delivered two boxes of paper every month to that address over the past year. "This particular paper is made for a laser printer commonly used with computers. We sell a lot of it," Compton stated in response to Dunwoody's questions.

All Dunwoody had accomplished was to establish that the delivery consisted of paper used for a computer, a point which was not even in dispute. Yet, Dunwoody winked and drooled at the jury as he returned to the counsel table, convinced that he had just scored a vicious slam dunk that would resonate all the way from the county courthouse in Clayton to the Vineyard.

Joshua needed only two questions to wipe the smirk off Dunwoody's face at the start of the association's defense. "Isn't it a fact, Mr. Dunwoody, that your petition in this lawsuit was prepared by you on your computer?" Dunwoody stared at the judge, his eyes pleading for help.

"Don't look to me for help," the judge said. "Just answer the question."

After a long pause while Dunwoody surveyed the courtroom, he said, "Yes, but that was for . . ."

"And isn't it also a fact," Joshua pressed, "that your computer sits in your dining room in your townhome?" Dunwoody squirmed, slumped, and slithered down the witness chair, like a child after dinner who wants to escape the harsh glare of the adults.

A parade of neighbors testified on behalf of the association that they didn't see, hear, or smell anything that might be a nuisance coming from the "subject townhome." Besides, they said, everybody in the Vineyard had a plumbing, furnace service, or other truck pay them a visit on occasion. A realtor testified that there were no measurable damages to the value of Dunwoody's unit. In fact, according to the appraiser, values could easily diminish if the Vineyard enforced its policy of prohibiting home offices.

An expert testified about offices in the home. She said that downsizing of big companies had forced thousands of skilled professionals to run businesses from their homes and that some of the most successful companies, like Apple Computer and Microsoft, had started in the home. An estimated forty million Americans worked in a home-based business, using a computer for word and data processing for their business, doing research on the Internet, telecommuting, telemarketing, or communicating via email with customers. "Today, home workers account for nearly forty percent of the work force," the expert said, "And it would be unreasonable to enforce a restriction to prohibit home offices in view of the tremendous popularity of this form of business."

The jurors barely had time to elect a forewoman before they sent a note to the judge that they had reached a verdict. They filed back into the courtroom, returning to their assigned seats in the jury box, avoiding Dunwoody's gaze. In language of double negatives picked up from the jury instructions, the forewoman announced that the association had not acted unreasonably in not enforcing the restriction in this case and, thus, the jury had found for the defendant association. As Joshua thanked the jurors, Dunwoody could only stare at the floor, as if he might discover some misplaced fact in the carpet that would salvage his case.

Dunwoody's photographic exploits passed into the lore of the community. Thenceforth, J. Thomas Dunwoody would be known as "the Worm of the Vineyard."

10

In the course of the Great Home-Office Case, as the clerks at the county courthouse liked to call it, Angela and Joshua had learned from judges and other attorneys that Dunwoody was a courthouse fixture. Some of the bailiffs saw him so much that they thought he was a licensed attorney and allowed him to venture behind the bar and even into the judges' sacred chambers.

Joshua's research in the legal files of the clerk's office showed that this case had been Dunwoody's eighteenth lawsuit, all *pro se*. A sampling of defendants included the newspaper and two TV stations, the State Department of Revenue, a local magazine gossip columnist, the County Division of Health, and Midwest Power Co. His suit *du jour* was either libel or intentional infliction of emotional distress. Dunwoody had lost every lawsuit he had brought, although he successfully defended himself against two speeding tickets.

On Tuesdays and Thursdays, when the second floor of the courthouse was teeming with a zoo-like assemblage of DWIers, DUIers, speeders, road ragers, careless lane changers, excessively loud mufflers, driving school dropouts, and others answering the long traffic docket, Dunwoody could be found in the hallways offering counsel and tips on trial strategy to these mangy defendants in exchange for cigarettes.

Among the more interesting items uncovered in Joshua's search was Dunwoody's three-year old conviction for child molestation. The board members at the Vineyard were concerned about having knowledge of this conviction, and worried that they might be liable in the event one of the children in the Vineyard was molested by this degenerate psycho. After vigorous debate, the board decided to notify the owners in a carefully worded memo, which they asked Joshua to draft. As was customary, Michelle handled the mailing, and PSM sent out the memo on its postage machine. A copy of the court record of the conviction was stapled to the memo.

Two days after the board's notice appeared in mailboxes throughout the Vineyard, Dunwoody filed suit against each board member—personally—claiming violation of his constitutional right to privacy, libel, defamation of character, and intentional infliction of emotional distress for publishing the information. For good measure, and looking for the deep pockets of the legal malpractice insurer, Dunwoody had added Angela and Joshua, alleging that they had authored the memo with the "conscious and willful intent" to defame him and to "inflict upon him severe and permanent emotional distress." And for spite, he had named Michelle for her role in mailing the notice. The petition alleged his damages at an even two million dollars.

Settlement discussions were attempted, but both Dunwoody and the Vineyard board were too polarized to negotiate anything. Joshua had called the meeting at his office to prepare the board for trial.

"Well, counselor, every time Dunwoody files a new lawsuit against us, the claim is crazier and the amount of damages is higher. How serious is this one?" George Belt, the association president, asked Joshua. Like many of the owners at the Vineyard, Belt was a blue-collar worker, punching a clock at the auto plant. "You know, Joshua, I think it's time to go fishing, and I'm ready to put the Worm on my hook and drown him down at the river," Belt said.

Maxine Midland, the association secretary, said, "George, you drown all your other worms, so that would probably do the job with Dimwitty." Maxine was in her mid-sixties and clerked at the factory outlet store a few miles away from the Vineyard. "But, that would be too good for him. He should do community service, like cleaning the urinals at the state pen." She shook her head in mock disgust. "The inmates would enjoy watching him in those shorts."

"Look folks," said Joshua calmly, "we take every claim seriously and try never to underestimate the opponent, particularly when he's *pro se*, because judges have a tendency to lean over backwards for these people. Angela and I figure he's got the libel claim on his word processor and routinely files it on the average of every third lawsuit." Joshua studied the faces of each of the board members around the table. "In this case, Dunwoody can't prove libel unless he can show the court record was in error and that the board knew about the error. As for defamation, we should be able to prove that he had no character before the board mailed its notice, and thus he has none to be defamed."

"In other words," Michelle said, "we could win if we could prove that no one liked him before this happened?"

The third board member, David Daggett, stopped taking notes and looked up. "Can't we stop him from filing these lawsuits?" Daggett was treasurer of the association, a man in his early thirties, as handsome and charming as a systems analyst could be. We're not financially prepared to pay for such expensive legal work." Daggett recounted how much stress was placed on the association's budget by the costs of defending the lawsuit. "Dunwoody's going to send the association into financial ruin, even bankruptcy. And, mark my words, people, that's exactly his strategy."

"David, the association can't block an owner from his day in court," Joshua answered. "The essence of this case is that the jury will decide whether the interest of all the owners in knowing about this conviction—which is a matter of public record—outweighs whatever privacy rights Dunwoody might have under these circumstances. Our position is that the association is entitled to what the law calls 'qualified privilege' to communicate with our owners, who are members of the association, on matters of common interest to the entire community."

"We have all the faith in you, Joshua," said Daggett, "but, as treasurer, I'm concerned that we simply can't afford to continue this lawsuit."

After Dunwoody's previous suit, the insurance company had notified the board that the association's directors' and officers' liability policy would not be renewed. The D&O insurance policy provided coverage for claims against the association based on the board's decisions or actions. "So, we got caught between policies, and now we're self-insured. We're on our own." Daggett handed out copies of the mid-year financial statement he had prepared. "You can see that, without our D&O coverage, we've been dipping into our reserves to pay attorney's fees. We've had three substantial special assessments in the last two years, and I, for one, don't want another financial surprise. Why don't we try to settle this by offering an apology and retraction?"

Michelle and Joshua exchanged nervous glances down the length of the conference table. Joshua remembered that Michelle had walked into the meeting with a hacksaw, and he wondered whether one of the board members would use it on Daggett.

George and Maxine were all too familiar with Daggett's personal financial problems. Daggett's divorce thrust him over the precipice of bankruptcy within six months, and he had been free falling since. The bank started to repossess his Chevy Vega, but reconsidered when the repo agent arrived at the parking lot and saw the vehicle. Daggett had been late paying his general assessments and was constantly three months behind. He still hadn't paid two of the special assessments. Yet, he refused to resign from the board despite direct requests from the other board members to do so.

George and Maxine listened to Daggett in stony silence. In their minds, Dunwoody was no better than a terrorist, with no concern for community values. They refused to negotiate with terrorists. They wanted the Worm squashed at any price. They wondered whether Daggett was more interested in fostering the association's interests or protecting his own precarious financial condition.

Joshua's meeting with the board ended that evening at eight-thirty. The Vineyard board had filed out, leaving Michelle and Joshua alone in the conference room. Joshua stuffed papers back into their files. "I'm starved, but I don't want Chinese takeout for the third time this week. You want to grab some dinner?"

Michelle straightened her papers and reached under her chair for the hacksaw. Turning to Joshua, she said, "I'd go home, but I'm afraid to open the fridge. Last time I checked, some of the leftovers were moving and making squishy sounds, like a compost bin."

Glancing at her files on the conference table, Michelle reflected on his invitation for dinner. Professionally, her work was all-consuming. She had been on a roll at work, and was not looking for the distraction of a relationship right now. Nevertheless, to be honest, she had entertained thoughts of Joshua in the past few months—he was certainly attractive and seemed to be nice. *If anything comes of this, it's going to be at a pace I'm comfortable with, slow and sure.* His invitation was cleverly disguised, sounding casual and spur-of-the-moment, not giving her much time to think of reasons to reject it. She vowed to herself that she would be cautious. "I'll join you, but only if it doesn't affect our professional relationship." She picked up the hacksaw and said with mock seriousness, "Or, you'll get *this*." She moved the hacksaw alongside her neck in a sawing motion. "This dinner is not a date. Is that understood?"

"Absolutely. Oh, I couldn't agree more," Joshua responded without hesitation. *Anything is a start*, he thought. "This is an *un*-date. We're merely continuing our meeting over some food. A simple matter of mutual convenience. A concession to the fact that great minds think on their bellies. Nothing extravagant, I assure you. How about Bertolio's?"

Joshua started turning off the lights as they walked out. B.J. Page was still in her office, mired in electronic legal research involving the campaign lawsuit filed against the Cove, determining whether a candidate's right to political speech extended to a private community that prohibited solicitation. Sticking his head through the open door, Joshua said, "B.J., we're done for the night. Why don't you get going, or are you sleeping on the couch again?"

She looked up from her computer and blinked. "Joshua, you know I'm just a paralegal," she said in her low gravelly voice. I have to stay on top of this rapidly evolving field of law. If I choose to sleep over on the couch, it's because I'm dedicated to my job, and it has nothing to do with the ugly fact that I may lack a personal life outside the fourth floor of this old warehouse." B.J. waved a glossy magazine in Joshua's direction. "I was just reading an article by this techie lawyer in the *State Bar Journal*. It's called 'How a Scanner Changed My Life.' Pretty exciting stuff," she grinned. "Oh! I just remembered, did you get this email from Angela?" B.J. handed him a printout.

"Thanks, B.J.," Joshua said, glancing at the email, then folding the paper in thirds and slipping it into the inside pocket of his jacket. "See you tomorrow."

11

It was after nine o'clock p.m. when Michelle and Joshua arrived, in separate cars, at Bertolio's Ristorante. They were seated at a small table in the back of the crowded, dimly lit restaurant. The maitre d' produced a tall candle on their table, lit it with a wooden match, and disappeared. Joshua looked around to make sure no one was within eavesdropping distance.

Michelle looked at the candle and smiled. "This table reminds me of a song by Leonard Cohen that I used to play when I had time to practice my guitar. The song is called "One of Us Cannot Be Wrong," and it starts like this:

> I lit a thin green candle
> To make you jealous of me
> But the room just filled up with mosquitoes
> They heard that my body was free.

"I don't get it," Joshua said, his brows furrowed. "It's nonsensical. What do you think it means?"

"Life is nothing more than people taking little bites out of you."

"Well, it's either way over my head, or way under it. I think it's about a man who tries to attract a woman with his mind, but he can only get women who are incapable of appreciating him. Who wrote it? Leonard *Who*? Never heard of him," Joshua said with a renewed frown.

"Leonard Cohen was a noteworthy writer of folk songs in the late sixties, a Canadian, actually, but other performers made his work popular, like his best-known song, 'Suzanne,' which I think was recorded by Judy Collins." Michelle paused then gave Joshua a very serious and penetrating gaze. "Tell me you're kidding—you've really never heard of Leonard Cohen? Where's your appreciation of American culture?"

"Look, when we decided to have dinner, I didn't know there was going to be a pop quiz. I would have been better prepared."

Michelle feigned a contemptuous look then turned to glance around the restaurant. "Nice place," she said, looking at the alluring photographs of Tuscany that covered the walls. "Some day, I'll visit Venice," she said with a sigh. "It was nice of you to invite me to dinner, but this is definitely not a date."

"All right. Message received." Joshua looked her in the eye and said, "What makes you think I would invite you to dinner, anyway?"

"Because you just did."

"Did not."

"Did so."

Always trying to position himself to have the last word, Joshua said, "Michelle, if I thought I could trust you, I'd have written up a memorandum of understanding, with all the particulars. We could stipulate to no dates, and no pop quizzes."

"We could call it the Un-Date Agreement."

"Exactly."

"Bet you wouldn't sign it."

"Would so."

"Would not."

A polite throat clearing at Joshua's shoulder brought

a temporary halt to the verbal skirmish. They looked up and saw the waiter, eager to promote the chef's specials off the dinner menu. When the waiter finished his recitation, describing the fresh pasta and spedini dishes, he handed them a pair of menus and hurried off to the kitchen.

Joshua leaned across the table and said in a loud whisper, "How can you not want one of the chef's specials when they're described with an Italian accent?"

Michelle smiled. "It's probably true—some women are overcome by a foreign accent. So, what do you recommend in this joint?" Michelle teased, studying the menu by pointing her finger to each entree as she devoured it mentally.

"I really don't know. This is my first time here."

"Once again, why don't I believe you?" She feigned a pout. "You probably take all your dates here."

Joshua picked up a thick slice of Italian bread and drowned it in a plate of olive oil. "Only the mean ones. Let's just say that my personal life isn't quite that exciting. Although I love practicing law and couldn't think of anything I'd rather do at this point in my life, it seems to have sucked all my energy. It makes me burn a quart of blood a day. It drains me of any free time to have a social life. How about you—anybody special in your life?"

Michelle pretended to be preoccupied with the menu. *Sounds like a familiar refrain.* She raised her eyes to look at Joshua. "Dozens," she finally said. "Actually, I don't have two minutes to think about it. Erin, a friend of mine, nailed it when she told me, 'time is the new poverty.' "

"And, you're one of the new time poor? Just for the record, this is not a date," Joshua said, the words bursting out in a deliberative staccato. He closed his menu and looked around for the waiter.

When their dinners arrived, they smothering the table with wonderful aromas. The waiter distributed the food with a practiced flourish, clasped his hands to his chest with pride, bid them *buon appetito*, and scurried away.

Michelle took a small bite of her beef spedini, marinated in butter and garlic and charbroiled to perfection, just as the waiter had described. "This is superb," she said, reaching for her glass of chianti. "I'm glad you ordered the pasta because I knew it would be fun watching you eat it."

Joshua's face was hovering just above his plate, his fork at his lips, trying to reduce the distance over which he had to coax several uncooperative noodles into his mouth. He glanced around to the neighboring tables to see if anyone was watching his battle with the recalcitrant pasta. He examined his tie and observed with pride that no sauce had found it yet.

Joshua remembered Angela's email that he had tucked into his suit pocket. He unfolded the single sheet and skimmed the memo. First, he read Mac's email, recapping the suspected break-in, the police investigation, and the fact that nothing appeared to be disturbed. Angela's reply followed, recommending that Joshua help Michelle and Mac explore possible motives and strategies.

"This break-in business is really weird. What's your gut tell you?"

Michelle related her analysis. She described her two scenarios, noting that there were so few facts, she could only speculate. "But, I can't just dismiss it. Jenni may be a complete ditz sometimes, but my gut tells me that we should assume she set the alarm when she locked up Friday night. If so, someone got in, disarmed the system, and then left without setting it again. The question is, was anything taken? If nothing was taken, then what was the person looking for?"

"It would be easier if you could identify something that was taken," Joshua said. "But, it sounds like you don't know what happened because you can't find anything missing.

Let's start with why. Maybe we can list some reasons why someone wanted to get into PSM's offices. What are the usual motives? Money? Revenge? Information?

"Information? That's so abstract. We have a ton of information and data, but what exactly do we have that would be so valuable that somebody would break in to get it, yet we can't find anything missing?"

"Did you check your files?"

"Of course," Michelle said, her voice edgy. "We went through our files three times without finding anything out of order. All the cabinets were locked, just like they always are, and we didn't see anything missing."

"Do you keep a safe?"

"Yes," Michelle said, wearily. "And it was still locked, but we looked inside anyway, and we took inventory of all the keys we keep in there. We're certain no one got into the safe."

"How about your desk drawers?" Joshua asked with a serious look, which suddenly turned into an impish grin. "Sorry. You already told me that nobody wants to get into your drawers."

Michelle instantly kicked him in the shins under the table. "You're asking for this, you know," she said as she renewed her sawing motion along her neck with an imaginary hacksaw.

Joshua grimaced in pain, and a wounded cry of "Ouch!" streamed from behind clenched teeth. With one hand, he rubbed his bruised shin. With the other, he prepared his next attack on the pasta. He rotated the fork slowly, carefully, meticulously. Two stubborn noodles trailed eight inches from his fork. Giving up for the moment, he said, "So, we don't know what was taken. Perhaps nothing, at least, nothing tangible. Suppose that it's got something to do with information. Yeah, information that would be part of a larger motive. Money, revenge, or power. Maybe leverage for blackmail. Maybe it was something out of a James Bond movie, where this spy uses a high-tech miniature camera to take pictures of documents. Then he puts the file back in the cabinet, and nobody ever knows he was there."

Michelle's face was scrunched up. "What comes first? The why or the who?"

"That will give us something to work on at our next un-date, like tomorrow night?"

12

Angela and Philip strolled, arm in arm, up the gentle incline of Rue Mouffetard, flanked by a rainbow of colors along both sides of the narrow, cobblestone street in central Paris. Peaches, bananas, black cherries, tomatoes, melons, and other fruits and vegetables, sausages, chickens, and breads were overflowing their stalls in this vibrant outdoor market. They picked out some apples, grapes, and pears for a picnic lunch. Further up the street, they found a *maison de frommage*, a *boulangerie*, and a *magazin de vin*, where they loaded up with cheese, a baguette, and a bottle of Haut-Medoc.

"Feeling more like a Parisian now, Phil?" Angela asked as they spread their picnic on a nearby park bench.

It seemed cool for July, and Philip was grateful for the cotton sweater he had bought at the department store, Printemps. "Hard to tell. It looks like most Parisians devote themselves to devouring heavy sauces, drinking espresso, and smoking cigarettes all day. And they're all thin. Back home, it seems like about eighty percent of Americans are overweight. But, I love the way the French elevate eating to an art form, a process rather than an event, that must be savored one tasty morsel at a time. I could adapt to that." He paused to take a bite out of a shiny, dark red apple. "So, what's new at the office?"

"Actually, one item is pretty interesting, Phil. We have this gated condo, about three hundred units, real upscale. Lots of important people live there, and all the others aspire to be important. Wealth, power, influence, or all of the above. The president of the condominium association aggressively wants all of those things. He's built his own little political machine in the condo. He's the head rooster out there, the king cock." Angela paused to spread some brie on a piece of baguette. "P.S., the association's reserves are pushing the million dollar mark."

"Sounds like a king with a very rich fiefdom," said Philip.

"More complex than king. Add ward boss, imperial ruler, and dictator, and you get a better picture of this guy—his name's Curtis. Anyway, the primary election is coming up for one of the county council seats, so what does our president do? He lets his favorite candidate, the incumbent councilman, come through the gate, and even walks around with him to knock on doors and press the flesh. Brand X is the challenger, an attorney in the prosecutor's office named Brandon Mason—not someone to be taken lightly. Mason hears about this and demands equal rights to go into the Cove, canvass door-to-door, leave brochures, and do all the normal stuff that politicians like to do when they run for office."

"Let me guess," said Philip. "The king stands in front of the gates and refuses to let Mason enter." He re-filled their plastic cups with wine.

"You can go to the front of the class. Not only that, but the gate guards—we call them attendants so the board doesn't get sued if some owner gets mugged—are under strict orders from Curtis to refuse entry to Mason."

Angela looked up at Philip, who was shaking his head in bemusement. "Oh, it gets worse. You'll love this! King

Curtis issued what he called an 'executive order'—more like a royal edict—stating that the president, between board meetings, has the authority to determine who can solicit within the community."

"Wasn't there a recent case in New Jersey where the board in this high-rise condo used its newsletter to endorse one candidate, and refused to let the opposing candidate distribute his own literature to the owners?" Philip asked.

"Exactly. And the board lost that case. All our guy had to do was pick up the phone and call Joshua or me and we could have avoided this dispute. But, of course, our clients hardly ever ask for preventive lawyering. There are three reasons why they don't."

If work is her aphrodisiac, Philip thought, *I can go along with it.* "And, what might those three reasons be?"

"Okay, smartie, here are my three reasons: One, it's because the board members are unpaid, untrained, and unsmart. Or, two, they hate to spend money on attorney's fees, which is a false economy. Or, three, they would rather do whatever they want without a nagging attorney raising questions. By the time they wake up, they've dug themselves into a big hole, and it's often too late. You know the ad for the oil filter—'pay me now, or pay me later?' It's a shame, but it keeps us in business." Angela selected an apple, polished it on her sleeve, and took a tentative, juicy bite.

Angela continued, "So, the Cove board was served with a monster lawsuit—a TRO, temporary restraining order—and injunction, seeking the right to enter this gated community in order to carry out campaign activities under protection of political free speech guaranteed by the First Amendment. The judge immediately granted the TRO, and there's a hearing in ten days on whether a preliminary injunction should be granted. Well, seven days, now."

"I assume you have a Laclede Multi-Part Defense Plan?" Philip asked with a laugh.

"Definitely," she said. "First, I'm sending an email to B.J. so she can put the insurer on notice of the claim. I doubt there'll be coverage, though, because King Curtis placed the Directors' & Officers' liability policy with one his cronies, and I'm sure it doesn't have non-monetary defense against injunctive actions. Second, I'm sending Joshua an email, with a copy to Mac and Michelle, suggesting a personal *tete-a-tete* with King Curtis to tell him he's really shot himself in the foot this time and see if he'll back off. We might be able to settle the whole thing before it gets in the news. Third, I better think about who we'll have as witnesses at the hearing."

13

The blond-haired man sat up and rubbed his eyes as the train rolled into the Hauptbahnof, Zurich's Central Station. His suit didn't fit well on his slender frame, and he looked uncomfortable wearing it. Other passengers were getting up from their seats, gathering their bags, and standing in the aisle. He ran his hands through his wavy hair, straightened his regimental striped tie, and patted the inside pocket of his jacket to make sure his passport was secure. He held onto his briefcase tightly, retrieved his shoulder bag from the overhead rack of the second-class compartment, and stood with the other passengers waiting for the train to come to a halt by the platform.

As he waited, his fingers felt the new business cards in his shirt pocket. He liked the nickname given him by Vinnie the Bug, and he had printed new business cards that referred to him as a global business consultant.

The Consultant found a café in the train station and ordered a latte and a hard roll then washed and shaved in the men's restroom. The matronly attendant slowly worked at mopping the floor. With no apparent need to rush, her measured sweeps of the tiled floor were almost effortless, slow-paced and methodical. He thought it curious that the men using the urinals didn't seem concerned that a woman was in the men's restroom, making their business her business.

Refreshed but growing anxious as he anticipated the task ahead, the Consultant decided he should get some local currency. He found the currency exchange window, expecting to get the new euro. But, the Swiss were not in the European Union, so he would get Swiss francs at the exchange rate of 1.00 CHF to .6100 USD. CHF was shorthand for Confederation Helvetica Franc. He pulled out a tiny calculator the size of a credit card, and he figured that if he exchanged one hundred U.S. dollars, he would receive one hundred sixty four Swiss francs, less commission.

Walking out of the train station, he paused in the Bahnhofplatz, the large plaza on the south side of the station, to enjoy the fresh, cool air. He found a bench near the statue of the Swiss statesman, Alfred Escher, and made a mental note to research Escher to see why he was a national hero, worthy of such a statue. Someday soon, he would have the time and money to spend doing such frivolous things. But, for now, he had far more important tasks on his mind, and he studied the large street map of Zurich that was posted on a kiosk.

The Consultant's travel to Zurich had been carefully, intricately designed to ensure he was not followed. He had suffered the five-hour train ride on Amtrak to Chicago, and had taken the El from the Loop to O'Hare. Next he had taken a direct Lufthansa flight to Frankfurt and then transferred to the overnight train to Zurich. During the entire trip, he had nervously glanced around and behind him, looking for anyone who seemed to be following him. While not convinced that all these precautions were actually necessary, he had enjoyed immensely the detailed, meticulous planning involved and making all the reservations on the Internet, particularly the electronic ticketing. He congratulated himself on a successful completion of the first leg of his trip. Now for the critical second phase—to open a numbered bank account in Zurich.

He thought fondly of his darling little applet, Special Assessment, that he'd left at PSM and gave a silent prayer that she was sleeping quietly and unnoticed in the web browser. There it would hide until someone logged on to PSM's computer to make an electronic contact with the user's bank. Once that occurred, the applet would awaken and be activated in the Master Bookkeeper software. The applet would make an electronic snapshot of each password by memorizing the keystrokes of the user. Then, it would wait silently for further instructions.

That's when the Consultant, as the applet's master, would log on, enter the password for a particular account, and then send an instruction to the user's bank. The user's software would not be able to distinguish the source of the instruction, and it would assume the instruction came from its customer. PSM would not discover the transaction until the next bank statement arrived and possibly even later. If the transfer was timed to occur shortly after the user's bank closed its records to prepare the monthly statement, the user might not learn of the theft for up to four weeks.

My darling Special Assessment. Clever or malicious? Malicious or clever?

But, what he needed now was a new account at a different bank. A discreet bank, one in which the employees didn't ask any questions. The best way to overcome the sheer fear, nervousness, and anxiety of trying to conduct business in another country, particularly opening a foreign bank account which, of course, he had never done, or even dreamed about for that matter, was to anticipate, to plan, and to be prepared.

What would the bank want to know on its application? He had made a detailed list of accounts to demonstrate his credit worthiness, although the list was a bit short, with only one credit card and a checking account. He was prepared to impress the bank officer with the success—or at least the promise of success—of his global high-tech consulting business, and he had practiced and rehearsed his presentation countless times on the plane and train en route to Zurich. He had made an outline, then drafted the entire presentation on his computer, then reduced it to a synopsis, and reduced the synopsis to a series of bullet points, and recited the presentation under his breath at least fourteen times until it was committed to memory. He was as prepared as he would ever be.

The clock tower in the Bahnhofplatz began a series of gongs. The Consultant looked up and saw that it was ten o'clock. If anything, he could rely on the famed accuracy of Swiss clocks. He synchronized his watch. *Perfect timing, the banks will be open now.*

He walked leisurely down the Bahnhofstrasse, a tree-lined street reserved for pedestrians that was bustling with activity. Windows on the upper stories were decorated with bright red geraniums. Passing elegant shops and department stores, he wrote down the name and address of several banks, studied the appearance of each, trying to decide which one he should approach. *This city reeks with the sweet smell of money.* Reaching the Paradeplatz, he saw the stately facade of the Zuricher Zentral Banque. It did not appear to be too imposing. Gathering his courage, he walked in.

"*Guten Morgan,*" he began nervously to the attractive, young receptionist seated behind a handsome mahogany desk.

"Good morning, *mein Herr*, how may I help you?" She greeted him in fluent English with a German accent.

He paused, wondering why the receptionist immediately knew to greet him in English. Even so, he was greatly relieved that he could proceed without a language barrier. "Well, I'm here…" he began unevenly, "to open an account for my consulting business. I regret not calling ahead for an appointment, but I would be happy to wait until someone is available to see me."

The receptionist invited him to have a seat while she busied herself on the phone. After a few minutes, another woman dressed in a dark business suit approached him in the lobby, introduced herself as Herr Gottlieb's assistant, and led him down an interior corridor bordered with dark wood paneling and cloth wallpaper to the private offices of the bank officials.

A heavy-set, bald man with gold-rimmed glasses, a black three-piece suit, and a full walrus mustache that hid his upper lip walked around the desk with his hand outstretched. "Good morning, sir, I'm Heinrich Gottlieb." The Consultant introduced himself and presented a fresh business card to the bank officer.

"May I offer you some coffee?"

"That would be very thoughtful, thank you."

As Gottlieb brewed fresh coffee in a silver coffee press on the sidebar, he turned to his visitor and said, "Please, have a seat. I understand you would like to open an account." Gottlieb parked his considerable bulk back in his banker's chair.

The Consultant chose one of the three luxurious leather wingback chairs, placing his shoulder bag and briefcase on the thick Oriental rug. He took a deep breath, retrieved the mental image of the bullet points he had rehearsed on the train, and began. "That's correct. I've not had the need for an account in Europe, up to now at least, but my consulting business has grown so rapidly. You see, the field of high-tech, computer-based consulting for global corporations is quite the growth market these days.

I find it's time for my banking relationships in Europe to grow and mature also."

Herr Gottlieb reviewed the business card. "Your offices are in St. Louis?"

"That's correct. The main campus of our global headquarters is in St. Louis. The area is becoming the Silicon Valley of pharmaceutical and plant science research in the United States."

"Ah, although I am of Swiss descent, I know that St. Louis has a rich heritage of German settlement and influence. Most noteworthy, perhaps, are your breweries."

The Consultant decided that it would be better not to bring up the rich French heritage of St. Louis. "Indeed, Herr Gottlieb, and the tradition lives on in our annual Strassenfest."

"Very well," Gottlieb said as he carefully inspected the business card. An uneasy prolonged silence ensued.

The pause in the conversation made the Consultant nervous. *Was Gottlieb stopping to allow time for a hidden camera to scan my face for Interpol? Maybe Gottlieb simply expects me to continue. Okay, here goes, bullet point number three.* "My consulting business is based on developing the latest in software programs for very sophisticated, high technology research operations, such as biogenetic technology applications…"

Gottlieb jumped out of his seat, holding both hands up as dual stop signs. "*Bitte, bitte, mein Herr,*" he said firmly but not unpleasantly although his thick German accent was sufficient to make him sound authoritarian. "At the Zuricher, we do not pry into our customer's affairs. It is enough that you entrust your money with us," he chuckled in his bass voice. "We do not need to know your business. We would prefer not to know. Even so, a word of friendly advice. Many Europeans highly suspect biogenetic technology being imported by you Americans. If this is really your business, I suggest you do not advertise it outside your business partners. Mad cow, and all that. No, we do not need to know how you make your money. We are a bank. You have money. We provide banking services for your money. It's really quite simple."

The powerfully built banker sat down again, removed his gold-rimmed glasses and placed them gently on the top of the large mahogany desk. He pinched the bridge of his nose then stroked his mustache at the corners. The Consultant glanced around the room, from the desk to the matching paneling, which ran from the floor to a chair rail around the room, above which was a gallery of photographs showing former bank presidents looking rather stiff and prosperous.

Gottlieb continued in a soft, pleasant voice laced with his German accent. "Allow me to explain the banking laws of Switzerland, enacted by the Federal Assembly, which, of course, govern our Zuricher Zentral Banque. Switzerland is remarkable in today's global economy for stable currency and international trading relationships. Our banks are instrumental in maintaining these desirable elements of stability and predictability, which allow our country to attract trading partners abroad in every aspect of the economy."

The banker walked with a deliberate motion to the sidebar and refilled the Consultant's china cup from the large coffee press. He returned to the desk, but did not sit down. "We operate in the strictest of confidence and with the utmost discretion. After today, you will be a valued customer, but only a number as far as any future dealings and transactions are concerned. It is possible for our customers to make virtually any transaction, including deposits, withdrawals, and transfers, as your needs may require. We honor transactions twenty-four hours a day, by phone, fax, or electronic transfer. Therefore, in the future, you need never visit us again, although that is not to say you would not be welcome at any time. No appointment, no waiting."

The Consultant slowly sipped the strong coffee. "And my identity, as well as the existence and status of my account, are absolutely protected against discovery by others?"

"You may be assured that we practice the highest standards of privacy and confidentiality for our customers. It is our reputation. It is what our customers rely on. Not only for your protection against third parties, but also within our institution. The name of the account holder is coded and secured even against discovery by our clerical staff. Plus, unlike your American banks, we do not mail monthly statements, for several good reasons. First, we find that such a practice is unnecessary when we are dealing with sophisticated businessmen like yourself. Second, it is unnecessary when we have such a vast array of electronic means for communication that are faster and more efficient. Third, printed statements may invite snooping eyes to inspect the paper in your trash." Gottlieb's stern face relaxed into the hint of a smile. "So there. All you will need after today is your secret number. Do you have any other questions?"

The Consultant took another sip of coffee and sat the china cup gently on the small table next to his leather chair. "I think you've exhausted my questions, Herr Gottlieb, thank you very much."

"Very well, then." Gottlieb looked across the desk at his visitor. "And what amount and currency will you be using to open the account today?"

The Consultant hesitated. The one question he had

not anticipated. "Actually," he stalled, "I don't like carrying large amounts on my person, in any form. I trust you understand my sense of caution in view of the intense security at airports these days. I'm planning to transfer certain funds to the bank within the next several days, and continuing far into the future. Electronically, as you suggested, perhaps over five million in U.S. dollars. However, if a deposit today is required, I can provide…uh…a token amount, merely a gesture to satisfy the bank's formalities." He reached in his wallet and removed a note for one hundred CHFs he had obtained earlier at the Hauptbahnhof, and placed the bill on the corner of Gottlieb's desk, observing Gottlieb as the banker's eyes followed the money. The Consultant quickly changed the subject. "And, I assume, there is a written application or some procedural form that must be completed for the bank's records and to assign a number to the account?"

"Of course, but our application is discreet and highly confidential. Customary information, mostly, such as banking references, sources of credit, a summary of assets and liabilities, and so forth. My assistant will provide the form, and you may fill out the information in one of our private rooms. If you are free to return after fourteen hundred this afternoon, we will have your new account number ready. That would be two o'clock, American time."

Gottlieb retrieved the Swiss francs from the corner of his desk with a perceptible look of disdain, as if it were beneath him to handle such a small amount of money in his bank. He walked over to his visitor and they shook hands again. "It has been a pleasure, *mein Herr*, and we look forward to a long and prosperous relationship for both of us. Enjoy our wonderful city of Zurich. Will you be staying long?"

"Oh, uh, well…I have a few appointments here," he lied, "but I'll return soon, I expect."

The banker led them out of his office and to the desk of his assistant, the woman in the stern business suit, where he handed over the note for one hundred Swiss francs and asked the assistant to attend to the needs of their new customer.

The Consultant sat alone in the private room, studying the one-page application form as he refilled his cup from a freshly brewed coffee press. Gottlieb had overstated the information requested on the form. Back home, it's easier to open a bank than to open an account. Here, they just want your money. *They don't care who you are or what you do for a living, unless you're dumb enough to try biogenetic technology in Europe. All they care about is the money you have for them, particularly if it's hard dollars from the good ol' U.S. of A.*

14

"Mr. Carlton," the taller man began, "our company has a very substantial presence in the community association industry back East, and we're looking to expand in the Midwest, starting right here. We think the growth prospects in St. Louis, both in terms of urban renaissance and suburban migration, are excellent for a company that is well positioned, like ours. We provide a full range of management services, and if you'll look at our proposal for Estrella Cove, you'll find our rates very competitive." The two men sitting across from Curtis' desk were dressed in matching black business suits, their dark hair slicked back with an abundance of gel. Beside their chairs were parked matching, slim black briefcases. The shorter, stockier man fondled a small gold loop in his left ear.

Curtis wore his favorite golf shirt, a shade of yellow that he described as "school-bus mustard." It wasn't tucked into his brown slacks, as Curtis had given up years ago any attempt to circumnavigate his ample girth.

He leaned back in his new chair, comforted by the smell of new leather, and thumbed through the literature presented by the businessmen from the East Coast. Curtis was proud of his new office. He had agonized over whether to greet today's business visitors over at the coffee table with the Queen Anne couch and wingback chairs or at his aircraft-carrier-sized walnut desk. The office featured Curtis' own private restroom and shower, equipped with the finest fixtures, down to the washers, all furnished by Carlton Wholesale Plumbing Supply. A collection of miniature fixtures adorned his desktop, symbols of the family business—a brass bidet, a crystal bathtub, and a gold plated faucet to light his cigars.

The computer sat on the matching antique credenza next to a laser printer and was fully linked with PSM's system. Curtis had chortled aloud when he scrolled through the association's financial records for the first time.

He admitted to himself that Michelle had done one helluva job. She had been on site every day to supervise the construction of the office and select the furnishings. Simply telling her how well she had done was insufficient. He'd send her a dozen roses, he thought, to show his appreciation for the outstanding job. And take her to dinner at the Pride of Maine Restaurant, where he could appreciate her finer points over lobster with drawn butter. His eyes half closed, Curtis was overcome by a fantasy: *How can I get into her tight…schedule?*

He scanned his visitors' business cards for the third time, as if some hidden negotiating edge were present, if he could only find it. Curtis prided himself on his skill in evaluating people at first glance. He studied the business card of Theodore 'Ted' Kosankis, Vice-President, Logistics. *Kosankis wears an earring, doesn't say much, looks like the muscle of this pair, not too bright.* James R. Bedford, Vice-President, Marketing. *The taller one. He's the mouth and the brains.* The black-suit twins were with Central Management and Investment Services, Inc. No letters after their names. No professional credentials or certifications noted.

"We've had the same management company here since control was transferred from the developer," Curtis said, glaring suspiciously at Bedford, trying to measure the businessman across from him. Behind Curtis' intense gaze, the engine of a competitive mind was running at full throttle. He explained that the Cove had plenty of reserves, and the physical plant was well-maintained. "We're content, things are going great, the buildings are well maintained, the grounds are green, the owners are happy, and they're paying their assessments. Everything is just peachy. So, why change?"

"You can't afford not to change, Mr. Carlton," said Bedford, returning the volley with an equally intense gaze. "We can save you money. We can make more money for you. If you've had the same manager for several years, it's time to change. We've done our homework, you see, and we know you're using PSM and that they're charging you fifteen dollars per door. Frankly, they're a small operation with limited resources. It's time for new thinking, new blood, new energy. You don't know how successful this place can be until it's under experienced management by the type of people who have a creative vision of how management should function." Bedford leaned forward with a slight smile. "I'm sure you understand what I'm talking about."

Kosankis grunted his approval, his head down, staring at Curtis through a single row of thick, dark eyebrows.

Curtis fingered the slick brochure of CMIS. It was in a handsome binder with a spiral comb and divider tabs. The cover page featured a photograph of one of the gates, with the name and the signature of the Cove. But otherwise, the brochure appeared to be nothing more than a generic marketing piece, stored in the company computer and regurgitated with slight modifications for each new prospective client. It was mostly about how great the company was, the number of clients, the wisdom of the CMIS approach to managing community associations, and glowing quotes from a variety of satisfied clients, all of whom seemed to be located on the East Coast. Curtis turned to the final tab marked Proposal.

Bedford could see that Curtis had reached the meat of the marketing piece. "Now, Mr. Carlton, the rates contained in our proposal reflect our absolute commitment to be competitive. In fact, we'll wager that we can save you money as well as beat the competition, but we would need to review your detailed financials for the past two years. Then we could see where we can economize on your expenses." Bedford straightened his tie and shifted toward the front of his seat, using his Mont Blanc to point to the rates quoted in the proposal.

Curtis studied the proposal. "Tell you what. I've got the financials right here on my computer and can print them out for you," Curtis beamed proudly. He wheeled around to face the credenza and kept talking. "Got this baby just a few days ago, and it's plugged directly into PSM's system." Curtis struck several keys, moved his mouse and clicked, his eyes fixed on the monitor. "It's a great setup because I can track our finances in real time. The owners pay their assessments directly into a lockbox at the bank. So, I can monitor revenue from the minute the funds are credited by the bank to payment of bills and transfers to reserves. I can even move blocks of reserves from one account to another to take advantage of higher interest rates. I can do it on a daily basis if I want."

Curtis moved the mouse and clicked again. The laser printer started humming. He handed the papers to Bedford. "You gentlemen are welcome to use the conference room next door to look over the financials."

Twenty minutes later, just as Curtis was finishing a

phone call, Kosankis and Bedford knocked on the open door and strode into his office.

"Here's what we can do for you, Mr. Carlton," Bedford began, setting his pocket calculator and notepad on Curtis' desk. Bedford noticed the miniature brass bidet with a gold nameplate that announced "William Curtis Carlton, President," if anyone was uncertain. "PSM has three permanent maintenance personnel for routine repairs and maintenance, but you're outsourcing all other work to contractors and vendors. You're not only outsourcing, but the other thing you're doing wrong is that all your major projects are put out on competitive bid. Again, that's on top of your three full-time maintenance people. We can cut costs from ten to fifteen percent by using our own maintenance company for everything. You'll deal with one set of people who are intimately familiar with the needs of the development, and you won't have to waste time getting all those competitive bids. They're always more expensive anyway."

Curtis bristled at the idea of firing his maintenance people, one of whom was his wife's sister's kid. He was twenty-two, and didn't have enough brain cells working even to keep a job as a pipe cutter in the family plumbing supply business, so Curtis put him on the maintenance crew at the Cove. Curtis' wife, Evelyn, would have to explain it all to her sister, and he figured that he'd never hear the end of it. *Life's too damned short*, he thought. "Well, we might be able to do business, but our maintenance crew are good people, and they're familiar with the property. We just can't let them go."

"That's understandable," Bedford said. "Look, you and I are businessmen, so let's be frank. We came here because we've heard great things about your community. We want your business. And, to show you our commitment, we can make it worth your while—sort of a signing bonus just between us—if you can bring Estrella Cove on board."

Boy, is this guy a smooth closer or what? He studied Bedford, wondering whether the Easterner's eye twitched or whether that was really a sly wink. "Well, we can talk some more if you like," Curtis finally said, trying not to appear overly anxious. *What the hell,* he thought, *I'll shove it down their throats and see what comes out.* He remembered the words of his grandfather, "If you don't ask, you don't get."

Curtis passed a hand through his thinning red curly hair as he reviewed his notes. "Why don't you gentlemen go back next door to the conference room? You come up with your best offer, but I'm telling you what we need if you want to be taken seriously. Here's the deal. First, I want you to beat PSM's rate by three dollars per door."

"That's twenty percent," Bedford complained.

"Do you want the business, or not?" Curtis shot back. He was pushing a take-it-or-leave-it proposition. "Second," he continued, jabbing a stubby finger at the proposal, you guarantee a fifteen percent savings the first year in maintenance costs, but one of our three maintenance people stays, at my sole discretion. You'll get part of this savings by using Carlton Wholesale Plumbing Supply as your sole source supplier for all plumbing repairs. I'll guarantee a good price." Bedford had to look away to camouflage a smirk that acknowledged the transparency of Curtis' greed.

"Next, you'll be responsible for getting me out of the PSM contract without a lawsuit, and you pay any cancellation fee. Of course, a change in management would be subject to board approval, and we can never predict what they'll do." It was Curtis' turn to reveal a sly wink. "One other thing," Curtis said, turning to Bedford, "If we go with you guys, although I'm far from certain at this point,

I really don't want to see your ugly mugs at my board meetings. Don't you have any good-looking girls in your firm? In fact, I'm going to add one more contingency, that you hire that Michelle girl away from PSM. She's pretty damn good, and I'm sure she'd like more money for dealing with the likes of me."

Curtis stood up to signal the end of the meeting, his hands came to rest on his considerable middle, his fingers drumming his belly contentedly. "Last," he added, wagging a finger at the proposal, "I haven't forgotten what you said about a signing bonus."

The black-suit twins exchanged sidelong glances as they rose in unison from their seats. "Mr. Carlton," said Bedford, extending his hand, "I think we see eye-to-eye on these business matters. I know how to take care of my partners." Kosankis showed a toothy grin.

"Mr. Carlton was my father. You can call me 'Curtis,'" he said, shaking both their hands.

Bedford and Kosankis returned to the conference room. Bedford used his cell phone and called his office. "Tell the boss that the baby is in the cradle."

15

"Good morning, Jenni! It may be cloudy outside, but in here it's nothing but sunshine!" Sean Eastgate walked briskly to the reception desk and whisked a long-stem yellow rose from behind his back, holding it across the desk for her to smell.

"You're so full of it, Sean." Jenni Hiscock looked up to see Sean's face at the same time she picked up the ringing telephone and leaned forward to smell the rose. The phone cord snagged her mug and overturned it, jerking coffee across the desk. "Oh my god," she screeched into the phone, "I've sprung a leak!"

Sean dropped his shoulder bag, started grabbing dripping papers, and threw tissues on the small brown pond that had formed on Jenni's desk as she struggled to recover her composure. "Yes, this is Preferred Site Management," she gasped into the phone, while watching coffee cascade off the edge of her desk. "I'm sorry, she's on another line. Would you like her voice mail?"

"Sean, you really know how to show a girl a good time," Jenni smiled as she mopped up the desktop.

"If I'd thought that a single yellow rose would excite you this much, I would've gotten you a dozen," Sean laughed. "Hope that wasn't some dear client on the phone."

Sean Eastgate was the techie genius who had installed the computers and software systems at PSM. He had grown up in Southern California spending too much time at the beach. Still, he was bright and applied himself to earning a degree from Pepperdine in computer sciences and marketing. He had moved to St. Louis last year, for reasons that he preferred to keep shrouded in verbal ambiguity, and somehow survived on a rather hand-to-mouth existence while free lancing as a computer consultant. He was very good, but not perfect. Some glitch was always occurring in PSM's sophisticated data processing system. Sean had become such a weekly fixture at the office, troubleshooting and tracking down problems, that Jenni had presented him with a coffee mug of his own.

While any problem that slowed down PSM was always an annoyance to the staff, Jenni looked forward to Sean's visits. He was just under six feet tall, blonde, good looking, mid-thirties, eligible, and seemed to show some interest in her. Unless she was reading the signals entirely wrong, which wouldn't be the first time.

Sean realized that Jenni wasn't the brightest light, but he liked her nonetheless.

He walked into the offices, found Michelle's workstation, and sat down in front of her computer. "Sorry I'm late getting over here, love," he said to her while looking at the monitor. "You know, I finished installing the computer at the Cove a few days ago, but Curtis called me at seven o'clock this morning and ordered me over there to show him how to run some new software he got. Anyway, let me play computer doctor. Take off all your clothes and let Dr. Sean check all your vital signs. Tell me where it hurts."

"Sean, you're just a hopeless beach bum! If I knew what was wrong, you'd be the first I'd tell. Whenever I try to get into my address book program, the computer locks me out." She gave Sean a helpless shrug, hands on hips. "As soon as I click on it, I get a window with a red stop sign that says Unauthorized Entry."

"Any problems with the other programs? What about Master Bookkeeper?"

"Well, nothing I've noticed," Michelle responded.

"Something weird is going on in this office," Sean said. "I can feel it. You've got a gremlin in your computer running around with a stop sign."

Michelle looked over his shoulder at the monitor. "Nothing would surprise me around here," she said. While she reached around Sean to answer the phone, he leaned back so that her breasts brushed against his shoulder.

"Excuse me," he lied, struggling to keep from smirking. "I didn't realize your keyboard had such a nice feel to it," he said, trying to stay busy tapping at the keys.

Michelle thought for an instant that Sean maneuvered into her intentionally, but she couldn't say anything, and turned her attention to the phone call. "Yes, this is Michelle." She paused, listening. "No, I'm sorry, we don't give out that information." Another pause. She ran her hand through her hair, a sign she was getting irritated. "Well, I'm sorry that you disagree, but you can bring it up at the next board meeting, if you like." She listened for a minute. "Well, goodbye to you, too!" She slammed the phone down. "Shit head," she burst and turned to Sean. "How totally rude. He hung up on me."

Sean watched the monitor and worked with the mouse as Michelle watched the screen over his shoulder. After a few minutes, Sean said, "I'm not sure what the problem is exactly, but it may be the circuitry. I'll have to get into all the computers in the office, which will take a more thorough investigation than I have time for right now."

"Sean, that caller really upset me. He's the treasurer of his association and an information systems analyst, and he'd like to track the association's finances on his own computer. He wanted to know when the reserves are posted on our system and when we receive the bank statements. Does that sound like a strange question to you, or is my radar too sensitive?"

"I don't know, Michelle," Sean replied. "Isn't that the same thing Curtis does at the Cove?"

"No, I don't think so because the treasurer's motives are not the same as what Curtis is doing," Michelle said. "Curtis told me he just wants to maximize yield on reserve funds, but the treasurer is concerned that his association is hemorrhaging red ink from a lawsuit brought by a crazy homeowner named Dunwoody. The treasurer, of all people, is delinquent in paying his own assessments, so he may have personal financial problems. And, he comes into the office weekly for financial data and to find out the latest status of the lawsuit. Half the time he spends BS-ing with Jenni. I'm wondering if he's making all these trips here on legitimate association business, or for personal reasons, like he's facing bankruptcy or he's hot for Jenni."

Sean studied the monitor, wondering if Jenni could be serious about this guy. "Michelle, this whole thing with your computer is off the radar screen. I haven't felt this strange since the ex-wife bid me adieu and ran off with her divorce attorney. He was a piece of work. Always wore white shirts and boring ties to remind everyone that he was a lawyer." Sean paused for a minute, reflecting on his failed marriage. "Anyway, back to reality. The problem with the computer is…is…well, it's like the duchess said in *Alice in Wonderland*, 'Tut, tut, my child. Everything's got a moral if only you can find it.' "

DAVID DAGGETT HUNG UP the phone and stared blankly at his computer monitor. He was analyzing the Vineyard's six-month income and expense statement, tweaking the figures to create alternative outcomes. In each scenario, the reserves were zeroed out. The only way to avoid another special assessment to defend the libel case with Dunwoody, the Worm, would be to defer even more maintenance until next year, transfer other expenses, and divert future contributions from reserves to professional fees.

He fought to control his rage, shaking his blond head. Why wouldn't that woman, Michelle, give him a simple answer to a simple question: "When are contributions to reserves posted?" *She's like all women*, he thought. *Irrational.* "May she rot in hell," he exhaled through his teeth.

He would drop by to see Jenni personally, charm her as much as necessary, and get the information. He would find the money. His scheme would work.

16

William Curtis Carlton admired himself in front of the hall mirror. He jutted his chin forward to see if that would tighten his jowls, and he attempted to smooth his curly red hair. Then, he turned to his wife of thirty years and said, "Ev, dear, I'm headed over to the office for a meeting with that young lawyer and the manager. First, though, Mrs. Lindholm wants to get a picture of me. It's a photo op for the Cove *Tattler*. I'll be back later."

Evelyn Carlton was busy warping her loom and nodded approvingly to Curtis as he left the condo. Their only child, Diane, had just graduated from the Theater Conservatory at Emerson College and would be staying in Boston to begin her acting career. When Curtis first retired, Evelyn had convinced him that the two of them should travel to faraway venues and broaden their cultural awareness. Evelyn really wanted to start rebuilding their marriage when Curtis retired. But, having spent his entire life with valves, toilets, and sewer pipes, travel for cultural awareness wasn't exactly his burning passion.

But he would do almost anything in the short term that would make his wife happy in the long run. Mostly, he would do anything to keep her occupied and out of his hair. He had reluctantly yielded to the fantasy of his dear

"Ev," as he affectionately called her, and soon the two of them had headed off on their first adventure since their honeymoon. After several days at El Tovar Lodge on the South Rim of the Grand Canyon, they drove through the high desert country of the Navajo Reservation, from Tuba City east to Kayenta and then south to Ganado.

It was in Ganado, with Curtis practically gagging from the hot, dry climate, that Ev begged him to drive west a few miles to Hubbell's Trading Post. Hubbell's was an historic site that had once served as an intermediary between the Navajo and the cavalry during the 1870's, and it survived as a thriving trading post for the Navajo and tourists, despite its isolated and desperate location. With rapt attention, Ev studied the Navajo women working their looms, creating rugs, blankets, and wall hangings. Ev discovered her passion for weaving.

Returning home, Ev took weaving classes at Craft Alliance, and Curtis grudgingly agreed to buy her a small floor loom, a twenty-two inch model from Harrisonville. *A rather expensive hobby, this weaving business, but it would keep her occupied while I'm busy with politics, doing the people's business.*

Ev's first work was a beautiful wool scarf for Curtis with black and gold stripes, the colors of Ol' Mizzou. Curtis examined the scarf and paused. Without emotion, he said, "Ev, with the loom and the attachments, and all the rest of your paraphernalia, I figure this scarf cost me over five thousand dollars."

She looked at the beautiful scarf and shook her head. "Curtis, it's always about you, isn't it?"

Ev devoted herself to the fabric arts and joined the Weaver's Guild. She was never so happy, warping and wefting her loom every day, banging her beater and pushing her threadles, turning out wall hangings, shawls, scarves, rugs, and other weavings. She became very particular about her yarn, contacting Hubbell's to find out how the Navajo make their yarn, only to learn that they bought it, all ready to weave, at a store in the tiny, dusty, wind-blown town of Sanders, Arizona. Ev called the store in Sanders, opened an account, and ordered a new supply of yarn.

Of course, Ev could buy all the yarn she could possibly use at Wanda's Weaving House, only a thirty-minute drive from the Cove. But, with her passion rapidly becoming an obsession, she continually sought new sources for the best yarns. First, there was the mail-order house in Reykjavik, which, of course, specialized in Icelandic wool. Next, on a trip to Hawaii, she found a yarn shop on Bishop in Honolulu that carried exquisite Italian yarn and opened yet another account. That was followed by a love affair with New Zealand yarn.

But, none of Ev's exploits exceeded the Carltons' trip to Paris, when Ev spent an afternoon touring Gobelin's, the legendary tapestry factory that has produced the huge tapestries hanging in castles and palaces throughout Europe. Ev watched with appreciation as the weavers worked at their looms, most of which were so huge that three weavers could weave a single piece at the same time. On the vertical looms, the weavers checked their work on mirrors that were placed behind the warp, which allowed them to see the other side, which was actually the front. Occasionally, the weavers referred to a full-size drawing of their work, called a "cartoon," that was behind them and served as a guide.

She spent the second day in Paris doggedly venturing from store to store in search of fine yarn, dragging Curtis along, ultimately finding her reward at the extensive display of Bon Marche, the huge department store on the Rue de Sevres.

Ev's total knowledge of French consisted of *"parlez-vous Anglais, s'il vous plait?"* The sales clerk darted from one shelf of yarn to the next as Ev pointed this way and that. The clerk was eager to please but, knowing little English, she soon scurried away in search of bilingual assistance. A young woman with a stroller volunteered but, when confronted with Ev and Curtis, could only struggle through a fractured exchange of broken English. Eventually, she threw her arms toward heaven in surrender, pursed her lips, and quickly fled, pushing her stroller until she disappeared into a canyon of towels and bedding.

After two full hours of examining every ball of yarn, considering the fiber and blend as well as texture, strength, and color, Ev sat down on a chair and sighed with content while she arranged her collection of yarn balls. Curtis suggested that they ship the bulky bags of Anny Blatt and Port Sur Carnet yarn, and they looked around for customer services. They wandered through the huge store, ascending and descending escalators, until they finally found Henri Dubois, an obstinate, dour clerk at the customer services desk on the top floor.

No people are better prepared to engage in dispute than the French. The exaggerated gestures, the feigned indignity, the wry smile followed by the coup de grace. But, few Frenchmen have had the opportunity to tangle with William Curtis Carlton, the plumbing magnate, a brute of a man who would get his way, one way or another.

Curtis began by leaning over the counter and, employing charades, gestured that he wanted to ship the yarn back home. Henri pointed to the bags of yarn, shrugged hopelessly, and responded, *"Je regrets, monsieur, ç'est impossible."* Curtis jabbed a stubby index finger into the unsuspecting face of poor Monsieur Dubois, waved his arms wildly, his voice steadily rising in volume. Curtis mercilessly berated Henri for not understanding him, and yelled at the poor clerk as if Henri Dubois was deaf rather than French.

Henri Dubois would not win this confrontation. Confused and frustrated, besieged and beaten, Henri finally consulted with another clerk in French and soon returned to Curtis, gave a final shrug of surrender and said, "*D'accord, monsieur, ç'est tout!*" Henri produced a form, handed Curtis a pen, and pointed to a signature line. "Insurance," was all he said. Curtis wiped his brow with a red bandanna and scratched his signature on the form, which was entirely in French. The yarn would be shipped back to the states, although the shipping and arrival dates were uncertain.

AS JOSHUA GUIDED HIS AGING '76 BMW 2002 up the winding blacktop road to the Cove's clubhouse, Michelle was sticking her head out the passenger window, gasping for fresh air. "Aren't you worried you'll die of carbon monoxide poisoning riding around in this old deathtrap?" She yelled through the wing vent.

"Michelle, it's unfortunate that you don't appreciate the maturation of a cult car. Old Blue may be over twenty-five years old, and she may have her share of warts and blemishes," he said, as exhaust fumes poured through the football-sized hole in the floor, "but this baby will be a collector's item some day, worthy of a good garage and driven only on Sunday." He patted the dashboard and said, "Don't listen to Michelle, honey, she's just jealous of your irresistible good looks."

As Joshua downshifted and Old Blue roared toward the crest of the hill, Michelle suddenly pointed to the right and said, "Look, isn't that Curtis?" Joshua lurched the car to the curb, and they both were stunned to see

Curtis emerge from a cloud of dust, riding a garden tractor and wearing a sweaty St. Louis Rams cap, his mouth a combination of forced smile and painful grimace. Denim overalls covered his favorite school-bus yellow golf shirt, and cowboy boots worked the tractor pedals and completed the eclectic ensemble. A dark visor covered his eyes. He looked like an overweight, country-western version of Darth Vader.

Michelle and Joshua stepped out of Old Blue and stood at the curb to watch Curtis finish the plowing. As Michelle shut the passenger door, the rear quarter panel molding clanged onto the curb. "Nothing to worry about," said Joshua as he threw the molding in the back seat, "just a little rust."

A few feet away Mrs. Lindholm, camera clicking, exhorted Curtis to smile as the next wave of dust swept over him. Michelle wondered whether Mrs. Lindholm was trying to take a picture of Curtis or the cloud of dust he had stirred up. More likely, Michelle thought, *Curtis forgot to zip himself*, and Mrs. Lindholm was turning the *Tattler* into a local version of its steamy tabloid cousin in Australia.

Curtis shut down the tractor, awkwardly dismounted the little monster as it belched, backfired, and farted a plume of black smoke from its metal behind. As men tend to do as soon as they put on cowboy boots, Curtis ambled over to where Joshua and Michelle were standing. He removed the visor and wiped a sweaty forehead with his favorite red bandanna. "Boy," he said, "it's really hot."

"What are you doing here, Curtis?" Michelle asked.

"Yeah, Curtis," Joshua said, "you're sweating more than Dan Quayle at a spelling bee."

Curtis proudly waved an arm toward the newly plowed area. "We're opening a new planting bed on the south forty, and Mrs. Lindholm wanted a picture for the

Tattler. So, do I pass for Farmer Brown, or what?"

Not quite, thought Michelle. She whispered in Joshua's ear, "He looks more like he's ready to make a pass at Farmer Brown's daughter."

"Curtis, in all honesty," Joshua lied, "you do bear a striking resemblance to the farmer in 'American Gothic.' All you need is a pitchfork and to lose a few pounds," said Joshua. "Come to think of it, have you lost some weight, or are you just wearing bigger clothes?" Perhaps because he was a lawyer, or simply due to his self-confidence, Joshua was one of the few people who was able to ignore the arsenal of intimidations that Curtis employed to cut down most other people. Joshua had established a relationship of mutual respect with Curtis the first time they met. He was unafraid to poke fun and make Curtis laugh at himself. Joshua relished trying to see how outrageous he could be with Curtis, and doing it all with a straight face.

Fanning her face against the swirling dust around her, Michelle said, "Well pardners, let's get in out of the sun, and mosey up to the farmhouse. You look like you could use a cool one, Farmer Brown."

Curtis waved goodbye to Mrs. Lindholm as she scurried off to finish the next issue of the *Tattler*. Curtis, Joshua, and Michelle walked toward the clubhouse, to Curtis' plush private office. They settled around the coffee table with their iced tea, except for Curtis, who had popped the tab on the can of a cold Budweiser. Joshua, eager to get started, said, "Curtis, we came here to discuss the campaign lawsuit filed by Brandon Mason."

17

Angela's call came in a few minutes after three o'clock in the afternoon, St. Louis time, which was ten o'clock at night in Paris.

"*Bon soir, Angela. Comment ça va?*"

"*Tres bien, Michelle. Et vous?*"

"Hold on, you two," said Joshua. "If you want to include me, you'll need to speak English. Otherwise, I'll know you're making up jokes and telling stories about me. So, how's Paris, Angela?"

"I got your email saying to call at this time. Sorry I'm late, but we just finished a three-hour gastronomic experience at a really delightful place called the Pub St. Germain on the Rue de Lancienne Comedie. I had the cotes agneaux that was the most delicious lamb I've ever had, and Philip had the...Well, anyway, as they say, the food is *ç'est si bon*."

"We didn't think you'd go to Paris alone. So, who's Philip?" Joshua asked.

Too late to correct her petit faux pas, Angela decided the best course was to plow ahead with an air of supreme confidence. "Phil is right here, pouring wine. If you must know, he's a manager in Boston. Also has offices in Philadelphia and somewhere in New Jersey. We've known each other a couple of years from the national conferences.

We were both bored at the Global Conference, so we took a little side trip to Paris. Anyway, Philip owns his own management company, very successful, very aggressive. He's very good at…uh…business," Angela said, winking at Philip over her glass.

"I suppose I'd have met him if you'd let me go to the national conferences," Joshua said. "What does he give away to have a multi-state management company?"

Eager to hear more about Paris, Michelle cut in, "Angela, have you been to the Louvre, yet?"

"Yes, absolutely. We set a land-speed record racing through the Louvre this morning, but we saw the three famous ladies: Mona Lisa, Venus de Milo, and Winged Victory. It was priceless, well worth the small fortune in the new euro, even fighting the crowds to see Mona."

"Angela, if we could steer this conversation away from you jet setters and back to paying the bills, for just a moment, we wanted to discuss the status of the campaign lawsuit. You know, the one where Brandon Mason is running against Curtis' favorite councilman, and Mason filed for a TRO and injunction so he can go door-to-door in the Cove," Joshua said, turning to his notes spread out in front of the speakerphone.

"Sure, Joshua, tell me what's going on."

"First, Michelle and I met this morning with Curtis, King of the Cove. In my best lawyerly fashion, I tried to persuade him to propose a settlement with Brandon Mason, but he just argued for an hour and refused to budge. I told him that his legal position is less than a winner and that the association doesn't have an absolute right to wall itself off from the rest of society, at least when confronted by a public candidate's right of political speech. Then, I emphasized that Mason was entitled to engage in the same campaign activities within the gates as the other candidates. Curtis refused to discuss settlement and kept saying that the president has broad discretion to adopt rules about solicitation. He said the job of a good attorney is to support his client, and threatened to fire me if I didn't argue his position instead of making him look like a wimp by settling the case. His real reason, I suspect, is that the judge is an old political buddy, and Curtis actually believes the judge is bought and paid for and will deliver the judgment."

"So, why am I not shocked? It sounds exactly like Curtis," Angela said.

"Wait, we're not done yet. Up to this point, all of Curtis' posturing was purely ego, selfish and disgusting. He knew he lacked a defensible position, but he kept plowing forward like a Missouri mule, ignoring reality. The entire show was vintage King Curtis."

Starting to laugh, Joshua continued. "But then it went from merely disgusting to certifiably crazy. I left Curtis' office and headed for the john—couldn't have been gone five minutes. When I got back, Curtis had done a one-eighty. Michelle, tell Angela how you negotiated with Curtis."

"Well," Michelle began, "Curtis was trying to be real nice and all. He was cooing, you know, trying to be all warm and cuddly. It was pretty repulsive. He told me how much he liked his office and everything. Then he says he'd like to thank me properly, by taking me to dinner. And he couldn't take his beady eyes off me, off my…uh…chest the whole time."

Angela laughed again. "How did you manage to keep a straight face?"

"So, I said to him, 'Mr. Carlton, if you believe your contributions to the judge in the past election translates into a ruling in your favor, you should analyze the political factor more closely. If the judge is in your corner, politically speaking, then he probably also supports your candidate in the council race. But, he knows that if he rules against Mason, it would elevate Mason into political martyrdom overnight.' Then, I said, 'Plus, if Mason lost, he would appeal, which would guarantee him free media coverage for a couple weeks, right up until the primary election in August. All of this attention would be political suicide for your guy. Bottom line: even if you win the case, you'll lose the election.' "

"I love it! Did Curtis get all excited or beat you with a drain pipe?" Angela asked.

"Curtis didn't say anything, he just stared at his boots for the longest time," Michelle continued. "Then he put his fat hands on his fat stomach, starts this thing he does, drumming his belly with his fingers, and says, 'Michelle, you've got a point. I'll agree to a settlement, but only if you'll agree to have dinner with me.' "

Michelle had to pause because Angela was laughing so loudly. "Then he says, 'how about this Saturday night?' I told him, 'Mr. Carlton, you'll settle because it's the politically smart thing to do. As for dinner, thank you very much, but I already have plans.' But, I tried to end on a positive note, telling him, 'let's talk about it again after we get the settlement put to bed.' "

"Whoa, let's hope that's just a poor choice of words," Angela said. "Michelle, have you and Mac made any progress in figuring out who might have broken into your office?"

"Not yet, but Joshua is helping us."

18

"Where do we start?" Joshua asked, as he arranged the napkin in his lap.

"I suggest you start with the dills," Michelle said, reaching with a fork into the glass jar filled with green monster pickles.

"That much I figured out, thank you very much." Joshua grabbed a pickle with his fingers. "How did you discover this place? It's cool."

Michelle and Joshua were meeting for dinner to continue their collaboration on the break-in of PSM's offices. They were seated in Dr. Berman's Delibar, a long, narrow restaurant with a high ceiling, exposed ductwork, vinyl tablecloths, and the best sandwiches and German potato salad in St. Louis. Dr. Stanley Berman and his wife, Shelley, opened the trendy Delibar last year on Euclid in the fashionable central west end, after Stanley suddenly quit his psychiatric practice. Stan's friends wondered whether he had finally lost his sanity or had finally recovered it.

The dinner hour found the restaurant packed with professionals, eager to sample the micro-brews and vanquish the demons they dealt with all day in their offices. "Well, you picked your favorite place last time," Michelle said, "so it was my turn now. Don't eat too many pickles, you'll get sick," she warned Joshua as he reached for another green monster.

"What I meant was, where do we start making ..." Joshua paused to look at the surrounding tables and, turning back to Michelle, whispered, "a list of prospects, or perps, or whatever they're called?" He tried to make it sound serious, but when the words stumbled out so awkwardly, both he and Michelle could hardly keep their composure.

She reached in her large shoulder bag for her pocket organizer just as their brisket sandwiches, potato salad, and draft beers arrived. "I think we're working on a list of suspects." Michelle hesitated while the college-age waiter, wearing blue jeans and a Dr. Berman's t-shirt, finished placing the dishes of food and mugs of beer on the table.

Joshua hoisted his beer while Michelle concentrated on a blank page of her notepad. "Let's start by listing motives across the top and suspects down the side," Michelle said, as she began writing. We'll label the motive columns with money, power, revenge, and other. All we need is gluttony, and we'd have most of the seven cardinal sins. The first candidate," she said as her lips tightened into a frown, "is almost too obvious. Our old friend, Dunwoody, the Worm. 'His pen is breathing revenge.' "

"A famous quote, I suspect," said Joshua.

"Those were the words of Alexei Tolstoi, the pre-revolutionary Russian novelist. Anyway, the Worm is literally drooling for revenge. Besides, nobody knows how he makes a living, so he should also be in the money column. Oh, you probably were too busy trying to control the crowd at the annual meeting, but Dunwoody was wearing these really short shorts, and, well, I shouldn't mention any details right now since we're in the middle of dinner."

"How about this?" Joshua interrupted. "Dunwoody has us tied up in a serious lawsuit. What if he was looking for the litigation file, with all our correspondence relating to legal strategy, witnesses, testimony, and everything else we're planning? Wouldn't he love to get his hands on that file?"

"Point well taken, counselor," Michelle looked at Joshua. "I knew there was a reason I brought you along tonight."

"Okay, Michelle, you got to pick the top draft choice. Now, for the next pick, I say we go with David Daggett. What little we know about him, he fits the profile. He's the treasurer at the Vineyard, and he shows too much interest in the association's finances. Also, he's an information systems analyst, so he's computer smart. And, he's got a ton of personal financial problems."

"Plus, Daggett is creepy." Michelle related the phone call she had received from Daggett requesting information about posting dates for reserves. "I think he hates women, which could be the result of his divorce."

"Or, maybe the cause," said Joshua, his eyebrows arched. "Your turn now."

Michelle was plunging her fork into the cole slaw when Shelley approached the table. "Michelle," she said, wiping her hands on her apron, which was already decorated with a rainbow of splotches and stains, "I knew you were a smart girl. You're courting this handsome young man by giving him a good, home-cooked meal!"

"Joshua, I want you to meet Shelley, my mother-in-fact," Michelle said. "So, try to put on your best table manners. And, while you're at it, tell Shelley why you haven't touched the best German potato salad in all of St. Louis."

When Michelle and Joshua later left Dr. Berman's in her Ford Explorer Joshua was driving. It was a compromise between them, worked out after some friendly debate.

She hated riding in Old Blue, and he couldn't stand being a white-knuckle passenger while she drove the huge, lumbering Explorer.

"Look, Michelle, it's about nine o'clock, but if it's not too late for you, I think we should try to continue working on the list tonight. Do you want to stop for coffee?"

"What is this business about it being too late for me? I'll bet I get less sleep, work longer hours, and I'm less grumpy than you."

Joshua pulled the Explorer into a vacant space outside Freddy's. "This is a coffee un-date," he said as he shut off the engine. "I'd get the door for you, but the rules of un-dating prohibit me from any activity that could be construed as a display of affection."

"Maybe we should renegotiate the agreement, expanding the restaurant-hopping to include you being a gentleman. Now, there's an idea."

"May I remind you, Michelle, that you're the one who insisted on retaining a professional relationship. I'm doing my best. Besides, if women want equal rights, you can open your own door. Chivalry is not a forgotten kindness: it's dead because modern women have killed it."

They walked in silence to the door of Freddy's. "Well, Joshua," Michelle finally said, stopping in front of the door, "Have you gotten that out of your system? Why don't you just tell me what's on your diminished mind?"

Joshua stopped and faced her. "I've been giving this arrangement some serious thought. Would you be interested in renegotiating the un-date agreement to include a movie Saturday night? I might even agree to let you sit next to me, if you're nice."

"What makes you think I'd want to sit next to you?"

Freddy's was always bright and busy. They found a table near the door and studied the people coming and going until their menus arrived. Michelle ordered decaf and Joshua asked for chocolate ice cream and a cappuccino.

Joshua didn't mention the movie again. He had hoped Michelle would stop the bantering, but instead she stopped him from pushing for a date.

Michelle brought out her pocket organizer and opened it to her notes. "So far, we've got Dunwoody, of course, and David Daggett. What about the treasurer at the Cove—the guy with two first names?"

"Allen Russell," Joshua added. "He's a finance guru, but too clever by half. An article in the *Business Journal* said that he left himself exposed in the big merge, although the company called it corporate downsizing or restructuring, just to be polite. They were top heavy in bean counters, and Russell, of all people, should have known about it. Then, there are the rumors that he's been piling up huge gambling debts. Let's put him on the list, but I'll check with an old friend down at the casino—she's a dealer—and see how much truth there is to the rumors."

"So, who is this old friend, the dealer? I'll bet she's fabulously beautiful, especially in those skimpy, push-up outfits they wear down at the casino."

"Oh, Bits? She's just an old friend. Do I detect a little jealousy, Ms. Un-Date?"

"Don't flatter yourself. Look, Joshua, let's talk frankly about King Curtis. I think he bought above his means. The guy who knows everything at the Cove is Bruce the concierge. Ex-concierge, I should say. The board terminated him, with two weeks notice. Of course, he knew Curtis was behind it, that Curtis single-handedly dictated the decision."

Michelle stopped to sip her decaf. "Anyway, there's no love lost, and Bruce has mentioned that he's heard incredible stories about Curtis shaking down different owners for campaign contributions and pumping suppliers and contractors for bribes and kickbacks. If Curtis can afford to live at the Cove, what does he need with campaign contributions? Where does the money go? Does Curtis have financial problems we don't know about? Is this money going to the judge's re-election or into Curtis' pocket? Either way, something stinks."

"I knew there was a reason I brought you along tonight," said Joshua, his face deep in thought. "Add to that Curtis' insistence on getting a computer that's linked to PSM's system, and I'd say he has more than a passing interest in the Cove's funds."

"But, Joshua, Curtis' big thing is…well, I don't know anything about his thing, big or small, and I hope I never find out." Michelle explained her observations that Curtis was dominated by an insatiable hunger for power and influence. "He loves being president, dominating the board members so they become loyal followers who cower at the monthly meetings and issuing edicts to all the subjects in his kingdom. His favorite expression is, 'I'm the president, and the buck starts here.' Community associations are supposed to be democratic sub-societies, but Curtis' version of politics and governance is definitely not something that was taught in high school civics class. Even so," Michelle asked, "what would motivate Curtis to break into our offices? For what purpose? Money? All of the Cove's records, particularly the financials, are no further away than the touch of his fat fingers. I mean, he can monitor them, but he can't manipulate them."

"You should know. You linked him to PSM's system."

"I wonder." Michelle remembered Sean Eastgate's comment about being called out to the Cove at seven in the morning to install a new program for Curtis.

Joshua gazed thoughtfully out the window. "Maybe he hired one of his cronies to break into your office. Paid the guy with cash right out of the secret president's fund, or whatever he calls it. With Curtis, anything's possible," Joshua added, savoring his last spoonful of ice cream.

"Which reminds me, you remember Curtis' huge antique desk? I'll tell you how he got it." Michelle recalled her trip down to the LaSalle Antique Trading Company on South Broadway, meeting Ernie Buggieri, telling him that Curtis Carlton sent her, and that she was searching for the "largest antique walnut desk in existence" for Curtis. "Joshua, this guy Ernie has only a handful of pieces in this tiny store, mostly replicas, but he raised his eyebrows when I mentioned Curtis' name and said that 'he'd look around and call me.' Two days later he called, and I went back down to the store, and there sat the walnut desk and credenza, completely restored to mint condition. When I got both pieces moved to Curtis' office, I checked the desk inside and out, you know, to list it in the inventory, but couldn't find any model number, serial number, factory name, place of manufacture. Not a trace. It had all been completely removed."

Joshua looked at Michelle and said, "You can learn a lot of strange things just hanging around the courthouse. The Buggieri brothers operate barely within the law and occasionally venture to the other side. In fact, the word is that Vinnie has been a suspect in various sleazy crimes, like planting eavesdropping equipment for lawyers handling big divorce cases, but the prosecutor hasn't been able to get enough evidence for an indictment. As you suspect, the antique store is probably a legitimate front for their more illegitimate activities. Ernie and Vinnie Buggieri are slimy bottom-feeders. So, the question is, do they have any connection with Curtis the sewer pipe magnate?"

19

Sean Eastgate paced around the tiny living room in his loft apartment, located in the old garment district of the city, at Washington and Fifteenth. The apartment was hot and steamy. His long blond hair was soaked with sweat. He popped another can of Busch while he paced the floor, stopping on each passage to inspect the data on the monitor of his computer.

Leaving California was the last resort, an act of true desperation, but he had no real choices. Ten years out of Pepperdine had seen him still bouncing around from one job to the next, until he had developed the concept of his boutique computer store in Newport Beach. He opened the business with equal portions of advertising fanfare, high expectations, and heavy debt—designing and selling upscale computer systems for high-tech businesses would be his ticket to quick and easy wealth.

Sufficient cash flow never materialized. He started demanding payment in advance, which he turned around to pay the suppliers who screamed the loudest. The lawsuits weren't far behind. First, the landlord sued for back rent, then three clients sued for refunds, followed by a half-dozen suppliers who filed suit to collect the money Sean owed on account. The legal claims started to snowball and soon became a deadly avalanche. He was so hopelessly in debt there was no way out, save for a disgraceful bankruptcy. His wife of five years wasted no time filing for divorce.

A divorce was one thing, but bankruptcy was beyond his self-image. Sean decided to change his name and disappear, trying several cities until he arrived in St. Louis practically penniless. He knew he couldn't get a job with a computer company. Most employers in the field would want a full background check, where all he had was a black hole. He decided to combine his greatest expertise with his greatest attribute—knowledge of computers and charm. A trip to the Women's Business Network—the ol' girls network—landed him a list of small businesses owned and operated by women. He started knocking on doors. It had taken over a year, but he had wooed a handful of good clients.

His favorite client was PSM. Sean enjoyed working there because Michelle and Jenni were so good looking and the business handled a lot of money for a bunch of condo associations. Jenni Hiscock, in particular, was responsive and seemed ripe for the picking. It hadn't been difficult to conjure up reasons for dropping in once a week to make sure everything was going okay with the computer system, and to have a conversation with Jenni, Michelle, and the other women. Except Mac. He didn't click with Mac.

He remembered that he owed PSM a return service call to open up all their computers to see if he could catch what he had described as a gremlin. He squeezed the empty beer can and sat down to work at his computer.

BARELY FIFTEEN CITY BLOCKS to the east of Sean's apartment, on the levee of the Mississippi River, Allen Russell, the downsized comptroller and finance whiz who was treasurer of the Cove, studied his cards at the hundred-dollar blackjack table of the Riverboat Belle Casino. He drew one card and counted his total—on the margin.

He was confident the program he designed on his computer could beat the house. In blackjack, theoretically, the house would win fifty percent of the dealings over time. And, theoretically, the odds of the house winning any particular hand were fifty percent. But, Russell knew this result didn't occur in a predictable, uniform pattern where the house won every other hand. However, he also discovered that it didn't occur in random chaos. Using computer modeling, he had plotted the results of thousands of blackjack hands, and he found that a pattern could be discerned in which the house won four or five hands in a row, then the player won four or five hands in a row, back and forth, separated by transitions.

All Russell had to do was track the results of each hand, bet aggressively when the run was in his favor, and bet conservatively when the run favored the house. He figured that applying his program would increase his odds from fifty percent to two-thirds, and that he could reach as much as seventy-five percent if he could accurately predict the gray transitional areas when the momentum of a run starts to turn.

He held his cards close to the green felt of the table, pondering his position. Unconsciously, his hand scratched his head of thick, wavy blond hair. He had won two hands in a row, so the odds based on his secret program were heavily in his favor in this hand. Yet, he was nagged by the fact that he drew a hand of fifteen, which suggested the game was at a point where the cards were in transition, and the house might be starting a run of its own.

The dealer was a curvy young woman named Bits, who hardly needed the benefit of the push-up bra that she stuffed herself into (she called them the "girls"). Bits had the queen of spades face up on the table. Russell looked at the queen and thought the old lady was staring back at him with a smirk on her lips. Bits had another card buried beneath the queen, tempting Russell to think that Bits was probably somewhere between seventeen and twenty-one. On the other hand, it was possible that Bits only had twelve. Russell was counting the cards, as any good blackjack player does, and knew that the probability of drawing a six or under was less than one in three. His bet of ten thousand dollars was already on the table. *It would be a close call, but that's why I love the science of gambling.*

Russell lightly scratched the felt with the bottom of his cards, signaling to Bits that he wanted another hit. He watched the girls as Bits leaned forward and gently tossed another card toward him. A four came, face up, giving him a new total of nineteen. His heart pounded, but Russell disguised his elation.

Now, he studied Bits and the girls, who had the queen of spades showing. He figured she would stay. Surprisingly, Bits dealt herself another card, face up, a five. A total of fifteen was now showing across the table. With one card down, it was more likely than not that Bits and her girls had busted. She turned her hidden card face up, revealing the five of diamonds. *She had twenty. Shit! Double shit!* Bits smoothly scooped Russell's chips off the table, all ten thousand dollars' worth, and watched out of the corner of her eye as a look of anguish swept across his face, leaving skeletal, ashen features.

Russell walked away, shoulders slumped, hands deep in his pockets, perhaps searching for loose change. Not for the first time, he thought of the Cove's reserve account—eight hundred thousand ways to take care of his gambling debts.

TEN MILES AWAY IN SOUTH COUNTY, a computer screen reflected the sneer and the drooling scowl of J. Thomas Dunwoody—the Worm of the Vineyard. Surrounding the computer, arranged in neat stacks on the perimeter of his dining room table, were heavy brown books containing the *Missouri Revised Statutes*, a soft-back copy of the *Rules of Civil Procedure*, various form books, and the growing file of "Dunwoody v. the Vineyard Townhouse Association, et al." He popped the tab off a fresh can of Bud, lit another cigarette, and reviewed his copious notes on the monitor.

Thoreau wrote, "The mass of men lead lives of quiet desperation." That was an understatement, for totally hapless and hateful was the life of J. Thomas Dunwoody. His neighbors found him disgusting and repulsive. In turn, he found them to be part of a misguided society, which inflamed his paranoid view of the world and fueled his theory that *they were all out to get him*.

The court records about the child molestation charge were all wrong. After all, he had pleaded guilty and served his probation under a "suspended imposition of sentence," so how could it be a conviction? He hated the humiliation he felt when a copy of the conviction was sent to all his neighbors. The children of his neighbors in the Vineyard, sternly warned by their parents, fled from him whenever he approached. It made him feel like a leper.

He wondered how the Vineyard's finances were doing, particularly in view of the outrageous legal bills racked up by the Law Offices of Angela Laclede. He had a weekly routine of dropping by PSM's offices to get a printout of the latest financial statement to see how fast they were bleeding to death. He didn't need the information at PSM—he already had his own source. But, he stopped at PSM several times a month to let them know that he was always watching and would stop at nothing to irritate them. He had just obtained a copy of the June report, which would be useful in the deposition. And, it gave him a chance to visit with that cute little receptionist, Jenni. *Did she kind of like me, or was she being nice just to humor me?*

Dunwoody paused to flex his spindly arms, admiring the tattoo depicting the face of Florence, his first wife, on his left bicep. He popped his knuckles and continued his slow, methodical hunting and pecking on the keyboard. He figured that the weakest link on the board was Maxine Midland, the secretary, who seemed to be the board's rubber stamp. Maxine was a plump woman in her sixties who clerked at the South County factory outlet. He had scheduled her deposition to begin at nine-thirty tomorrow morning. He could take all day if it suited his pleasure. *My dear Mrs. Midland, you won't know what hit you.*

He wished he could have seen the look on that cocky attorney's face—Joshua was his name—when he read the notice of deposition of Maxine Midland. Dunwoody drooled at the thought. He watched the computer monitor as he finished preparing the questions he would ask at her depo.

As the laser printer began producing copies, he logged onto the Internet.

Just like McArthur, Dunwoody thought, *I shall return. And sweet shall be my revenge.*

20

Angela and Philip were studying the menu at a sidewalk café in Vieux Lyon, the historic district of France's second largest city. It had taken barely over two hours for the express TGV train, at 186 miles an hour, to whisk them from Gare de Lyon in the heart of Paris to the city best known for its pleasures of the palate, its gastronomic excesses.

After considering the menus at several restaurants and bistros, they decided to try the Chez Papillon Restaurant on Rue St. Jean. The waitress, a leggy, dark-eyed beauty from the countryside, came to their table with two menus. Angela turned to her and said awkwardly, "*Quelle est la specialite de la region?*" Without hesitation, the waitress responded, in very acceptable English, that the restaurant featured several special dishes of the Lyon area. As soon as she realized her patrons were Americans, the waitress excitedly described her trip to California last summer, explaining how amazed she had been that any *sane* person would want to live in Los Angeles. Philip responded that she had just answered her own question. Her puzzled look gave way to a wide smile and a giggle. Angela proudly mentioned to the waitress that Lyon was a sister city of St. Louis.

The waitress patiently responded to the numerous questions from both Angela and Philip about various dishes on the menu, lyonnaisse cuisine, and local *vins rouge*. They took fifteen minutes to plot a coordinated dining experience, with the appropriate wines to add the right tastes, *a la Francaise*.

Philip casually watched the waitress as she left with their order. "I'm in love," he sighed. "So, Lyon is the culinary capital of the world—the food here should be better than in Paris!"

"This trip has been just what I needed, Phil. It's been so relaxing, and we've been to such romantic places. And so are you!" Angela was looking forward to after dinner, when they would return to the hotel.

"You want another massage, don't you?"

"A woman can't be too careful, Phil. What if the doctor missed something? And, it's good therapy—I've hardly thought about work."

"How can you say that? Everywhere we go, Angela, you carry your pager and your cell phone, and you haul your laptop around your neck like an albatross. You're never out of contact with your office. Even in the W.C. I'm surprised you haven't developed a case of techno-stress."

"Actually, I'm relieved that things at the office are okay. It looks like we've been able to reach a settlement of the campaign lawsuit, so we won't need to prepare for a hearing. Michelle, the manager, persuaded the Cove president that he'd be doing the challenger a favor by defending the suit. It had nothing to do with the law. The president figured out that it didn't make sense to win the lawsuit and have his candidate lose the election. More likely, he'd lose both."

Philip took a sip from his glass of Bordeaux. "You work with a lot of management companies in St. Louis?"

He tried not to sound like he was fishing.

"Sure, most of the better companies. The company at the Cove is Preferred Site Management, or PSM for short, and they're very good. They have four managers handling a total of about two dozen communities, so that each one has only six properties. They've been careful to avoid growing just for the sake of being big. With some exceptions, they've concentrated on getting quality, upper-end communities."

"You mentioned before that the Cove was out of developer control for only a few years, but had good reserves. That's a real success story. Are the rest of PSM's associations as accomplished in building reserves?"

Angela finished swallowing a slice of baguette and considered the question. "We've worked with all the managers to develop an aggressive program to build reserves, and PSM has been quite successful. If a community can afford it—and most of their clients can—the owners are paying gradually into reserves, but the funds accumulate quickly. It's much preferred to the more popular alternative—charging special assessments whenever it's time to replace the roofs or siding. That's nothing but a failure to plan. PSM has some associations with more than a half million dollars in reserves."

"Incredible." Philip busied himself with a slice of baguette. "Do you think PSM would consider a buyout?"

Angela was surprised and puzzled by the question. But, before she could respond, the leggy waitress approached with their dinners.

After their leisurely dinner at the Chez Papillon, Angela and Philip strolled, arm in arm, soaking up the evening twilight of Lyon. They walked to the Soane River, one of the two romantic rivers that meander through the city, and they stood on the Pont Bonaparte to watch the lingering sunlight play on the skyline of Vieux Lyon, topped by the Basilique Notre-Dame de Fourviere high on the hill to the west.

Heading back into the narrow streets of Vieux Lyon, they found a bench on the Place St. Jean where they admired the gothic cathedral built between the 12th and 15th centuries, with its signs of the zodiac on the front portals. The Place was surrounded by residences painted in pastels and highlighted with bright shutters. The weather was ideal, and the Place was filled with couples sharing an intimate moment and hundreds of pigeons scrabbling for handouts.

"Angela, it's time for my daily call to the office," Philip said.

"Now, tell me which one of us is techno-stressed?"

Philip formed his lips into a silent kiss directed to Angela. "I'm sure you don't want to hear my boring shop talk, so I'll just walk over there by the church. Be back in a few minutes." Philip began tapping the numeric pad of his cell phone as he walked across the Place toward the church.

The black-suit twins were seated in their hotel room in St. Louis when the phone rang. Bedford answered, "How ya doin' boss?" Kosankis walked into the bathroom and picked up the other phone, blasting a "hello!" that echoed through the bathroom. Bedford asked, "Are you making any progress with that woman lawyer?"

"I'm mixing as much business with pleasure as I possibly can with Angela," Philip said. He knew that most of the management companies would consult Angela if they were offered a buyout. "I need to get on her good side. But, if I pump her for any more information, my randy little traveling companion is going to get suspicious."

Bedford answered, "We're sure it's tough duty traveling around France with a good looking woman, but somebody's got to do it. Right, boss?"

"I got your message about Estrella Cove—you said the baby was in the cradle. Tell me more."

"Okay, about the Cove," Bedford continued, "we're confident that the president—his name is Curtis Carlton—likes our proposal. I mean he really likes it. And we know what part he likes the most. If we read him right, he wants a hand in the reserves till, but he wants it to be our hand, so his fingerprints aren't on the deal."

Kosankis stammered, "We got a small problem, Boss."

Bedford interrupted, signaling Kosankis to shut up. "Here's what's happened. We've hit a little bump in the road, just a hiccup, really. Not with any money issues. Carlton wants us to steal the woman who now handles the account with the current management company—PSM. We tried to tell him that we couldn't even approach her unless we knew we had the account. He said no deal without a personal guarantee from her that she's switching companies."

Philip asked, "So, you're at an impasse. Is her name Michelle?"

"That's it," answered Bedford. "Michelle Gratiot. Hey, how'd you know her name?"

"That's why I'm in charge. Any other prospects?"

"Nothing," said Bedford, "we made a list of the dozen biggest associations in the entire St. Louis area, figuring they'd have the biggest reserves. We've had initial meetings with them, but they're real slow to make decisions. Cold prospecting isn't any good. We need somebody inside."

Kosankis jumped back into the conversation. "Boss, what if we tell Carlton we'll deliver the girl only if she delivers?"

"Mr. K," Philip said into the cell phone, "you've got the brains of an army cot. But, you've given me an idea about the Michelle woman. I'm not sure whether she's part of the problem or part of the solution, but she might be the bait. Listen up: here's the plan. But, if it's going to work, you've *got* to make Curtis think it was his idea."

21

"Joshua?" It was Sedona's cheerful voice coming through the intercom on his office phone.

"Hi, there." Joshua's voice was hoarse and husky. "I may be here in body, but I'm not sure about the rest of me. It was a long night of legal research at the law library. You know, the law is mostly boring, don't you? Who's calling at this ungodly hour of the morning?"

Sedona was the spunky receptionist who drew her name from the scenic red rock town where she was conceived by her honeymooning parents twenty years ago. Sedona was notorious in the office for coloring her hair differently every week in shades that couldn't be found in nature. This week was maroon.

"The man first asked for Angela," Sedona said, "and when I told him she was out of the office, he asked for you. Said you'd want to talk to him. He's on line one. Are you okay?"

"I desperately need some coffee before I can be expected to sound like a lawyer at eight o'clock in the morning," Joshua said hoarsely. "Ask him to hold for just a minute, then I'll pick up." Joshua struggled into the kitchen, where he filled his favorite Science Center mug with black coffee, then buried his nose in the mug to absorb the full aroma. When he returned to his office, he picked up his phone and pressed line one. He cradled his throbbing head in his hand. "Hello, this is Joshua."

"Good morning. We met once at the Cove, but I don't know if you remember. My name is Bruce, and I'm the concierge there. Well, until a few days ago, when I was fired."

"Sure, Bruce, I remember you. I'm sorry to hear about the job situation, but our office didn't have anything to do with your…ah…separation. If you're calling to file an employment grievance…"

Bruce interrupted Joshua, "No, no, not that, although it did cross my mind, truth be known. Someone needs to bring that obese dictator down. I'm calling you about something much more juicy. But, I only have a minute now. I'm standing in the backyard of my house, using my cell phone, because I'm worried that Curtis might have bugged my home. For that matter, he's probably intercepting this call. He has friends who can do that sort of thing, you know. Can we meet later today, privately, say five-thirty?"

"Can you give me a hint as to what this is all about?"

"Well, who do you represent? Do you represent Curtis, or the board, or what?"

"None of the above. We represent the entity, Estrella Cove Residents' Association."

"Good! Then I'll give you a brief summary, and it's gonna be quick. Curtis has a dozen scams going. He's been hauling in money from just about everybody. Payoffs, bribes, kickbacks, you name it. He sends it out of the country, then brings it back. And another thing, I think he's got plans for the reserves, and they're not community plans, you know, they're not what you'd call in the best interests of the association, which you represent. Also, he's been having private negotiations with some powerhouse management company from back East, very secretively, very quietly, without the knowledge of the other board members. I think I know what that's all about. It's much more complex than just changing management companies."

"Bruce, how did you get your information? Are these just more rumors from the Cove Information Center? I mean do you have some hard documents or other tangible proof?"

"It's difficult to say right now." Bruce glanced around nervously, his voice hushed. "Curtis doesn't know it, but I've got a key to his new office. He's got lists of names, money received, and other stuff. Can't you subpoena his computer?" Bruce was pacing nervously in his small yard. "Look, I'm probably sounding paranoid, but I'm worried that Curtis will send somebody after me. I'll bring this stuff to you. I live in the Soulard District. Meet me at McGuire's Pub at five-thirty. And, be there. I'm counting on you."

The line went dead abruptly ending the conversation. Joshua checked the calendar on his computer. He was free at five-thirty. He tapped out an email to Michelle, asking her to meet him at McGuire's.

THE EARLY MORNING SUN coming through the windows was like a thousand bright and powerful floodlights, creating a blinding glare behind Curtis' bulk as he sat at his desk in the presidential oval office at the Cove's clubhouse. The smoke from his morning cigar rose gently until it diffused with the horizontal rays of sunshine pouring through the miniblinds. It created a thick blue-gray haze, making the office look like a steamy sauna.

Curtis had intentionally arranged his office so that the large windows were directly behind him and purposefully left the miniblinds open this morning to maximize the effect. He believed the backlit effect of the sun in his visitors' eyes gave him an edge during mano-a-mano negotiations such as he was having this morning.

"First, gentlemen," Curtis said, tapping the ash from his cigar into a crystal ashtray the shape of a bathtub, "I'm glad I caught you this morning, and I want to thank you for getting on this problem so quickly. This thing with Bruce, needless to say, came as a real surprise. As I told you on the phone, he got into my office last night. My other…uh…business associates don't really have the background for this task, so I thought that you guys might be interested. What do you think is the best approach?"

"Well, Mr. Carlton," said Bedford, squinting into the sunlight and through the haze in the general direction of Curtis' bulk, "as we suggested on the phone, we could pick up Bruce and talk to him." Kosankis occupied himself by staring off into space and fondling his earring, his dark, slick hair glistening in the rays of sunlight.

Bedford continued, "We have an associate here named Leo, does odd jobs for us, not too bright, but very dependable. All we need to do is call Leo, and he'll pick up Bruce in a few hours. Leo knows about this abandoned cottage in the Ozarks we can use, and he'll help us babysit Bruce. It's about a three hour drive from here."

Curtis was shocked. "That sounds like kidnaping, I won't be a part of that."

"Not exactly. Look, Bruce lives alone, and we'll just need him overnight. No one will miss him, and the police won't do anything unless a person is missing for over twenty-four hours."

Curtis reflected on the proposed arrangements, his hands folded across his belly. "That makes me feel better. You need to know what created this little problem. Gentlemen, the information I'm about to tell you is highly confidential." Curtis stood up, casting a long shadow across his desk and gestured with his arms fully extended. "Look around this office. Go ahead, get up and walk around. Take a good look, and tell me what you see."

The black-suit twins glanced uncomfortably at each other and began a slow procession around Curtis' office, carefully examining the walls, vents, and light fixtures. They gently moved paintings and looked under lampshades and picked up ashtrays and other movable objects. Their eyes focused on one item then the next, uncertain of what they were looking for.

Having completed their inspection, they returned to stand in front of Curtis' desk, still without much of a clue. Bedford ventured a shrug of surrender and sat down. "Okay, Mr. Carlton, we give up. What's the point?"

Curtis nodded with approval. "You've made my point. Even when you're looking for something, you can't see it. This room is equipped with state-of-the-art motion-activated video camcorders. The cameras are so well hidden that even a trained eye can't see them. And, they're soundproof. They're so quiet you can't hear them."

Continuing with unabashed pride, and trying to impress his visitors with his grasp of new technology, Curtis said, "My good friend, Vinnie, installed these. Now, there's a specialist, a pro with considerable talent and discretion to match. I first met Vinnie years ago, when he tried to sell me a truckload of brass fittings. Only problem was, they were all hot. I was gonna call the police on him, but instead, we became good friends. Now, he does little favors for me. He put these devices in when the office was built. Nobody knows about them, including the carpenters and the drywall installers who worked on this place. It wouldn't be any fun if everybody knew about them, now would it?" Curtis sat down again and sent another plume of smoke into the sun's rays.

Kosankis leaned over the desk into Curtis' face. "Are you sayin' that all of our private conversations here in your office have been videotaped? I don't like that." Kosankis stared angrily at Curtis.

"Relax, Kosankis." Curtis, unruffled by the sudden outburst, stood up and sucked generously on his cigar. He then exhaled an enormous plume of smoke into Kosankis' face. "You've got nothing to worry about. You think I got here by being dumb?" *Like you?* He almost added. "I always destroy the videotapes after your visits here." Kosankis retreated from the desk, wiping his eyes, and slowly returned to his chair.

Bedford, who had been listening calmly during the heated and smoky exchange, suddenly bolted upright in his seat, his eyes looking like a light bulb had just clicked on in his head. "You've got Brucie on candid camera! You caught the mousy traitor on tape with his little red-handed paws in the till."

"Precisely," Curtis beamed proudly. "Bruce sneaked in here late last night, went through my desk, and looked at my files." Curtis swiveled in his chair and waved at the credenza. "And, if that wasn't enough mischief, he poked around in my computer."

"Why would Bruce want to get into your files, Curtis? What was he looking at, or looking for?" Bedford asked.

Curtis handed Bedford a black videocassette. "Here's the tape. You should look at it a couple of times before you talk to him. There's no telling what sensitive information he got into. The tape shows he spent about ten minutes at the computer and made some notes, but he was standing in front of the monitor, so the cameras couldn't see what he was looking at. He also took some notes as he was going through my files."

Bedford looked over at his partner. Kosankis simply stared off into space, playing with his earring. "Any idea why little Brucie would do this?" Bedford inquired. "That would help us figure out what he's planning to do with the information."

"You want to know why he did it?" Curtis paused to take a long drag on his cigar. "Bruce is probably pissed off, to put it mildly, because the board fired him. Our girl, Michelle, didn't have the balls to tell him, so I fired him myself. It was Wednesday, late afternoon. It looks like he came back last night. So, he probably wants some sort of revenge against me for firing him, even though I told him it was the board's decision. He could have information that, in the wrong hands, you know, like the Feds, would make things well, potentially embarrassing for me, do you understand? If you're going to win, as Casey Stengel liked to say, 'you've got to keep the guys who hate you away from the guys who are undecided.' "

Kosankis had the look of someone who was completely lost. Bedford wasn't too sure, either, and said, "I'm not catching your meaning, Mr. Carlton. But, I do know this. Most amateurs who work a blackmail scam—or extortion, as they call it in more polite circles—are looking for easy money. So, have you considered that Bruce is setting up an exchange of some sort? It's not too complicated—under the circumstances, I doubt that he wants his job back, so I think it's more likely that he wants to extort some hush money. Call it a separation bonus to keep his mouth shut about all your dirty laundry."

"That may be possible," nodded Curtis, "but if I know Bruce, he's acting on principle, not for money. He's not getting his job back, I'll tell you that right now, and I have no idea what kind of payday he might be thinking about if it's extortion." Curtis paused to run a worried hand through his hair. "Boy, I sure miscalculated that little jerk. I never figured he'd do something so crazy. For all we know, he's headed downtown to that consumer reporter at Channel 4. Worse, he could be on his way to the IRS. Or, maybe he's going to the FBI, thinking they would put him in the witness protection program because he wants a new personality." Curtis chuckled at his own humor.

"Well, this background gives us more to go on," said Bedford. "Leo said that the cottage in the Ozarks is miles from anything. It's secure, and cute for being in the woods and all, and near a great fishing hole on the river. It should serve our purposes."

Curtis wasn't remotely in any mood for fishing or cute. As he listened to the black-suited, greasy-haired twins, his face slowly turned to a shade of crimson that should have informed them that he was not pleased. "You've got to interview him, and do it fast." He stood at his desk while his closed fist punctuated the air with exclamation points. "That little patch of pond scum should spill his guts in five minutes with a couple of pros like you. Find out what he knows, what records he got into. See what he was going to do with the information. Find out if he's got money on his mind and, if so, how much. Do what it takes, which shouldn't require much. Just get him to talk. Get all the information you can, then get back to me."

"Mr. K. here can be very persuasive. He prefers electrical probes to the genitals, but he can also break fingers without blinking."

"No way." Curtis said firmly. "I may be mean, but I'm not malicious. All you need to do is scare the shit out of him. Threaten him if you must, but don't hurt him."

Bedford was making some notes in his pocket memo pad. He looked up at Curtis and said, "Okay, my friend, we'll try to do it your way. But, before we go, and this will just take a minute, there's one other thing our boss wanted us to discuss with you."

"By the way," said Curtis, still red-faced, looking Bedford straight in the eye, "when will I have the pleasure of meeting this mysterious boss of yours?"

"He operates behind the scenes, that's just his style, you know." Bedford squinted toward Curtis through the blue haze.

"To put it frankly, Mr. Carlton," Bedford continued, "we're taking care of this potential embarrassment for you. We're doing you a little favor. Where we come from, that means that you get to do us a little favor in return. After all, that's what business is all about, isn't it? We don't have to draw you a picture, do we?"

Curtis felt his stomach turn. "I'm listening," was all he could manage as he gingerly sat down. His apprehension mounted as Bedford and Kosankis stood up. The black suits walked around the desk until they were standing on either side of Curtis.

Bedford leaned over to avoid the glare from the window, his lips inches from Curtis' right ear. "We know your computer is linked into PSM's system," he said slowly, quietly, and firmly, very much under control. "And we know that your darling Michelle would do just about anything for you if you only could figure out how to ask her, because she wants to keep the account. All we want is a list of all PSM's clients, their annual income, and their reserves. And then you could access this information through your computer."

Curtis fought to retain his outward composure, but his voice sounded more like a squeaky plea. "Well, if you know all that, you must also know that my computer is only linked to the Cove's accounts. I can't access anybody else's account." Curtis was relieved to have this honest response, since he needed to stall while he figured out where the black-suit twins were heading with this "little favor."

Kosankis reached for Curtis' cigar that was still smoldering in the crystal bathtub on the desk and held the glowing tip inches from Curtis' left eye. "I don't think I like you," he grunted.

Bedford whispered in Curtis' ear. "You know, Mr. Carlton, for a smart guy, sometimes you aren't really very bright. Connect the dots—do you hear me? This part is where your cute little Michelle comes in. You treat her right, and I'm sure she'll understand that cooperation is in her best interests. And, if not, she might join Brucie for some fun down at the summer cottage."

Inching closer to Curtis' right ear, Bedford whispered, "You do understand this little favor, now, don't you?"

Kosankis sucked on the cigar and exhaled blue smoke in Curtis' face.

"Wait," Curtis said, waving the smoke from his face. "I have a better idea. How would you guys like to buy a management company? Lock, stock, and reserves?"

22

Joshua walked into McGuire's Pub & Grill and had to pause inside the door to allow his eyes to adjust to the dim lighting. The Beatles' "Sgt. Pepper's Lonely Heart's Club Band" was on the pub's stereo system, straining to be heard over the din of what seemed like a thousand patrons.

McGuire's was a storefront watering hole in the historic Soulard District, which was originally developed late in the nineteenth century as housing and neighborhood shops for working class families who labored at the factories, breweries, and warehouses near the levee of the Mississippi River. The success of McGuire's, mirroring that of the entire Soulard District over the past twenty years, reflected the rediscovery of this historic neighborhood, with its sturdy housing stock ready to be lovingly rehabbed by the Yuppies and DINKS—Double Income, No Kids. The patronage of McGuire's also reflected the residents of the District—an eclectic mix of young and middle-age business people and professionals of every political and sexual persuasion.

Joshua groped and fought his way through the throng, walking along side the well-worn, lacquered bar on his left, looking for the familiar face of Bruce or Michelle at one of the tables to his right. It was a short drive from his office, still he noted that he was ten minutes late. No sense spoiling his perfect record of never being on time. He would celebrate the twin accomplishments of keeping his record in tact while, at the same time, arriving ahead of the others. The om-pah beat of "When I'm Sixty-Four" thumped in the background. *Will you still need me, will you still feed me...* Joshua found an empty stool at the bar, ordered a wheat beer, and contemplated whether the tiny local micro-breweries were making any money trying to compete in the shadow of the Anheuser Busch Brewery.

As he was draining his second glass and emptying the bowl of peanuts, Joshua was ready to concede that the micro-breweries had a competitive product, but were surviving only at the mercy of the larger, established brewers. Just then, he felt a hand squeeze his right shoulder. He looked around to see Michelle sitting next to him.

"Come here often?" She teased him.

"Only when I get hushed calls from frightened concierges before my morning coffee," Joshua said. "Nice to see you. Was traffic horrible? I've been waiting since five-thirty," he lied with a coy smile.

"The despised Cubbies are in town, and everyone is headed to Busch Stadium. Must be a sellout. At least, Highway 40 is a parking lot, and everybody is wearing red." Michelle conducted a brief scan of the pub and patrons. "Bruce told me that McGuire's was his favorite neighborhood pub. It certainly has its own energy. Tell me exactly what Bruce said on the phone."

Joshua signaled the bartender for two more beers. "Like I said, he sounded very scared on the phone. Bruce had implied either documents or records existed to get Curtis in a lot of trouble, although I wasn't sure whether Bruce meant that he had actual documents, or copies, or just made notes. Whichever, Bruce was concerned enough that he was afraid to use his home phone. Most of all, Bruce was very concerned that someone was following him."

"Joshua, who would be following Bruce? He's not exactly the sort of person who would attract sinister types. Except he's an hour late. Either he decided against meeting with us, or he was detained so he couldn't meet with us. In view of his panicky call to you, I doubt that he whimsically changed his mind. Now, I don't feel like eating, and I don't feel like waiting. I'm worried."

"Bruce mentioned that he lives right around here. Let's look up his address and go over there."

When they found Bruce's address in the phone directory, Michelle and Joshua realized his house was less than two blocks away. They walked briskly along Sidney, the old-fashioned street lamps throwing disks of pale light along the sidewalk. As they approached the four-family row house, they saw a large man walking toward them from the opposite direction. The man walked under a street lamp, and they could see he stood at least six-foot-two, was dark-skinned, and was dressed in a tank shirt and shorts, carrying a gear bag on his shoulder. His biceps bulged out of his shirt. Although the man didn't look particularly menacing, the night was dark and he was very big.

Arriving somewhat awkwardly at the wrought iron fence at the same as the hulking stranger, Joshua said, "Good evening. We're looking for Bruce's house—do we have the right address?"

"Close enough," the stranger said cautiously. "Are you two friends of Bruce?" Michelle and Joshua introduced themselves and said they knew Bruce from his work. "Nice to meet you. I'm Ardice Hamilton Godwilling, and I live next door," the man's deep baritone voice was guarded, but he offered his hand, first to Michelle.

"I knew it." Joshua said, pointing his finger at the man's face. "Your nickname is Ham, and you played defense for Northwestern in Chicago. Right?"

"Yeah, man, that was me," he said and cast his eyes away with a shy grin. "I started at middle linebacker for four years, and all four years we were the doormat of the Big Ten. Then I graduated—in pre-med—and they went on to the Rose Bowl. Anyway, what brings you down to Soulard—I hope it's social. Bruce has been sort of edgy lately, not like himself. He could use some cheering up."

"Um, not exactly social, although we've been concerned about him also," Michelle said. She told Ham about how Bruce had asked to meet Joshua and her for a beer at McGuire's and failed to show up after an hour. She omitted the details of Bruce's panicky phone call and any reference to his fear that someone was following him.

Ham said, "Well, I'm just getting home from my shift at the hospital. I'm a resident there. I got off early tonight, so I stopped at the gym for a little workout on the way home. Gotta keep this off, you know," he said, patting his flat, hard stomach. "I haven't talked to Bruce all day. Why don't you guys come in. Maybe he's lost in his Beethoven, or captured by some cookbook from the south of France."

Michelle and Joshua followed the broad-shouldered Ham through the gate and stepped aside while Ham unlocked the door. "We're trusting neighbors down here—we all have each other's keys." No one said anything about being afraid of what they might find inside the house. Ham unlocked the deadbolt and then the doorknob.

"Bruce? Bruce, you home?" Ham's robust voice carried though the house like thunder. He turned to switch on the foyer light.

No answer.

The rest of the house was dark. Ham slowly walked into the living room and flipped the wall switch. "Bruce?"

No answer.

The wall switch had turned on a table lamp in the far corner, bathing the living room in soft light. Ham stopped and stared, with Michelle and Joshua peering on either side around his broad shoulders. The three of them were speechless as they surveyed the ransacked room. The empty shelves on both sides of the fireplace, books tossed on the floor, the couch and chairs overturned, their cushions ripped open, pictures torn off the walls.

"Son-of-a..." Ham's words were interrupted by a scraping noise upstairs. "Sounds like a window," he whispered and headed for the stairs leading to the second floor. Joshua followed a few cautious steps behind him. Ham suddenly stopped to pick up the bat and glove left at the bottom of the stairs between softball games. He carried the bat menacingly in his right hand and handed the glove to Joshua. "I'll crank him, you catch him," Ham winked as his muscular legs bolted up the steps.

Moving quickly up the hardwood steps to the second floor, with Michelle close behind, Ham and Joshua couldn't hear anything but their own footsteps and labored breathing. Ham raced into one of the bedrooms and crashed over two drawers strewn in the doorway, landing in the middle of the floor with a painful thud and a few choice oaths from his locker room days.

Joshua groped for the light switch and quickly saw the open window. Ham was back on his feet, clutching his right shin and hobbling to the open window, where he was joined by Joshua wearing the outfielder's glove on his left hand. Michelle broad-jumped the scattered drawers and squeezed in between Ham and Joshua at the windowsill.

A man, dressed in dark clothing, was running through the backyard and down the alley, slipping quickly out of view.

Ham massaged his shin as he surveyed the mess in Bruce's room. He led the way, limping, as the three of them walked through the second floor rooms, turning on all the lights, shocked by the desk drawers, papers, clothing, and furniture that were strewn everywhere.

23

The scorching temperatures and relentless humidity, so typical of summer in St. Louis, had finally broken. A cool front of Canadian air came into the area on a brisk northern breeze. The Consultant turned off the air conditioner and opened the windows to let the welcome breeze bring fresh air into his small apartment.

After his return flight from Zurich, he was eager to get back on his computer. He was now intently watching his computer monitor as he analyzed the financial files. *Hello, my darling little Special Assessment. I know you've been asleep, awaiting your master's voice. It's time to make some money, my little friend.* He awoke the applet and found the list of passwords. *This was too clever for words*, he thought. *Or, maybe just merely malicious.*

After he entered the passwords, the accounts appeared on the screen in the same spreadsheet format as he had seen on the computer in PSM's offices. He scrolled through the accounts, reviewing each of the names and amounts against the list he had made at PSM. Perfect, it's all here, he thought.

He had memorized the all-important number of his new account at Zuricher Zentral Banque, but he had to review again the bank's instructions for electronic transfers. He reached in his wallet and unfolded a sheet of the bank's letterhead, which explained the magic instructions in four languages. It seemed that his heart was beating more loudly as he read the required steps in the English version.

A trial run would be appropriate. I'll start with one hundred thousand dollars, then check with the bank to make sure it went through.

He scrolled back through the accounts until he found Estrella Cove, which showed a new reserve total of slightly over eight hundred thousand dollars. He highlighted the account number and entered the figure of one hundred thousand dollars. They don't need it, and they won't even miss it. Then he entered his new bank account number at the Zuricher in the appropriate space and highlighted it. He moved the cursor to "transfer" and held his breath as he clicked the mouse. The computer quietly whirred, hummed, and clicked, like a cyberspace cash register.

Clever or malicious? Malicious or clever? A difficult choice, indeed.

According to the bank's instructions, electronic transfers could not be verified for two hours, although further instructions could be sent to the bank. Such further instruction, in his case, could be a transfer to yet another foreign account, which he might decide to open in Geneva. *One step at a time*, he reminded himself. For now, he just wanted to make sure the one hundred thousand dollars was transferred to the Zuricher, where he could collect it personally in hard cash. What started as a poor dreamer's fantasy was getting closer to rich reality.

He flipped the tab on another Busch and flopped on the couch to watch TV. And the clock. And wait until he could confirm the transfer with Zuricher Zentral Banque.

24

At the same time the Consultant was popping the tab on another beer, Joshua and Michelle were pulling up in front of Joshua's house, squeezing the Explorer into a tight parking space on the narrow, tree-lined street in the city's central west end. Looking at the stately brick homes, Michelle said, "I love this street, with these solid houses and mature trees." With the unique architectural detailing of each home, the entire street looked like an outdoor museum.

Joshua hoisted two briefcases out of the rear storage compartment of the Explorer, which was filled with Michelle's tools for emergencies, such as flashlights, plumbing wrenches, shovels, work boots, hammers, a stepladder, and her hacksaw.

They reached the front porch, where Joshua opened the door and entered his code to disarm the alarm. "Michelle, meet my steady girlfriend for the past five years, Amourette." The Golden Retriever wagged her tail furiously and rolled over, paws waving in the air, begging to have her belly rubbed. "She has her own private dog door in the basement, so she comes and goes as she pleases."

"Did you name her 'little love affair' after anyone in particular?" Michelle looked up at Joshua as she petted Amourette's underside.

"I'll ignore that. Let me show you around." Joshua sat the briefcases on the floor in the foyer, next to the antique coat rack, and guided Michelle through the rooms on the first floor, explaining the tedious restoration work he had completed on the first floor of the century-old house. They stopped in the kitchen.

"I can see you've done a lot of renovation in the kitchen. This six-burner range looks commercial. It's… uh…really unusual."

"Well, I like to cook, although I'm not that good. Actually, I just wanted a dramatic centerpiece, and I saw some magazine pictures of commercial gas ranges in home kitchen settings. Gas is the only way to go if you're serious about cooking. But, it got a little complicated because this range requires a commercial hood and vent, so the contractor had to open a huge hole in the wall. See there?" Joshua said, pointing. "That's right where the flue runs, which is about a foot thick and all brick. The neighbors probably thought I was opening a restaurant because they came over and asked for a menu. Anyway, now I can boil six pots of water at the same time."

"This is really wonderful, Joshua. And, since you offered to cook us dinner after we get done working, how about we get started on the files?" Michelle said. Joshua opened two Michelobs and handed one to Michelle. When they were both seated with a beer at the kitchen table, Joshua emptied the contents of his briefcases into two stacks of files.

He opened the top file and said, "I asked B.J. and Sedona to pull all the files that contained complaint letters or threats from condo owners who didn't appreciate our taking legal action against them." Joshua explained that the files they had gathered were recent or pending collection and enforcement actions, where PSM was the managing agent, where the lawyers had filed suit, and the owner had threatened the lawyers in some way. The threats were made either by sending hostile letters or making abusive calls to the office, or making threats in person at the office or the courthouse, which has happened more than once.

"These two stacks represent the two dozen current files we have that fit those criteria. We can go back further if we need to," he said. "But then, of course, I wouldn't have time to make dinner for you."

She opened the first file. "How could we overlook the Sanford case?" Michelle asked, reviewing the minutes entered in the front of the file. "The Quivering Oak Condominium Association sued him to collect a special assessment of fifteen hundred dollars to replace all the roofs, which he refused to pay because his roof didn't leak, as if we could replace only half of a roof. He lost at trial. On appeal, his main legal argument was that the special assessment was invalid because the board was elected without a quorum. He lost again. The whole dispute cost the association over twelve thousand dollars in attorney's fees, which he couldn't pay. He filed for bankruptcy and moved to an apartment. Then he moved out of state. You're still trying to collect the debt in bankruptcy court in Texas—the special assessment of fifteen hundred, plus regular assessments of six thousand dollars during the four years of litigation, which he didn't pay, of course, plus the twelve thousand in legal fees for the trial and the appeal, plus the legal fees we're now incurring trying to collect all that. When should the board concede that it has done enough to collect this?"

"Some boards just refuse to let go," Joshua said glumly. "Oh well, I shouldn't complain; after all, it pays the bills." He opened a file and said, "Here's the Thomas file.

This guy refused to pay his assessments at Magic Woods Condominium because his wife didn't like one of the women on the board. We filed suit, then took a consent judgment. Thomas sends us a check for fifty dollars every month. And every time he sends me a love letter. In this one, he says, 'I hope you die of a brain tumor that explodes through your eyeballs.' "

"Stop, you're making me ill." Michelle already was skimming the minutes of the next file. "Talk about puking, here's a case involving a dog in a second story condo."

"Oh, yeah, what a fun case," Joshua said. "The woman had a very active social life and a German Shepherd that urinated on the deck because she was too preoccupied to walk it. That routine went on for months until winter, when the lady downstairs complained about the 'yellow icicles' hanging from the upstairs deck—and growing bigger every day. We settled the case, and she paid the association to replace the wood. Then she sold the unit and moved. On balance, a good result for the community, but a significant disappointment for all the guys who lived there."

"I remember that woman. She was a real knockout," Michelle observed. "I got the impression you had a thing for her."

Joshua ignored the taunt and started into the next file. "This one involved Stately Sycamore Estates Homeowners' Association, a jilted lover, and a macho truck."

Stately Sycamores had a restriction against parking trucks larger than half a ton on the street. Unfortunately, one woman's live-in boyfriend owned a one-ton, dual-axle truck that wouldn't fit in the garage, so he parked it on the street. She feared he would leave if he couldn't keep the truck.

"There was no way to settle the case," Joshua continued, "It was all or nothing because this woman's entire life was hopelessly intertwined with the fate of this stupid truck. We won at the trial level. Then they appealed, contending that our private truck restriction wasn't enforceable because the streets were public. They lost again, and they refused to pay the modest sum of four thousand dollars in attorney's fees that we spent on the appeal. We got a judgment for the fees, but he moved out and disappeared, sticking her with the judgment. Hey, what's true love for, anyway? So, now we're garnishing her wages. She hates us for causing her to lose her boyfriend and for garnishing her wages. She's threatened the board and sent us five hate letters."

Michelle and Joshua carefully reviewed the remaining files, adding another half-dozen names to the growing list of suspects.

"I'm starved," Michelle said as she helped Joshua organize the files and remove them from the kitchen table. "So far, you've refused to tell me what we're having for dinner. What's the surprise?"

"Fresh pasta, and I mean fresh. We'll make the sauce and mix in some onions, mushrooms, and tomatoes with a few selected fresh herbs. It's my secret recipe—the sauce that made the walls of Jericho come tumbling down. The key to Italian cooking is fresh ingredients, keep it simple, and don't spare the olive oil." Joshua paused and held up an index finger. "But, we cannot create Italian cuisine without appropriate background music. Do you prefer Verdi or Puccini?" He headed toward the living room.

"Do you have *Il Trovatore*, with Pavarotti as Manrico?" Michelle called out over her shoulder. "That's one of my favorites."

"We only have the highlights version, if you're not offended," Joshua said, as the CD player started the music from Act One of Verdi's opera.

"It's so sad, in the first scene of Part Four, when Leonora takes the poison that she secretly hid in her ring."

Returning to the kitchen with a bottle of red wine, Joshua used a screw-pull to uncork it and filled two glasses.

"I hope you like this. It's a very smooth pinot noir that should go well with the Port-Salut cheese. Here's to good company, even if it is an un-date," he offered in toast.

Be careful, Michelle. One step at a time, take it slow and steady, stay in control of the pace. "And, here's to the value of a professional relationship," she responded a bit more firmly than she intended. "And don't you dare forget it," she added, sawing her neck with her fantasy hacksaw. Joshua thought he saw her wink, but he couldn't be sure.

"Let's see what kind of personality we have here," Michelle said, and held the glass up to the light to observe the color of the wine. Then, she swirled it gently to coat the sides of the glass and delicately addressed the bouquet. She sniffed once, then again. At last, she took a modest sip. She swallowed, cocking her head to one side and said, "A complex personality, aggressive yet with a subtle edge, a little difficult to swallow, with a hint of surprise at the end." She turned to look Joshua in the eye. "And now, I'll tell you what I think about the wine."

It was a rare occasion when Joshua let his guard down, but Michelle's subtlety took him completely by surprise. His face wore the smile of embarrassment. It made him appreciate how much he admired her quick wit and engaging humor. At the same time, he acknowledged that she was capable of carving him up with a quick glance. He considered the symbolism of the hacksaw.

They clinked glasses and eyed each other cautiously as they drank.

Joshua found a pair of matching aprons in the drawer next to the sink. "You know, of course, that the world is full of great female cooks, but the world's great chefs are all men," he said. "Nothing sexist intended, but I'll be the chief chef tonight, and you can be the prep chef." He helped Michelle tie her apron behind her neck, which made him remember tying his lab partner's rubber apron in chemistry class back in high school, when he accidentally dropped one of the strings and impulsively reached to retrieve it, but succeeded only in grabbing her right boob. *What a fine mammary.*

He poured a jar of marinara sauce into a pan and brought it to a slow simmer. Michelle prepared the pasta dough in a large stainless steel bowl.

Joshua placed a thick maple cutting board on the countertop and sprinkled the surface lightly with flour. Then, he cut the ball of dough into quarter-inch slices. Next, he fastened an old-fashioned, chrome, hand-cranked pasta slicer to the edge of the countertop and explained the different settings to Michelle. They started by feeding the slices of dough through the rollers, adjusting the settings until the slices were rolling out as thin sheets. They adjusted the crank to the setting for fettuccini and began feeding the slices of dough into the narrow slot.

"You're putting it in crooked," Michelle said. "Let me feed it and you turn it."

"This requires teamwork, so don't start cranking at me. Cutting pasta dough may look easy, but it's tricky and delicate, and you've got to feed it straight, then crank fairly quickly and steadily with one hand and catch the pasta strips as they come through with the other hand. That's why you need four hands to do this. You'll get the feel of it."

The first two attempts resulted in a growing mound of broken bits and pieces of pasta. But, as they finished their second glasses of wine, Joshua and Michelle were giggling and elbowing each other and cranking out perfect strips of fettuccini, which they placed over a pasta drying rack.

Joshua looked at the pasta. "It's nice to know you need me," he said. "See, it takes the lawyer to tell you what's straight and what's crooked."

Michelle then diced the huge portobello mushroom and chopped an onion while Joshua turned on a high flame under the five-quart pot of water. He peeled two garlic cloves and sliced them in half. They added a twelve-inch sauté skillet to the range and covered the bottom with olive oil. Michelle sautéed the chopped onion for a few minutes, then added the sliced portobello, garlic, crushed Roma tomatoes, and fresh basil. The kitchen soon was filled with rich smells being released by the sauté. They gently placed the fettuccini in the boiling water and Joshua sliced the fresh loaf of coarse Italian bread he had picked up earlier at the Missouri Bakery in the Italian neighborhood called simply, the Hill. Michelle broke up some romaine lettuce and prepared a caesar salad.

Amourette sauntered into the kitchen from the basement, and began scouring the floor for any morsels of food that had escaped the countertop. Then, she sat next to her food bowl and stared expectantly at Joshua. "You're a good girl, Amourette, you're so eager to please, and you ask for so little, unlike some other women I know," Joshua said loud enough for Michelle's benefit.

"Are you trying to communicate with me through the dog?"

"Some guys will try anything," Joshua responded, as he scooped two cups of Science Diet into Amourette's dish. He then filled the dog's water bowl with fresh tap water and placed both bowls by the French doors, where she wasted no time assaulting her only meal of the day.

Michelle and Joshua had dinner in the formal dining room, sparsely furnished with a large antique table and chairs and little else. "You could say I'm a minimalist," Joshua explained. More accurately, he didn't have any time for frivolous activities such as shopping for furnishings. The table was adorned simply with two tall red tapers that flickered brightly, a bottle of Classico Chianti from Tuscany, and a bottle of Evian. The overhead chandelier was set to dim. Joshua sat at the head of the table, with Michelle on his left.

They ate leisurely, the frantic and stressful pace of the past week slowly washing away, layer by layer, as they savored the flavors, textures, and aromas of the pasta and wine. They talked of new movies they wanted to see, new books they'd heard about but didn't have time to read, and places they wanted to visit. They didn't talk about work. *Il Trovatore* had ended, and it was replaced by Puccini's *La Boheme*. Montserrat Caballe was singing *Mi Chiamano Mimi*.

"If you ever decide to stop practicing law, Joshua, you should consider a second career as a gourmet. You and your six burner commercial range." Michelle sipped the last of her glass of wine, her plate clean. "This meal was far superior to any restaurant. I'm full. That was marvelous. How about a stroll around the block? Is it safe?"

"We'll take the d-o-g for a w-a-l-k," Joshua whispered.

They cleared the table and loaded the dishwasher then started for the front door. Amourette was waiting for them, her leash in the middle of the foyer's oak floor. "You can't fool this dog," Joshua said. "Not only can she lip-read, but I think she knows sign language, too."

Joshua fastened the leash to Amourette's collar, and the three of them headed out the door, Joshua getting a flying start as he was jerked down the walk by the dog. "She'll slow down in a few minutes," he shouted over his shoulder at Michelle, who had to jog to keep pace. They turned to the right and, half jogging and half walking, headed east down the sidewalk.

Unlike the last two weeks, the evening air was pleasant and dry. A light breeze rustled the tops of the pin oaks and sycamores. Joshua made a mental note to open the windows when they returned home.

Amourette's burst of energy spent, the trio assumed a more leisurely pace as they reached the corner of the block. "So tell me, Joshua, why did you decide to live in the city? Aren't you concerned about crime and safety? Why didn't you join the suburban sprawl?"

"Actually, my first place was a new home in the 'burbs. I was the perfect SHIPWOK, and I craved the American dream, or at least, I thought it was the right thing to do."

"What's a SHIPWOK?" Michelle asked with her eyebrows furrowed.

"Oh? I thought you'd heard that term by now. A SHIPWOK is a Single High Income Professional Without Kids. Anyway, I fell for it. I was brainwashed. I listened to the real estate agent and blindly swallowed the so-called conventional wisdom that life in the suburbs was the American way. You know, a new house on a large lot. Well, I soon learned after moving in that the quality of construction was shameful, at best. It's amazing to think that a whole house could be built on a Monday morning. I'm not just talking nail pops. Half the house settled two inches. The roof leaked with the first hard rain. That's when I learned that the shingles on the rear portion of the roof had been installed backwards. After only two years, I had to paint the exterior because the original paint job washed away. The siding warped with moisture. I was a such a naive consumer. I didn't consider all those things when I bought. It looked good, so I thought it was good. After three years, I realized I didn't know any of my neighbors, except to wave at them when we happened to mow our yards at the same time. And, if all of that wasn't enough, I faced a horrible forty-five minute commute twice a day on that parking lot we call Highway 40."

Joshua stopped while Amourette sniffed the marking of another dog at the base of a huge pin oak. "Here, the houses are all brick, built to last, and they all have wonderful architectural detailing and stained glass. The style of each house is different. Each front doorway is distinct. The homes have large front porches that aren't far from the street, which invites you to talk to the neighbors. All of that is missing in new construction in the 'burbs. Here, you get to know your neighbors because the houses are so close together. You can smell your neighbors' cooking and listen to the Cardinals' ballgame on their radio. You can walk down to the corner market, the drugstore, movies, or a variety of restaurants, without getting in a car and driving to West Jesus. Frankly, I think it's more a community than most of the new developments that dot the landscape of suburban migration. And, I'm willing to bet you, community associations will begin to rediscover the importance of diversity. Urban planners and community builders will start to re-engineer, re-invent, and restructure suburban communities to recapture the diversity of the traditional urban neighborhood."

Michelle was admiring the diverse detailing of the cornices atop each of the houses. "Walking down your street is like exploring a museum of architecture, full of embellishments. It's unfortunate that no one is building new homes today with this level of charm. I chose to buy my condo as a matter of convenience, and because it's the most affordable way to become a homeowner and get out of renting forever. But, you're right. My condo has shoddy construction. I can hear my neighbors flush. Worse, I can hear their pillow talk. I had to rearrange my bedroom so the bed is on the other side. And, I don't know any of my neighbors, except to wave when I'm taking out the trash."

They arrived back at Joshua's house. He ground fresh espresso beans and turned the steam valve on his Gaggia to froth a pitcher of skimmed milk. "Just water for me," Michelle said. They sat down at the kitchen table as Amourette curled up under it with a long sigh of serenity.

"Amourette sounds like I feel. Exhausted and content." Michelle stared distantly at her glass then looked up to study Joshua's face. She took her napkin and wiped a froth mustache from his upper lip. Neither spoke for several minutes.

"Well, Michelle, it's nearly midnight." Joshua finally broke the silence as he looked at the wall clock. He stretched. "Tomorrow is Saturday, and I have a hockey match in the Men's Catholic Church League. I play for the local parish, although Father Ragazzi won't even pass the basket so we can get matching jerseys for the Battling Beagles. The past three years, I've played in a Sunday afternoon men's basketball league, too. It was just a group of guys who got together and formed a team so we could join a league, but we couldn't find any business to sponsor us, so we invented a sponsor. His name was Jack. We started as Jack's Warm Car Wash, and the next year we were Jack's Used Dental Hardware. Last year, we started the season with a terrible slump, losing our first eight games. Then, Jack suddenly died, poor guy. He was so loved by all the players. It was a tragic loss, and we all wore black armbands in token mourning, and told our opponents that our beloved sponsor, a great humanitarian, had died. We finished with eight straight wins." Joshua glanced at a tired-looking Michelle. "Oh, I'm sorry—this trivial drivel must be boring."

"No, it's not boring at all. You know, you never talk about yourself. I'm not sure why, so I guess it's just because deep down, you're really shy. Let me take advantage of the opportunity. Tell me, do you date much?"

"Excuse me?"

"Do you have selective hearing? I asked if you date much?"

"Okay, I heard you. I just don't know what to say."

"What part of the question don't you understand?"

"The part that sounds like a date question, but I'll try to answer it anyway. The dating department really hasn't seen much activity after an accumulation of failed relationships. A few years ago, I dated this woman, a nice woman, so I thought at first. It seemed like we really clicked, you know, lots of things in common. But she was a social worker, and every time we had a date or got together, she'd ask, 'How are we today?' It was like she worked full time micro-managing the relationship instead of just letting it happen. I broke it off and focused on my work since then. Now, I'm date shy."

Michelle paused. "So, you just unilaterally decide that if you think a relationship is too much work, you dump it. You hide behind your law practice, which, conveniently, can be as busy as you choose to make it. Is that about right?"

Joshua studied the dregs in the bottom of his cappuccino mug. "But, I really enjoy what I do, and if I don't have time to date, so be it." He stopped and looked up at Michelle. "On the other hand, perhaps the right woman would change that scenario. So, now, it's your turn. You tell me something personal about yourself. It doesn't have to be too revealing. Were you a cheerleader in high school? Do you have a crush on your car mechanic?"

Michelle stalled for time, glancing sheepishly around the kitchen, looking for a hint of how to begin. "Well, I haven't dated anyone seriously for about two years. Before that, I went through a flurry of men. I mean, I was a serial dater, recklessly in search of a secure relationship, what a stupid fantasy that was. Let's see, there was a stockbroker, who would call me with hot tips, so I got into the stock market. That relationship didn't last more than six months, long enough for the market to go south. I sold the stock and broke off the relationship, losing a few hundred dollars, and a lot of self respect, in the process." Michelle paused to take a sip from her glass of water. "Then, I dated one of our contractors, I'm embarrassed to admit, but he remodeled my bathroom before he dropped me for a woman he picked up at a bar. I must say, though, he did good work." Michelle looked up at the ceiling, squeezed her eyes tightly, and tried to recall the next episode. "I met this lawyer who did estates work, and he insisted on drawing up a will and trust for me. We broke up because all he could talk about was planning for death. It was like dating a mortician."

Joshua smiled when she finished. "So, let me guess how you bought your Explorer."

Michelle regretted that she had left herself open for Joshua's comment. "That's a mean thing to say. Actually, I did get a great deal on the Explorer. And, I'm not having a relationship with the mechanic. But, I will tell you something else." Michelle turned away, but Joshua caught an embarrassed look on her face. She scratched the back of her head while she thought. "Promise you won't laugh?"

"I don't want to sound too lawyer-like, but it depends."

"You're hopeless. May I borrow your guitar? I know that's a very personal request, almost like borrowing a toothbrush."

"That's not a problem. It's just that it's been ages since I've even picked up my own guitar." Joshua walked into the living room trying to remember the last time he played his Goya six-string acoustic guitar. "We'll need to wipe the dust off first," he told Michelle.

Michelle took a seat on a kitchen stool and tuned the guitar. She began strumming and picking a soft melody, full of melancholy, then began singing softly, her voice now deeper and more resonant than her speaking voice, as mournful as a cello:

> A tiny bird trapped in a cage,
> She couldn't fly to her goal,
> The bars of her cage took her breath
> and stole her soul.

She continued the melody on the guitar, until it drifted into the air like the essence of her subtle perfume.

Joshua remained silent as Michelle finished the last chords. "That's a really haunting melody, a beautiful song. Who wrote that? Your Leonard Cohen?"

"The night we had our first un-date," she explained, "I couldn't sleep, you were so heavy on…It was probably too much coffee. Well, I began writing this song. That's as far as I've gotten."

"How does it end? Does another bird come along and free her from the cage?"

"You'll just have to wait and see." Michelle looked up into Joshua's eyes then sat the guitar in the corner.

They sat across the kitchen table, breathing quietly, occasionally venturing an uncertain glance at each other, too exhausted for conversation but not wanting the evening to end, unsure about what would come next. Joshua realized that the un-date had gone as far as he could expect. "Um, look, it's late, and you must be very tired. It's time to take you back home to the 'burbs. If we leave now, we might get there before tomorrow."

As they walked out of the house to Michelle's Explorer, they didn't notice the dark sedan parked across the street, a shadowy figure slouching low behind the steering wheel.

25

Kosankis was driving the black rental car, a new Ford Taurus, south on Highway 19, while Bedford was riding shotgun and checking the map. They had left St. Louis nearly three hours ago, driving south on I-55 most of the way, until they turned off onto the narrow, two-lane state highway. The cool weather had quickly yielded to July's customary heat and humidity. The late afternoon sun was low in the sky, and the trees sent long shadows across the pavement.

"Slow down," Bedford said, pointing at the map, "the turnoff should be somewhere up here in the next mile, on the left. Remember, Leo said that it's just a dirt road, and it's unmarked." They crested a hill and Kosankis turned left onto the narrow road, barely wide enough for the Taurus. They drove another fifteen miles through a canopy of oak and hickory, the car kicking up billows of white dust as it bounced and jiggled along the primitive dirt road.

They pulled up in front of the small stone cottage, built in the 1930s as a private summer home by a long forgotten family from St. Louis. When the Current River was made part of the Ozark National Scenic Riverway several decades ago, the cottage was taken over by the U.S. Forest Service. But, the Forest Service chose to establish their local office in Eminence, thirty miles away, which was the closest town of any size. They never used the cottage because it was too far away, too small, and too inconvenient. Sometimes, the locals stayed over night during their winter hunting expeditions. The original name of the cottage—Seldom Seen—became increasingly appropriate as the years passed, especially in the summer.

Leo, the south side mercenary who had been guarding Bruce, just in case Bruce turned dangerous, strode out the front door of the cottage. He was dressed in a t-shirt, jeans, and hiking boots, and waved to Kosankis and Bedford as the dust settled around the car. "How's Brucie?" Bedford called out to Leo.

"Oh, I'd say we're getting along just fine. We don't exactly have friendly chats. He don't say nothin' to me, and I don't say nothin' to him. Ya know? I keep him locked up in the bedroom with a TV. There are some old paperback novels on the bookshelf, but he don't strike me as the Zane Grey type."

Zane Grey? Kosankis wondered.

Bedford asked Leo quietly, "Has Bruce volunteered any information about you-know-what?"

"He's just whined about being here and called Curtis a bunch of locker room bullshit, but he hasn't spoken a word about anything else. And I didn't ask him nothin.' I've been babysitting, just like you asked me to, until you got here and could take charge of the interrogating."

The three men entered the cottage. Kosankis retrieved two small overnight bags from the trunk and carried them in, while Bedford carried two shopping bags and the videocassette. Leo had brought in a twenty-one-inch color TV and VCR and had put them on a table in the living room. Bedford popped the cassette into the VCR, and Leo pulled three cans of frosty Budweiser from the cooler and passed them around. The three men stood and watched the videotape.

The tape started with the door of Curtis' office opening slightly, allowing a sliver of light to enter the dimly lit room. The shadow of a man crept cautiously into the office. As the figure drew closer to Curtis' huge desk, the lamp illuminated his face. They could plainly see that it was Bruce. Standing over Curtis' desk, Bruce appeared to look at papers on top of the desk then opened the drawers, peering into them with a penlight held in his mouth. He made some notes on a paper he pulled from his shirt pocket. Then the tape showed Bruce turning on the computer behind Curtis' desk, looking at the monitor for about ten minutes, and making a few notes. He shut down the computer and appeared to tiptoe out of the office.

"Back up the tape, Leo," said Bedford. "Go back to where he's standing by the computer." Leo reversed the tape. All three men watched intently. "There—freeze that!" Bedford was pointing at the image on the screen. "You can't see it because his back is turned, but doesn't it look like he's reaching into his shirt pocket? Okay, Leo, advance it frame-by-frame." The three men watched the screen in silence, as Bruce made tiny, jittery movements in each frame. Bedford pointed again at the screen. "Right there—see his right hand? Doesn't it look like he's putting a diskette into the computer?"

Leo moved closer to the TV until his nose was inches away, his eyes peering into the screen. "Could be, Mr. B., but that whole area is in a dark shadow, and I can't tell for sure. He could just be putting his hand on the top of the computer while he's looking at somethin' on the screen."

"How about you, Mr. K?"

"Naw, I don't see it, Mr. B. I gotta agree with Leo."

"You guys would make terrible detectives. I'm telling you, he's putting a diskette into the computer."

Leo advanced the tape to where Bruce was shutting off the computer, but the view was totally obscured by Bruce's back. "Look there," said Bedford, "he's taking the disk out of the computer and putting it back in his shirt pocket."

"You're seeing things, Mr. B."

Leo asked if the two other men wanted him to heat up the canned beef stew that he'd brought in. "Leo, how about you getting a fire going in the barbeque?" Bedford said as he unlocked the bedroom door. "We got three huge t-bones down at Ralph's for us. Save the stew for Bruce, if he can keep it down."

Kosankis and Bedford walked through the door and into the tiny bedroom. It was furnished with a twin-sized bed, one straight-back wooden chair, and a low dresser with a thirteen-inch, black-and-white TV sitting on top, its ancient rabbit ears straining for a signal. The small double-hung window, with security bars on the outside, was pushed open as far as it would go, letting the hot afternoon breeze come in. Bruce was sitting up in the bed, staring at the TV. "And how's Bruce doing this fine day?" Bedford asked sarcastically.

Bruce didn't say anything, his eyes remaining fixed on the microscopic TV screen with its scratchy picture. Through the snow, he could barely decipher the NBC nightly news with Tom Brokaw.

Bedford approached the bed. "It's your lucky day, Bruce. Look what we brought you." Bedford reached in the Banana Republic shopping bag and pulled out a t-shirt and a pair of plaid boxer shorts. "We didn't know your exact size, so we hope these fit. If not, we'll be happy to exchange them so you'll look suitably fashionable in your next life."

Bruce refused to take the clothing held out by Bedford at arms length. "Don't you idiots realize it's the middle of July, it's at least ninety degrees out there and probably twice that hot in here? Are you trying to sweat me to death? Why did you bring me to this insect-ridden hovel with no air conditioning?"

Bedford sat the clothing down on the bed. "What a wimp, hey Kosankis? Well, Brucie, maybe you should file a complaint with the local Fair Housing Council. I'm sure they'll come out and talk to the landlord about the conditions." Bedford smiled in appreciation of his own wit, while Kosankis managed a grunt of approval. "Surely, Bruce," Bedford said, sharpening the blade of his sarcasm, "you didn't expect the Ritz, did you? Are you getting a bit testy, or are you merely trying to develop a sense of humor?" Kosankis thought that was the most hilarious thing he had ever heard.

Bruce was ready to spit, but was too thirsty. "Frankly, I don't find any of this very humorous. Curtis and both of you...you gorillas...can jump into a vat of nuclear waste, for all I care."

Bedford stood at the end of the bed, blocking Bruce's view of the TV. "Now, there's an idea we overlooked. We brought along some implements to make your testicles glow in the dark, electrical clips that plug into the wall and attach to your prick, or we could try an old favorite, the electric probe that's useful for hemorrhoids. If you prefer simplicity, we can be more basic, like breaking a few fingers. But you know, Bruce, you've got a much better idea. If these things don't work, I'll run down to the power plant and get a vat of nuclear waste. How's that sound to you, Mr. K?"

Kosankis smiled a toothy grin. "Sounds like fun."

Turning back to Bruce, Bedford said, "Look, Bruce,

we got you pegged. This is not some spy movie or a Grisham novel. You're not a man who's got a storehouse of machismo, you hear what I'm saying? You're here alone, and this is reality. You'll spill your guts at the first sight of blood, the first broken finger, the first cup of boiling water on your tender testicles. In fact, I'll bet that you'll squeal at the mere vision of the electric clips on your prick, or the mere thought of the electric probe up your butt. My dear friend, Mr. K., is a certified specialist at interviewing techniques. You're going to talk, one way or the other, so why don't you just make it easy on yourself? All we want to know is what information you saw in Curtis' office."

Bruce had decided the only way to deal with these fellows was to deny everything. He had no idea how far they'd go, and until he found out, he'd deal with them his way. "I've never been in the royal offices of his highness, King Curtis, and even if I have, I didn't see anything. So, you can just go ahead and torture me. I've got nothing to tell you." Bruce paused, his lower jaw defiantly jutting out, his mouth turned downward at the corners. "And you guys should know you're making a huge mistake. You're making a mistake of epic proportions."

"Brucie, why does it sound like everything you say is written down somewhere?" Bedford held up the videocassette for Bruce to see. "Did you know that you're on Candid Camera? It's all here, my friend, in living color, the complete saga of your little adventure in Curtis Carlton's office. Maybe we should make some popcorn, sit back, and watch the movie." Bedford waved the cassette in front of Bruce's face. "No, it's you who'll be making a mistake of epic proportions if you don't start talking. Tell you what, we're going to take a short break for a little something to eat, some thick t-bones charbroiled on the grill and a couple of beers. And, when we're done, we'll come back to see if you've reconsidered your position. Meantime, Mr. K. will give you a little something besides the heat to think about."

Kosankis grabbed Bruce's left hand, holding the little finger tightly.

"No, no, don't. Please, I beg you, don't do that," Bruce pleaded as he struggled to free his hand from Kosankis' grip.

"Bruce," said Bedford gently, "today, we're in the information access business. We want information from you." His face devoid of any expression, Kosankis avoided looking at Bruce and began to apply pressure to his little finger.

"Hold it, Mr. K. Let's wait until after dinner. Brucie can think it over in the meantime." Kosankis reluctantly released Bruce's hand.

The black-suit twins left the room, Bedford pausing to blow a kiss to Bruce. They locked the door behind them. It was eight o'clock, and dusk was settling in on Seldom Seen.

Leo finished grilling the steaks and passed another round of Buds to Bedford and Kosankis. Starving after a long day of hard work, they devoured the food with little conversation, save for the fraternal belching and farting.

Kosankis and Bedford returned to Bruce's room and saw that he was lying in the prenatal position. Kosankis flourished a black gear bag and sat it on the floor next to Bruce. "You feel more talkative now, Bruce?" Bedford asked. "I must warn you that Mr. K. is very good at his interviewing technique. Would you like a demonstration?" Kosankis hovered menacingly over Bruce.

Bruce had been reconsidering his position. *I'd better give them something. They could be serious about this broken finger stuff or the electric probe.* He shifted his body just thinking about where they'd insert the probe. "Okay, okay, I'll tell you what you want to know." A long pause as Bruce struggled to steady his breathing. "Okay, so maybe I looked at some files. They were in his desk and on the computer. I saw that you puke heads are with a big management company back East. I saw your fancy brochure and Curtis' notes. It looks like you nice gentlemen are trying to take over management of the Cove. You're trying to screw PSM. Next, you'll probably screw the Cove."

"Mr. K., do you think that's all he found, or should you give him more encouragement?" Kosankis reached for the black gear bag.

"No, please, you don't need to torture me." Bruce pleaded. "That's it…that's all I saw. I'm telling you the truth."

"What did you take?" Bedford stood over Bruce on the opposite side of the bed.

"Is that a trick question or something? I didn't take anything. If you have a tape of the whole thing, you'll see that I didn't take anything."

"We know you're lying, so stop wasting our time," Bedford said. "We know you took some notes."

"Oh, that. Yeah, I took some notes. I just told you what was on the notes. About your proposal to take over the Cove's business. Oh, I remember now, Curtis wrote Michelle's name down on your proposal and put a big question mark by it."

"Come on, Bruce," Bedford pressed, "you're not being very cooperative." Kosankis slowly opened the zipper of the black gear bag and inspected its contents. "Make it easy for yourself, you know that you won't stand up under pain. Tell us, where are the notes?"

"I destroyed them. The notes are all in my head, like I told you. I don't need notes. I've got a great memory. Just ask Curtis. I've told you all there is to tell."

"You're a spineless little wimp, Bruce." Bedford kneeled over him. "Why did you go to all that trouble?"

"Because he fired me from my job, didn't he tell you that? He's a despicable, obese monster, and I hate him. Most people are merely afraid of Curtis, but I affirmatively despise him. And you can tell him I said that."

Bedford, arms folded across his chest, looked at Kosankis, who now had one hand in the black gear bag, eager to demonstrate his skills for extracting information. Bruce was lying on the bed, worried about what Kosankis would pull from the gear bag. Bedford nodded toward the door, and the black-suit twins began to leave.

"We'll be back tomorrow, Bruce, to see what else you can remember," Bedford whispered at the door. "Say your prayers, because your memory better improve by then."

26

The rattling elevator stopped at the fourth floor, and Joshua hurried into the suite of the Law Office of Angela Laclede. Sedona was occupied with incoming phone calls, so Joshua waved and picked through his faxes and the pink slips of phone calls. It was Monday morning, and his bin was brimming with messages that came in over the weekend. He stopped to scan them quickly, recognizing some of the same clients who had phoned him at home on Saturday, not that they had a real emergency, just hoping they would not be billed because they didn't talk to him at the office. He was looking for a message from Bruce.

"You've got a call holding on line two, Joshua. Guy says his name is Ham. Said you'd know who he is and that it's urgent." Sedona passed a hand with deep copper painted nails through her long hair. Joshua counted at least four rings on her hand.

"Looks like we're getting the new week off to a fast start. Hey, Sedona, what do you call that strange and exotic hair color you're wearing today?"

"Magenta, with sienna highlights, can't you tell? Can I get you some coffee?"

"You know that I don't expect you to get my coffee, but thanks." Joshua hurried into his office, walked behind his desk, clicked on his email and picked up the phone in the same motion. He struggled to remove his suit jacket without dropping the phone and watched the computer monitor while the gods of cyberspace breathed electronic life into more messages. *If our clients would just stop calling me, I could get some work done.*

"Josh, this is Ham." The rich baritone voice resonated over the phone.

"Hey, guy, how are you doing? Hear anything from our friend?"

"That's why I'm calling."

"I hope it's good news."

"That's difficult to say…uh…right now, but it'd be worth a quick meeting. I've got two more procedures scheduled this morning. Can you come down here about eleven o'clock?"

"I've got a motion docket in the city, Ham, and I probably won't be done until noon. How about McGuire's?"

"That'll work. See you at noon, buddy."

Joshua entered the appointment on his computer calendar, appropriately called "Time & Chaos." Then he clicked back to read his email as Sedona came in with a cup of fresh black coffee, a hearty blend he got from Starr's. The regular mix was called "Lawyer's Blend," which consisted of one-third French roast, Colombian, and mocha java. But Joshua made the mix even more robust by substituting Italian espresso beans for the French roast, and Starr's dubbed it "Barrister's Blend" in his honor. Joshua's email inbox showed two new messages, one from Angela, the other from Michelle. He sipped his coffee and clicked first on Michelle's email:

> I haven't heard a word from Bruce, how about you? Are you as good at other things as you are with pasta…? Have a great day!

That made him smile, and it brought back fond memories of last Friday night. Not one to push his luck, Joshua had decided not to ask Michelle out over the weekend. He re-read her message and could feel his body temperature rising, but a clever response would have to wait until after court, and now, after lunch. He would leave her a voice mail on his way to court to let her know about the lunch meeting with Ham. He clicked on Angela's message:

How's the case with the gay-basher?

He thought, *Angela, I sure hope that Judge Freeman understands community association law.*

Joshua stuffed the Mayfair Court file and a legal pad into his brief case and ran out the office, telling Sedona over his shoulder that he would be downtown at city court and wouldn't be back until after lunch. "Call me on the cell phone, if it's an emergency, but I'll have it turned off in court." Joshua hurried to the MetroLink stop and waited on the platform, enjoying a calm moment to gather his thoughts. He would have ten minutes on the train to review the file.

Mayfair Court was a private street in an exclusive area of the city's south side, one of the oldest and most fashionable neighborhoods, where some of the most expensive homes were located. This early planned community, or "private place" as it was known historically, included approximately fifty turn-of-the-century mansions on huge lots, with a wide median strip of green space and trees in the center of the street. Neo-Gothic stone pillars adorned each corner at the entrances, one of which was large enough to serve as the residence of a grad student in philosophy. The main entrance was controlled by a pair of ancient, ornate, steel gates that hadn't been opened in years, the owners preferring instead to use the side street for access into their exclusive enclave.

The governing documents dated back to 1910, with a few "new" amendments that were only sixty years old, and they featured an array of antiquated restrictions on the use of property within Mayfair Court. Most remarkable was the prohibition against owners selling their homes to "anyone of the Negroid or Mongoloid race." *Thankfully, the 1948 U.S. Supreme Court case of Shelley v. Kraemer had preempted that ugly vestige of racism*, Joshua thought, as the train slowed for his stop at Eighth and Pine.

Joshua engaged a brisk pace to cover the three blocks to the civil courts building. He walked up the steps to the aging courthouse, which, to put it most kindly, was guilty of functional obsolescence. The structure was in general disrepair as the result of decades of deferred maintenance. Cosmetic repairs were continually made under the banner of renovation. The last attempt at a bond issue to fund a restoration effort failed miserably. The lawyers who practiced in the city courthouse blamed the result on the judges, who in turn chastised the media for failing to get the message out.

One of the newspapers ran an editorial after the bond election, hailing the paper's own in-depth, seven-part series on the deplorable conditions at the courthouse as sufficient exercise of its journalistic responsibility. The editorial blamed the pathetic result on an apathetic body politic that didn't care about the quality of the justice system until they got personally involved; and, even though the number of civil and criminal actions being filed was mushrooming, the number of people directly affected was still relatively small. The results didn't surprise anyone: the courts ranked down with libraries in terms of priorities for public spending.

Joshua passed through security and the x-ray machine and headed for the elevators. The creaky old elevators, however, only went to the tenth floor, at which point he had to wait an uncertain amount of time for another elevator to the twelfth floor or walk two flights of steps. He headed for the stairs, taking two at a time, passing the peeling green paint, the leaky pipes, and dim light bulbs in the stairwell.

Finally, he reached Division 39, Judge Luther Freeman. The corridors weren't air conditioned, but the huge windows were open, allowing the early morning breeze to blow gently into the hall. During the worst of the heat, the courthouse had became so hot that the clerks placed fans in front of the fuse boxes to keep them from overheating and blowing.

Thankfully, motions today were being heard in the judge's air-conditioned chambers, rather than in the sauna that served as his courtroom. Joshua recognized and greeted a few of the other attorneys, who were mostly standing and shuffling around, or trying to get comfortable in the hard wooden chairs. A few were practical, having removed their suit jackets. Some attorneys were sipping the rancid courthouse coffee from Styrofoam cups. Others huddled by the open window, smoking cigarettes and quietly sharing courthouse gossip. The rest discussed their disputes or the terrible burdens of their caseload, or read the morning paper while they waited for their cases on the motion docket to be called.

Joshua's opponent, a highly successful personal injury lawyer named Frederick von Humbolt, was already seated. Humbolt was from an old St. Louis family and claimed to be a direct descendant of the German scientist, Baron Alexander von Humbolt, after whom a street was named. He was widely known for his pompous and theatrical style in the courtroom, which provided much material for the gossip columns, and for the questionable tactics he used in the dark and dangerous back alleys of discovery, where lawyers were unleashed to take depositions of opposing parties, demand documents, inspect property, and intimidate opposing counsel. Today, however, Humbolt would not be engaged in his personal injury specialty, but would be representing himself as an owner of one of the most ostentatious limestone palaces on Mayfair Court—where he was known among his neighbors as Little Adolph. He had fostered a reputation for hating everyone who wasn't what he called a WHASP—a white, heterosexual, Anglo-Saxon Protestant. Humbolt was unrelenting in his mission to make America pure.

With all chairs taken, Joshua found a place to stand and opened his file to review his notes and research. He knew he was prepared to argue the law, but less sure he could handle Humbolt's style of mud wrestling. At least, he remembered to wear his protective gear.

Once inside chambers, Humbolt began in his usual, full-of-himself manner as he and Joshua seated themselves in front of Judge Freeman's desk, "Your Honor, this is a simple case of the trustees of a private place failing to enforce a single-family restriction." Humbolt's first tactic was to take the offensive, starting the oral arguments although it was Joshua's motion to dismiss. But, Joshua didn't mind in this case. He hoped Humbolt would dig himself into a hole by demonstrating the depth of his conservative beliefs in front of this young, African-American judge.

"I'm a homeowner in Mayfair Court, representing myself in this action," continued Humbolt, speaking louder than necessary to overcome the noisy window air conditioner. "Two unmarried men purchased the home next door to me last January. Within a week, I wrote the trustees, advising them of these facts and of their duty under the trust indenture to enforce the restriction because these two men are obviously not a single-family. Now, here we are in July, and the trustees have failed or refused to enforce the restriction, leaving me no choice but to bring this action against them for breach of their duties. Here's a copy of the restriction for your review, and a copy of the *Philby* case, which controls in this issue. *Philby*, as I'm sure the court recalls, defines the term 'single-family' as being related by 'blood, marriage, or adoption.' The two men living next door to me, and I might say that my wife is even more disgusted and repulsed than I am, cannot begin to meet any of these three elements."

Humbolt, a self-righteous, arrogant expression fixed on his face, handed the documents and court cases to Judge Freeman. The judge turned to Joshua, "What of it, counselor?"

"Have you finished your argument, Fred?"

Humbolt barely nodded, unwilling to concede even a common courtesy. "My name is 'Frederick,' not 'Fred.' "

"Your Honor," Joshua continued, "what's before you today is the trustees' motion to dismiss for failure to state a claim." Joshua looked directly at Judge Freeman. "Essentially, we have three points in support. First, the trustees have considerable discretion in carrying out their duties, including deciding how and when to enforce the restrictions, or deciding not to enforce. The basic standard of review in Missouri is whether the trustees' decision is reasonable.

"Second, *Philby* is a 1972 decision that dealt with four young men who were attending college together. The parents of one of the boys owned the house, but the boys were unrelated to each other and were rooming together solely as a temporary economic arrangement. Thus, *Philby* is readily distinguished on its facts. In our case, two adult men are living together in a union, as domestic partners, as a single-family unit. For our last point…"

Frederick von Humbolt cut off Joshua's statement. "Your Honor, our legislature, like virtually all states around this great country of ours, does not officially recognize same-sex marriage, or union, or whatever the gays and lesbos want to call it. It's un-Christian and against God. It violates the sacred principle of motherhood. It's against the flag." Humbolt sighed and turned a wistful eye to the Stars and Stripes standing against the wall behind the judge's desk.

"Excuse me, Fred," Joshua implored when Humbolt had finished. "I listened patiently while you spoke first, even though it's my motion that is being heard. Then, I extended the courtesy of asking whether you were finished, and you indicated that you were. Now, I would appreciate the same courtesy from you, if you've finished interrupting me."

Humbolt grunted audibly. "I may not be finished interrupting you. That depends on what idiocy you say next." He returned his gaze to the flag and straightened his posture. Joshua could see the earlobes and the back of Humbolt's neck turning crimson.

Joshua turned to Judge Freeman. "As I was saying, Your Honor, the last reason is that each homeowner, including Mr. von Humbolt, is authorized in the indenture to bring such an enforcement action directly against his neighbors, which demonstrates that he is not without available remedies. He just wants the trustees—and now this court—to carry on the dirty task of acting out his prejudices." Handing some photocopies to the judge, Joshua said, "Here are three recent cases in support of each of our points."

Judge Freeman looked back to Humbolt, who was fuming, his eyes ablaze, his hands trembling. He was a self-confident man and would not have his values easily disparaged. He could barely stop himself from crossing the border of self-control. "Judge, if you would just read this particular restriction," Humbolt pleaded, jabbing at the documents, "you'd see that it was intended precisely to prohibit the use of property by any persons who do not constitute a traditional single family. To meet this restriction, the occupants cannot be unrelated by blood, marriage, or adoption. And, that's exactly what we have in this…this…abomination."

Joshua was quick to reply. "Your Honor, this is not a question of Talmudic intricacy. The restriction was intended to prohibit rooming or boarding houses, not domestic partners. We're living more than a full century after this language was written, and this court may take judicial notice that growing numbers of unmarried people choose to live together as a single-family. Some do so out of love, companionship, or other personal reasons that this court should not be forced to inquire into. Some of these people are males, some are females, and some are mixed-sex. If the courts take a homophobic approach and adopt a bulletproof test to prohibit people from living together as a single-family merely because they are not related by blood, marriage, or adoption, our society would be branding a scarlet letter H on thousands of fine citizens. It would open the floodgates of litigation that could drown the justice system. It would turn the clock back to *Shelley v. Kraemer*. And, I'm sure that I need not remind the court that *Shelley* arose in a private street not far from this very courthouse." Joshua couldn't resist referring to that not-so-subtle landmark case and watching Humbolt wince. "That's all I have, Your Honor. Thank you."

Frederick von Humbolt huffed. "But, judge, the plain language requires you to…"

Judge Freeman stood. "I can read the plain language, thank you, Mr. Humbolt, and I've heard quite enough. The matter is taken under advisement so that I may review the documents and authorities you have presented to the court. Gentlemen, please prepare a memo and leave it with my clerk." As the two lawyers stood to leave, there was silence in the room, violated only by the screeching and whirring of the window air conditioner.

Humbolt glared menacingly at Joshua then spun on his heels and stalked out of the judge's chambers, leaving Joshua standing by himself. Judge Freeman glanced over at Joshua and said, "Good day, counselor," with a wisp of a smile that disguised his inner thoughts, but Joshua caught a thumbs-up peeping out from the sleeve of his black robe.

27

Lunch hour at McGuire's Pub was elbow-to-buttock with men and women stylishly attired in business casual jammed into every nook, cranny, alcove, and bay window. Joshua glanced at his watch, noticing that he was fifteen minutes late, the borderline of professional discourtesy, as he worked his way to the back of the restaurant. Over the din of conversation, he could hear the sound system carrying the voice of Eric Clapton. *Leila, you got me on my knees, Leila. Beggin' darlin' please, Leila.* Excusing his way through the restaurant, Joshua finally found Ham at a small round table barely adequate for the two men.

"Hey, Ham, what's happening?" Joshua pulled out a downsized wrought iron chair and seated himself. He smiled at Ham. "How are the shins?"

"Man, I've got a bigger hematoma on my right shin than I ever got playing football."

"Does that mean you have a bad bruise?"

"Yeah, it hurt like hell the first day." Ham reached into the rear pocket of his slacks and pulled out a business-size envelope. "Look, Joshua, this came in the mail on Saturday, inside another envelope addressed to me." Ham handed him the envelope with a handwritten note on the outside.

Ham, please hand-deliver this to Joshua Fyler. He's the Cove's attorney.

Joshua carefully opened the envelope. Inside was a small piece of paper with some notes and a computer disk. Joshua inspected the note, handling it by the edges. He turned the note on the table so it faced Ham. "Is this Bruce's handwriting?"

"If not, it's a great imitation."

"Well, let's see what it says." Joshua used a cloth napkin to turn the note so that both men could read it. The note looked like a list of letters and numbers:

L-D?

M. G. ??

#J-213-978-M-0097

7-14 King

The waiter was hovering over their table, and Joshua hastily gathered up the note and disk and opened his menu. After the waiter took their orders and hurried away, Joshua returned the note and disk to the table.

Ham explored the stubble of his beard with his fingertips. "Who's L-D?"

"I can't think of anyone with those initials. Ham, did Bruce talk to you at all about anything that was going on at the Cove just before he disappeared?"

"Sure. That's why he was so upset. It must have been last Wednesday or Thursday that Bruce called and told me they let him go. Man, was he pissed. All he could do was spit obscenities about Curtis. He called him King Curtis, and, for some reason, he mentioned the French Revolution. Said Curtis had lost his mind. That pretty well sums it up. You think Bruce's firing is connected to this?" Ham asked, gesturing to Bruce's note.

"Will Northwestern beat Notre Dame? If these things aren't connected, it's the biggest coincidence since Monica Lewinsky got spots on her dress."

"What about the police?"

"I've already talked to them. They don't think we have any tangible evidence, and they'd just file this as a missing person case," Joshua said. "Now, look at this note because Bruce is trying to speak to us. I'm wondering who's L-D? It's somebody's initials. Bruce is referring to somebody, maybe a person who was working with Curtis, maybe one of the people responsible for Bruce disappearing."

The arrival of their lunches made Joshua put the note and disk back in the envelope, which he placed in a pocket inside his jacket. Both men were silent for a few minutes while they devoured their food and thought about the code in Bruce's note.

"Josh, maybe it's not who. Maybe it's what. Like, the living dead. Or, how about long-distance phone calls?"

"Very good, Ham. So, what did Bruce mean by that? Everybody's got a long-distance phone service. Is Bruce telling us that Curtis had a private long-distance service?" Joshua pulled out a piece of scratch paper and wrote, "L-D = long-distance phone?"

"You're on the right track. The long-distance carrier sends out itemized billings, with the phone numbers of all calls made," Ham said around a mouthful of grilled chicken.

"It sounds like a long shot, but let's try it." Joshua reached into his pocket for his cell phone and entered the number of PSM. "Jenni? Hi, it's Joshua. I was wondering..." He paused, listening. "It's very nice that you think I'm responsible for Michelle being in such wonderful spirits this morning, but... She thinks I sent them? Sorry, but I didn't send her a dozen red roses. It must have been someone else. Jenni, stop for a minute, please. The reason I called is to ask you if PSM receives the monthly statements from the long-distance phone service at the Cove. Oh, that's good news." Joshua nodded at Ham. "Okay, could you locate the past…say, three to six months, and you and Michelle look them over? No, I don't know what we're looking for. Anything out of the ordinary, I guess. Thanks, Jenni, I'll talk to you soon. Yes, I'm sure I didn't send the roses. Yeah, you too. Bye."

Ham was finishing his salad. "Were you talking about Michelle, the woman who was with you the other night? She's one fine lady. You better send her some roses, before you lose her to that other guy who's obviously got more sense than you."

Joshua rolled his eyes. "You, too? I just got an earful from Jenni. Michelle is an intriguing possibility, but I'm not sure I'm ready to invest in another relationship right now. Anyway, some other secret admirer must have sent her roses." *Who the hell could that be?* "At any rate, Michelle leads us to the next item on Bruce's list, the letters, M.G. Those letters may be the initials of Michelle Gratiot, or the classic British roadster, which is doubtful unless Bruce was kidnaped by a sports car buff. But, why Michelle?

"And why the emphatic pair of question marks?" Ham asked.

28

"Hey, Curtis," Bedford said, as he and Kosankis took their seats and coffee at Curtis' aircraft carrier. Bedford glanced around the office and said, "You know, this place is twice as big as the first apartment I had when I went to college."

The sun again was glaring harshly through the window behind Curtis, but this time, Bedford and Kosankis were prepared. They both put on their sunglasses. "We drove up to give you a personal status report, to let you know we're on top of things," continued Bedford. "We…uh…*interviewed* Brucie last night."

"Oh? How's my good friend, Bruce?" Curtis asked through clenched teeth, barely disguising his disgust. "Tell me some good news."

"We had a little chat with Bruce, and we reached an understanding, although he does not send you his best regards. He's scared, and I don't think he appreciates our hospitality," Bedford said. Bedford related that Bruce had admitted seeing the management proposal and Curtis' handwritten notes. "He knows that we're trying to get the Cove's business."

"That's all?" Curtis was surprised. "Last time I checked, there was nothing immoral, illegal, or fattening about changing management companies. It's a free country. But, what about the computer—what did he see?"

Bedford crossed his arms defensively. "Well, when I looked at the videotape, I thought for sure that Bruce inserted a disk, and after a few minutes, ejected it and put it back in his pocket. Kosankis and Leo claim the video was too dark to be certain."

Curtis turned in his chair to look at his computer. "But, suppose you're right, Bedford. Bruce could have copied anything that's on this baby," he scowled and pointed with his thumb toward the computer. "Bruce certainly had enough time to download a lot of data. So, we've gotta think he did it—he's got a disk. You asked him, right?"

Kosankis adjusted his bulk on the chair. "Uh…not exactly."

Curtis fumed at the thought of a disk floating around with his personal financial dealings on it. "What you mean is that you didn't ask him in the right way," he boomed. "And I thought you guys were pros!"

Bedford put a hand on Kosankis' arm as a signal not to say anything. Turning to Curtis, Bedford said, "By 'not exactly,' Mr. K. simply means that we haven't got that far in the interview."

Curtis put on his reading glasses and opened his desk calendar. "Look, I'd like to call a special board meeting within two days to approve your contract. If I see fit. But the contract won't get on the agenda if you don't get that information from Bruce. Now, do you want our business or not?"

"You're forgetting one little detail, Curtis." Bedford stood up and leaned across the desk. Have you gotten that list yet from Michelle? We've got a tail on her, so we're ready to move if you don't produce."

Curtis flashed a reassuring smile. "That won't be necessary. Let me handle her. I know how to do it. I'll call her and move that along. Meanwhile, you guys better get your butts back down to Seldom Seen. Let's meet again tomorrow."

AS BEDFORD AND KOSANKIS SETTLED into the black Ford Taurus for the three-hour drive down to the Ozarks, Bruce examined the sturdy bars on the small window in his room. He couldn't budge them.

The stone construction of the cottage kept his room stifling and hot because the stones absorbed heat through the day and radiated it through the night. A new day, even with a cool, early morning breeze, did little to mitigate this process. Today, there was no breeze into his room, despite the open window with the screen and the steel grate.

His cell, for all practical purposes. Bruce wondered if he should start making marks on the wall to number the days of his confinement, or he could rip out pages from this sorry collection of paperbacks. Maybe he should leave a coded message depicting the final bitter dregs of his captivity in case some future traveler ever came by the cottage.

Bruce found that the coolest spot was on the concrete floor. There he sat, trying to read another Western adventure, in his Banana Republic boxer shorts and tennis shoes, when he heard the Taurus crunching on the driveway in front of the cottage. The driveway was topped with a layer of chert, or Mozarkite, the official state rock. Bruce listened as Bedford and Kosankis slammed the car doors, walked up the path, and opened the cottage door. He could hear Leo speaking in a low voice, but couldn't understand the conversation. Then Bedford and Kosankis, their suit jackets abandoned, abruptly burst into the room. Bruce didn't move, look up, or otherwise acknowledge them.

The black-suit twins stepped into the corner where Bruce was slouched against the wall and stood over him menacingly. Bruce continued to ignore their presence, feigning interest in his paperback. "Good afternoon, Bruce," Bedford finally said. Out of the corner of his eye, Bruce could see Kosankis rolling up the sleeves of his white shirt, revealing a tattoo of a red scorpion on his beefy forearm.

Bedford held out a tan paper sack with golden arches on it. Bruce had vowed years ago never, regardless of how poor or famished he might be, descend to eating a fast food hamburger. "Look, we brought a hot lunch for you," Bedford said.

"Eat it," snapped Bruce, still looking down at the paperback.

"Bruce, you're not being very grateful, especially in view of the trouble we went to get this gourmet-to-go meal for you." Bedford let the sack fall to the floor between Bruce's legs. "Look, like I said before, all we want is for you to tell us what you know. If your memory hasn't been revived by our last discussion, Mr. K. has a few conversation pieces that you might find stimulating, maybe even shocking. The problem, as I'm sure you're aware—because you're not a stupid person—is that Mr. K. has a very limited vocabulary. He's mostly a non-verbal sorta guy. You know what I mean?"

Bruce stared at the matching black wingtips, now coated with a thin layer of gray dust from the chert road, stationed on either side of him. "You can try whatever vocabulary you have, whatever language you want to use, whatever tone of voice you think fits, but I can't tell you what I don't know."

Kosankis muttered "fuck it" under his breath and reached into his black gear bag. He unwrapped a coil of electric wire and found the outlet where the TV was plugged in. He held the alligator clips in one hand and inserted the plug in the wall receptacle with the other. Next, he pulled out several lengths of rope from the gear bag. Kosankis was intent on deploying his tools of torture, like a surgeon preparing his instruments. He avoided eye contact with Bruce and was silent during the entire ritual, concentrating his full mental capacity on the task at hand.

"Now, Bruce," said Bedford softly, "Mr. K. is going to take this rope and tie you to that chair so tightly that you won't be able to move a muscle, particularly your precious family jewels. And then, Mr. K. is going to attach one alligator clip to your finger and the other to your little peenie. But first, Mr. K. will give you a demonstration of how this simple device works."

Kosankis groped on the floor for the two loose ends of the electric cord, each with a metal alligator clip attached to it. With a theatrical flair that Bruce couldn't appreciate under the circumstances, Kosankis stood to his full height and stretched his arms in front of him, one alligator clip in each hand. Bruce could see the red scorpion, its curled stinger twitching in rhythm with the flexing of Kosankis' forearm. Slowly, Kosankis brought his two hands together, the distance between the two alligator clips gradually narrowing, the mere sight enough to make Bruce's skin tingle. When the alligator clips were almost touching—not more than an inch separated them—Kosankis paused to increase the dramatic effect.

Bedford said, "Would you like a drum roll, Mr. K?"

Finally, the brute brought the two alligator clips together, but instead of the controlled electrical flash he expected, Kosankis ignited a display of shooting sparks and a bolt of electrical energy that sent ripples through his body. He was rocked by one spasm after another and shook uncontrollably as he stood there, struggling in vain to separate the alligator clips, which had welded themselves from the intense heat. The television went into mortal shock, and the tiny screen went dark as black smoke curled from the rear panel.

"Shit, Kosankis!" Bedford yelled, "you've blown a fuse."

The wires, like the TV, were now dead. Kosankis stared blankly at his burnt hands and fingertips. The still air filled with the rancid stench of burning hair. Kosankis' body continued to convulse, the veins in his thick neck pulsating, the red scorpion on his forearm still twitching its stinger. Bruce, in a state of rapidly increasing anxiety, thought he saw black smoke belching from the brute's ears. But, Kosankis recovered quickly and before Bruce could react, he found Kosankis' huge right shoe pressing down hard into his chest, forcing him into a position flat on the floor. It was hard to breathe.

"Be reasonable, Bruce," Bedford pleaded in a comforting voice. "We know that you put a disk into Curtis' computer, that you downloaded some information, and saved it. And we know that you put it back in your pocket, and you had it when you left Curtis' office. I'll ask you real nicely, but just once. Where is the damn disk?"

Bruce was so scared he stopped breathing. "I really hate to disappoint you guys," he gasped, "after all the trouble you went to in getting my lunch. But, I don't know what disk you're talking about." *And that's the truth*, Bruce thought.

Kosankis pressed his foot harder into Bruce's chest. Bruce struggled to push the heavy foot aside, but couldn't budge it. With a nod from Bedford, Kosankis reached down and singled out the index finger on Bruce's right hand. "Oh jeez, no!" Bruce shouted. "I've told you everything. Don't do this!" Then, he clenched his jaws, preparing for excruciating pain.

Kosankis stared dispassionately at Bruce, lying prone on the floor, and tightened his grip on the index finger. "Brucie," Bedford said, "the reason Mr. K. is so good at what he does is that he has no conscience. He doesn't feel your pain."

"You guys are sure tough. It takes two of you to break my fingers."

"Listen, smart mouth," Bedford said cooly, "that's the last lip we want to hear from you. The next noise out of your mouth will either be some answers or some squealing from having your thumb pointing in the wrong direction. How about it? Did you make a disk?" He nodded again to Kosankis, who took a grip on Bruce's thumb and twisted the joint backwards. "Last call, Bruce," said Bedford.

Bruce felt the pain rising in his hand. "Okay, Okay," Bruce panted. "You're right, there is more. There is a disk. But, it's encrypted, and I'm the only one who knows the encryption. I'm the only one who could decode the disk."

Bedford looked surprised and puzzled, hands on his hips. "So, that's your insurance policy? We can't kill you because we need you to decode the disk? That's clever, my friend. Too clever by half. You can do better than that."

Kosankis released Bruce's thumb and threw the limp arm down hard on the concrete floor, and the two men left the room. Bruce gasped for air and massaged his thumb, grateful that it was still attached.

Bedford paused in the open doorway. "Bruce, we're going to relax and have a few Buds. Do a little fishing down at Bird's Hole, below the bluff. But, we'll be back in a few hours. You'd better tell us where that disk is. If you cooperate, maybe we'll cook you a nice fish dinner. Otherwise, Mr. K. has a piece of pipe outside, and he's eager to make your shinbones sound like a pipe organ."

Kosankis grunted with approval at the thought of brandishing a steel pipe. At least it wouldn't give him an electric shock.

Bruce heard the door slam and the deadbolt close. He exhaled a long sigh, wondering what they would try next, and what he could say to stop them.

BRUCE SQUINTED MINDLESSLY THROUGH the bars of his window. His body was sticky and squishy with sweat. His eyes weren't quite focusing, but he could see that the sun's rays were lower now. It must be late afternoon—his captors should be returning soon.

Bruce thought he heard scuffling along the dirt road, but from a different direction than the path down to the river. He thought he heard voices, but he couldn't see anyone. "Hey, out there!" he said in a breathy stage whisper. "Help me!"

The voices stopped. More scuffling steps could be heard, slower but louder now and more distinct.

Bruce tried again. "Over here. At the window. Help me!"

The faces of two young men with long hair appeared outside the window. Bruce judged them to be in their early twenties. They wore fishing vests and carried rods and gear. "Hey, you guys look like lifesavers," he burst. "I've been kidnaped by these mafia guys. These goons are coming back soon to kill me."

The shorter fisherman, with his mouth open and a puzzled look on his face, studied Bruce's pleading face through the bars on the window. "How do we know you're not some dangerous criminal, being held by the FBI or the CIA or Sheriff Cooper, or somebody like that? Sheriff Cooper is nobody to mess with. He'll arrest us, too, for aiding and abetting."

Bruce sighed. *A couple of college kids.* "Look, we can talk about what-ifs all day, but I only have a few minutes. Three goons are down the bluff, fishing. They look like they just escaped from prison or a zoo for mafia gorillas, and they're coming back at any time. You've gotta believe me. You've gotta help. They'll kill me, I'm sure of it."

The young men looked at each other. "What the hell?" They tried the front door, but it was thick and heavy, and firmly locked. Returning to the window, the shorter one said, "We'll find something to get these bars loose. Don't go away, we'll be right back."

Don't go away. What a sense of humor. Bruce waited anxiously.

The bolts holding the bars to the frame began to move under the prying of the galvanized steel pipe they found behind the cottage. The young men were strong, but both of them had to put all their weight against the pipe. The bolts screeched as they slowly came free from the wooden window frame. They managed to remove the bolts on one side, which allowed them to pull the entire grate enough to create an opening. They slashed the screen with a fishing knife, and Bruce threw his torso into the hole, landing painfully on his forehead and causing a bad bruise above his left eye.

Bruce got to his feet and shook both their hands impulsively. But his celebration of freedom ended abruptly when he heard voices on the trail leading up the bluff from Bird's Hole, two hundred feet below. "We've got to get out of here. Right now!"

"What do you mean, *we*? My buddy and me, we've done enough Boy Scout deeds for one day. You're on your own, pal."

Bruce started running for the woods. "I'm outta here," he called over his shoulder. "What are you planning to do?

Stay for dinner with these guys? I don't recommend it."

The two young men exchanged frightened looks as the rustling sounds from below the bluff grew louder. "I'm outta here, too," the shorter man said and chased after Bruce. The three of them were soon out of the clearing, running as fast as they could through the trees and brush, the fishing rods catching the low branches and slowing them down.

Bedford, Kosankis, and Leo had pulled several nice bass out of Bird's Hole. They were fishing on a gravel bar at the bottom of the bluff when they heard the screeching sounds of metal against wood. They couldn't see the cottage or the clearing at the top of the bluff, but they readily guessed something was wrong. They threw down their fishing rods and ran up the narrow, winding trail that led to the top of the bluff. Their wingtips were no match for the steep and slippery dirt trail, and they soon were clamoring up the bluff on all fours, clutching at the brush to pull themselves up.

They arrived at the top of the bluff, gasping for air, sweat pouring off their faces, to notice the open bars on Bruce's window. They looked around the clearing and turned just in time to see Bruce and his long-haired friends disappearing into the dense woods. The clearing was only fifty yards across, but in the thick forest, such a lead could be difficult to overcome.

"I'm John," said the shorter one between deep breaths as they hurdled a fallen tree trunk. "This here's Tom. We've got a canoe about a mile down the river. That's our best bet."

"My name is Bruce, and I won't forget this for the rest of my life, which, at the moment, appears to be extended. Will your canoe make it to the Gulf of Mexico?"

John and Tom looked back at Bruce. "You're kidding, right?" said Tom.

"I hate to tell you guys," John panted, looking over his shoulder, "but they've spotted us, and they're only about forty-fifty yards back."

Bruce slowed his pace to a jog. He glanced along the sides of the trail thinking, *It's an age-old trick, but it's worth a try. Here's a perfect spot.* "Tom, give me your fishing rod and help me with this." Bruce pulled several yards of ten-pound test from the tip of the rod and wound the line around the base of two oak trees on either side, eight inches above the ground. The fishing line was invisible in the growing dusk. Tom threw the rod into the bushes.

Their hearts racing, Bruce, John, and Tom hurried silently further into the woods. After about ten seconds, they heard the noisy report of a pileup back on the trail, as Bedford, Kosankis, and Leo tripped over the fishing line and entangled each other in a heap of arms and legs. Then they heard the thunderclap of a shotgun blast.

"Hey, guys," Bruce said, "Did I mention that they had guns?" The thought of being gunned down from behind by a shotgun propelled Bruce forward. Followed by John and Tom, Bruce scampered recklessly down the bluff, half-running, half-sliding on the steep slope toward the canoe. Tom got in the back, Bruce took the middle seat, and John pushed them off the gravel bar into the current. There were only two paddles. John and Tom began paddling hard, and soon the canoe was moving swiftly downstream. Bruce, feeling vulnerable and exposed in the middle of the river, paddled furiously with his bare hands and scanned the bluff for a sign of Bedford and Kosankis. But, night was settling in rapidly, and it was becoming hazy and dark now.

Suddenly, two shotgun blasts came from the riverbank, buckshot kerplunking into the water around the canoe. "Shit," John said. The three men in the canoe paddled harder and breathed harder. No one spoke for a few minutes. Finally, when they rounded a sharp bend in the river, John said, "Good thing they just had a shotgun. If they'd had a rifle, 'specially with a scope, we'd be done, for sure. Bruce, if it's okay with you, we'll drop you off in the next town. It's only about two miles downstream. I'd like to say it's been fun, but…we really don't want to see you again, or your friends with the shotgun, if it's all the same to you."

ON THE BLUFF, KOSANKIS WRITHED in pain. When he tripped over the fishing line, he shot his right foot.

29

"Michelle, Mr. Carlton is here for your lunch appointment." Jenni's voice came through the intercom as Michelle was just finishing a phone call. "Please ask him to wait a few minutes, Jen. I'll be right out."

She clicked on her email and saw three new messages, two from clients and one from Joshua. She read the client messages quickly and saved them, then clicked on Joshua's message, which was sent earlier in the morning.:

> Thanks for the dinner invite—you're on! I'll bring the vino and see you at 7:00 p.m. at your place, unless the Worm's depo runs late or I get a migraine going out to the burbs. Watch your back at lunch!—j.

Michelle smiled and clicked on Reply and typed a quick response:

> You know what he'll be watching. Good luck at depo!—mg

She deleted the personal messages then checked her makeup and clothes in the full-length mirror she had installed on the inside of the closet door in her office. She was wearing her favorite summer outfit, blue linen slacks with a pink cotton top, and sensible navy flats. Satisfied that everything was in order—professional and attractive, but not provocative—she headed toward the lobby.

Curtis was studying the framed photographs on the lobby walls. The pictures were black-and-white candids of people, not models and not posed, the very old and the very young, at work and at play, at life. He turned to see Michelle as she entered the lobby. "Hello, Michelle. Wow! You sure light up a room when you come in!" Curtis gave her the full once-over. "It must be your energy. Jenni was just telling me that this is your photography. You have a keen eye for capturing the character of your subjects. I'm just an amateur, but I'd really like your opinion, see if you think my pictures are any good." He paused to examine a photograph of a young mother and her daughter walking on the beach. "You know, you should exhibit your work. If you're interested, I have close contacts in the gallery business—some old friends who owe me a few favors. I'm sure we could get you a show."

Curtis had friends all over, Michelle thought, trying to fake a smile that didn't betray her distrust.

He admired Michelle's mouth, until he realized he was licking his own lips. His eyes slid down to her neck, then lower still for an unabashed admiration of her breasts, a lingering leer, an intrusive undressing of erotic expectation. Finally, his gaze bobbed up again to her face. "I think we should do it. Exhibit your photography, that is. Well, anyway, thanks for taking time from your busy day. Are you ready for some lunch?"

Curtis is pandering again, Michelle thought, *looking for ways to get into my…good graces, although my photography is good.* "It's my pleasure, Mr. Carlton. After all, you're our favorite client," she said, rolling her eyes at Jenni as Curtis held the door open for her.

After helping Michelle into the passenger's seat, Curtis eased his bulk into the driver's side. His stomach pressed against the steering wheel. His blue aloha shirt, incapable of containing his considerable girth, pulled open to reveal a hairless belly. He put the Buick in gear and rolled out into the heavy traffic of Lindbergh Boulevard.

Michelle arranged the shoulder strap across her chest and tightened her seat belt. "So, Mr. Carlton, where are we going for lunch?"

"Let me surprise you." Curtis continued his appraisal of Michelle with a lengthy sideward glance, making her exceedingly nervous in the heavy traffic. Her eyes remained fixed on the road, her feet were pressed to the floorboard as if she could slam on an imaginary brake pedal should they head into a collision. "Speaking of surprises," Curtis continued, concentrating on one more sidelong ogle before returning his attention to the road, "Bruce hasn't come in to work for several days, although we gave him a full two weeks' notice. Have you heard anything from him?"

"Are you shocked?" Her response was quick, her tone sharp. "After all, you fired him without cause. Did you expect a thank-you note? Flowers?" Michelle studied Curtis' face and could see his jaw tense and his neck redden, and instantly regretted her tone. She continued, less strident, more gently now, "Bruce ran the entire clubhouse, and he did it flawlessly and without a single complaint from the residents. I hope the operation doesn't suffer, because Bruce will be extremely difficult to replace."

"If I want to fire somebody, I fire him. End of story. He can take his fussing act down to the Soulard District, where he can be with his own kind."

"Mr. Carlton…"

"Please, Michelle, call me Curtis," he cooed softly.

She took a long pause to gather her thoughts. "Mr. Carlton. Understand that I wouldn't defend Bruce if he hadn't done his job properly. But, you should know that he's not gay. He told me just the other night that he was hoping to meet some women his own age."

"Really? Well, he sure acts like a fag."

"Exactly," Michelle responded quickly. "The women love the attention he gives them and, at the same time, they don't feel threatened by him. But, did you ever hear him with a group of men? It's a totally different experience. He can talk business, Wall Street, sports, you name it. And, he's got quite a locker room vocabulary."

"My intuition is never wrong."

"Intuition is not enough to fire someone. And that kind of decision can't be based on testosterone level. Look, Mr. Carlton, I want you to do what's right, like you did in settling the campaign lawsuit. You should meet with Bruce and get all this out on the table and give him a chance to respond. I'll set up the meeting. Okay?"

Curtis didn't say anything for a few minutes. He concentrated on steering the big Buick through the traffic. He had no intention of re-hiring Bruce, so what harm would a short meeting be? More importantly, he didn't want to create negative feelings that would poison the atmosphere at lunch. He finally said, "You're a persuasive woman, Michelle. I'll think it over."

"That's a cop-out, and you know it. You've treated Bruce shabbily, and the least you can do is meet with him. Will you do it?" Michelle pressed.

Curtis needed Michelle to be in a positive frame of mind at lunch. "Well, if it's that important to you, Michelle, then I'll do it."

"Thank you, Mr. Carlton, that's all I ask."

"Now will you call me Curtis?" He pulled into a parking space at Michael's Italian Restaurant. "Oh, by the way, did you get the roses?"

"Um…yes…um, Curtis, they're very lovely. They really brighten up the office. But, I was just doing my job, and you don't need to send flowers." Michelle was pleased at her hard-fought victory for Bruce, but she was worried by his disappearance. She didn't know why her instincts kept her from mentioning to Curtis that she thought Bruce was missing. Curtis may be an egomaniac, but she had never considered him dangerous. She looked forlornly out the passenger window, wondering if lunch would be like a tightrope act—without a safety net.

THEIR MEALS FINISHED AND the plates cleared by the waiter, Michelle ordered an espresso and Curtis got a cup of coffee. Up to this point, lunch had been accompanied by a pleasant conversation, mostly about his business experience and political activities. Curtis was so self-involved, it wasn't difficult to get him to talk about himself.

Michelle allowed herself to relax a little. *Perhaps I've overestimated his lust. Maybe he's just interested in being seen with an attractive woman.*

Curtis reached for the sweetener and examined a pink packet and a blue packet. "The pink stuff tastes bitter. My dear wife, Ev, says the pink stuff makes me flatulent," he said, faintly smiling, as he stirred a blue packet of sweetener into his coffee. "The main reason I wanted to meet personally with you," he continued, still looking into his coffee, "is that I have a serious proposal for you. It could mean a significant boost in your career, and I do mean significant."

Uh oh, here it comes. Michelle studied his face intently.

Curtis looked up to exchange Michelle's gaze. He spoke slowly, in measured phrases. "I've been authorized by a client, who cannot be disclosed at this time, to make an offer to purchase PSM." He paused for a minute to let it sink in. "What do you think? Are you at least interested?"

Of all the scenarios racing through Michelle's mind, selling the company was not one she'd anticipated today.

She struggled to find a reasonable response to such a ludicrous idea and wondered how she could even mention it to her partner, Mac. She delayed a response by taking a sip of her espresso, letting the demitasse cup linger at her lips. "Curtis, you couldn't possibly know how hard Mac and I have worked to build up PSM. We invested every cent we had, and we worked brutal hours to make it successful. It's not just a job, it's our entire professional lives. It's our unique creation—not just a product that we've developed in order to sell it. It's what we are, what makes us feel special. Why do you think we'd sell?"

Curtis pulled a set of papers from his leather attaché case. "Because, you and Mac are smart business…" He swallowed with difficulty as he struggled to be politically correct, "…women. And, smart businesswomen, like smart businessmen, shouldn't be in love with their businesses. It's a business, not a love affair." He stopped and looked Michelle in the eye. "You're right, you deliver a professional service, not a bunch of products. But, what does it matter? When opportunity knocks, the smart businessperson should be prepared to respond. This offer could be the opportunity of a lifetime to put six figures in your bank account. And—this is the best part—you could stay in the management business."

"Working for someone else, right?"

"Or, take your six figures and do something else. You're certainly young enough to start a new business."

"So long as it's not community management, right?"

"Michelle, you stand to make a lot of money. A real bundle for a woman your age. Let me walk you through the proposal, and you keep an open mind. Remember before lunch, you told me to keep an open mind about Bruce. Now, you do the same. That's all I ask, Okay?"

"No. I want to know what your interest is in this deal."

"Fair enough. You know that I have many contacts in town. If I can put two parties together in a mutually profitable deal, I'll do it. I'm just acting as a business broker." Curtis looked up from the papers. "You should remember, Michelle, that I'm not the sort of person you want to get on your bad side. Don't be disrespectful to me. It doesn't cost anything to listen to this proposal."

"Since you put it that way, Curtis, I'm all ears."

Good girl. "Now then, here's the deal, as they say. Even though under the law it's the buyer's offer, we've left the contract price open. We'll let you tell us what you think is reasonable. The buyer will need to conduct his due diligence, so you'll need to furnish a list of current clients and any that you have in the pipeline—you know, any boards that you have pitched or given proposals to during the last sixty days. In addition to the list, you furnish annual financial statements for PSM and for each client. We'll need to review the assets and reserves of each of your clients, as well as PSM. The buyer doesn't want any surprise liabilities."

Curtis stopped to take some coffee. "Next, you will be able to stay and run PSM at a nice salary if you like, or you may leave, at your option, but you would be subject to a covenant of non-compete for five years. You give me your response to our offer by the fourteenth, and my client would have ten days to review the financial statements and agree to a contract price. Last, my client would have another ten days to review your lease and UCC filings and take care of all the other administrivia in such a transaction. If the price is right, it would be a cash deal." Curtis placed the printed documents in front of Michelle.

"At the risk of appearing ungrateful, Mac and I simply can't do this." Michelle used her middle finger to gently push the papers back across the table. She was pleased with the symbolism of her gesture, although it escaped notice by Curtis.

However, Curtis did see that he would have to take the gloves off. "Young lady, you are not being reasonable. This kind of offer doesn't come around every day." Curtis' earlobes turned red. "Look Michelle, for the huge majority of people, even very successful people, it hardly comes in a lifetime. You'll have enough money to invest in other businesses, the market, who knows what? And let your money work for you, instead of the other way around. Most of all, you don't want to offend me or lose the Cove's business—it's your bread and butter. Don't forget that, young lady." Curtis wagged a finger in Michelle's face. "You will consider this offer and let me know." He picked up the papers and forced them into Michelle's hand. "If you have any reasonable concerns, I'm sure my client is open to negotiate such matters. And, if you agree to sell and we can reach a deal in the next two days, I'll split my commission at closing or throw in a new Z3—you know, the BMW roadster—in the color of your choice. Trust me, Michelle, it will be the beginning of some real money for you."

JENNI HISCOCK HAD WORKED through lunch at her desk in PSM's lobby. Freddy's special, the jerk chicken plate, was sitting half-eaten on a paper plate next to her notes. A thick pocket file containing the Cove's bills and invoices was spread out on her desk. She found the packet of phone statements, picking out the most recent six months. When Michelle arrived back from her lunch meeting with Curtis, Jenni was able to tell her that she had completed a review of the information as Joshua had requested.

Michelle and Jenni met in the large conference room, which was used primarily for those occasions when client board meetings were held at PSM's offices rather than on site. Jenni spread the itemized long-distance bills on the table, arranging them chronologically. "Joshua wanted us to review the past three-to-six months, so I looked at those bills, then compared them to the earlier months in the file. There was nothing out of the ordinary, until I got to last month's bill, which shows six unusual calls within the last ten days of the billing cycle. All of these calls were to the same phone number. I looked up the area code. It's Boston."

Michelle studied the billings in silence. When she finished the most recent one, she looked up and said, "Jen, you're right. All of a sudden, there's a flurry of activity with somebody in Boston. Shall we see who it is?"

Michelle carefully entered the number on the telephone in the conference room and put it on speaker. The call was answered on the third ring. "Good afternoon. CMIS, may I help you?" Jenni and Michelle exchanged shrugged shoulders. "I'm sorry," Michelle responded into the speaker, "I may have misdialed. What company is this?"

"You've reached Central Management and Investment Services," said the voice through the speakerphone.

"Sorry to have bothered you," Michelle said and hung up.

Jenni was still staring at the phone. "Was that Central Management as in community management? If so, who at the Cove is having numerous conversations with a management company in Boston and why? What prompted Joshua to have us look at these long-distance bills?"

"Slow down, Jen, too many questions." Michelle found the member directory of the Organization of Community Associations on her shelf and turned to the manager section. "Well, in answer to your first question, here's the listing for Central Management and Investment Services, in Boston. The phone number is a match. The name of the CEO is Philip Palmer."

"Never heard of them." Jenni wrinkled her nose, as if the information had a foul odor. "But, whoever they are, it smells."

"No, Jenni. You smell with this," Michelle said, pointing to her nose. Then, pointing to the phone bills, she added, "*This* stinks."

JOSHUA PARKED OLD BLUE along the curb on South Broadway. He left his suit jacket in the car, loosened his tie, and walked down the sidewalk to the storefront of LaSalle Antique Trading Company. It was another hot afternoon in St. Louis, and Joshua hugged the shade under the shop awnings. He tried the doorknob, but found it locked, so he knocked. While he waited, he peered through the window at the several desks and armoires inside.

Finally, the door opened a crack, and Joshua could see a short man with a rotund stomach and a pencil neck peering through the opening. The man spoke in a low voice. "If you're looking for antiques, Ernie is out right now. He's on a buying trip. Come back tomorrow." He abruptly closed the door.

Joshua put up his hand. "Wait, are you Vinnie? Curtis Carlton told me that you were the man to see for special projects."

"Why didn't you say Mr. Carlton sent you? Come on in."

"Actually, it was a friend of Curtis," Joshua said under his breath as he walked into the small shop. A small window air conditioner was pushing the humid air around with little improvement. The hardwood floors were in need of restoration, and threadbare Oriental rugs covered the central area of the store. Joshua looked around at the antique furniture, trying not to appear too nervous. He pulled an envelope from his pocket and handed it to Vinnie, who opened it far enough to see two crisp, new fifty-dollar bills inside. "Please accept this as a courtesy from me to you, in respect for our mutual friend."

Vinnie checked the contents of the envelope again. "Grant's not exactly my favorite president. It's a nice introduction, but the amount of the courtesy will relate to the scope of the request." Vinnie spoke softly, with a slight smile that contradicted his penetrating gaze. "So, what can I do for Curtis' friend?"

"I'm an attorney with a very special client." Joshua said with the most serious of expressions. "A very wealthy client who, through no fault of his own, is in a lot of trouble. As in domestic trouble. Beyond that, I'm not at liberty to say due to attorney-client privilege. What I'm looking for is a...well...a professional hacker, a computer expert, someone with state-of-the-art knowledge and skills, to gain access to the most advanced hardware and financial software. He'll be well compensated, but he must be discreet. I'm sure you understand our situation."

Vinnie folded his arms across his chest, and an index finger touched his nose. He was deep in thought. "Maybe we can help you," he said finally. "Wait just a minute," he said, gesturing for Joshua not to follow. Vinnie disappeared into the back of the shop. After a few minutes, he returned and handed Joshua two business cards.

"Both of these guys are very good and very discreet. Like me. I've worked with both of them on occasion, special projects like you described. If one of them isn't available, you've got a backup." Vinnie handed the envelope back to Joshua. "You keep this, but tell Curtis he owes me one."

Joshua shook Vinnie's hand and walked out onto the sidewalk, listening to the sound of the deadbolt as it clicked home behind him. The hot afternoon sun was scorching. Even the weeds in the sidewalk cracks were wilting. Joshua inspected the business cards and walked back to Old Blue.

30

"Curtis isn't going to like it when we tell him Bruce got away," Bedford said as he steered the Taurus along the dirt road, the silhouette of Seldom Seen rapidly disappearing behind a cloud of dust. It was dark now, and Bedford drove as fast as he dared through the ruts and washouts.

"Right now, I really don't care what Curtis thinks." Kosankis groaned from the back seat of the car, a towel with ice cubes wrapped around his right foot. "This thing hurts like hell, so why don't you just shut your face and get me to a hospital. Besides, I didn't have nothin' against ol' Brucie."

"Let's get out on the interstate, then we'll stop at the first Podunksville with a hospital sign. But listen, Mr. K., there's no telling what Curtis is going to do when he finds out that Bruce is running around loose." But mostly Bedford wondered where Bruce had stashed that damn disk of Curtis' files.

"Couldn't happen to a nicer asshole," Kosankis moaned in he back seat. "Every time we talked to Curtis, I had the feeling he was doin' it to us. You know what I mean? Every thing we asked for, he'd put us off. Little by little, bit by bit, that fat fart sucked us further into his mess. Now we've got nothing to show for all our work."

"So, what are you saying?"

"What I'm saying is that we're trying to spoon feed this deal with Curtis, and in return he's spoon-fucking us. That's what I'm saying." Kosankis stared glumly out the car window at the blackness of the woods along the highway. "What are we going to tell Curtis about Bruce?"

"We'll come up with something by tomorrow morning," Bedford said.

"All right, Mr. B. You always got all the answers. And, what'll we tell the boss?"

"Jesus, Phil will really be pissed. I can hear him now. He'll want our heads."

"Before or after Curtis kicks our butts?"

"What did you say about our butts? Maybe that's it," Bedford said under his breath. He saw the blue H of a hospital sign and exited the interstate, looking for directions to the hospital.

"Maybe what's it?"

"Maybe that's it, Mr. K." Bedford steered the Taurus into the circular driveway of the small 1950's brick building that advertised itself as the Tri-County Regional Hospital. "It would buy us some time to find Bruce. Yes indeed, that's the solution."

"Whatever you say. All I know is, we're being spoon-fucked."

CURTIS WAS FEELING GOOD about the new day. He took a refreshing shower, put on his extra-wide slacks with the industrial-strength suspenders, and slid into a pair of comfortable deck shoes. He savored the forthcoming events of the day. He was eager to call Michelle. *I hope she'll agree to meet me for lunch to discuss the offer.* At ten o'clock, Bedford and Kosankis were due in from Seldom Seen. *I hope they'll have the disk, and I won't have Bruce to kick around any more.* Curtis couldn't wait to get over to the clubhouse and sit down at his desk with his coffee and a morning cigar.

Ev was happily humming as she tied a warp on her new loom. She checked her heddles, worked the treadles, and practiced moving the beater back and forth. Curtis figured it was cheaper to buy the huge, fifty-inch loom, bigger than an upright piano, than to pay for another trip to Paris. He wondered how he got stuck with those alternatives. *I guess I taught Ev too well.* "Don't forget your hat, Curtis dear, to keep the sun off your head," she chirped happily, "and take an umbrella. They say it could rain later."

Curtis gave Ev a peck on the cheek, grabbed his fishing hat off the rack by the door, and walked briskly to the clubhouse. His first stop was the Cove Café, where he picked up a cup of freshly brewed Colombian. He sat down at his desk, inhaled deeply of his mug of coffee, and slurped noisily. He opened the top drawer, pulled out his appointments calendar, and confirmed what he already knew for the morning of July 14:

9:30—Call Michelle re contract.

10:00—B & K O/C

He checked the clock on his desk. *God, I want to do this deal so bad I can taste it. What other leverage points would get Michelle to sell PSM?* He reached for the phone and called PSM's number. When Michelle came on the line, he cooed. "Good morning, Michelle, how are you today?"

"Just fine, Curtis." *He's more slick than usual,* she thought. "But, I only have a minute because I'm headed out to a property. You caught me with one foot out the door. Actually, a whole leg."

The metaphor struck Curtis speechless as his mind flashed to the image of Michelle's beautiful, sleek, tanned legs peeking at him from under a short skirt as she sat down for lunch with him. He shook himself into reality, quickly realizing that it would not be an opportune time to discuss the contract if she were in a rush. "Can you meet me for lunch later—about one o'clock?"

She read his mind. "If you want to know about the contract, I can tell you quickly. Mac and I have considered the offer, and our price is $999,999.99. And that's firm."

"Well, you girls do think big, don't you?"

"You did say six figures, didn't you?"

"It better be negotiable, little lady."

"Don't bet on that, Curtis," she shot back.

"I'll convey this to my principal," Curtis murmured with a disappointed tone that masked his elation that a counteroffer was actually on the table. Now, at least, the boundary lines were drawn on the playing field.

"Just think of the handsome commission you'll get. But, you need to move quickly, while we little ladies are in the mood. We'll send a messenger to drop off the contract later this morning. Your principal has forty-eight hours to respond. As always, I look forward to hearing from you." With that, Michelle disconnected.

Curtis stared unbelievingly at the telephone, then placed the handset back in its cradle. *Gutsy girls. I bet they're just playing hard to catch.* He walked out of his office to get a refill on his coffee. He stopped to tell the waiter that he was expecting a package to be delivered by courier, and he wanted it brought immediately to him, wherever he happened to be when it arrived.

As Curtis was giving these instructions to the waiter, he looked up and saw Bedford walking through the foyer, with Kosankis several steps behind, hobbling awkwardly on crutches. Bedford spotted Curtis, waved, and approached him in the café.

Curtis could barely conceal his amusement as he watched Kosankis faltering on his crutches and bandaged foot. Curtis turned to Bedford. "What happened to your buddy? Somebody finally step on his toes?" He chortled, impressed with his version of quick wit.

Bedford examined Curtis for a minute. "Actually, Mr. Carlton, Kosankis finally shot himself in the foot."

"Whoa! Hey, that's a great line, Bedford!" Curtis was tickled. "I'll have to remember that one. Finally shot himself in the foot! Ha!"

Bedford wasn't sharing in the joke. "We bring some good news and some bad news for you. But, let's go into your office to talk."

"And I have interesting news for you as well. You'll be very pleased at the latest development," Curtis said, staring Bedford straight in the eye.

Just as Kosankis caught up with them in the café, Curtis and Bedford hurried away to Curtis' office, and Kosankis turned and bravely hobbled after them, knocking over a mahjong table with his crutches in the process.

The three men seated themselves at Curtis' desk. An extra chair was moved over to Kosankis, so he could elevate his right foot. "Gentlemen," Curtis began when everyone was settled, "What's the news from Seldom Seen? Did you get the disk from Bruce?" Curtis chuckled optimistically. He was in such an easy mood. But, Bedford and Kosankis were impassive, merely exchanging sidelong glances of impatience. Kosankis fondled his earring.

"Here's the situation, Mr. Carlton." Bedford recited slowly. "We had another discussion with Bruce, which was much more productive." He turned to Kosankis, who grunted in agreement, forgetting his ill-fated experiment with electricity.

Bedford summarized the last interrogation, resulting in Bruce's admission that he downloaded files from Curtis' computer, and encrypted the disk with a secret code. "Bruce thinks he has an insurance policy, that we won't hurt him because he's the only one who knows how to decode the disk."

"So, you took the disk from him, right?"

"Um, not exactly," Kosankis mumbled under his breath.

Curtis was tiring of hearing this response. He leaned forward in his chair, and said, "Just what exactly is meant by 'not exactly?' "

Bedford put his hand on Kosankis' shoulder to keep him from another stupid statement. He said, "Mr. K. simply meant that we hadn't got that far in the interview."

"So, Bruce thinks he's got himself a life insurance policy, does he?" Curtis asked rhetorically. "Well, I bet we got our own insurance policy. If Bruce is the only one who could decode the disk, and if he isn't around anymore to decode it, then it doesn't matter where the disk is. No one could read it anyhow, without Bruce."

"Curtis, that's elegant in its simplicity!" Bedford nodded as he grasped Curtis' logic. "A brilliant strategy."

"Of course. That's why I'm the president. That's why the buck starts here." Curtis' fingers stabbed the top of his desk for emphasis. "Now, boys, that should streamline your mission. You're not going to hurt Bruce, but you'll need to get the disk."

A long pause settled over the meeting. Finally, Bedford spoke, "That brings us to the other news. We took a little break between interview sessions, so Bruce could refresh his memory." Bedford embellished the escape story. "When we returned to the cabin there was these five or six guys that looked like they were a genetic mix of Deliverance and paramilitary radicals from a training camp in the Ozark backwoods. They were heavily armed with double-barrel shotguns and hunting knives.

They'd pried the security bars off the window, kidnapped Bruce, and they were running into the woods."

"A bunch of local yokels sneaked up on you and helped Bruce escape? Seldom Seen is not so seldom seen?" Curtis' neck was turning red as he fought for control. "Is this the good news—that Bruce got away? More like stupid and dumb, I'd say." Curtis was glaring at Bedford.

"No telling what those guys will do with Bruce."

"As in…?"

"They could go all the way."

"And the problem would…uh…go away? But, how did Kosankis get hurt?"

"Oh…well, when they saw us, they started firing. We chased them into the woods, trying to save Bruce…" Bedford pointed at Kosankis' foot resting on the extra chair. "But, not before one of them shot Mr. K. in the foot. That's why we were late getting back. Mr. K. paid an unscheduled visit to County General Hospital."

Curtis studied both men with an incredulous gaze. "You guys are a couple of big-city boys. Today, you get shot in the foot. Tomorrow, you'll step on your own dicks." Curtis stared hard at both men.

"But, the problem of Bruce is taken care of, and you don't have anything on your hands. When they get done with Bruce, they'll probably throw him in the river."

"It seems to me," Curtis said, glaring at the other two men, "that the problem hasn't been solved at all. We don't have the disk and we don't know where Bruce is."

"We'll go down there and find him."

"Yeah, you better do just that."

"Obviously, we'll need more time."

The three of them sat in silence for a few minutes, trying to stare each other down.

Finally, Bedford broke the silence. "Curtis, you mentioned that you had made some progress."

Curtis picked up his notes and installed his reading glasses on his nose. "Well, your company is looking for ways to get a toehold in this market, and you could do so either by picking up major accounts, such as the Cove. Or, as I mentioned to you before, you could buy your own management company directly. So, guess what? PSM is on the market! At a real bargain price, I might add. Under a million dollars."

Bedford looked at Curtis with a mixture of bemusement and amazement. "A million bucks? No kidding! Hear that, Mr. K? Only a million bucks, the man says. Curtis, you're developing quite a sense of humor."

"Keep your pants on, Bedford," Curtis implored. "Any smart businessman knows you gotta spend money to make money. Look at their assets." Curtis' mind suddenly flashed to Michelle's assets, but just as quickly, he clicked back to the contract. *I've gotta drive this thing to the finish line.* "PSM has access to client reserves of ten million dollars, maybe more. That's my guess about the amount of reserves under the control of those two girls. Can you believe that? Ten million bucks controlled by those two broads. That's easy pickings. Once the company is in the hands of a whiz kid like your boss, and yourselves, of course, there's a return on investment of ten-to-one, or even better. You can't beat that for an honest day's work."

Kosankis scribbled a note and held it out for Bedford to read. "More spoon-fucking?"

"Look," said Curtis, "I'll show you a small sample of the wealth that will soon be at your very fingertips." Curtis wheeled his chair around and turned on his computer. But, before he could proceed into the financial program, the intercom interrupted him. He picked up the handset, listened for a moment, and said, "Good, have him bring it in immediately." There was a knock on the door, and the courier appeared with a large shipping box and a manila envelope. He tore open the box, only to find it full of balls of colorful yarn that his wife apparently had ordered. Then he opened the envelope, glanced at the contract, and handed it to Bedford. "Gentlemen, this paper is better than a winning power ball lottery ticket."

Curtis returned to his computer. "As I was saying," he beamed, "let me whet your appetite with a little morsel from one of the many nourishing reserve accounts at PSM, our very own Estrella Cove." He clicked enter and watched the screen.

The usual program window did not appear on the monitor. Instead, as the three men turned to watch the screen, a muscular cartoon Bruce, dressed entirely in black, slowly emerged on the screen. The three men were now studying the monitor with anticipation and anxiety etched on their faces. A cartoon Curtis appeared, wearing a school-bus yellow golf shirt and overalls. The outline of a tall, menacing guillotine took shape in the center of the screen. The cartoon figures started moving. Bruce pointed to the guillotine, and Curtis' image knelt and placed his head in the notch under the huge, glistening blade. Then, Bruce swung a massive sword, slashing the rope that held the blade suspended. Curtis' head went rolling across the screen, coming to rest when Bruce stopped it with his foot. Curtis' eyes were wide open in horror.

Then, Bruce's voice came through the speakers as if he were standing next to the computer: "Ha, ha, ha, King Curtis. Your hard drive is dead."

31

"We're in Cannes, now, on the Cote d'Azur. I'm on the French Riviera, and I can't believe it, a dream come true." Angela was standing on the balcony of the hotel, watching the lights of the harbor reflecting on the still black water. The cord on the hotel phone was stretched as far at it would reach.

It was six o'clock at night in St. Louis, and Joshua and Michelle were huddled over the speakerphone in Joshua's office. Michelle sat in his executive chair while Joshua rested on the corner of his desk. "Describe it for us," Michelle said.

"It's more enchanting and romantic than I had ever dreamed."

The Hotel Splendid overlooked the harbor, situated between the old and new sections of town, and the morning sun gave life to the pastel buildings terraced on the hillside of the old town, Vieux Cannes, until they glowed. During the day, the water of the harbor was aquamarine and so calm it looked like a mirror. Now it was dark, and Angela marveled at the sight of the full moon—it was the middle of the night in Cannes—lighting the masts of expensive yachts and sailboats. "I'm sorry, but I'm in love, and I'm not coming back."

"So, what's there to do on the French Riviera," Joshua said, "besides look at wealthy people, expensive shops, and topless women on the beach?"

"Well, we saw Bill Cosby walking his dog today. Do you know what today is in France? It's Bastille Day, of course. That's why I'm up so late—we just had to do our share to help the French celebrate properly. But, let me tell you about…"

"That's it!" Joshua said. "Bastille Day is July 14. That explains one of Bruce's notes, the one that says '7-14.' It's the day that the French celebrate their revolution, the toppling of the monarchy. But, what's that got to do with Curtis?"

Angela was too excited to wait for Joshua to finish his thought. "Let me tell you about Grasse. Yesterday, we rented a cute little Volkswagen and drove up to Grasse, the *parfum capital de tout le monde*—the perfume capital of the world."

A half-dozen perfume factories were located in this small town in southern France. Angela and Philip had toured the Fragonard plant, where they saw the entire manufacturing process, from extracting the essence of roses, lavender, and other scents, to the final products, including bars of soap, cologne, and *apres rasage*—after shave lotion.

"We sampled sixteen different scents, and I fell in love with Rendezvous, which is a simply delightful fragrance. So, I bought a few bottles of perfume and cologne and some soap. In fact, I did all my Christmas shopping. I was going to ship it back to the States, but I decided to take it all with me."

Michelle nodded to Joshua and asked, "Angela, we need to talk very privately with you. Are you somewhere that Philip won't hear this conversation?"

"Actually, he just received a call on his cell phone. He's in the room, and I'm out on the balcony."

"HEY, BOSS, IT'S BEDFORD and me," Kosankis bellowed in a voice loud enough to carry across the Atlantic on its own. "How's it goin'?"

"Just great," Philip groaned sarcastically. "Let me give you a small sample. Yesterday, Angela wants to go perfume shopping, so we have to rent a car, and we wind up with this gutless, micro-compact that we drive through these mountains with all these crazy French drivers. She drags me into a perfume factory, for Pete's sake, where she's just gotta sample everything. We must have tried two dozen different odors, only they call 'em 'fragrances.' We sprayed and sniffed, sniffed and sprayed, until my olfactory glands are bursting and I get a headache and my nose starts running. I mean I'm going crazy. She buys a ton of this stuff called "Rendezvous"—probably because it's the only one she understands in English. She spends enough dough at this place to jump-start the new euro.

"I told her she should ship it home rather than carry it all over Europe. Good idea, but, the factory doesn't ship its own products for some unknown reason, but this gorgeous salesgirl tells us that the Poste, as they call it, is just up the hill. 'Go to the circle in the middle of town, you can't miss the sign,' she says. So we drive up to the circle, which seems like the busiest intersection south of the Arc de Triomphe, and we drive around it about four times looking for a sign to the Poste. Well, let me tell you something, my friends. The circle is really a race track with three lanes, and here we are in this gutless little rental car, and everybody else has a Mercedes or a BMW zooming around the track, racing in from about half a dozen different highways. Finally, she's getting dizzy and ready to barf the French croissant she had for breakfast into her bag with all the perfume, so I got the hell out of there. Going north instead of south, of course."

"But, what about them topless beaches?" Kosankis asked. "Do the babes really lie on the beach half naked? Is it really that cool?"

"Take it from me, the French women are *tres* cool. More naked flesh in one place than you could handle, that's for sure."

"ANGELA, WHAT ABOUT THE BEACHES? Did you dare to go topless?" Michelle asked in a teasing voice.

"The beaches of the Cote d'Azur are fabulous. No doubt about it, the beaches are full of well-tanned and well-oiled flesh in great abundance. About one-third of the women on the beach go topless, and about half the men are either stepping on their dicks or they're taking pictures. The other half? They don't seem to even notice. In one sense, it's an enormous culture shock, but in another way, it's interesting, and probably healthy, that the Europeans don't have such a hangup with the female breast. I doubt that Americans, both men and women, are culturally or socially mature enough to handle it. We saw young topless mothers with their children, as well as old ladies, all blissfully enjoying the beach. One woman sat on a towel busily chatting on her cell phone, oblivious to the fact she was topless and a bunch of strangers were sharing the beach. Phil called it 'Boob Beach,' and insisted that he wasn't gawking, but somehow managed to shoot two rolls of film."

Joshua was starting to feel uncomfortable with this discussion, so he tried to change the subject. "How's the food, Angela?"

"The food is *tres fantastique, mon ami*. But, it's easy to make a mistake if you don't know the language. After the

Fragonard factory, we drove to Antibes to see the old fort on the cliff that Picasso used as his studio in 1946." The Grimaldi Chateau, now the Picasso Museum, held a collection of fifty works that Pablo Picasso created there and overlooked a fabulously beautiful stretch of the Mediterranean.

"We stopped for lunch at a restaurant on the beach. Sat down next to a foursome from Great Britain, and it was fun to be able to speak English with strangers for a change. As you might expect, the menu had a lot of fish dishes, so I decided on an entree that literally translated into 'little fried fish dish.' The waiter confirmed, without any elaboration—he didn't speak English very well—that it was, indeed 'little fried fish.' So, the waiter comes out with this enormous wooden bowl brimming with fried sardines, complete with the heads, tails, and everything in between. Even drowning them in tartar sauce couldn't disguise them. I simply couldn't get these little guys to go down. Nor could I give them away to the British folks, who were supposed to be used to eating fish and chips, but even they clearly had better tastes than that. I mean, these people merely looked at my bowl of these little suckers, and begged off. As soon as Phil finished his sautéed salmon, I rushed to the nearest sidewalk sandwich stall to get a reliable *croque monsieur*—toasted ham and cheese."

"So, what are your travel plans now, Angela?" Joshua asked.

"We may stay in Cannes another day or two, then take the train to Monte Carlo, then Venice. Definitely Venice. So, tell me Joshua, what's going on at the office? Everything under control?"

"The practice of law has its moments, Angela. In fact, I still remember one from last year." Joshua paused to see if anyone caught his dry humor. He reviewed his checklist of agenda items and began by summarizing the Mayfair Court hearing and reporting that Judge Freeman had ruled in favor of the trustees and dismissed the case.

Joshua outlined the discussions underway to settle the campaign lawsuit, which would allow the challenger, Brandon Mason, to campaign door-to-door in the Cove or, at his option, obtain a mailing list of all owners and sponsor a rally at the clubhouse.

"Next," Joshua continued, "we're getting ready for the depositions called by the Worm in his defamation case. In addition to all that, however, Michelle has some more interesting things for you on yet another matter."

"Angela," Michelle began, "we've been real concerned about Bruce—the concierge at the Cove. You know, Curtis terminated Bruce then he suddenly disappeared. Somebody ransacked his row house in Soulard. But, apparently, just before he disappeared, Bruce mailed a disk and some notes written in cryptic code to his neighbor, Ham Godwilling. Ham passed them to Joshua. We're pretty sure the notes represent information that Bruce saw in Curtis' personal files, either in his desk or his computer. Joshua's got the details."

"Now, this is very important, Angela," Joshua said, his voice lower now. "Is Philip still out of range? Are you sure he can't hear you? If he can hear, I'll just ask you 'Yes' and 'No' questions."

"It's okay, Joshua, he's still inside," Angela whispered, just to be sure.

"Good. Listen carefully." Joshua read Bruce's notes to Angela and related the findings of the long-distance record review done by Jenni and Michelle. "Bottom line, Angela, is that it appears Curtis is engaged in a serious flirtation with another management company, an out-of-town firm, located in Boston. I really hate to be the one who tells you this, because you're so involved emotionally, but the name of the Boston management company is Central Management and Investment Services."

"Isn't that Philip's company?" Angela asked.

"That's right, Angela. The CEO is none other than Philip Palmer."

Angela steadied her grip on the phone. Each word was like a jolt of electricity. She looked over her shoulder into the room and saw Philip reading on the bed. "Maybe I'm missing something, Joshua, but so what? It's probably just part of some marketing that Phil's company is doing. You can't leap to the conclusion, based solely on some long-distance phone bills, that something sinister is going on between the Cove and Philip."

"Angela, I don't blame you for wanting to dismiss this information. So did we, at first. But, listen, it's not just the phone calls. Remember that Bruce told me on the phone that a management firm back East had given Curtis a proposal to manage the Cove. And, on top of that, Bruce made a special note about the Cove's reserves. Curtis has a computer that is linked to PSM, and we all know how much interest he's shown in the Cove's reserves, which, you must admit, are fat and could be tempting to anybody who wants to take over a well-heeled community."

"Joshua, I simply can't believe it. Management companies don't go into other states and raid clients. It's probably just an aggressive sales person in Philip's company who's telemarketing to OCA members, and Philip doesn't know anything about it."

Joshua pulled two business cards from his shirt pocket. "Here's another item, although I'm not sure what to make of it, except it needs to be on our growing list of evidence."

"Circumstantial evidence," interrupted Angela.

"At this time, I'm not persuaded that anything should be sugar-coated. Angela, you remember the name of Vincent Buggieri—Vinnie the Bug? Does that ring any bells with you?"

"Isn't he the guy who was granted immunity by the district attorney so he could testify that he was hired to plant illegal listening devices in a couple of high-profile divorce cases?"

"That's him. Anyway, and apparently unrelated to all this, Michelle learned that Vinnie the Bug and Curtis the King are close. When Curtis wanted first-class antique furniture for his office, he sent Michelle to see Vinnie. We don't know what the connection is, at least we don't know yet. So, between Vinnie's reputation in the use of illegal electronic devices, and some kind of connection he has to Curtis, Michelle and I thought that Vinnie might know guys in town who are computer experts. You know, professional hackers who could break into sophisticated computer systems. I go down to the Buggieris' little antique shop on South Broadway—what a joke—I whisper something out of the corner of my mouth like 'Curtis Carlton sent me,' and Vinnie treats me real special. He gives me two business cards and refuses my money. Vinnie gives me a wink and a nod, and says he's used both of these computer experts and they're really good, 'very discreet,' in his words. One of them, I never heard of, some guy named Scarpo. But the other one is none other than Sean Eastgate, the techie who installed the entire computer system at PSM. Michelle tells me that he comes into PSM's offices at least once a week for trouble-shooting or to put out some fire or another in their system."

Angela poured another glass of wine and tried to enjoy the cool breeze on the balcony while digesting the latest batch of disturbing information. "You think that maybe Curtis hired Sean Eastgate to break into PSM's offices and steal something? More specifically, to get into PSM's computers? But, what for? You just said he's in their computers all the time as part of his service. Why would he bother to break in, in the middle of the night, when he's there in the daytime?"

"Maybe he didn't want to be seen doing whatever he was doing there?"

"Suppose you get that other hacker Vinnie mentioned. Fargo, or whatever his name is. Make sure he hasn't done anything for Curtis, so you could use him as an independent computer consultant to check out PSM's system. Tell him to run all the data and financial systems. See if anything's missing or, better yet, if maybe something's there that shouldn't be there. But, he's gotta have no ties to Curtis."

Michelle jotted a few notes. "Good idea, Angela. I'll call this guy, Scarpo. You know, the computer is about the only place we haven't looked to see if anything is amiss due to the break-in. Jeez, I just can't imagine it could be our computer."

Michelle paused, remembering another question for Angela. "There's something else, another really weird incident you should know about. One of the notes left by Bruce had my initials, followed by a pair of question marks. Two days ago, out of the clear blue, Curtis calls up and is very insistent that I go to lunch with him. He picks me up at the office and we go to Michael's, you know, the very upscale Italian restaurant that opened about two months ago? Anyway, Curtis gives me this story that he represents a principal that he can't disclose, but whoever it is, somebody wants to buy PSM."

"You're kidding. So, are you going to sell?"

Michelle rubbed the tip of her nose, an unconscious signal of uncertainty. "Curtis hands me a written contract, says I will be rich—as in six figures rich—and wants Mac and me to fill in the sale price!"

"Hey, everything is for sale at the right price. So, what are you going to do with the contract?"

"Mac and I decided to make a crazy counteroffer. We kept it under a million dollars: $999,999.99, to be exact. We know it's totally outrageous, and we're sure they'll reject it. That's what we expect, but, who knows? It's a counteroffer, and if they're stupid enough to accept it, well then…"

"Oh, I see where you guys are going. You think that the principal behind Curtis' offer is Philip—or his company? That's absurd, don't you think? I mean, why would they want to buy PSM? Look at the industry. Community management companies are traditionally local operations, not bought and sold by global conglomerates."

"Maybe not by global conglomerates," Michelle said. "But, just in the last year, we've seen a huge Canadian property management firm buy association management companies that are strategically located in high-growth markets. We may be seeing the beginning of the end for the traditional mom-and-pop operations. And small, women-owned businesses, like PSM."

Michelle paused, her eyebrows raised in a question mark, looking at Joshua for guidance. "Right now, Angela," Joshua said very slowly and deliberately, "we only have several pieces of a confused and confusing puzzle. The more pieces we find, the more complex it seems to get. First, we have the suspected break-in of PSM's offices, although we're not sure why somebody broke in. Curtis is featured prominently on our growing list of prospects, but he's not the only one. We also have

Dunwoody running a close second, then Russell, who's the treasurer at the Cove, and Daggett, who's the treasurer at the Vineyard. Curtis and Vinnie have some kind of connection, and so do Vinnie and Sean Eastgate. It's a syllogism with a possible connection between Curtis and Sean and between them and the break-in."

Joshua continued, "We can't explain Bruce's disappearance and the notes and disk he left. His notes aren't enough to identify the person who broke into PSM. They're more like clues in a treasure hunt that will give us some tips on where to look next."

"What's on the disk?" asked Angela.

"We have no idea yet," Joshua responded. "It's encrypted, and we can't decode it. But, why did Bruce suddenly disappear?"

Michelle asked, "Is it connected to his being fired?"

"Because he knew too much?" suggested Joshua.

"Who is the undisclosed principal who wants to buy PSM," Michelle asked, "and why?"

Joshua added, "If we can answer these questions, we'll be a lot closer to knowing why someone broke into PSM's offices."

Angela forgot she was in the south of France. Her view of Cannes' harbor from the hotel balcony might as well have been her office window. She was trained as a lawyer and that's how she thought about the mounting evidence and the tightening knot in her stomach, the one she felt whenever the facts in a case led her where she didn't want to go. Joshua and Michelle exchanged worried expressions, but didn't interrupt Angela's silence. Finally, Angela said, "What are the police doing?"

"Joshua talked to a detective," Michelle responded, "and, as you might expect, they don't think much of mere theories."

Joshua added, "The police want tangible evidence. All we have is a record of phone calls that might be part of a conspiracy but, by themselves, don't constitute criminal acts."

Angela, speaking slowly and deliberately, said, "Philip is a respected and reputable professional, with a large and successful business of his own."

"But, Angela," Joshua ventured cautiously, "how well do you really know Philip?"

"All of your questions can be answered by other factors. I don't see the problem."

Joshua's elbow rested on the desk, his forehead cupped in his hand, prepared to surrender to the unmovable object posed by his partner. He covered the mouth of his phone and whispered to Michelle, "She's in denial."

"Anyway, I love him very much," Angela said.

"Angela, you know how much I respect you. You're my mentor, my colleague, and my good friend. But, understand me, this is serious stuff, and I can't be less than completely candid with you. I hope I'm wrong and that you'll forgive me if this sounds insensitive." Joshua looked down as he carefully considered his next words. "All we're trying to tell you is . . ."

Angela cut him off. "That's really difficult to say, Joshua."

"What? Oh, are you telling us that Philip is nearby?"

"Yes, you could say that."

"Okay, we'll let you go," Joshua said. "You're right. We don't know what we don't know. But, Michelle and I are peeling the layers off. You take care of yourself. Understand?"

"*Je comprend, mes amis.* You do the same. *Bon soir.*" Angela disconnected the conversation. And she suddenly remembered Philip's question when they first met in London. Philip had asked, "How's Sean doing?"

PHILIP WALKED OUT ON the balcony just as Angela was saying goodbye. He moved a strand of curly hair to one side and gave her a peck on the forehead. "What's wrong, honey? You look so worried—everything okay at the office?"

"Huh?" Angela wondered how much his kiss was genuine and sincere. "Oh, I was just…uh…thinking about this…uh…new case we have in the office. Joshua was telling me about it."

"Well, I need to send some important emails to the office while I've got the information on the top of my head."

"Wait, Philip," she pleaded, taking his hand and pulling him close to her. "I love you very much." She hugged him tightly. "You know that, don't you?" After a long pause, she whispered. "You wouldn't hurt me, would you?" Her head nestled in the side of his neck.

"Honey, that's nonsense. Of course I wouldn't do anything to hurt you," Philip said softly, his eyes gazing beyond, to the lights of the harbor.

"Then, tell me you love me."

"Angela, I've got some urgent things to take care of. It will just take a few minutes. He gently pushed her away. He sat on the side of the bed, opened his laptop and typed in a short message.

> Re: Reserves Project. What's the Status?

32

Bruce stepped out of the canoe wearing the clothes he had on when he escaped the cottage, plaid boxer shorts and sneakers. The two long-haired young fishermen who had rescued him donated a t-shirt and five dollars and then hurried the canoe downstream, leaving Bruce standing alone on the river bank.

The sun had set about an hour ago, and Bruce guessed it was about nine o'clock or nine-thirty. The new moon was a yellow sliver low in the eastern sky. A light breeze gently rustled the huge leaves on the ancient sycamore trees that lined the riverbank.

The bruise on his forehead throbbed, and his stomach complained loudly. He stood on the gravel bank and looked up at the lights of a small town at the top of a bluff, relieved to have escaped Seldom Seen with the better part of his health. He worried that Bedford and Kosankis had an army of black-suited goons, armed with sawed-off shotguns and electrical probes, combing the hinterland in a plodding, relentless dragnet to hunt him down and do hurtful things to his body.

The alternative viewpoint, he could reason, was that his life was starting over. A chance for a fresh start. But, the fresh start wouldn't be easy. He wondered whether his first priority should be to get a hot meal, get some pants, get a place to stay, or get some ice on his forehead. The one thing he knew for sure, however, was that he couldn't go back to St. Louis. Not yet. He would go to the local sheriff, but first he needed the right plan and the lawyer, Joshua.

Bruce walked along the riverbank until he found an access point, followed the dirt road up the hill, and walked into the tiny town. A sign greeted him.

WELCOME TO CALVIN'S CREEK, GATEWAY TO OZARK VACATIONLAND, POPULATION 1500 (WINTER), 10,000 (SUMMER).

Walking down narrow Main Street, Bruce noticed the churches, banks, shops, and cafes that were typical of small town America, but not much different from the streets he walked in the Soulard District. One primary distinction was soon obvious: the street was bustling with summer vacationers, and the craft shops and restaurants were open and doing a lively business. He looked in the windows of the small cafés, which advertised fried chicken plates, pan-fried steak, fried mountain oysters, and fresh catch of the day, which would be prepared to your taste—so long as it was fried. Bruce pondered the cafés. *Why was this bustling burg trying to poison the tourists? Maybe I'll be safe with a slice of home-made pie and coffee.*

He had almost completed his tour of downtown Calvin's Creek—two blocks separated by a four-way stop—when he noticed a large cluster of bright lights on the outskirts of town. He walked about a quarter of a mile along the narrow county road where the outline of a resort came into view. The main structure was a large, two-story lodge that appeared to be new, but was artfully designed to have a worn, woodsy look. It was encircled by a vast parking lot.

Bruce hesitated then started up the expansive circle drive, merging among groups of tourists who were strolling toward the entrance. If he stretched the front of his borrowed t-shirt down so it covered the fly of his boxers, he appeared to be dressed much like the other tourists.

As he neared the lodge, he could see that half of the main floor was devoted to a restaurant, with two dozen tables set outside on the wide veranda, like a terrace café. The tables were brimming with diners sharing an enjoyable evening on the terrace. He could hear the buzz of lively conversation, and he noticed bottles of wine along with dinner plates on most of the tables. At other tables people were languishing over espresso, cappuccino, and after-dinner drinks. He nonchalantly glanced in the windows as he walked by and saw the main dining room, with small chandeliers that provided spot lighting on tables covered by white linen. The floor was black and white tile, a mature touch that appeared simple yet elegant. Patrons occupied all stations, and young waiters and waitresses dressed in long-sleeve white shirts and black vests hurried from one table to the next and back to the kitchen.

The Riverway Lodge. Bruce was intrigued.

Regretfully aware that the five-dollar bill tucked in his waistband wouldn't have much purchasing power in this venue, and stretching his t-shirt down as far as he could, Bruce held his chin high and entered. He was greeted by a small, squat man in a black tuxedo who twitched nervously and introduced himself as Christopher Doyle, the owner of the lodge. Doyle inspected Bruce from head to toe with skepticism, gestured vaguely at the reservation book on the counter in the foyer, and apologized that a table would not be available for perhaps an hour. Then he nodded half-heartedly to his left and suggested that Bruce could wait in the lounge.

Bruce found an open barstool and proceeded to devour a bowl of cocktail peanuts and a glass of water. He split his attention between watching the television mounted behind the bar and the attractive female attendant. But, he couldn't stop wondering why the owner was serving as the maitre d' and why he appeared so…so… disoriented, distracted? No, the man was frazzled.

Bruce had been around the hospitality business long enough and had hung out with enough waiters and waitresses to realize that his attendant would soon despise him if she thought that he was too broke to order anything or leave a tip. The possibility would soon become obvious in view of the fact that he was gorging himself on free peanuts and not ordering anything beyond tap water. Bruce disliked being despised by anyone, especially a woman who was on her feet all day, working hard for a living.

As soon as a small table opened at the rear of the lounge, Bruce tugged at his t-shirt, eased over, and seated himself. Soon the attendant walked over, *glided gracefully*, Bruce thought, to take his drink order. Peeking under the wet napkin he held to the swollen bruise above his left eye, he was struck immediately with her mystic smile and inviting blue eyes. "I'm waiting for dinner, and I want to be sober enough to enjoy it," he managed to squeak.

"Perhaps you'd like some hors d'oeurves while you wait. The kitchen is operating like an emergency room tonight, but if you're completely famished, I might be able to get you some extra appetizers. They're really excellent." Her badge advertised her name as Ronnie.

"Look, Ronnie," he said, leaning closer to avoid shouting, "apparently it may be awhile before I graduate to the main floor of the restaurant, so let me introduce myself. My name is Bruce, and this is my first night in town. I wasn't sure where to find a proper dinner around here. The cafés in town look like their meals come with a supply of barf bags."

"It's comforting to know you're so discriminating."

"And I appreciate your insight. Yet, there remains a somewhat embarrassing problem. You see, I had a near-death experience today on the river, and I don't have my credit cards with me. I'm on a limited budget."

"How limited?"

"Um…five dollars. This is really embarrassing."

Ronnie held her tray in her left hand and planted her right hand firmly on her slender hip. "Look, Bruce, no offense intended," she said sternly, "but five dollars won't even get you the aroma of one of our entrees."

"Be merciless if you must, but help me if you can. I'm absolutely starved."

"Who hit you on the head?"

"It's a long story."

"Let me see what I can do." Ronnie smiled and patted his shoulder then glided away ignoring her other tables and left the lounge. When she returned, she not only had the menu and wine list, but a plate of grilled portobello mushrooms and a glass of Pezzi King cabernet. And a linen napkin wrapped around crushed ice.

Bruce was amazed. "You deserve sainthood, Ronnie, and I'm going to recommend to the Pope that he put you on the fast track, just as soon as I can find my phone card so I can call the Vatican. I'll tell His Holiness that you're the spiritual leader of the Calvin's Creek Sisters of Mercy." He studied her face more carefully and guessed she was thirty-ish. She had long, dark curly hair, tied playfully in a ponytail. Her slender fingers were dressed with several rings of semi-precious stones, but nothing that looked like a long-term commitment. Her earrings were silver, probably Zuni or Navajo, he guessed. "So, tell me Ronnie, what do you do when you're not busting your butt waiting on tables and saving lost souls?"

"Don't laugh, but I'm an artist." She paused. "I paint and I'm into jewelry."

"What brought you to Calvin's Creek?"

Ronnie toyed with a ring on her left hand. "You might call me part of the great backwash. You know, went to California to seek my dreams, had my fill of the fast-paced phony life out there, moved back."

Ronnie had graduated with a degree from the Art Institute in Chicago and moved to Sausalito, across the bay north of San Francisco, to pursue art full time. "I did good work. No, I did *outstanding* work," she said, "but it's so competitive out there, and so, well, California. Mostly, I missed the seasons—the changing colors, the light, the mood. So, I packed up my little car and returned to the Midwest. Stopped here for gas, fell in love with the river and this little town, and decided to stay for a few days. I sold five pencil sketches and paintings in the first week. That was four years ago." A warm, natural smile flashed across her face. "Enjoy the escargot. It's on the house, Bruce." She touched his shoulder lightly again, then turned quickly and moved away to another table.

Bruce blinked as he watched Ronnie move so gracefully from one table to the next that it seemed her feet didn't touch the floor. Her mesmerizing smile was etched into his consciousness.

He held the cold napkin to his forehead and turned his attention to the menu. He admired the feel and texture of the burgundy-colored stock, handsome and durable, but not ostentatious. Printed on the front in a plain type style were the words, "Riverway Restaurant: French Cuisine at its Finest." Behind the type was a simple pencil sketch of the Eiffel Tower, signed by Veronica Pulaski.

He skimmed the list of hors d'oeuvres, including escargot de Bourgogne and fraise des bois. Three salads were listed—sallade lyonnaise, sallade niçoise, and sallade verte. The plats were divided into viande, poisson, and poulet. He located some of his favorites, steak au poivre, as well as other traditional dishes, like cote de boeuf, Carre d'agneau, and coq au vin. The wine list contained an extensive repertoire of French and California wines.

A separate list of pains featured demi baguettes and baguette au levain—sour dough—"baked fresh twice daily by the restaurant's own boulanger." Bruce recalled fond memories of the six wonderful months he had spent at culinary school in Paris several years ago, and he remembered that baguette means stick. According to Celine Debayle, author of *Les Pains et Leurs Recettes*, the origin of the word boulanger is a twelfth century noun, boulenc, which means "a round bread slightly flattened during cooking."

The menu was tantalizing and respectable for any establishment, much less one located on the outer boundary of civilization. Of course, a menu was only as good as the chef, particularly one who fashioned himself (or herself, Bruce considered) capable of producing a baguette that was qualified to accompany the fine cuisine represented on this menu. Although bakeries could be found on every street in Paris, the unwary consumer too often was lured into a mere bread depot. The true baguette must feature a crackling crust, the first texture experienced by the enthusiast, followed by a center that is not too chewy, but has integrity. Even the best boulangers, competing in the annual Paris baguette competition, were seen wringing their hands in frustration for some minor miscalculation or misstep in their preparation of the perfect baguette. If Mr. Doyle's chef is not a Frenchman, he (or she) at least should have substantial training at the best culinary schools of Paris or Lyon to make this menu a reality.

Bruce grew restless. It was well over an hour since he sat down in the lounge. He wandered onto the floor of the restaurant to look around. He was surprised to see that at least a third of the tables were empty, while the lounge was overflowing with patrons waiting to be seated. Many of the empty tables hadn't even been bussed. Two of the waiters were engaged in a heated argument as they lolled past Bruce, oblivious to the waiting crowd of patrons. A chorus of complaints was rising from the lounge behind him, and a foursome began walking out, muttering to themselves. Mr. Doyle, was nowhere to be seen.

Bruce stood against the wall, evaluating the chaos churning around him on the dining room floor, when Ronnie walked up. She stood there silently, arms folded across her chest and watched. "It's a mess," she said, a note of dejection and surrender in her voice.

"Where's the nervous Mr. Doyle?"

"Who knows? He has no idea about how to run this place."

"Well, I can't stand this any longer," he said. "This is absolutely unacceptable. Ronnie, could you take me to the kitchen? Please. Right now."

She looked at Bruce with a disbelieving expression, until she realized that he was quite serious. "What do you think you're going to do?"

"You'll see. Just give me a few minutes to get organized."

Bruce pulled his t-shirt down as Ronnie guided him across the dining area, swerving around the tables and onward through the double doors into the kitchen. They walked briskly past the two cooks who were busy at the ranges and cutting boards. "Over there," Bruce nodded to the far wall and quickly disappeared. Ronnie poured some coffee for herself while she waited. Soon Bruce returned wearing a black tuxedo jacket and a white apron that covered the front of his boxers. The sleeves revealed two inches of Bruce's wrists. The apron exposed a pair of white shins. Fortunately, nothing else was exposed. "*Voila*," he exclaimed, arms outstretched. "Ronnie, it's not perfect, but it will have to do for a maitre d'."

He strode over to the chef and introduced himself. "Hello, my name is Bruce, and I'll be directing traffic on the floor for a while."

The chef scratched his beard with the back of one hand, leaving a trail of burgundy sauce, while he studied Bruce with a raised eyebrow and look of supreme puzzlement. "Oy," was all he could mutter, with an exasperated shrug. Bruce guessed that the chef had served time in the Catskills.

Ronnie joined them. "Bruce, meet Pierre Des Peres, our chief chef, who's from France via New York and is still grappling with our language. Pierre, meet Bruce, whose last name I don't know." Pierre ventured a solitary nod and a look that said, *What do you think you're doing in my kitchen?* The short, squat chef turned his back and headed toward the range.

Bruce strode confidently out the double doors of the kitchen. First, he cornered the two busboys, a pair of defensive linemen with bulging biceps who played for the Mizzou football team. They held summer jobs at the restaurant, pumping iron during the day at the lodge's fitness center and clearing tables in the evening.

Bruce introduced himself to "Bruiser" Kowalski and "Tank" Tompkins. "Hey, have you ever heard of Ham Godwilling?" Their eyes grew wide when Bruce told them that Ham was one of his best friends. Bruce gave Bruiser and Tank a quick motivational speech about how the future of the restaurant, and their jobs, were at stake if they didn't clear all the empty tables in five minutes.

"Look guys," Bruce concluded, "we're down by two touchdowns in the fourth quarter, and they've got the ball. You know what to do. Take no prisoners."

Next, Bruce gathered the two waiters, the waitress, and Ronnie, and told them bluntly to stop bickering or they'd all be fired immediately. One waiter whined that they were short-handed and the busboys were slackers. Bruce put a comforting hand on the young man's shoulder and acknowledged the problem, but emphasized that they would need to pick each other up, that this was no time to sound like a loser. He cajoled the waiters, pointing out that it was one of the busiest times of the season. He would restore order, placate the patrons, and would help bus tables.

He looked out at the room and divided the floor into quadrants with broad sweeps of his arms. He took the area nearest the entrance and the lounge, and assigned the remaining quadrants to the other three. Bruce then turned to Ronnie. "Veronica, can you handle the terrace as well as the lounge?" He gathered the others in a tight circle around him, like a football huddle in which he was the quarterback. "Now, remember that we should always be courteous to our patrons, but we need to really pick up the pace. Okay team—let's go for it." Bruce had taken command of the floor.

Next, he hurried to the entrance, greeted two couples who were shuffling and fidgeting in the foyer, and showed them to the lounge as he swooped up the reservation book. Inside the lounge, he shouted the names of the first three groups at the top of the list and gave them an effervescent, "*Bienvenue a la Riverway Restaurant, monsieur et madam.* Your table is ready."

He glanced over to see Ronnie's smile, and gave her a confident thumbs up.

33

High above the Atlantic in a jetliner bound for Europe, the Consultant sat in the darkened cabin, his eyes wide open, his mind too busy for sleep. A different and more tedious route was planned this time. As with his first trip to Zurich, the scheme of plane and train connections was designed by his paranoid and meticulous mind to frustrate anyone trying to follow him.

Departing Lambert International Airport at St. Louis, he had looked around nervously to see if any suspicious eyes were giving him sidelong glances. He had taken a direct flight to Kennedy Airport in New York, where he located the international gates, searched the faces of passengers, and boarded his flight to Paris. He had seen no one that he thought was tracking his movements. Yet, his nerves were strung tight.

Far beyond the concern of being followed, he was more anxious about walking into the Zuricher Zentral Banque and making a cash withdrawal. It would have been far safer to verify with a computer entry that the funds had been transferred to the Zuricher. After all, what if he walked into the bank, and the account showed only the original piddly deposit of Swiss francs, less processing fees? And there were worse scenarios. What if the transfer had been discovered, and the police were waiting to arrest him? *What if? What if?* The thoughts made him wince in the dark. He took two Dramamine and fought their effect until he eventually slipped into a shallow sleep.

At Charles de Gaulle Airport outside Paris, he found the Air France counter and booked a seat on the next flight to Geneva. From Geneva, he would take a train to Zurich. His credit cards were maxed out, but after this trip, he could pay them off in full and still have a small fortune left over.

The train pulled into the Hauptbahnof precisely on schedule. He was exhausted from the long trip, but energized by the familiar sights of the Zurich train station. As he walked along the platform, he glanced anxiously around him, trying to identify any faces that were on the flight from Paris to Geneva. There was none.

He bought a latte and headed for the men's restroom to shave. It was getting to be a routine he enjoyed. He didn't even mind the presence of the matronly cleaning lady in the restroom. She always appeared to maintain her gaze on the floor that she was incessantly mopping, but he began to notice how she would work her way toward the end of the urinals, mopping slowly, leisurely, to remove some invisible smudge from the floor, and then peek at the men's plumbing over the top of her glasses without raising her head. It was a technique reflecting great finesse, which she had obviously perfected over a long period of devoted training.

He changed into his suit and put on a fresh dress shirt and tie. *This afternoon I'll treat myself to a new suit at one of the expensive boutiques in Zurich.*

The Bahnhofstrasse was more beautiful than he remembered. It was formerly a street, but had been transformed into a pedestrian mall. It was full of energy, with businessmen dressed in expensive suits walking briskly, shoppers strolling leisurely, and dozens of sidewalk cafés filled with people who apparently had nothing more pressing to do than gawk at others as they moved up and down the pedestrian avenue. Street vendors offered everything from cut flowers and silk scarves to huge pretzels and wiener schnitzel.

He avoided looking into the elegant shops, preferring to focus on the task at the bank. Why should he be worried? After all, he'd withdrawn money hundreds of time at his own bank. But, never in a foreign country, never a numbered Swiss bank account.

He finally reached the Paradeplatz and saw the familiar entrance to the Zuricher. He paused in front of a shop window, where he used the reflection in the glass to straighten his tie. His hair was too long, he noticed, and he tried to organize it with his fingers. He breathed deeply three times, counted to ten, and strode as confidently as possible through the glass doors of the bank.

The cute, young receptionist smiled as he approached her desk. "It's nice to see you again, *Herr Consultant*. Welcome back to Zurich."

He returned the smile warmly. "*Bitte, Fraulein*. It's wonderful to be back and to see your lovely face again. Indeed, much lovelier than this mere token of my appreciation for your kind assistance during my last visit," he said, and he whisked a long-stemmed red rose from behind his back and handed it to her across the desk.

"This is a pleasant surprise, thank you. I must put it in some *wasser*. How do you say…?"

"Oh, do you mean water?"

"*Ya*, of course. I must get some water. Do you wish to see Herr Gottlieb?"

"Now that I have an account with you, I came in to make my first transaction. Could you direct me to the clerks?"

"Of course. The windows are there, and you will find deposit and withdrawal slips on the counter along the wall." She nodded and used the rose to point across the lobby. He followed the direction of the red bud.

He stopped at the counter, found a withdrawal slip, and filled it out for seventy-five thousand dollars. *That's seventy-five thousand in U.S. of A. dollars, mind you.* Then he approached the row of mahogany-paneled windows, stopped at the second teller, and handed her the slip. She greeted him and inspected the paper then turned to make an entry in her computer. After about two minutes, she excused herself and disappeared through a large wooden door behind her.

As he waited, he realized he hadn't taken a breath since he approached the window. He tried to concentrate on normal breathing without looking too conspicuous. He knew the bank must have surveillance cameras, and he struggled against the urge to look up or around for them.

The teller returned after a few minutes. "Here we are, *mein Herr*," she said, as she counted the money out in thousand dollar bills. "And, if you will please sign this receipt and initial your account number to confirm that all is correct."

He was reviewing the receipt when he suddenly heard the deep, guttural voice and felt the bulky presence of Heinrich Gottlieb at his side. "I was advised that you had returned for another visit. I hope you are not having any problems, *Herr Consultant?*" Gottlieb, attired in his severe, black three-piece suit, leaned closely into the window, one elbow resting on the narrow counter.

The Consultant was startled by the interruption and gathered his thoughts as he listened to Gottlieb breathing through his walrus mustache. The bullshit smile flashed across the Consultant's face, and he extended his hand.

"So nice to see you again, Herr Gottlieb. Everything is going fine, I believe." They shook hands.

Gottlieb nodded at the stack of thousand dollar bills. "That is a rather large amount of cash money you have." Gottlieb lowered his voice to a husky whisper and fingered the tip of his mustache with his thumb and index finger. "You are aware, of course, that your country's currency laws require us to report transactions involving over ten thousand dollars. It seems that your government is particularly interested in persons who bring large sums of cash back into the U.S. Naturally, we hope you'll invest it here in Zurich, rather than the Bahamas." His voice emphasized Bahamas, and one eyebrow went up expectantly. "Such a silly law, *ya*? If you leave your funds in Zurich, you wouldn't need to worry about such silly things." Gottlieb's eyes drilled into the Consultant, the type of gaze that commands a direct response.

Does he think I also have an account in the Bahamas? Or, is he bluffing? The Consultant embarrassingly was not aware of those intrusive requirements, which the government used in the hope of catching drug dealers. "You needn't worry, Herr Gottlieb, because that is not my business." He slipped the cash into both inside pockets of his jacket and shook Gottlieb's hand. Gottlieb didn't relinquish his grip. His head tilted back and his eyes locked onto the Consultant's face, searching for the lie behind the casual exchange. Their eyes locked before Gottlieb finally released the Consultant's hand.

Gottlieb's smile masked an unconvinced expression. The Consultant was uncomfortable under the penetrating inspection, but outwardly maintained his confident look. "*Bitte, Herr Gottlieb. Auf Wiedersehen.*" He flashed his bullshit smile again, but its usual sparkle had dimmed.

On the sidewalk, outside the Zuricher, the Consultant breathed deeply and patted the inside pocket of his suit jacket. The bulge on either side brought forth an excitement, an exhilaration, and finally a confidence he couldn't quite understand. For the first time in his life, he had some real money, and this seventy-five thousand dollars was just the beginning. He walked briskly, but not hurriedly, glancing behind him occasionally, as if he expected Herr Gottlieb and the police to be running after him. *What if they came galloping after me on horseback, like a scene from Butch Cassidy? Who are these guys?*

He reached the next block and entered a small café, bypassing the sidewalk tables in favor of a seat inside, next to the window, where he could keep a vigilant and nervous lookout. Businessmen in expensive suits were hurrying by, eager to be on time for their next global deal. Beautiful young women strolled by, dressed in the latest fashions from Paris and Milan, carrying shopping bags from chic boutiques. He sipped his latte and watched them all come and go from his window in the café, envying the wealth and desiring the women. It was a simple recipe, wealth and women. He would soon have the first ingredient. And, the second wouldn't be far behind.

His heart, which had been pounding in the bank as if he were running a marathon, was finally returning to normal. Not knowing how long he might need to be in Zurich for the transaction, he had intentionally decided not to make return travel reservations. Even with no plans for his trip home, he knew he must carefully consider an appropriately confusing route. Feeling the twin bulges in his jacket, he suddenly decided that, for the first time, he would play it by ear. He realized that he needn't be in a hurry. He might stay in Zurich a few days, or take the train to Lausanne and then to Geneva, or simply take it one day at a time. He didn't need to worry. The bulging pockets in his jacket comforted him and gave him the release he craved.

He paid the bill in Swiss francs and walked out the front door of the café, merging easily with the strolling shoppers on the pedestrian avenue, heading in the direction of the train station.

A computer and electronics store caught his eye—Der Electronika—and he walked closer to examine the equipment and ads displayed in the window. He could tell that this store was high-tech, with next year's hardware, better than anything he was familiar with in the States, better than any mail-order catalogs for techies he had seen. The window displayed notebook computers that he had only read about back home. The bulges in his jacket spoke to him, *you deserve some new toys*.

Inside, he wandered over to a table that contained advanced multi-media equipment that could make a videotape of a meeting, or instructions, or dazzling women in skimpy swimsuits, and then scan the tape into the computer, allowing others on the Internet to click on their email and view the tape. *Surely, I could find a good use for such a neat scanner.*

At another table was a wide range of the latest laptops. A busy executive couldn't live without a notebook computer to use during those times he was away from the office. While he was concentrating deeply on a brochure, a young woman approached. "May I help you select a notebook today?" She spoke pleasantly with a German accent.

Her words were perfectly businesslike, but her voice sounded sexy. A hint of huskiness, perhaps. He looked up and saw a slender, blonde woman, mid-twenties, almost as tall as he. Her eyes were blue. Not merely blue, but the blue of a Swiss lake, deep yet inviting, shimmering as in the sunlight. He fumbled with the brochure until it slipped from his hand, and he apologized for his clumsiness while she knelt to retrieve it from the tile floor, revealing a well-rounded cleavage that disappeared into a black lace brassiere. He feared the money in his jacket pockets might spill out if he leaned over to join in the scramble for the brochure, but not wanting to miss any of the sights, he kneeled.

"Tell me, *Fraulein*, how did you know to speak English to me? I don't recall saying anything since I came here."

She stood and said, "Ah, then, you are an American." With this pronouncement, she smiled and spoke in German to the cashier. She took his hand, placed the brochure in it, and clasped his fingers around it. "It's a game we play when we're not too busy." Her lips were thin and glistened with a deep red lipstick. Her smile was warm and inviting, her body radiating with sensuality. "We have so many customers from other countries, and many from the United States. Some are handsome businessmen, like you." She turned her head slightly, avoiding his eyes, as if embarrassed by her admission. "So, Gretchen and I make a small contest—a bet, I think you call it—to guess what country a customer is from. I hope you aren't offended by our little game?"

"Well, I am offended, *mein Fraulein*," he answered with mock seriousness. "But, I would waive the offense if you would help me select a few items. First, you must tell me your name."

"My name is Anna."

"And my name is…uh…Ralph. Now then, Anna," he continued, "since you enjoy games of chance, I will bet you that, when we are done, you will agree to have dinner with me tonight."

"*Rolf*? Most of the Americans I meet know more about computers than women." Her lips feigned a pout, but her enchanting eyes remained fixed on his face, closely monitoring his expression.

"It depends on what they learned about first."

"Is that why you're looking for a notebook computer, Rolf?" Her lips opened into a sly smile.

"It's all about clicking, isn't it?" He wet his lips with an exaggerated motion of his tongue, and left them slightly parted. He was enjoying himself immensely. *Back in the hunt*, his bulging pockets spoke to him. And he loved her style of flirting. *Are all European women this open?*

They spent the next two hours together, comparing capacity and specifications of a dozen notebook computers, flirting and counter-flirting, brushing up against each other in feigned casual encounters. "Excuse," he would say as his arm brushed her breasts while he reached for a mouse. She didn't seem to mind, he noted. Anna demonstrated several models. He tested them and finally selected a Pentium V-Plus model that operated at a dazzling 1,000 megahertz and came with built-in ports and internal modem. "But, are the menus and directories in German?"

"Now, you're being silly. The default language is English, but the software allows you to select another language if you want. Is there anything else you would like to see?"

"Perhaps later," he responded, with a flash of the bullshit smile.

"Ah, but there is something else you must see. You will be one of the first in America to have this." He followed her to the glass showcase, and couldn't help notice the easy roll of her hips beneath her short black skirt. She displayed a watch on the countertop.

"I already have a watch," he said. He picked up the timepiece and closely examined it. "What's so special about this one?"

"You have an ordinary watch, one with a design and capability that dates back several decades. Now, look,

Rolf," she said, pointing at the watch with a ruby fingernail, "this one is a 'smart watch,' made by a Swiss company, Swatch AG. It has a computer chip that allows you to do all kinds of things, like pay for merchandise." She reached over the counter and gently took the watch from him. "See this part?" The ruby fingernail reappeared to caress the watch. "This tiny window is a scanner, the same idea as the ones used in supermarkets. You could go to your ATM to make a withdrawal then pass the watch across the scanner, and the amount of the withdrawal is electronically sensed by the chip in the watch. You could even open a locked door with this watch—a door with an electronic security code."

She leaned over the counter, noting the features of the smart watch. He followed her description attentively, appreciating all the fine points she displayed on the countertop.

Instinctively, he reached for his wallet to get a credit card. Then he remembered the bulge of cash in the breast pocket of his jacket. Sure, although the items cost over five thousand dollars, he would pay cash. A rush went through his body and made his fingers tremble. He had never felt such security. *I can pay five thousand dollars, cash, for a few toys!*

Anna finished placing the new laptop in its padded carrying case made of supple black lambskin with a shoulder strap. She picked up the watch. "I'll set the alarm to ring at 1830 hours, which is six-thirty in American time. That's when you should return so we can go to dinner. Here, put it on, let's see how it looks."

"One last thing. Can you recommend a good hotel? It looks like I'll be staying overnight in Zurich."

Anna paused for a moment, her nose wrinkled in thought. "Ah, for you, the Hotel Baur Au Lac. It's on the lake in a private park. It is most elegant, and it is close to everything."

He put his leather case over his shoulder and waved as he walked out. "See you then," he said. Anna responded, "*ciao*" and waved back.

As soon as he was out the door, Anna joined Gretchen behind the counter. They exchanged spirited high-fives. "Did you see that thick bundle of American dollars on him?" Anna asked, her eyes rolling in amazement.

34

"Please state your full name for the record."

"Maxine M. Midland, 1432 *Pueh-lak*, Unit C."

The court reporter asked her to spell the name of the street. "P-a-u-i-l-l-a-c, she said each letter slowly. But most people spell it Puehlak, just like it sounds." Maxine nervously scratched the top of her left hand while she awaited the next question.

With that simple question and nervous response, J. Thomas Dunwoody, the Worm, unceremoniously launched his deposition of the association secretary in his great defamation case, *Dunwoody v. The Vineyard Townhome Association*. In his lawsuit, Dunwoody claimed that the association had "viciously and intentionally defamed and maligned his good character by reason of the board sending a written notification to all the unit owners in the Vineyard, which notification stated that he had been convicted of child molestation." Attached to the memo was a copy of the court record of the conviction, which Dunwoody alleged was "false, erroneous, and without any veracity whatsoever."

Since he hadn't retained an attorney, and since he had no office, Dunwoody held the deposition in the kitchen of his townhome at the Vineyard. The space was cramped and humid. A naked fluorescent light cast a harsh glow over the room, the globe long since destroyed by the errant heave of a cutting board, toaster, or pot. Dirty dishes and skillets filled the sink. A bowl of half-eaten chili on the countertop was drawing a crowd of flies like cops to a donut. Two cartons of Chinese takeout were oozing a thin stream of soy sauce, which had formed a brown pond near an open container of microwave tortellini. A package of hotdog buns was quietly turning green. A mousetrap poised silently and patiently in the corner of the countertop, its morsel of cheese swiped long ago. A small tin pot on the range was drowning an orphan hotdog in a puddle of murky water.

The kitchen table, a 1950's metal affair, only had space for four chairs. The top was Formica with a marbled look that was gouged and scratched from years of abuse. The original chrome edge had been painted and now was chipped and dented. Dunwoody sat at one end of the table dressed in his favorite old gym shorts and a t-shirt that exhibited evidence of recent skirmishes with the microwave tortellini. The tattoo of his first wife Florence revealed itself on the pale bicep of his left arm. She smiled when he flexed and frowned when he relaxed—a fitting remembrance. Maxine, Joshua, and George Belt, the association president, occupied the other chairs.

Becky, the court reporter, teetered on a tall, wobbly barstool at the corner of the table, squeezed between the microwave oven and a black-and-white TV. The stool was vintage thrift shop and it thrust her knees high above the tabletop. She perched at the end of the table opposite Dunwoody, her short skirt a certain diversion for his meandering attention. However, at the moment, it was Murphy, Dunwoody's mangy dog of uncertain gender and breeding, who was meandering under the table, loudly sniffing and inspecting Becky's premises and occasionally snorting with approval.

"Does anyone want coffee?" asked Dunwoody, gesturing toward an old percolator on the gas range.

"Is it fresh?" Joshua inquired.

"Just made it yesterday." Dunwoody filled his mug with thick black liquid. "Coffee is like sex. Even at its worst, it's better than none at all." He winked at Maxine.

Dunwoody busied himself shuffling through a stack of papers, searching for a powerful follow-up question for Maxine to maintain his momentum. Not finding what he wanted, he scattered the papers on the table and examined each page briefly, scratching the stubble on his chin and caressing the scar that drooled from the corner of his lower lip. He paused to adjust the black Walgreen's reading glasses on his nose. He gathered the papers up into a new arrangement and repeatedly tamped the stack on the table, like preparing to deal a deck of cards.

Dunwoody's mind was difficult to divine. Quite possibly his intent was to stall for more time, or to draw attention to himself, or to drag out the deposition until everyone around the table was sufficiently punished. In any event, on the third or fourth attempt to straighten his papers, Dunwoody missed the edge of the table with the uneven stack, and papers fluttered in a half-dozen directions beneath the table. He dived after them.

Murphy was also quick to pounce on the papers, sniffing loudly to determine if anything was edible. Joshua bent under the table to get a better look at the mess and estimate how long Dunwoody would torture them with the clean up. Dunwoody snarled, "Counselor, these are my client's *notes* we're dealing with here, prepared for my eyes only. They are protected by attorney-client privilege. You may not look at my notes."

Dunwoody then disappeared completely below the table to retrieve his notes, scuffling with Murphy who was standing on the papers and chewing the section labeled, "Board Records." From somewhere below the table, originating in the vicinity of Becky's skirt, Dunwoody snapped, "Let's go off the record, please, while I confer with my client." Becky could feel Dunwoody's hot breath on her ankles. After several minutes of Murphy's snorting and Dunwoody's grunting from below, Dunwoody's face re-appeared with a drooling sneer above the table. He clutched the papers close to his tortellini t-shirt as if he were guarding a hot hand in a high-stakes poker game.

Joshua had opened his pleadings file and was vacantly flipping through the papers bound at the top. "The last time we checked the file, Mr. Dunwoody, you had no attorney in this matter. Has this situation changed in the last sixty seconds?"

"Excuse me counselor, but this is my depo, and I'm asking the questions here." Turning to Becky, Dunwoody barked another order. "The court reporter is instructed to strike any more long-winded objections or speeches by defense counsel."

"Don't worry, Dunwoody," Joshua smiled, "we're still off the record—assuming you'll get around to making one at all."

"You know," Dunwoody drooled to no one in particular, "I've been to four funerals in the past two weeks. Then, I went to my niece's wedding." He paused for a drag on his cigarette. He exhaled, scratched an armpit, and stubbed out the cigarette. "Yep, four funerals and a wedding. And you know what I concluded? Funerals are better—at least you don't need to bring a gift."

There was stony silence around the table. Joshua rolled his eyes. "Dunwoody, are you planning on continuing this depo any day soon?"

As Dunwoody removed a disk from his files and inserted it into a notebook computer, it reminded Joshua of Bruce's mystery disk. He had time now, so he decided to try again and see if he could decode the data that Bruce had encrypted. Joshua cleared a spot on the countertop, opened his WinBook computer, clicked on Corel Word Perfect, and inserted the disk. Only one document was on the disk, "Sewerpipe.wpd." The electronic hourglass turned while the WinBook whirred for a few seconds. The document appeared on the screen:

Rec%#$$$$knkkiel¨¨¨{22j/lm890006^^st.j.ðenðio vmeosa/<?

Αχχουντλεδγερσ, ρεχειπαβλεσ,μονεψ τρανσφερσ,παψμεντσ.

□↗↗♦≈□□♏♋♍□♦■♦♦⊁■♦♦ℯ⌁□≈♦ ○♋■♎ ♌♋≈♋○♦🖉 acctsrec'bledepositsandtransferscontractsπαψαβλε.

It still looked like gibberish. Joshua glanced over to see what Dunwoody was doing. The air in the tiny kitchen was trapped in a thick blue-gray fog. Judging by the overflowing ashtray, Dunwoody must have smoked half a pack of Marlboros before the depo started, and it was only ten in the morning. With the devotion of a religious ritual, he now tapped out another, and lit it with an ancient Zippo butane lighter, cupping the flame as if he were in a windstorm.

Joshua stared at the screen on his WinBook. Pure gibberish. He closed it with a heavy sigh and returned to the deposition table. He had no idea how to decode Bruce's data.

Dunwoody exhaled over the top of his notes and adjusted his reading glasses lower on his nose, still pondering his next question for Maxine. He reached for his cup of coffee and slouched lower in his chair, seemingly to concentrate on his shredded notes, but more likely to get a better glimpse of the view across the table. Becky eyed

Dunwoody suspiciously then tugged at her skirt.

The silence continued around the table while everyone watched Dunwoody with growing boredom and dwindling patience. They followed his eyes focusing on his notes then darting above his reading glasses toward Becky's hem. The hint of a drool appeared, then his eyes drifted downward again. Finally, he took a long drag from his Marlboro and asked, "Ms. Midland, are you an officer of the Vineyard Townhome Association?"

Joshua sighed loudly and did nothing to stifle a yawn. *We'll be here all day.*

Dunwoody spent the first two hours on Maxine's education background (high school, two years of community college) and work history (fifteen years at the South County factory outlet, where she never rose above the position of sales clerk). He had prepared meticulously, without regard for getting to the facts at issue, content to irritate by duration if not relevancy. Had he chosen a career in law, he would have done well defending cases for insurance companies.

By one o'clock in the afternoon, with the questions finally becoming relevant to the issues in the case, Joshua requested a break for lunch. Dunwoody waved off the request with a drooling smirk. It was his show, and he was eager to stay in control and use his control. *Today, for a change, these people have to respect me*, Dunwoody thought. He held the pages that had been chewed by Murphy, and slowly and carefully, as if he were putting the final strokes on *Whistler's Mother*, he marked several lines of a paragraph with a yellow highlighter pen. He reviewed his highlights with a drool. His mouth opened slowly, and out rolled another mundane question about how the board minutes were maintained.

Maxine, still nervously scratching the top of her

hand, was poised to answer when Joshua held up his hands to signal a time-out in the proceedings. He turned to Becky and spoke in measured words and with a calm voice, "We can all hear the court reporter's stomach rumbling. In compliance with the Rules of Civil Procedure of the State Supreme Court, protecting court reporters from deposition-abuse, and in the spirit of humanitarianism, we're declaring a recess of ninety-minutes for lunch. Let's go off the record."

Becky finished tapping Joshua's statement, immediately stopped her stenography, and reached for her purse before Dunwoody could utter an objection. Joshua, Maxine, and George stood up as if on cue, gathered their files and walked out, with Becky right behind them. They all jumped into George's minivan and sped away in search of a restaurant. Dunwoody looked blankly at the empty chairs scattered around the kitchen table, his focus finally stopping at the barstool where Becky's long legs had perched a minute ago. Murphy whined at the door, wanting to be let out, too. "What rule was that...?" He muttered and reached for his rulebook.

35

It had been a long day at the offices of Preferred Site Management. Joshua had given Michelle the business card of the computer expert referred by Vinnie the Bug. After she completed a complicated series of calls, relays, and messages on pagers, he finally returned her call and agreed to a consultation at PSM's offices. He arrived precisely on time at 9:00 a.m., announcing himself to Jenni at the reception desk with a brusque, "I'm here to see Michelle."

Michelle met him in the lobby and led him to her office. He was short, slightly built, and bald, with pale skin that looked like it had only seen sunlight vicariously while watching movies. His clothes were casual and cool—a short-sleeved white linen shirt, tan linen slacks, and light brown loafers. His movements were quick and self-confident. His speech was terse.

Once inside Michelle's office, he sat his briefcase—more like a postal carrier's bag—on the floor. "My name's Scarpo, and I understand you have a problem. If you were referred by my dear friend, Vincent, I'll do everything possible to help you." He pointed a thin finger toward the business card in Michelle's hand. "As stated on my card, I'm a Forensic Information Technologist. In my business, we just call it a FIT. Some people have their offices swept for unwanted listening devices planted by competitors, or enemies, or by authorities who like to snoop. But, if your computer is suffering from a virus or other illness, you must have a FIT. My specialty is investigating computer systems for viruses, bugs, and other nuisances. I'll cure this ailment because I'm very good at what I do. And, I'm not inexpensive, my consulting fee being two hundred dollars an hour. Now, enough small talk, tell me about your business, your software, and your problem." He listened attentively, intensely, his eyes fixed on Michelle, while she answered his question.

"The individual homeowners at our associations send their assessment checks directly to a lockbox at our bank. The bank deposits the checks into our separate client accounts and enters the data and then sends an electronic report so that we can see the deposits on our system. We then move portions of these deposits into reserves by sending instructions back to the bank. All of this activity is done electronically."

He interrupted with one question, "When you had the new system installed, did you also get a web security system?" When Michelle said "yes," his eyebrows arched. "It must have been an off-the-shelf anti-virus program. A smart hacker can get right through those."

Scarpo started with Michelle's computer, his lithe fingers flashing over the keys. He called up one program after another, running each for a few minutes. He paused occasionally to ask Michelle a question about the functions of the data on several of the spreadsheets that appeared on the monitor. But, for the most part, the next hour in Michelle's office was silent except for the tapping on the keyboard. Scarpo's face was impassive as he devoted total concentration to his work. He broke his silence once to say, "Hmmm. That's interesting." Finally, he stood and said, "Show me the server."

Scarpo opened the tower of the server with a battery-powered screwdriver. He examined each of the boards and chips with a magnifying glass he kept in his postal pouch. He traced all the wiring with his fingertips. He examined all of the computers in the same manner, running programs and inspecting the internal wiring. After requesting a ladder from Michelle, he removed tiles in the drop ceiling and traced the DSL wiring. He was full of quiet, controlled energy and an insatiable desire to track down every potential avenue of trouble.

After six hours of nonstop forensic information technology analysis, Scarpo returned to Michelle's office with concern on his face. He sat down and looked her in the eye. "You have a serious problem, one that could cost you over five million dollars in losses—if it hasn't already. You have no time to waste." Michelle called Mac, and the two women huddled with Scarpo in the conference room.

"Based on my inspection and tests, I believe you have a form of virus in your computer system. You have one of the better web security systems, but none of these systems provides one hundred percent protection. Whoever installed this virus had to be very knowledgeable and clever. Very clever, indeed. It's called an 'applet,' and here's how it works…"

JOSHUA KNOCKED ON THE DOOR of Michelle's condo. He held a bottle of wine for the dinner that Michelle had offered to cook for the two of them.

"Hi, there." Michelle greeted Joshua in the doorway with a warm smile, a cold can of Michelob, and a hug. It was a friendly hug, not an intimate hug. He pondered whether Michelle's hand was teasing the hair on the back of his neck during the brief embrace. "I'm glad you could come over," she said, a hand still on his shoulder, "It's been quite a day. The FIT came in to analyze our computers, and I'm eager to tell you what he found." He tried to kiss her lightly on the cheek, but he delayed slightly, and in that instant of indecision, she turned away.

Joshua stood there a second, disappointed that he missed an opportunity to kiss Michelle. He took a gulp of beer and loosened his tie. "It's seven o'clock already, and I drove straight over here from Dunwoody's. He succeeded in exhausting all of us, taking over eight hours for a depo that should have lasted forty-five minutes. Poor Maxine! He even asked her where she had her hair done, and had she mentioned the incident at the hair salon?"

Joshua walked with Michelle into the living room. She looked sensual in her Sun Devils football jersey, her breasts swaying gently beneath the fabric, her nipples firm and noticeable through the thin cotton. No bra?—he hoped.

Michelle handed him a black t-shirt and said, "I thought you might want to get out of your stiff shirt and tie and get more comfortable. He unbuttoned his white dress shirt then turned his back to her while he removed it. She watched, without trying to be too obvious, and admired his narrow waist and the muscles in his back. He slipped the t-shirt over his head, looked down to see the gold seal of the University of Missouri and said, "This is more like it."

"So it was a marathon depo. But, you were able to take some breaks," Michelle asked, deliberately keeping the conversation light. She knew the mood would change as soon as she brought up Scarpo's report.

"Sure, we stopped for lunch. Oh, and we took a break in the afternoon, when a roach crawled out of Dunwoody's papers and ran wild on the kitchen table. Maxine was so repulsed we had to stop for half an hour. Not to mention that we all inhaled enough secondhand smoke to kill a dozen lab rats. Come to think about it, that's probably how Dunwoody controls the mice at his house."

"Do you think he got anything that hurts our case?"

"No way, although he'll probably file a motion for summary judgment, because that's his style as a wannabe lawyer. The only exhibits he used were the court's copy of his conviction and the board's memo to the owners. Oh, and he tried to use year-to-date financial statements, but I objected to those. Bottom line, no surprises."

They moved to the kitchen, and Joshua rested his elbows on the kitchen countertop. "After he finished with Maxine, I took his depo for about an hour. He couldn't name a single person in the Vineyard that he considered a friend before all this occurred. He didn't have any friends there before and he doesn't now. And I asked him to specify the alleged damages he suffered in the forty-eight hours that elapsed between the board's memo and when he filed suit. His answer was, 'that hasn't been determined yet.' He couldn't name a single person who would testify that his character was defamed. No one has said anything to him or written nasty letters." Joshua finished his beer and crushed the can.

Michelle brought another Michelob from the refrigerator. "Based on the depo, do you still think Dunwoody should be on our list of suspects for the break-in at PSM?"

"Indirectly." Joshua explained as he flipped open the tab of the beer can. "I asked him about his computer background, skills, training, and so forth. He's self-taught, and claims that he's limited to 'hunting and pecking' in word processing, but has no training or proficiency in financial or bookkeeping software. However, he said that he goes to PSM's offices every week to get a fresh printout of financial statements. He said, 'I do it mostly to irritate Michelle and to keep reminding the board that I'm always watching them. Not just the cost of the lawsuit, but everything else, from asphalt resealing to zinnia mulching.' At least, that's what he said."

"So, what's your conclusion?"

"On the surface, Dunwoody has all the credentials to qualify as a suspect. He's smart, clever, hateful, and vengeful. He has the twisted mind of a mad genius. But, I'm not sure he has the sophistication to break into your offices and not leave a sign. As for money, he doesn't appear to have any, but it doesn't seem to bother him. He acts on principle, not greed. The depo was a terrific waste of time, but at least we now have him on record that his case is a bunch of hollow bullshit brought by a lonesome, paranoid asshole who lives in a stinking, rotting kitchen with an undisciplined dog and repulsive cockroaches."

For a moment, Michelle considered Joshua's analysis. "If everybody is entitled to his day in court, does that include the psycho-weirdoes like Dunwoody? He's like a serial plaintiff. Isn't that a senseless waste of taxpayer dollars?"

"Our judicial system is like a Rube Goldberg device. It generates a lot of energy, but only enough to keep going around and around without actually getting anything done."

"Joshua, let's go over to the table," Michelle said. "I need to talk to you about what the FIT found when he came in today."

"The what?"

"You know, Scarpo, the computer expert. He's the guy referred by Vinnie the Bug. He calls himself a forensic information technologist because he dissects computer systems that have been compromised. Scarpo is a FIT."

"Michelle, I'm really upset with you. Why did you let me ramble on about that stupid depo I had today, while you're sitting on this major news event?"

"Well, you looked tense, and I thought you needed to unwind first."

"Sometimes you're too gracious. So, what did he tell you?"

"Do you know what an applet is?"

Joshua looked puzzled. "A dwarf apple?"

"Yeah, with a big worm in it. It's a viral program that can be hidden inside another program where it waits for instructions. The applet takes control of your software functions. Scarpo told me about a group of European hackers, called the Chaos Computer Club, who invented this sneaky virus, but he didn't think it was capable of electronic transfers without a lot more refinement. He said that although the stories are only anecdotal, with no actual reported cases, the applet may be a way to commit the perfect bank robbery." Michelle paused for a sip of beer.

"How does it get into your software? How does it work?"

"From what I now understand, someone inserts the applet in your Internet web browser, such as Microsoft's Internet Explorer or Netscape's Navigator. Once in place, it searches for a financial program. In our case, an applet has been hiding in our Netscape, waiting to attach to Master Bookkeeper, the accounting software that we use for client accounts. Scarpo said that the applet is programmed to exploit a security gap in Master Bookkeeper. The way he explained the process it all seems possible."

"So, what does this applet do?"

"Well, according to Scarpo, the applet was planted in our web browser and sat there passively, waiting for instructions from its master. As soon as we made any transaction in Master Bookkeeper, which is every day, the applet was poised to take instructions from an off-site computer."

Joshua finished his beer. "Based on what I learned at the depo, that's way over Dunwoody's level. He may reek revenge, but he's just a mouse potato when it comes to computer software. But, it sure fits Curtis, because he's in love with power, and he sees PSM's reserves as the path to power. Curtis would need help on something as sophisticated as planting the applet, of course, but he has access to that kind of expertise from Vinnie the Bug and his friends. You know Allen Russell, the financial wiz, could also do it, and he has a strong motive—he's racked up heavy debts at the casinos. And, let's not forget David Daggett, with all of his fiscal problems."

"You're right, Joshua, this little applet is really sophisticated. It's not just a program on a disk that you can install by inserting and clicking. Scarpo told me that we have a first class web security system with no obvious signs that it was penetrated. That's why we had no idea that anything was wrong. Whoever did this had to know exactly how to penetrate our web security system. This plan could only have been carried off by a very clever hacker."

"Okay, but how does an off-site computer send instructions to this little guy, the applet, hiding inside your computer?"

Michelle got up from the table and started pacing. "First, our accounts can only be accessed by a code. Each client account has its own password."

"Of course, you have passwords," Joshua said. "That would explain the break-in. Someone wanted to steal the passwords."

"No, I don't think that was the reason for the break-in," Michelle said, pacing harder now. "Whenever we would enter a password to access an account, the applet would memorize it."

"So, somehow, the hacker contacts the applet from a remote computer and gets the passwords What happens then?"

"The hacker could use a password to access an

account and instruct the applet to transfer reserves out of that account to another bank. From there, the funds could be transferred to yet another bank. At that point, it would be next to impossible to trace."

"So, who's got the off-site computer that directs the applet?" Joshua asked.

"That's the five million dollar question, isn't it? I asked Scarpo where the off-site computer could be. He said that since the applet is planted in the web browser, it could be anywhere. That means the computer could belong to Curtis, or Allen Russell, or David Daggett, or Dunwoody, or even Philip Palmer's computer in Boston."

"Scary stuff. Can you tell if any reserves are missing?"

"Not yet. Until now, we've relied on electronic transfers and our computer for day-to-day information. But, if there have been transfers out of reserves through the applet, they're not showing up. There's only one way we'd be able to discover unauthorized transfers that didn't show up in our daily transactions. When we receive the bank statement, we verify and reconcile all the transactions in our accounts."

Joshua now stood up. "But, that's only once a month."

"That's what makes it even worse. We don't know how long the applet has been there. It's been three weeks since the last batch of bank statements. So, Mac and I are going down to the bank tomorrow morning and, we'll go over all their records and compare them to our current printouts."

"Are you going to notify your insurance company?"

The conversation paused, each of them deep in their own thoughts. After a few minutes, Michelle said, "Well, how about dinner now?"

Joshua opened the bottle of wine he brought, Havens merlot 1998, and poured two glasses in the small dining room of Michelle's condo. He lit two long white candles on the table. In the kitchen, Michelle stuffed a roasted pork tenderloin with a mixture of sautéed portobello mushrooms, yellow bell peppers, sun-dried tomatoes, and zucchini, and then sliced the tenderloin into medallions. She stirred the braised asparagus and drained the angel hair pasta, then tossing it with extra virgin olive oil. Joshua came in and sliced a fresh baguette, using diagonal cuts.

They sat next to each other at the dining table. "I think it's time we should get this over with. Get it behind us."

"Get what over with?" She was genuinely puzzled.

"This," he whispered and leaned over and kissed Michelle on the lips. Stunned, she involuntarily allowed his kiss then returned it lightly.

"Oh, that," she said, suppressing a smile. "And who gave you permission to kiss me?"

"You did."

"Did not."

"Well, your eyes did. Anyway, listen, now that our first kiss is out of the way, maybe we can deal in a mature way with this sexual tension I'm beginning to feel between us. Besides, I like that," he said, reaching for his fork. "For starters, we should maintain that as our little tradition."

"What little tradition?"

"The tradition we just started—kissing before dinner. You fashion yourself as not being romantic, but I know better," he insisted.

She raised her wine glass and shielded her eyes behind it. *Slow and steady, Michelle. He's going too fast, slow it down. Stay in control of the pace.* "You have a vivid imagination."

"Why can't you admit it—that you're hopelessly in love?"

"In your dreams. Anyway, you're the one who's afraid of the C word."

"Ha. Look who's talking," Joshua paused, feigning

disbelief. "Well, maybe both of us are. But, at least I'm working on it. Are you?"

"I'm working on it, but it's not a high priority. I'm the original Sisyphus where relationships are involved," Michelle groaned. "You have to understand, Joshua, that right now, I'm totally consumed by this applet thing. I can't think about anything else right now. Do you realize what this problem could do to my reputation? And Mac's? A theft of millions of dollars of client funds, right out from under our noses. Can't you see this is a career-ending crisis? Our credibility would be destroyed. All our clients would flee to our competitors. I'd probably never get bonded again. The end of PSM and probably my career in community management. Just like that. *Punto final.*"

Joshua listened carefully to Michelle's words. "I'm so sorry, you must think I'm terribly insensitive. I want you to know that I'm here to help, however I can."

"You're not being very helpful if you're trying to get me into bed because you think I'm some poor woman caught in a moment of weakness." Her voice was rising. "You're like all other men—it's all about what you want. Not about my needs. I enjoy your…friendship, but…" Her lips quivered as her words trailed off.

Joshua looked stunned by the accusation. And, just when he thought he was making progress with Michelle, she uttered the one word a man in love fears the most, when the woman says "I just want us to be friends."

"…and right now," she continued, near tears, "my whole career, everything I've tried to build, every dream I have of the future, is hanging on some invisible hacker stealing our clients' funds, doing it right through the computer on my desk using a sneaky little virus called an applet…"

"Look, Michelle, you can't blame me for creating this crisis," Joshua said. "Tomorrow, Mac and you are going to the bank. You'll know better if any funds have actually been transferred out of your accounts."

Michelle looked wounded and disappeared into the bathroom.

After a few minutes, she rejoined Joshua at the dining table, dabbing her eyes with a tissue. The rims of her eyes were red. Trying to brighten the dark mood in the room, Joshua turned his attention to dinner. "So, what do you call this strange, exotic dish?"

"Well, since you ask," she sniffled, "you take a pork tenderloin, make a slit through the inside with a thin knife, creating sort of a hollow pocket that's open at both ends. Then you pack it full of yellow bell peppers and other stuff, and *voila!* Pork tenderloin with yellow bell peppers and other stuff."

Joshua devoured his first mouthful, washing it down with the Havens merlot. "Wow, this dish is really different. I didn't know food could taste like this. You could go on Martha Stewart's show, although you need a little work on the verbal presentation."

"Wait, we forgot to make a toast," Michelle said, reaching for her wine. As they raised their glasses, Michelle looked glum. "Here's to finding the missing reserves. I hate to think of the alternative."

"Here's to insurance coverage."

They somberly clinked glasses. Then the phone rang.

36

"Who would be calling at nine o'clock at night?" Michelle wondered out loud.

"It's probably one of those long-distance phone companies trying to get you to switch," Joshua said. "They don't care what time it is."

The phone rang again.

Michelle looked longingly at the food on her plate. "But, we finally sat down to eat."

"Ask them for their home phone number, so you can call them when they're eating."

Another ring.

"Maybe it's an emergency from work."

"I've never seen an emergency that couldn't wait until the morning. Including a board president who called me from jail at three in the morning."

And another ring.

"I have to get it." Michelle dropped her napkin and jogged into the kitchen. "Hello? Yes, just a moment." She carried the cordless handset into the dining room. "It's for you. It's Ham Godwilling. How did he get my number?"

Joshua finished chewing and took a gulp of water. "I put my phone on call forwarding to your number." Taking the phone from Michelle, he said, "Hey, Ham. Hear anything new?"

"That's why I'm calling, man." Ham's rich baritone voice filled the phone. "Guess who's alive and well and staying in an undisclosed location?"

"You serious? Wait a second, Ham, I'll put you on the speakerphone so Michelle can hear." Joshua grabbed Michelle's hand, walked into the kitchen, and put the phone on speaker.

"Hi, Ham," Michelle said. "We've met, remember? The night we chased the burglar at Bruce's row house, and you banged your shin." She smiled, remembering the incident.

"How could I forget?" Ham laughed. Listen, guys. Our friend called a few minutes ago and left a voice mail at the hospital for me. I figure he thought that was the safest place to call. Said he was detained and threatened by a couple of…let me see my notes…he called them 'assholes in wingtips.' Says he's okay. Except for a bruise on his forehead, no clothes, and no money. He's not in the city, but he's not far away. He wants you to call him tonight between eleven and midnight. Here's the number."

Joshua wrote down the number, noting that the area code was out of state.

"The other thing he said," Ham continued, "is to make sure your phone isn't bugged."

"Bugged? Is he for real, or just being paranoid?" Michelle asked.

Ham responded, "Hey, I'm just the messenger."

"How did he sound?" Joshua asked.

"He talked fast, which is unusual for him, you know, but he didn't sound panicky or anything. I heard a lot of clatter and noise and voices in the background, like dishes and stuff. Sounded like he was in a restaurant or a bar."

"Ham," Michelle said, "We think you should be on the call, also. Can you conference with us at eleven o'clock?"

"Consider it done. The hospital has conference calling, so I'll just stay here at work for a while and place the call. Remember to check your phones and the house for bugs." Ham said goodbye and disconnected.

"Is that incredible or what?" Michelle was excited as she and Joshua returned to the dining table. "Detained and threatened. He didn't say kidnaped and tortured. Who would have expected such high adventure from Bruce, of all people?"

"I wonder if he escaped or they let him go?"

"I wonder who kidnaped him and why?"

"The threshold question," Joshua said, "Is whether he was really detained by these guys, these 'assholes in wingtips'? Maybe he just decided to disappear, for reasons unknown at this time, and now he thinks it's time to reappear, so he comes up with this crazy story."

"Joshua, you're scaring me. What are you saying?"

"At this point, everybody is a suspect until we're sure they're not."

"You don't know him like I do."

"Maybe not, but I know, for starters, that he's computer literate." Joshua cut another slice of the medallion of pork tenderloin, sorting out the bell peppers and leaving them in a small yellow mound on the side of his plate. "Let's be objective. He was fired by the Cove, so now he's got the classic motive of revenge. We know he got into Curtis' computer, which is networked to PSM's system. Suppose he planted the applet at PSM, then got into Curtis' computer and used it to transfer funds out of the Cove's reserves? Wouldn't you agree that such activities would be a good reason to disappear for a few days? He could have gone out of town to collect the cash he stole."

"But, why would he come back?"

Joshua paused with his mouth full. "But, he hasn't

really come back, has he? We're just going to talk to him on the phone. We don't know where he is and, actually, he could be anywhere. Isn't that a fact?"

Michelle looked uneasily at Joshua. "Would you stop playing the lawyer? You just have to question everything."

"Well, I thought you wanted my help." Joshua paused. "Now, we certainly have a memorable evening, what with our first kiss and our first argument."

"And, all within ten minutes," Michelle said, looking down at her unfinished dinner.

They glared at each other and completed their dinners in silence.

After they finished clearing the table, Michelle said, "What's this about checking for bugs? How are we supposed to do that?"

"You've seen them do it on TV. Let's take both of your remote phones apart and see if there are any bugs. Once we're sure your phones are clean, we'll just take them outside and talk."

At five minutes after eleven o'clock, Ham's conference call was ringing somewhere out of state. Joshua and Michelle were sitting outside on her deck with the two remote phones.

Joshua was surprised when a woman's voice answered. He said, "I'm sorry, we must have the wrong number."

"Wait. Is this Joshua?"

"Maybe. Depends on who wants to know." He looked over at Michelle and shrugged his shoulders.

"Good. This is Veronica and I have your friend right here, safe and sound. I'll put him on the line."

"Hello, Joshua? This is *me*. Just refer to me as your friend."

"How do I know it's really you? Tell me something that only my real friend would know, like his mother's social security number."

"Hey friend, this is Michelle! I recognize your voice,

so ignore Joshua, he's just kidding. We've been worried sick about you. It's great to hear from you. We were wondering if we ever would again."

"And this is Ham—how you doin' friend? Now that we've all introduced ourselves, who's the woman who answered the phone? Is she a new friend of the friend?"

"Her name is Veronica, and she's a beautiful human being. Ronnie's letting me stay at her place for awhile." Bruce was sure that nothing had been said thus far that would give away his location. "Did you all check your phones for listening devices? Are you far away from any possible bugs?"

They all assured Bruce that everything was okay, and that he could talk candidly.

"It's a fascinating and exciting adventure, so fasten your seatbelts, my friends," Bruce began. "I'll give you all the gory details of capture, torture, escape, and revenge. Well, that may be a bit embellished. Please hold your applause until the end." He recounted everything from his unauthorized inspection of Curtis' office to becoming the maitre d' in a nice restaurant. "Only in America, right?" Bruce ended his story.

"Bravo, my friend," Michelle shouted.

"Sounds like your first novel. I want a part in the movie," said Ham.

"You'll all have a role to play," Bruce laughed.

Then it was Bruce's turn to listen as Joshua, Ham, and Michelle took turns relating events since his sudden disappearance.

"So, please tell us, friend," continued Joshua, "What exactly did you find in Curtis' office that started all this commotion?"

"Well, after Curtis fired me, I noted that he was having several meetings with these two guys who wear black suits and too much gel on their hair. Later, I learned their names were Bedford and Kosankis. And, Curtis had lots of long-distance phone calls back and forth with them. I wanted to find out what the meetings and phone calls were all about."

Bruce described the proposal from the East Coast management company that he found in Curtis' office, and his own attempt to install a virus, called 'the guillotine,' in Curtis' computer. The virus was set to take effect on the fourteenth, which, of course, Bruce pointed out, was Bastille Day. He admitted that he didn't know how it worked, but happily described the guillotine scene that signaled the death of Curtis' hard drive. "Do you guys know if the virus worked?"

Michelle looked at Joshua and said, "Curtis hasn't mentioned anything about that. Now we know why. It might implicate him in the hiring of Bedford and Kosankis."

"Friend," Joshua said, "do you know if these goons are still looking for you?"

"I have no idea, but I'm on alert, twenty-four/seven. I'm sure they are. These guys were so determined to find out what I saw on Curtis' computer and to get the disk that I downloaded from his files, that I'm sure Curtis would stop at nothing."

"Well, we have the disk, but we haven't been able to decode it," Michelle said. "What information is on it?"

Bruce paused before responding. "It has something to do with all the money Curtis has taken through bribes, extortion schemes, kickbacks, etc. No wonder he loves being president of the Cove. He's making more than he did selling sewer pipe."

"First, he bought his election," said Michelle. "Now, he's buying his retirement."

It was Joshua's turn. He explained how he opened

Sewerpipe.wpd on Bruce's disk, but it was distorted. "It looked like the data you copied was encoded in Curtis' computer."

"No, that's not it. I encrypted the data on that disk, and that's why you can't read it. And only I have the key to the code. That's my ticket to stay alive. Even if somehow they got their hands on that disk, they'd need me to decode it."

Joshua said, "So, if the data on the disk is Curtis' financial affairs, he may have some serious problems with the IRS. He's worried that the information you have could create tax headaches for him. Not to mention some attention from the FBI."

"You're right, Joshua. Curtis may have a huge tax problem, even criminal charges," responded Bruce. "That's why Curtis was wetting his pants, that's why he hired those two fart mouths to get the disk."

"On the other hand," Michelle ventured, "If you were dead, they wouldn't worry about the disk. No one else could read it."

Bruce said wearily, "Okay, so maybe there's a small hole in my analysis."

A long silence ensued. No one knew what to say. Finally, Ham spoke. "Friend, when are you coming back to…uh…never mind. Just when are you coming back?"

Bruce looked at Ronnie, who was sitting next to him on the couch. He reached out and put his arm around her shoulder. "What would I do if I came back now? I'd be looking over my shoulder all the time. Here, at least, I'm reasonably safe in a relatively remote area and, on top of that, you guys should know that I'm having the time of my life down here. First, I've got a chance to take over as concierge of the entire place. Frankly, they need me desperately. Second, Ronnie and I want to be together, maybe see where this thing goes. Third, remember that I mentioned *revenge* at the beginning of my story? Listen to this plan, my friends, and tell me what you think. Each of you will play an important role in this little drama."

Bruce summarized his plan, describing to his friends what each of their roles would be. Michelle would set the trap, Joshua would enlist the sheriff, and Ham would be in charge of reparations.

It was well after midnight before Joshua finally left Michelle's condo and walked tiredly across the dimly lit parking lot to the visitor spaces where Old Blue was parked. His mind was so busy sifting through a dozen strategies that he didn't notice the dark sedan, its driver slouching behind the steering wheel, carefully watching Joshua's movements.

37

Curtis cradled the phone to his ear with one hand and held a fat cigar in the other. He leaned his leather chair back as far as it would go. "Look, Bedford, it seems to me that there's really no comparison between the options. Behind Door Number One, if your company takes over as the Cove's manager, you get our business and access to reserves, but that's only one account. Behind Door Number Two, if you acquire PSM, you get all their accounts. That's two dozen accounts, with access to all their reserves, including the Cove." Curtis reached for his coffee. "The difference is quite simple. What part don't you understand?"

From the back of Curtis' office, trumpets announced the opening movement of Bach's *Magnificat*. Curtis rested his cigar in the brass ashtray shaped like a bidet and conducted the orchestra with his free hand.

"The difference is simple," responded Bedford while he tapped on his calculator. "The difference is it takes one million dollars to get the prize behind Door Number Two. And that's not chump change."

"But the potential gain is exponential. Instead of servicing one account, you'd own a company with two dozen accounts—that's twenty-four associations with a total of about seven thousand units. Instead of dealing with eight hundred thousand dollars in the Cove's reserves, you'd be dealing with over five million dollars in reserves, given all the accounts at PSM. Plus, you'd become a major player in the Midwest community management market overnight. As my granddaddy used to say, 'You gotta spend money to make money.' "

"Yeah, yeah. Look, Curtis, you can skip the lecture in Economics 101. What's your interest in all this?"

"What's my interest?" Curtis repeated the question, stalling to divine an appropriate response. The *Magnificat* had ended, and he paused to admire a woodwind solo introducing the "Domine Deus" movement of Vivaldi's *Gloria*. *Sounds like an oboe*, he thought. "Let's just say that I'm a guy who likes to broker profitable deals."

"What about this Michelle? Why should we keep her? We only hire our own people because they're more loyal and easier to control."

"Bedford, I thought you were smarter than that. How do you think we're going to get them to agree to the sale? We tell the Michelle girl that she's important to keep the business going, so we're willing to double her salary." Curtis was starting to rock anxiously in his chair, sensing that he was nearing the finish line on this deal.

"It's way too much money," Bedford persisted.

Fashioning himself as the consummate dealmaker, Curtis couldn't play the role without a cigar clenched in his teeth. He exhaled a plume of blue smoke as his mind clicked through the factors. *I just need one more carrot for these guys. Maybe I could cut my commission on the front end and get a percentage of the take on the back end? Or, take an equity interest in the parent company? That way, I'd be a silent partner and have a hand in the reserves.* "I'll tell you what, Bedford," he said, accenting each word as his lips worked around the cigar. "Let's give the Michelle girl two options, either of which would be attractive to her. We'll force the girl to choose between two financial scenarios she likes. It would be better for us."

Bedford interrupted him mid-sentence. "Why do you keep calling her a 'girl?' I've never met her, but she sounds like a pretty shrewd woman to me."

"Last time I checked, it wasn't discriminatory to refer to any female by the word 'girl.' Although the way this country's going, that's probably the next thing the courts will put into a protected class, and they'll make it illegal to leer or say 'tits' and 'ass.' We already got girls in the Army and on our submarines, don't we?"

"Curtis, you're in the wrong era. You belong in the nineteenth century."

"Anyway, as I was saying, we give her a choice between two options, both of which she'd like. It's better than forcing her to choose between 'yes' and 'no.' We make a counteroffer, say, at five hundred thousand dollars for PSM if she doesn't stay and six hundred thousand if she does stay, with double her salary."

"It's still way too much money," Bedford objected. "Here's the deal. You counter at two hundred thousand, and we'll see where it goes from there. Leave Michelle out of it. We're interested in buying PSM, but only if we can steal it. And, you've gotta keep all the contingencies about reviewing their books and accounts—that's our escape hatch because we can kill the deal and still have the information on their other clients."

"No, here's the deal, pal." Curtis bolted upright in his chair, his face turning the color of his hair, his veins pulsating in his thick neck. Jabbing the air with his cigar for emphasis, he bellowed, "We offer the scenarios just like I said. One more thing, I get a percent of the take, plus an equity interest in your company. And, if you don't like that, you can just kiss my rosy…"

"You shut up and listen, Curtis. You have no idea what you're doing or who you're dealing with."

"No, you listen to me. You don't know who *you're* dealing with," Curtis roared. "Just let me run with this thing. My business instincts are solid. I know exactly what I'm doing, and don't you forget it." Curtis leaned back in his leather chair. He took a long draw from his cigar, exhaling the smoke slowly. The triumphant strings and trumpets echoed through his office, concluding Vivaldi's *Gloria* with the final movement, "Cum Sancto."

Curtis had reached his favorite point in negotiating a business deal—the stare down where one side or the other must blink. It would not be him. He stared into space contemplating his strategic plan. Involuntarily, his fingertips began to drum lightly on his belly.

IT WAS TWO O'CLOCK in the afternoon in Zurich. The Consultant could hardly bear to open his eyes as he lay sprawled in the king size bed at the Hotel Baur Au Lac. His mouth felt like it was filled with cotton balls. A heavy weight seemed to be on top of him, pressing him into the bed, preventing him from getting up. He groaned painfully as he tried to roll onto his side. His head was being pounded by rotating hammers that exploded each time they struck his brain, and they were synchronized with the bolts of sunlight that shot into his eyes. Everything above his toes ached. His clothes were somewhere, but he couldn't remember where. His only thought was that he had been drugged.

Rubbing his eyes, he mustered enough strength to drag his body out of bed and thrash about until he found the bathroom. He splashed cold water on his face and reached for a linen towel furnished without extra cost. His suite at the lovely Hotel Baur cost six hundred dollars a night. But, it was on the lake. In a private park. The memory of last night was starting to return.

He wandered back to the bedroom, holding a cold washcloth on his throbbing forehead. Glancing down at the bed, he could see an indentation still in the pillow where the woman had been. He sat down on the edge of the bed, dim fragments of last night coming into focus. There was dinner with—Anna, that's her name—at a very nice restaurant. There were drinks and dancing at an upscale disco nightclub. The last dance was slow, and she held him tightly with various body parts rubbing together. Then, back to this hotel room.

On his second trip to the bathroom, he saw the note on the dresser, and he groped across the room to pick it up. It was handwritten on hotel stationery.

> Rolf, you are a wonderful dancer and lover. Thanks so much for the smart watch. I just love it. And thanks for the money—you're much too generous. I left enough to pay for the hotel and your flight back to the States. Ciao, Anna.

Followed by a postscript,

> Don't bother looking for me at the shop, yesterday was my last day. And my name is not Anna.

An overwhelming feeling of panic struck as he found his suit jacket on the floor of the closet and searched the inside pockets. All that remained of his money was a pair of one thousand dollar bills. He felt his wrist and found it bare. Next, he grabbed his wallet and inspected the contents. Thankfully, she didn't take his credit cards. Suddenly his stomach churned, and he could taste the bile in his mouth. The currency floated to the carpet as he bolted to the bathroom, where he violently retched last night's dinner into the six hundred dollar bidet.

THE CONSULTANT FASTENED HIS seatbelt for the flight from Zurich to New York. His mind raced over the events of the past two days, always ending with the same refrain. *How could I have been so stupid? I've got to start thinking with the right muscle.*

The little diversion at the Hotel Baur had cost him a small fortune not to mention his pride, but he couldn't exactly report the theft to the police. How would that play? *A whore-thief stole the money I stole?* It would also cost him precious time. An old song ran through his mind, "Mama said there'd be days like this…"

From now on, he would be all business. He'd go home, transfer the rest of PSM's money and disappear.

THOUSANDS OF MILES AWAY, Michelle and Mac were leaving the bank, adjusting their eyes to the noon sunlight. They'd spent all morning reviewing the bank's records of daily transactions. Everything appeared normal. All deposits, checks drawn, and transfers to reserves were accurately reported, until a transaction that occurred several days ago in the bank's computer records. Michelle was the first to spot it, an unexplained electronic transfer of one hundred thousand dollars from the Cove's reserve account.

The bank officers, who looked at the printout and thought it was another inter-account transfer of PSM funds, had been just as surprised as Michelle and Mac. They called in the bank's CITO—the Chief Information Technology Officer—to review the computer printout. The analyst could only determine that the funds apparently were sent electronically to an eight-digit account at another bank. The officer in charge of international transactions thought the recipient account resembled the system used by the Swiss, but she couldn't obtain any further information due to the strict confidentiality maintained by Swiss bankers.

Mac and Michelle headed across the parking lot toward Michelle's Explorer and drove the four blocks back to the office. Mac was flipping through the computer printout while Michelle drove. After a few minutes, Mac said, "We're really exposed on this. Whoever planted the applet was able to transfer a hundred thousand dollars out of one of our accounts, right under our noses. He must know there's over five million dollars in our reserve accounts. He could be transferring more money out of our accounts right now, as we talk. Why would he stop at a piddling one hundred thousand when he could get five mil?"

Michelle's face scrunched up. "Any ideas about what we should do first?"

"Well," Mac ventured with uncertainty, "suppose we bring Dr. FIT back, and have him transfer all our data to a new hard drive. To get rid of the applet, we may need to terminate the web browser, then re-install a whole new system. Very complicated, very expensive."

"And, it could mean that we wipe out the only information we've got to catch the hacker and recover the money." Michelle gathered her thoughts. "So, what about this approach? We keep right on with our present system, with the applet in place, and use it to follow the money. It's the only way we're going to catch him."

"And, it's probably the only way we're going to recover the funds. But, we're racing against time. The applet could be shuffling our funds right now."

"I'll drop you at the office," Michelle said, "I'm due to meet His Lowness for lunch in a few minutes. He called first thing this morning. He was in rare form even for Curtis. Said he had made exciting progress on the sale contract and practically demanded lunch today. I'm meeting him at

Michael's Restaurant again. I'm sure he'll have a counteroffer to convey. Which will work out just fine, because I've got a message for him—from Bruce."

"You know," Mac mused, "I don't want to sell PSM now, not at any price. We're just getting our business to the point where we can really increase our client base and our profit margin. But, in view of what we learned at the bank, this might be the right time to sell."

THE SETTING SUN CAST a glow of rose, pink, and lavender hues through the strands of clouds in the western sky and onto the buildings. The Grand Canal reflected the sky and buildings in a waterscape swirled into a kaleidoscope by the wake of boats. Throngs of tourists pushed their way across the crowded Ponti de Rialto. Below, vaparettos, the waterbuses of Venice, plus motorboats used as water taxis, and timeworn gondolas churned their way through the murky waters of the canal.

Venice might be rotting slowly into the sea, but it still managed to extend its special magic, its poetic enchantment. Venice's 70,000 residents were overcome by twelve million tourists who choked the city's alleys and Campos every year and gratefully left behind hundreds of millions of dollars. Philip and Angela beheld the awesome, almost religious beauty of the sunset from atop the the Ponti de Rialto, one of the four hundred bridges that crossed the more than one hundred fifty canals that connected, or separated, Venice.

"Ah, Venice, I love you," sighed Angela, her head turning slowly to see everything, letting her senses absorb all the sights, sounds, and smells, "and I see your great beauty locked in a death struggle with decay."

Philip was preoccupied surveying the dark canal below. "Yeah, but you won't love this. Just look where their garbage goes. It's like one huge sewer filled with water."

"I'm hungry—take me to dinner in Venice." Angela took Philip's arm, and they walked down the east side of the bridge, heading into the labyrinth of narrow passages that they hoped would lead to Piazza San Marco.

They entered a narrow alleyway just before the piazza, where they encountered a group of street vendors, three African men dressed in their native clothing—long robes of bright colors. Several dozen leather purses were displayed on a large red blanket covering most of the alley, making it difficult to pass. As Philip and Angela approached, one of the men blocked Angela's path, holding a purse in front of her face. With a heavy British accent he extolled the beauty of a brown leather purse. "Soft leather, pretty lady, for you half price, only fifty dollars." Trying not to be rude, Angela casually inspected the purse. Philip walked on.

"My brother and I have just arrived from Ethiopia, and we hope to make some money to send for our families," he pleaded.

Looking up, Angela didn't see Philip. She became nervous and turned quickly to leave. But, the purse man blocked her way, "Wait, you're such a nice lady, I'll sell you this purse for only forty dollars." Growing anxious, she thanked the purse man, squeezed past him and hurried down the alleyway. The purse man ran after her, "Please, I can't go back to Ethiopia, just give me twenty-five dollars for this lovely purse."

Angela saw Philip waiting at the corner. "Where were you? Didn't you see I needed some help back there?"

"You weren't attacked, were you?" Philip said. "So what's the big deal?"

"Your sensitivity is underwhelming," said Angela, staring into Philip's face.

Dusk lingered on the piazza like a thin veil of pale

yellow silk, shrouding the alluring beauty of San Marco. The gold mosaic of the basilica was still brilliant where a streak of sunlight broke through. Under the watchful eye of the great bell tower, the piazza bustled with activity. Thousands of visitors stood mesmerized by San Marco, loitering in quiet conversation or enjoying wine at one of the numerous terrace cafés.

A long line of tourists waited outside a shop to buy gellato, the thickest, creamiest ice cream known to kiss human lips. Hustlers practiced their slick scams on unwary tourists. Street vendors stood at their carts on the piazza and hawked sacks of birdseed, which parents bought to quiet their pestering children. Invariably, the parents would then whip out their cameras and memorialize the cute kids feeding pigeons on their shoulders while San Marco was relegated to a blurry background.

"Pigeons are really disgusting," Philip said. "The pigeon is the birds' answer to donkeys."

They stopped for dinner at the Florian, a small café on the piazza and ordered the sampler of seafood for an antipasto, followed by filetto de sogliola—filet of sole—and an order of spaghetti alle vongole, which they divided. A bottle of chianti and a basket of dense local bread with a small plate of seasoned olive oil completed the meal.

They concentrated on their food and, unlike their previous days in Paris, conversation was forced and uncomfortable, occurring in fragments. Philip mentioned something about the exchange rate between the dollar and the euro, and said, "Before the new euro, Italians used a wheelbarrow to carry their lira around."

Angela responded, "Venice is known for its fine glassware. Can we take a waterbus to Murano tomorrow?"

The quiet was interrupted by the sounds of men running outside the restaurant. Startled and curious, Angela looked up to see the three Ethiopian purse men galloping by, their colorful robes flowing behind them, one of them carrying the red blanket full of purses like a giant knapsack bouncing on his shoulder. A few seconds later, two black-uniformed Italian policemen, batons clutched in their hands, huffed by in pursuit.

Philip complained about the mosquitoes. Angela coveted the linens. Philip abhorred the stench. Angela longed to hear the choir singing in the Basilica San Marco. Philip had just commenced a detailed and disgusting description of the rats in the canals when the waiter arrived with tiny glasses of grappa, the potent liqueur that has its unique origins in Venice.

Outside, a string quartet played Rossini overtures, creating a perfect picture of romance in Venice. Yet, Philip and Angela strolled in silence across the piazza under a black sky and a dark mood. The rising tide created large pools of water on the piazza. The upside-down reflection of San Marco reminded Angela of how much Philip had changed in the past two days. She noticed that the pigeons had deserted the piazza, deciding it was time to roost.

Back in their room at the Hotel Flora, Angela collapsed on the bed and watched old American movies that had been dubbed into Italian and were shown through the night on TV. Philip, accompanied by the sounds of gurgling plumbing in the ancient hotel, tapped out a short email on his notebook computer.

Re: Project Retirement: Again, advise status ASAP.

38

Michelle was twenty minutes late for her lunch meeting with Curtis. She hurried across the parking lot, threading her way through parked cars, carrying her linen suit jacket over her arm, and checking her face in her compact mirror as she walked toward the entrance to Michael's Italian Restaurant.

It was sweltering. No surprise in the middle of July, in the middle of the day, in the middle of an asphalt parking lot, in the middle of St. Louis. Her pantyhose were sticking in all the wrong places. *It's sure hard to look cool when it's so damn hot.*

Once inside the air-conditioned restaurant, she paused to calm herself. She took several deep breaths. All she could smell was the heavenly aroma of garlic. The headwaiter, wearing a black suit with a red vest, gently took her elbow and said, "Mr. Carlton has a table at the rear. Please come with me."

As Michelle approached the table, Curtis scooted briskly out of the booth, arms fully extended toward her as if they were lovers meeting for lunch. His eyebrows arched and his full lips smiled with anticipation. *Oh, no, he expects a kiss!* Before she could dodge aside, Curtis had his thick arms around her back, pulling her body tightly against his. The delightful garlic aroma that filled the restaurant gave way to Curtis' disgusting cigar breath.

"Michelle, it's sure good to see you," he exhaled into her neck. "It's been awhile, and I've missed you. How *are* you?"

All she could think of was the football player from Tulsa who lusted after her during her sophomore year at Mizzou, whose idea of an "Oklahoma Hello" was five minutes of pawing her. "Yes, Curtis, it's sure been a long time. Everything's fine. How's Evelyn—is she still enjoying her weaving?"

Curtis helped her into the booth, which was small and elbow shaped, with barely enough room for two people. Their knees touched under the table. "Ev is weaving up a storm. It's wonderful to see her so engaged in a hobby. She loves staying home with her warp and heddles and whatever. It leaves me free to do my business. How about you—been keeping busy?"

"No, Curtis, I've been loafing a lot lately. Usually, I just put my feet up on my little desk, between the stacks of files, and take long naps."

Michelle looked up to measure his eyes. Curtis, not knowing if he should take her seriously, returned her gaze with an expression that was both bemused and amused. The waiter appeared with the menus and described the day's lunch specials. Michelle settled on the caesar salad and iced tea. Curtis ordered a steak, medium rare, grilled baby potatoes and a draft Michelob.

After they had ordered, Curtis watched Michelle intently. Although she averted his gaze, Michelle knew his hot eyes were on her breasts and it made her anxious. Suddenly, he placed his heavy hand on the inside of her knee and said, "You're really beautiful, do you know that?" She thought she might puke. "But," Curtis continued, "as my granddaddy always used to say, 'business before pleasure.' Ha, ha."

Michelle reached down and firmly removed his hand from her knee. She picked up her glass of water and swallowed slowly, trying to keep her stomach, and her head, clear. *How will I ever get through this?*

He placed a copy of the sale contract in front of her. She glanced down at it, but the printing was blurry. Curtis was droning on about some of the minor changes to the transaction. His words became dim and fuzzy, his voice seemed far away, as if he were speaking through a long pipe. Michelle, suddenly realizing that she was lightheaded, interrupted, "Curtis, I feel like I'm going to hurl." She abruptly excused herself from the table, holding a napkin to her mouth, and rushed to the ladies room.

Michelle splashed cold water on her face, and crouched with her head between her knees, holding a damp paper towel to her forehead. As the color gradually returned to her face, she lingered in front of the mirror and put on fresh lipstick. Her thoughts returned to that vulgar octopus in the restaurant. She promised herself that she would regain the high ground and be more aggressive. She wondered about Curtis' so-called "undisclosed principal." *Why were they so determined to buy PSM, and what were their motivations? What was the connection between Curtis' rush to buy PSM and the theft of reserves? The two events didn't seem compatible. Why would someone want to acquire PSM if he knew that all the reserves were gone?*

Michelle returned to Curtis' table after a few minutes. Curtis stood at attention as she approached and offered a hand while she scooted into the tiny booth. Michelle looked embarrassed and said, "Sorry about that, it must be that I was outside in the heat so much this morning. All of a sudden, I didn't feel well, but now I'm much better, refreshed. You were saying?"

Curtis drank half of the glass of Michelob in two gulps. "I'll summarize the highlights of the counteroffer." He emphasized the optional terms. She could design her own position with the company. "The buyer is a sophisticated management company, located…uh…out of town, so it's not one of your competitors. And, they're smart enough to know that you'd be vital to the continued success of the company, so they'll double your salary if you'd stay to manage your accounts. Especially the Cove. Ha, ha."

Michelle looked at him. *His smirk is even more disgusting than merely putrid.* "What's in it for Mac?" Michelle felt a rise of anger, but kept her voice level and low. "What do I tell her? This offer looks like I'm selling her out."

"Mac?" Curtis was momentarily stunned. He had focused so much on Michelle that he had completely overlooked her partner and the possibility that Mac could have objections. "Ah, Lindsay McPherson." *The other girl at PSM*, he thought. "Well, uh…" he stammered, "what do you think she wants to get out of this?"

"Mac doesn't want to sell at all. Not at any price. And I certainly can't force her to sell, nor could I sell only my share without her consent. Not that I'd even think of doing that to my partner."

"She'll get a nice package. You tell her that."

"What if she doesn't want 'a package?' "

Curtis stuck out his chin. Beads of sweat were forming on his forehead, and he wiped his face with his red bandanna. Michelle could see the blood vessels in his temples beginning to pulsate. "No, that's not an option," he boomed, his voice rising and detonating like thunder in a fast-moving summer storm. "That's not how business people make a deal."

He found it difficult to control his temper. *When will women learn how to negotiate like men?* "You don't just say 'no!' " The storm had now reached its full power,

Curtis' fists pounding the air for emphasis. Michelle retreated to the side of the booth, trying to get as far away as possible until the worst of the storm passed, silently vowing not to subject herself to such abuse again. "You make a reasonable counteroffer, that's how it's done," Curtis thundered. *You dumb broad*, he seemed tempted to add. His eyes were menacing, his expression full of disdain. "And, as you can see, there's a deadline for your response. You have forty-eight hours," he said.

"Surely, my cup runneth over." Michelle looked at him from the corner of her eye.

Curtis leaned back and studied Michelle's face for a moment. "You and Mac would get a helluva lot of money for a company you started with nothing. You'd get a huge return. Sell and move on with your lives. You'd both be rich. Just let me know in forty-eight hours."

Michelle held up her copy of the contract. "You're overlooking Section 27, which I added. It provides, and I quote, 'Notwithstanding any other provision herein to the contrary, this Contract is further contingent upon review and approval by Seller's attorney not later than ten (10) days after the date of Seller's acceptance.' "

Curtis reached for the contract and read Section 27 to himself, a frown curling his lips downward. The red bandanna appeared again as Curtis swiped at his forehead. More likely, he was stalling, trying to navigate a path out of the attorney's review. Just then, the waiter arrived with their food.

They ate in silence for a long while, exchanging glances of lust and distrust.

Finally, Curtis ventured to break the silence. "Did I tell you that the board at the Cove is thinking of sending the guards for CPR training? What do you think?"

Grateful for anything else to talk about, Michelle

responded, "Probably not a bad idea, considering the age of some of the residents. Of course, if the board goes ahead, make sure your people—they're attendants, not guards—are appropriately trained and competent. And, remind the residents that it's not a substitute for calling 911 immediately."

But, Curtis wasn't paying attention. His mind was far away, dreaming of Michelle giving him CPR if he were to collapse on the couch in his office.

"Speaking of your people," she continued, trying to get Curtis' attention, "I heard through the grapevine that Bruce is working down at the Riverway Restaurant. Isn't that great news—that he got a good job?"

"Huh? What did you say about Bruce?" Curtis lumbered out of his fantasy, back into the reality of Michelle's startling disclosure. "I thought Bruce was ... You say he's working? Where?"

"At the Riverway Restaurant."

"Really? Isn't that part of some fancy lodge down in the Ozarks?"

"That's the one. It's outside Calvin's Creek. He works the dinner shift."

"Yes, that is wonderful news. Very interesting, indeed." Curtis' eyes opened wide and shifted to the windows. His gaze was far away, his jowls rolling with tremors.

"Curtis, do you feel okay?"

39

Curtis' focus finally returned to the restaurant, to the tiny elbow shaped booth, and to Michelle sitting next to him. He abruptly said something about needing to get back to the office, and quickly paid the luncheon bill in cash.

A few minutes ago, Curtis had all day. Now, suddenly, he's a man in a big rush, Michelle mused.

He waved goodbye to Michelle in the parking lot, then padded as quickly as he could in his deck shoes to the big blue Buick. As soon as the engine was running, his stubby finger was jabbing at his car cell phone. He switched on the air conditioner as he waited for an answer.

"Bedford? Dammit, it's about time you answered. Do you have any idea how long I've been bouncing around your phone system?"

"Curtis? That's why we've got voice mail. Why didn't you use it? You need to get with the twentieth century, man. On second thought, you missed that one. Better try for the twenty-first century now."

"Screw your damn voice mail. And screw your buddy with the earring. And while I'm at it, screw you, too." Curtis was sitting there in his hot car, fuming and screaming into the hands-free microphone.

"Slow down, Curtis, and just tell me what's wrong now."

"You know damn well what's wrong, Bedford."

"Is it the sale contract? Is it dead?" Bedford covered the mouthpiece on his phone while he waved for Kosankis to come in.

"No, not that," Curtis stormed, "you *putas* told me that you didn't know where Bruce was because a local gang took him. But, you caught a break. I found out where he is."

Bedford strained to listen. "What do you mean, you know where Bruce is?"

Kosankis limped into the office and, hearing Bedford's last remark, hissed under his breath, "Oh, shit."

Curtis continued his rage, pounding the steering wheel. "Don't you screw with me. Brucie is alive and well, working in a fancy restaurant. And I still don't have that disk you promised to get. Now, I'd suggest that you get your butts…"

"Hold on, Curtis," Bedford interrupted, "Kosankis just came in. I'll put you on speaker."

"Hello, Mr. Carlton," Kosankis grunted. "What's this about Brucie?"

"Skip the crap, boys. You gotta finish the job, and you know it." Curtis' face was red and the veins in his temples were bulging. "I promise that I'll deliver the sales contract for you, but you've gotta get me that disk. You do that, and I'll split my commission with the two of you."

"Why not give us the whole commission, you cheap bastard," Bedford said.

Ignoring Bedford's last comment, Curtis continued, "Bruce is at the Riverway Restaurant, outside of a small town called Calvin's Creek, working the dinner shift. It'll be like shootin' fish in a barrel. Just don't get caught, for Chrissake."

Bedford snapped to attention, clicked his heels, and gave a mock salute to the telephone. Kosankis simply gave the one-finger salute. They hung up, grabbed their suit jackets, and goose-stepped out of the office.

JOSHUA DOWNSHIFTED OLD BLUE into third gear to finish the climb up a long hill in the rugged Ozarks. It was late in the afternoon, but he was only about thirty minutes from Calvin's Creek when his cell phone rang.

"Joshua? This is Michelle."

"Hi, there! Good to hear your voice."

"I can barely hear you," Michelle shouted. "It sounds like you're in the middle of a hurri- *crackle*. Do you have the windows down, or what?"

Joshua responded loudly. "I love a drive in the country. Beethoven's Third is on the CD player, turned up to thirteen, of course. The muffler developed a little problem, so that explains the growling noise you hear in the background. The A/C isn't working, that's why I've got the windows down, and that explains all the static on the line. It's just the wind."

"Oh. Are you sure that's all?"

"Well, Old Blue still starts, runs like hell, and stops. What more should I demand of her?"

"I'm just concerned that if Old Blue broke *crackle* where you are, you'd never find a mechanic to help you. Please think about getting a new *crackle*. You could keep Old Blue as your Sunday car."

"Don't worry, Michelle. That's why I keep a trunk full of spare parts. I've got fan belts, hoses, a gas pump, a *crackle* pump, alternator…"

"All right, Mr. Stubborn." Michelle interrupted.

"…a complete set of metric wrenches, fire extinguisher, flares, sleeping bag…"

"Joshua, stop! Here's why I'm *crackle*. Actually, I have two things to tell you." Joshua turned down the volume on

Beethoven's funeral march. "Mac and I went to the bank this morning," Michelle said, "and we got some good news and some bad news." Michelle was sitting in her office, but lowered her voice anyway, just to be sure the staff didn't overhear. "The bad news first. Whoever planted the applet used an electronic transfer to move one hundred *crackle* dollars out of the Cove's reserves. Now for the good news: it was only one hundred thousand."

"I couldn't hear all of that," Joshua spoke loudly. "These digital cell phones really need more work. Who do you think it was?"

"It makes sense, doesn't it? Remember Bruce's notion that *crackle* has a scheme to get at the reserves? If Curtis can move the Cove's reserves around, why not out of the country?" Michelle related the bank's opinion that the funds were transferred to a foreign account, probably Swiss. "Curtis figures that if the Cove has fat reserves, so do our other clients. But, he can't get to the other reserves on his computer, so he plants the applet."

"Do you know if he's been to Switzerland recently? How can we find out?"

Michelle tapped her pencil on the desk as she pondered Joshua's questions. "I don't know and I don't *crackle*."

"While we think about that, what was the other thing you wanted to talk about?"

"Oh, Curtis called this morning. He was *crackle* to move the sale contract, so I met him for lunch."

"Now, I'm starting to get jealous. He sees you more than I do."

"Oh, sure, Joshua. It was a horrible, ghastly, *crackle* experience. I'm beginning to believe that any form of communication with Curtis is sexual harassment. Anyway, his undisclosed *crackle* made an interesting counteroffer."

"Really? No kidding?" Joshua paused, straining to hear Michelle, a puzzled expression on his face. Then he laughed. "Maybe it's a good time to sell, just when your clients' funds are being ripped off."

"That's funny. It's the same thing Mac said."

"There's something wrong with this picture, but I just can't put my finger on it right now. Why is Curtis pushing this deal?" His voice trailed off.

"My real agenda for my meeting Curtis today was to start Phase *crackle* of Bruce's plan. I baited the hook, and Curtis took it and ran. You should have been there to see the *crackle* on his face when I told him Bruce was alive and well and working at the Riverway Restaurant. I could hardly keep a straight *crackle*."

"Sounds great. But, how do we know for sure?"

"I *am* sure. You'd be *crackle*, too, if you'd seen his reaction. Anyway, I just finished a blind call to Boston, and asked to speak to either Bedford or *crackle*. Guess what?"

"I give."

"Both of the assholes in wingtips had just left the office 'on a business *crackle*,' and aren't expected back for a few days."

"Sounds like we're ready to start Phase Two."

"That's your part. I'll call Ham and let him know where we are."

Joshua removed his foot from the accelerator and let Old Blue coast down a long hill that would carry him through a narrow hollow and then to the bluff where the cozy town of Calvin's Creek was nestled. County seat of Lead County.

The narrow highway became Main Street as Joshua entered Calvin's Creek as scheduled, at five o'clock in the afternoon, and drove into the town square in the midst of rush hour traffic. He'd never given it much thought, but small towns had rush hour traffic, just like their big brothers and sisters. However, in the small town, rush hour lasts only five minutes.

He had to circle the town square, which was located appropriately in the heart of town, to find an open parking space where he eased Old Blue into an angled spot across the street from the Georgian revival courthouse of Lead County. The sheriff's office was in the courthouse, along with the offices all the other county officials.

He carried his suit jacket and loaded his black leather bag over one shoulder and his WinBook notebook computer over the other. Unlike his other legal files, for which he maintained careful notes, Joshua didn't have a single memo related to Bruce or the break-in at PSM. Even so, he was a lawyer, so he thought the attaché should accompany him. He couldn't walk into an appointment empty handed. It just wouldn't look professional.

He used the keyless remote to lock the car and arm the alarm, although he doubted that such precautions were necessary in small town America. On several occasions in the past, he'd left Old Blue on city streets, unlocked and with the keys in the ignition, hoping that someone would drive it away, but even those philanthropic efforts were defeated. Most decent car thieves in the city were more discriminating. They took his cell phone and stereo, but refused to touch Old Blue.

Joshua walked across the small park in the center of the town square. The shade of the huge old sycamore trees provided temporary relief from the afternoon heat. He strolled past a bronze statue of a war hero astride a great horse. Joshua guessed he had served in either the Civil War or World War I. That would narrow the possibilities to about fifty years. The plaque at the base announced that the statue had been placed there in 1925 by the Calvin's Creek Commission on Statuary Mounting and Erections.

Judging by the central business district, Calvin's Creek was small but stable. The streets were lined with two-story, red brick buildings that were well maintained and active storefronts housing a variety of businesses. There were no vacant shops. As Joshua crossed the street to the sheriff's office, he spotted a hardware store, a pharmacy, three craft shops, two churches, a coffee shop and several restaurants, a florist shop, and a newspaper office.

He opened the door to the sheriff's office and immediately spotted Bruce waiting for him in one of the plastic chairs in the lobby. Bruce stood up and walked toward Joshua, extending his right hand.

Joshua shook hands and inspected the purplish bruise on Bruce's forehead. Otherwise, Bruce looked fit and healthy. His sandy-colored hair was bushy and his beard was neatly trimmed. "We feared the worst, Bruce. Michelle and Ham and I were sure surprised and elated to hear from you. It must have been a terrible ordeal."

"Oh, it was really nothing," Bruce shrugged his shoulders, trying to look the reluctant hero. "But, now let's talk about the future." His expression was vibrant. "First, I want you to meet the woman who snatched victory from the jaws of defeat. Say hello to Veronica Pulaski, who has earned a badge of courage for coming to my rescue."

Ronnie, who had remained semi-hidden behind Bruce, now walked forward and shook Joshua's hand. "I've heard so much about you, it's good to finally meet you in person."

"Don't take it too seriously, it's all lies. Michelle couldn't join me for this trip, but she's been busy today, dealing with Curtis and Phase One." Turning to Bruce, Joshua said "Michelle met with Curtis, and she stayed with the script. She said his face suddenly screwed up when she told him the news about you being down here. Curtis grabbed the bait and literally ran with it. He immediately ran to his car and apparently called your two pals, because Michelle learned that they left Boston very abruptly on a 'business trip.' "

"What about Ham?" Bruce asked.

"Everything's cool."

"Great, perfect. Now, we just need to convince Sheriff Cooper. Did you bring the infamous disk?"

"You bet," Joshua said, pulling the disk from his shirt pocket.

40

Sheriff Cooper appeared in the lobby and introduced himself. Ronnie gave him a big hug as though they were old friends, which surprised Joshua. He turned to greet Joshua and Bruce. "Any friend of Ronnie's is welcome here," Sheriff Cooper said.

Joshua had expected the stereotypical small town sheriff—gruff, overweight, and undereducated—and an office furnished with hand-me-downs from the National Guard.

Instead, Joshua entered the sheriff's private office and glanced around in amazement. Sheriff Cooper had furnished the office with antiques he found at estate sales around the county. The main pieces were a 1920's mahogany roll-top desk and an enormous oak library table, which he used as his desk and conference table. Both pieces had been lovingly restored. A Pentium V computer, twenty-inch monitor, and HP VI laser printer were stationed on another, smaller library table. An antique oak dry sink was home for a large chrome espresso/cappuccino machine. The marriage of the wood antiques and the modern equipment was striking.

The sheriff's ego wall displayed degrees from Princeton and the University of Virginia School of Law, photographs of him shaking hands with three Presidents, and a variety of honors and awards. On the opposite wall were two oil paintings, one of the river at sunset and a portrait of a woman in her early sixties. Joshua walked closer to the paintings and saw they were signed by V. Pulaski.

Sheriff John "Jack" Cooper had retired five years ago, at 58, from a long and distinguished career at the FBI. He began as a field agent, but spent time in most of the sections as he rose through the ranks. His specialty was investigating white-collar crime rings, and he had spent the last ten years as an assistant director in Washington.

"Sheriff, please excuse my amazement," stammered Joshua, "but I just have to ask you the obvious question, how does a former assistant director of the FBI wind up as sheriff of Lead County?"

Sheriff Cooper stood five foot ten and was athletic, lean, and strong. His tanned face framed ice-blue eyes and a silver mustache. His graying hair was conservatively cut. He shunned the traditional tan uniform of local law enforcement officials in favor of a navy blue business suit with a French blue dress shirt and a blue-black tie with a geometric pattern. He looked more like a successful CEO of a Fortune 500 company.

As he began to speak, he peeled off his suit jacket and placed it neatly on a hanger, which he then hung on a brass hook fastened to back of the office door. "I'll give you the condensed version, which Ronnie already knows by heart because she made it happen." Sheriff Cooper eased himself into his chair behind the library table.

"The first half of my career, I must have lived in fifteen different places, mostly big cities. The FBI moved me around a lot. My wife, Emma—that's her portrait hanging on the wall over there—didn't much like that. Then, after nearly twenty years in Washington, D.C., fighting the congestion and the traffic and a job that never quit, we decided to find a nice quiet corner of this country. All I wanted to do when I retired was fish, hike, and compile the history of the FBI—not a kiss-and-tell thing, but a serious book describing the evolution of lab technology and the strategies we used to crack some of the biggest crime syndicates of our time."

Just then, the phone rang and the sheriff paused to answer it, speaking briefly and hanging up. "So, anyway," he continued, "Emma and I had been through this area years ago. We agreed to make another visit when I retired, this time to see if we'd be comfortable here. We rented an old house for six months, just to see how we'd like it. I'd fish a few hours at dawn every morning, then walk over to the coffee shop down the street for breakfast. Hell, you don't need a newspaper in a small town like this, you just go down to the coffee shop and find out all the news and gossip."

The sheriff stood and walked over to the window overlooking the town square. "It seemed like, whatever else was going on in town, the conversation at the coffee shop always turned to the growing incidents of crime. Lead County was fast becoming a mecca for tourists, and the local citizens had bought into the mantra of the Chamber of Commerce that tourism would reverse the economic decline around here. But, soon came the criminals, robbing tourists, stealing their cars, and so on. We were getting a bad reputation, and it was threatening to kill the dream.

"Well, a group of businessmen and the publisher of the local weekly paper formed a committee to look into how efficiently and effectively the sheriff's office was operating, and they asked me to serve on the committee. They told me I was a natural, with my background and all. So, despite Emma's disapproval and against my own better judgment, I agreed to help them in an 'advisory' capacity. I haven't worked on my book since then."

Cooper stopped his narration. "Pardon my bad manners. Can I fix you folks a cappuccino? I'd like one, so please join me."

The pace of a small town is definitely slower, thought Joshua. *The sheriff pauses in his busy day of fighting crime, hangs up his six shooter, and fixes a cappuccino.*

Ronnie, Bruce, and Joshua rose and moved over to watch Sheriff Cooper operate the fancy LaPavoni machine. "It's important to use distilled water, not regular tap water. The first step is, we let it build up a head of pressure," the sheriff said, as he turned on the steam switch. "Meanwhile, we get out the milk and fresh beans. I like the Italian roast—it's more robust than the French." From a carton of skimmed milk kept in the refrigerator he filled a stainless frothing pitcher about one-third full. The gauge on the LaPavoni was now at thirty PSI, indicating that the steam pressure was ready, and the sheriff rotated the handle until a blast of steam was working the milk into a frothy lather. He turned off the steam and scooped the dark beans into the burr grinder, which he set to the second finest grind. It whirred noisily for about ten seconds until the beans were reduced to a fine powder. "Next, we take this filter holder—the Italian word is 'portafiltro'—and fill it." He transferred the powdery results from the grinder into the portafiltro.

"The powder can't just sit in the portafiltro because the espresso would be too weak. So, we need to tamp it firmly. My friend, Derek, tells me that, with a good burr grinder, you should use thirty to forty pounds of pressure to tamp it down. He even made me use a bathroom scale to make sure I know what that amount of pressure feels like." The sheriff looked like he was tightening a screw as he pressed the powder down.

"Now, we're ready to turn on the pump and make

the espresso, like so." Steam sprayed, then the pump engaged, producing an aromatic, but small amount of rich, dark liquid, filling the cup about one-third. He poured the steamed milk, spooned out some froth, and topped it off with a dollop of whipped cream and a touch of chocolate shavings, and handed the cup to Ronnie.

A few minutes later, after the sheriff repeated the process another three times, they returned to their seats, lauding the quality of the effort. Bruce, in particular, was appreciative. "Sheriff," he asked, "who's your supplier of fresh gourmet beans? You certainly don't get them around here."

"I get them from Seattle by mail order."

"In that case," Bruce said, "the beans were probably roasted a few weeks before you receive the shipment. I've got some contacts in the city, so let me set it up so you get beans that are *really* fresh roasted. You can email your order and take shipment the next day."

"Great idea, Bruce. Go ahead and make the arrangements. Now, back to the saga of what I did in my brief retirement." Carefully wiping the froth from his mustache, Cooper continued. "Our former sheriff, J.R. Gillespie, truly defined the term, 'good ol' boy.' He had no formal training in law enforcement or any notion of modern crime-fighting techniques, but he got himself re-elected every four years because he ate a lot of fried chicken and cut a lot of ribbons.

"J.R. was a stereotypical small town sheriff—under trained and underwhelming. He excelled in belching, farting, and chewing cigars. He'd been in office for more than twenty years, and during that entire time he didn't change anything except patrol cars. Many doubted that he ever changed his uniform.

"One thing led to another," Cooper continued, "and the committee 'volunteered' me to run for sheriff against J.R. Again, Emma sternly reminded me that I was retired, but I'm so thick headed, I decided to run. The committee helped raise money for brochures, billboards, and signs, but my secret weapon was Ronnie, who agreed to be my campaign organizer. She got a list of eligible voters, found block captains, lined up speaking engagements, helped me go door-to-door, and designed our literature. She did it all. Without Ronnie, I'd have never won that election." He looked over at Ronnie and smiled. "Mostly, though, she's a helluva good painter."

Ronnie smiled back and said, "That was nearly four years ago, and now Jack is running for re-election this November."

Joshua said, "Now, you'll have to run on your own record, sheriff. How does it look for you? You ran as a reformer, but what's your campaign theme this time around, as the incumbent?"

"Ronnie, you're my spin meister," the sheriff said. "Joshua has asked the question that we'll hear most often in the next few months: 'Why should the people of Lead County re-elect Jack Cooper?' What's your response?"

Ronnie jumped at the opportunity without breaking stride. "When Jack was elected sheriff, the technology of this office was stuck in the 1960s. The deputies and officers had old-fashioned walkie-talkies where only two people could talk to each other. Now, any of our officers can make a conference call to everybody, and do it instantly. Before Jack, if a deputy arrested someone, the only way to find out his prior criminal record was to make a phone call to the state highway patrol headquarters in the capital. Now, we've got computers in all patrol cars, as well as the office, electronically linked to the computers in patrol headquarters and, of course, the FBI. Under Gillespie, there wasn't even a system for keeping local crime statistics. Now, we have a state-of-the-art electronic database, and it shows that Jack has reduced crime in all categories by an average of ten percent in each of the last two years. But, the job of bringing Lead County into the twenty-first century has just begun. Re-elect Jack Cooper to finish the job."

"I guess that says it all. The job I set out to do isn't finished yet." He paused as he looked at his desk. "But, it's been awfully quiet this summer," Cooper mused. "We could use a big bust heading into the fall election. Or, I may have to go back to working on my book."

"In that case, we may have a strong mutual interest to discuss, sheriff," Joshua said.

"I've been wondering what brought a big city attorney like you to a small town like Calvin's Creek," the sheriff said.

"Now, you're really starting to sound like a small town sheriff," Joshua said with a grin. "I'm here on behalf of my client, Bruce, who is prepared to file criminal charges for assault with a firearm, felony theft, and a smorgasbord of lesser charges, all of which occurred in your jurisdiction, right here in Lead County. Plus the kidnaping, which occurred in St. Louis and ended here. The perps are a couple of goons from Boston who work for a management company there. We think the mastermind is Curtis Carlton in St. Louis County, who, we believe, is using the Boston company to raid condominium associations of their reserve funds by way of sophisticated computer hackers."

"He's hacking into local computers to steal reserve funds? Using a computer in Boston?"

"Frankly, we're not sure about the location of the hacker, sheriff. Specifically, we suspect he's using what the techies call an applet. But, your point is correct. I haven't researched any cases on this, but since cyberspace is interstate, then the use of the Internet would constitute interstate commerce."

"How much are you talking about?"

"A bundle. Over five million dollars, and that's only the accounts we know about."

Sheriff Cooper exhaled audibly. "Wow." He was instantly intrigued and began making notes on a yellow legal pad. "Counselor, I'm listening."

Joshua wondered at the sheriff's last remark. *Is Cooper just being polite, or does he have a genuine interest?* "Bruce, it's time to tell your story."

Bruce, who had been quiet until now, launched into a detailed and colorful account of the events of the past several days. Cooper made a few notes on his legal pad, but didn't interrupt the narration.

"It gets better, sheriff," Bruce said. "I have a disk containing Curtis' financial transactions, such as payoffs, kickbacks, bribes, offshore bank accounts, and the like. You might call it a 'smoking gun.' "

"How did you get this disk?" Cooper asked.

"I downloaded it from Curtis' computer."

One eyebrow raised on the sheriff's forehead as he took the disk from Joshua.

"Now that the disk is in safe hands," Bruce said, "I can decode the data." The sheriff handed the disk back to Bruce and allowed him to load it into the computer.

Fifteen minutes later, when Bruce had completed the decoding, the sheriff asked, "Assuming all of this information to be true, I'm very interested in pursuing the assault which occurred in my local jurisdiction, and I'm sure the FBI up in St. Louis will want to talk to this Carlton fellow. But, the information on this disk, by itself, isn't enough to get a conviction. It doesn't have names. It just describes transactions, and the names are coded."

"Good point, sheriff," Joshua said, "The disk is not enough evidence to put Curtis away, at least not yet. Bedford and Kosankis need to be picked up first, for two reasons. Number one, so they don't kill Bruce trying to get this disk back." Ronnie squeezed Bruce's hand. "And, number two," Joshua continued, "these two goons are just mercenaries doing a job for Curtis, and we don't think they have any particular loyalty to him. If you could get them to talk, they'd give Curtis up in a blink. Now, it so happens that Bedford and Kosankis are coming into town soon—like tomorrow night. This is where you come in."

Bruce outlined his plan for the sheriff. "All you'll need to do is show up. And bring your cuffs."

MICHELLE HAD WORKED LATE at the office and didn't get home until after nine o'clock. It was dark when she turned the lock to open the front door of her condo. When she turned on the light, she was horrified at the sight. Everything inside had been tossed—drawers were scattered on the floor, furniture was overturned. Immediately, she shut the door and ran out to the parking lot.

She revved up the Explorer and roared out of the covered parking space in reverse. Tires squealing, she raced out of the parking lot onto the street, checking her mirrors to see if another car was following her. *God, I hope Joshua is back home from Calvin's Creek.* She tapped in his home phone number.

"Hello?" Hooray…it was Joshua's voice.

"Joshua, it's me. I just got home and…and it's… horrible. Someone ransacked my condo, turned it upside down. Can I come over right now? *I'm scared!*"

"Of course you can come over. But, you won't like it any better here."

"Don't tell me…"

"You got it, Michelle. I just got back in town, and it looks like a tornado went through here."

"Somebody's looking for something," Joshua replied.

"I wonder if they eavesdropped on our conference call last night with our friend."

"Yeah, but I thought we were really careful," Joshua said, glancing around at the mess in his kitchen. "And anyway, what could they expect to get from either of our places?"

"The disk!" Michelle concluded.

41

It was only six-thirty in the evening and too early for summer dinner at a world-class resort such as the Riverway Lodge. Michelle and Joshua nursed their coffees at a small table off to the far side away from the front entrance where they could observe guests entering the restaurant and have an unobstructed view of a small table near the kitchen, distinguishable as the only table with a "reserved" sign on it. Bruce looked elegant in his black tuxedo as he seated a foursome.

Joshua looked at Michelle with a puzzled expression. "So, how come you're so sure this is the night? I called three airlines and struck out. They wouldn't tell me squat."

Michelle was preoccupied circling the rim of her coffee cup with the tip of her middle finger. "It was really very simple. We have a 'good ol' girls' network. All I had to do was call my girlfriend at the ticket counter. Then, I confirmed it with another friend who works at the car rental company. Trust me, tonight's the night."

Dinner guests began arriving steadily. Families with young children sunburned from a long day of canoeing or tubing on the river and elderly couples wearing matching shirts, walking shorts, and straw hats, were seated at almost every other table.

Joshua pulled a business card out of his shirt pocket. "Michelle, I never got a chance to tell you about Sheriff Cooper," he said, handing the sheriff's card to her. "He's a career FBI man, retired now for several years. You should hear the stories he tells about working with Interpol in Europe investigating international white-collar crime rings. All the man wanted to do was quietly retire here in Calvin's Creek, do some fishing, and write a definitive history of the FBI." Joshua related Cooper's entire story, but time crawled while they waited.

By nine-thirty, Michelle and Joshua were getting hungry so they ordered salads, light sandwiches, and Cokes. The restaurant was full. Joshua checked his watch again and said, "I'm beginning to think that tonight's not the night."

"Trust me," said Michelle.

"Say, why did you bring your camera?"

"A good photographer never leaves home without her camera."

Joshua glanced at the maitre d' station in time to catch Bruce and see him roll his eyes and give a slight shrug of his shoulders. *No sign of them.*

Michelle watched Bruce control the bustling restaurant with calm efficiency. "Have you ever seen a man look more self-confident under such crazy circumstances?" She tapped Joshua's hand and said, "Recently, he told me his 'fantasy'—that he wanted to be in charge of a big fancy resort hotel. Bruce has found his fantasy."

Suddenly, Michelle's head jerked slightly to her left. It was ten o'clock. She looked over her shoulder and saw Ronnie escorting two men to the reserved table in the rear, which was currently the only unoccupied real estate in the restaurant. She elbowed Joshua. The shorter of the two men following Ronnie had the body of a bouncer and limped with his foot in a cast. Both men had their dark hair slicked back. Their matching black suits and wingtips stood out from all the other patrons. "We'll be right with you to show you the menu and tell you about tonight's specials," Ronnie said to the two men as they seated themselves, and then she returned to the front of the restaurant. As she walked past Joshua and Michelle's table, she gestured with her eyes to the table she had just left. As if anyone could have missed the assholes in wingtips.

Joshua squeezed Michelle's hand under the table. "It's finally show time," he whispered excitedly. "And now I have to pee from all that coffee."

"Cross your legs."

A few minutes passed, and Bruce strode across the floor of the dining room carrying two burgundy-colored menus. He walked at his customary pace, the same confident gait he always used when he was on the floor, quick but not hasty.

An African-American busboy was standing outside the kitchen doors, not ten feet from the table where the black-suit twins awaited Bruce's arrival. To the average patron in the restaurant, the muscular busboy was simply waiting to clear the next table.

The other two busboys on the far side of the floor nodded imperceptibly and started walking toward the kitchen doors. Joshua and Michelle watched the subtle, orchestrated movements intently, rose, and walked, as inconspicuously as possible, around the dining room, also heading toward the kitchen doors.

Bruce arrived at the rear table and feigned surprise when he recognized the two black-suited guests sitting on opposite sides of the small table. "Why, it's my old pals Mr. B. and Mr. K., but you're not letters from *Sesame Street*. You're looking smashing tonight, in your best casual outfits. How are those wingtips," Bruce said, intentionally stepping on Kosankis' good foot. "To what do I owe this pleasure? Did you run out of little old ladies to mug in Boston?"

"Actually, we came here for a funeral," Bedford said, in a low voice.

As Bruce extended his arms to put the menus on the table, Kosankis grabbed Bruce's right wrist in an iron grip. Bedford grabbed Bruce's left arm. Kosankis hissed under his breath into Bruce's ear, "I have a nine-millimeter cannon pointed at your kidney. Don't say nothin,' just walk with us. We'll go straight into the kitchen. I wouldn't hesitate for a second to blast you right now, so you better be a good boy, Brucie."

Bedford and Kosankis stood up on each side of Bruce, squeezed him tightly, yanked him off his feet, and maneuvered him through the swinging double-doors to the kitchen. Michelle watched them with a mixture of terror and anticipation. Then, she saw a uniformed deputy sheriff trotting across the dining room with a pistol in his hand. The deputy was making slow progress, doing his best to weave through the crowded tables where startled diners watched him with their mouths open.

As Bruce was being dragged through the swinging doors to the kitchen, he said loudly, "Maybe you guys would like to sample something in the kitchen? Tonight's pork special, perhaps?" At that cue, Ham leaped out from behind the swinging door and grabbed Kosankis from behind, pinning his arms in a hammerlock, causing him to drop Bruce's right arm. Kosankis struggled to free himself, the automatic pistol waving wildly in his left hand as the two men twisted, heaved, and grunted in a deadly dance. Kosankis swung his cast backwards, trying to pound Ham's shins.

Joshua bolted through the swinging doors a step ahead of Michelle. Sheriff Cooper burst into the kitchen through the alley door, but was still a good thirty feet from the heavyweight fight.

Bruce tried to twist Bedford's hand, but Bedford used a swift judo kick into Bruce's midsection to launch him like a rag doll against the heavy stainless steel freezer. Joshua jumped in front of Bedford and aimed a roundhouse right hook at his chin. Bedford deftly sidestepped, and landed a chopping blow with the side of his hand to the back of Joshua's neck. Joshua tumbled into a dessert cart, splattering slices of chocolate cheesecake and apricot delight in all directions. He landed in a heap in the corner, semi-conscious, his face half buried in a lemon meringue pie.

Bruiser, the football lineman playing first-string busboy, was waving a wooden rolling pin in front of his body as menacingly as possible. He advanced toward Bedford, narrowing the distance with slow, deliberate strides. Bedford assumed the judo position and eyed Bruiser. The two men, knees bent slightly, circled each other warily, each searching for an opening. It looked like a scene from a grade C kick boxer movie.

Suddenly, with lightning quickness, Bedford's right foot shot up into Bruiser's face. But, he deflected the kick with his arm and held Bedford's ankle high in the air. Then he swung the rolling pin and delivered a crushing blow where Bedford was fully exposed. He gasped loudly, then squealed in pain. He slumped to his knees, holding himself with both hands as tears came to his eyes. Tank came over and swung a copper sauté pan in an uppercut motion, catching Bedford's chin. The force of the blow knocked Bedford onto his back, spread-eagle and unconscious on the ceramic tile floor.

Kosankis and Ham were locked in a wrestling duel in the middle of the kitchen. Ham's tight hammerlock paralyzed Kosankis' arm so that the gun was pointed at the ceiling. The powerful Kosankis suddenly surged in reverse and maneuvered his lighter adversary backwards against the gas range where a five-quart pot of boiling water was ready for pasta. The flames began licking at the back of Ham's shirt. That diversion was all Kosankis needed to break free of Ham's grip. He took two steps to his left, found Bruce next to the freezer, brought the gun down to eye level, and focused his aim at Bruce's head.

Bruce froze, but out of the corner of his eye, he saw Sheriff Cooper leaping for Kosankis. Ham, the back of his shirt ablaze, was reaching for Kosankis from the other side. Instinctively, Michelle took a step forward and raised her camera. The sheriff flew through the air, grabbing Kosankis' hand as the gun exploded three times. The bullets ricocheted loudly off the copper saucepans hanging on the rack overhead. Michelle mashed her finger down on the shutter, the camera clicking continuously.

Ham tackled Kosankis and wrestled him to the kitchen floor while Cooper clung to Kosankis' gun. Tank and Bruiser piled on. It looked like a rugby scrum, a half-ton mountain of beef with bodies pushing and shoving, elbows and feet thrashing in every direction. Michelle was nervous, but kept her cool. *Step closer, focus, click, another step closer, focus…* Fearlessly, she moved to within feet of the fight and went down to one knee, keeping the camera steady and the shutter clicking away. Sheriff Cooper emerged from the pile with the gun raised over his head, oblivious to Michelle's camera, and stepped free of the brawlers. He calmly straightened his tie—just another day at the office.

The football players grabbed Kosankis under both arms and stood him up. Ronnie put a wet towel on Ham's back. When the sheriff's back was turned, Ham couldn't resist launching an elbow into Kosankis' left kidney. Tank joined in, kicking the side of Kosankis' knee, causing it to buckle and sending Kosankis to the floor.

"Sheriff," Bruce said, panting, "Your county is a pretty dangerous place. You can't turn your back around here without somebody getting mugged." Tank was reviving Joshua while Bruiser poured a pitcher of ice water over Bedford's head. Kosankis moaned helplessly on the floor. The deputy ceremoniously cuffed Bedford and Kosankis while Sheriff Cooper read their Miranda rights in a voice strong enough for all to hear.

A loud chorus of cheers and wild applause erupted from the dining room. The swinging doors of the kitchen were wide open, and patrons filled the doorway. Then, they started chanting, "Four more years! Four more years! Coop for mayor! Coop for governor!"

Sheriff Cooper was beaming and acknowledged the crowd's support with a self-conscious wave. Michelle's camera was recording the scene from various angles. Cooper then helped Bruce remove his jacket and shirt. Ronnie detached the wireless microphone from around Bruce's torso and removed a bulletproof vest. Cooper said, "Bruce, the microphone worked great. I was waiting out in the alley, and I could hear every word. But, it looks like your 'friends' from back East had a little dancing lesson in the kitchen before I could get here."

Joshua walked up to Bruce and Cooper, rubbing the back of his neck with one hand and wiping meringue off his face with the other. "So, what happened, anyhow? What did I miss?"

Bruce handed the tiny microphone and wire to Cooper. "It all went so fast, sheriff, I'm not sure what happened. But, it's true that many accidents occur right here in the kitchen. It can be a very dangerous place, with skillets and rolling pins flying everywhere. There's no doubt, though, that you got here just in time."

Cooper hesitated for a minute. "Law enforcement is mostly unglamorous hard work. And a lot of luck." He surveyed the food scattered around the kitchen. "I'm famished. Anybody ready for dessert?"

Coop led his group through the double doors onto the floor of the restaurant. The patrons erupted into another round of thunderous applause and shouts of "four more years."

42

The initial interrogation was taking several hours, running into the early morning. Sheriff Cooper was not about to be rushed in this critical process. Indeed, he relished a return to challenging investigative work. He questioned the suspects separately, alternating between them, using admissions from one against the other. It was two o'clock in the morning when Cooper started his third go-around with an exhausted, aching Kosankis. Coop had gotten little from Bedford.

"Sheriff," Kosankis groaned, "You gotta get me to a doctor. I tell you those goons broke my knee."

"Come on, now. I didn't see anybody hit you. And I don't see any part of you that even looks bruised. Besides, the nearest medical facility is a good ninety minutes away. We put in a call to the dispatcher but at this hour—so early on a Sunday morning—I'm just not sure how quickly the emergency paramedics are going to get here. You know how it is in a small, rural town like Calvin's Creek."

Cooper reviewed his notes and continued in a soothing voice, "There's just a couple of things that I still don't understand." He paused to look at his yellow legal pad, not that it was necessary to check his notes since he was a highly skilled interrogator, but more to allow his words to sink into Kosankis' thick and stubborn skull. "We know you held Bruce at Seldom Seen against his will and threatened him. What we don't know is who told you to do it."

"Beats the hell outta me."

"How do you know Curtis Carlton?"

"Curtis who? Never heard of him. I already told you that."

"You can stop denying that Kosankis, we've got a record of phone calls between Carlton and you. We can place you at his office on several occasions. And, we know that Carlton has secret recorders in his office and that all your meetings were audio taped." Of course, Cooper knew about the phone calls, meetings, and videos from Bruce, but the audio recording was pure invention, a hunch from years of experience. An inaccurate question could produce interesting results. *We'll see what happens*, Cooper thought.

Kosankis went into a rage. Suddenly he stood up and started limp-pacing back and forth across the small room. He shouted, "That fat slob never said nothin' about no tape recorders. He said he had video cameras, but he always destroyed the videotapes. He never said nothin' about no audio tape recorders."

"Yes, and we know about the video cameras, too," Cooper responded, pleased at how much information was spewing forth from this nonverbal muscle man. He made another note on his yellow legal pad. He liked to take notes during an interrogation, even though the entire session was being recorded on video by his own cameras placed behind two-way mirrors. Making notes by hand took time, which meant dead air, which the suspect often felt compelled to fill with more confessional material. It also gave the suspect more time to change his story, in which case he would be trapped by lies within lies. On this occasion, however, Kosankis simply grew more weary and impatient and started getting around to the truth. Cooper was a patient cop.

"Sir," Kosankis grunted more calm and subdued, "I really can't believe how this shit's coming down. Carlton had tape recorders, too? I knew he couldn't be trusted. I told Bedford that. I told Mr. B. just how we were being spoon-fucked by that fat fart."

"Look, Kosankis, we know from reliable sources and written documents that Carlton is making a deal for himself and your boss. Those two are in this together. The object of the deal is to buy PSM because it's rich in reserve funds. So, don't insult me, and don't waste my time trying to deny these facts. We also know that you broke into PSM's offices and planted a virus in their computers, so that you could secretly transfer funds out of their accounts."

"Huh? What have you been smokin', man? Do I look like the sort of guy who knows shit about computers? Huh? Do I look like a computer geek? Give me a break, sheriff!"

"Give yourself a break, Kosankis," Cooper replied. "It's time you start thinking about your own future, because no one else is. Where's Carlton—is he here, helping you out? And where's Philip Palmer—do you think he cares if you take the rap? We know that this wasn't your scheme—you were just carrying out the orders of Carlton and Philip Palmer. Unless you cooperate by giving us something about these two characters, we won't be able to help you."

Cooper stopped again to let Kosankis mull over his words. "Do you realize how deeply you're in this shit? Let me explain it to you. On top of the state criminal charges, we've got several federal crimes that have been committed.

The Feds have priority. What am I supposed to tell the FBI up in St. Louis?" Cooper paused again to make another note on his legal pad. "All you need to do is give us the details of how this deal is going down. Who planted the applet? Who is transferring funds? Where are the funds being routed? Otherwise, you'll have to take the rap all by yourself. Am I making myself clear?"

"It wasn't supposed to come down this way. I just don't understand."

"What part of it don't you understand?" Cooper barked. "The part about them throwing you to the wolves?" Cooper switched to his more comforting voice. "Look, Kosankis, I know that you were just carrying out their orders and that nothing was your idea. Well, now's your chance to get back at them. All we need is a little cooperation."

"I'm trying to cooperate. It was Carlton who hired me to threaten Brucie. That fat sombitch told me that Brucie had stolen a disk from his computer, a disk with Carlton's personal records. He hired me to scare the shit outta Brucie, just get back whatever it was that he took. But, all that other stuff? That was all their doing, sheriff. Carlton and Philip, they were cooking up something on their own, but I don't know nothin' about that stuff. In case you can't tell by now, sir, I ain't none too bright. Frankly, I'm just a dumb fuck, sir. Philip tells me what to do—he calls it the 'heavy lifting.' I'm too dumb to figure out computers and transferring funds and shit like that. Sir."

Cooper made another note: *Forrest Gump Defense— stupid is as stupid does. Sir.*

43

Michelle was enjoying the rare luxury of a leisurely, silky-soft bubble bath. The radio was playing country rock music. Mary Chapin Carpenter was singing, "Sometimes you're the windshield, sometimes you're the bug…" The fight scene in the kitchen at the Riverway Lodge replayed in her mind. She switched off the Jacuzzi, closed her eyes, and tried to just let her body and consciousness float in neutral for a while.

As usual, Bruce left no detail unattended. He knew that Michelle and Joshua would be in town late into the night when the business with Bedford and Kosankis was finished and that they wouldn't want to make the long drive home. So, despite the lodge's full occupancy on a popular weekend, Bruce arranged for a suite for Michelle and Joshua. He wasn't sure if he should reserve two rooms, or a suite with two beds. Either way, Bruce worried he might offend one of them. He opted on the side of optimism—a suite. Bruce took care of Ham, too, with a separate room.

It was two-thirty in the morning before Joshua left the sheriff's office, and he let himself into the suite with his electronic key. Seeing the bathroom door closed, he tapped lightly and said, "Hey, Michelle, I'm home! Are you asleep in there, or what?"

"I'm fine, Joshua. Oh, this Jacuzzi is fabulous."

"Are you hungry? Bruce was still at the restaurant when I got back from Sheriff Cooper's office, and he forced me to take some leftovers. We have some . . . well, I can't read the label because he wrote the name in French, but I think it's some exotic chicken dish. And it's still warm."

Joshua set the Styrofoam cartons of food on the table and uncorked a bottle of French margaux, compliments of Bruce. He was pouring the wine into two glasses when Michelle came out of the bathroom, her damp hair brushed straight back and gleaming. She was wearing an ASU basketball shirt that was so long it came down to mid-thigh, and the Sun Devil's pitchfork was aimed at her left breast. After her bath, it was clear that the shirt was all she wore.

"My hero," she said as she hugged Joshua, then examined the bruise on the back of his head, and lightly touched it. He could feel her firm breasts through the thin jersey.

"Yeah, some help I was. Knocked out before the fight even began. I can see the headline back home on my obituary—Local Attorney Suffocates in Cream Pie."

"And, the paper would have a black-and-white photo to go with it. I hope the pictures turn out okay. The one of you should be a great—you were airborne, flying head-first into the dessert cart."

"I can't wait to see it," Joshua laughed. He started opening the cartons of chicken and vegetables. It was three o'clock as they sat down to their midnight snack.

"Tell me," Michelle said, swallowing a bite of chicken orange, "What happened at the sheriff's office?"

"Bedford used his one phone call to reach Philip Palmer's attorney in Boston. The attorney called back half an hour later and said that legal services for Kosankis and him had not been authorized. Philip is out to save himself by sacrificing his trusted henchmen."

Joshua described the interrogation rooms, the two-way mirrors, and the video camcorders positioned behind them. He related the separate interviews, noting that Bedford was clearly the brains, that he held up well under the sheriff's questioning, dodging and weaving, giving up little information. The Kosankis interview was the more interesting of the two, even though he clearly was simply the muscle man of the black-suit twins and admittedly not too bright. "So," Joshua concluded, "it's ironic that Kosankis provided more information during his interrogation."

Michelle said, "You remember, when I called you on your car phone yesterday, you said something in this whole picture doesn't feel right? Well, tonight I was thinking, and now I think I know what it is."

"Let me guess," said Joshua. "Part of the picture is missing? Like Curtis hired Vinnie the Bug to plant the applet?"

"That's possible, but it's even more basic. It dawned on me while I was in the tub. Look, you and I know about the applet and the missing funds, but what did that bouncer-guy know about it?"

"Kosankis?" Joshua thought for a minute. "You're right, Kosankis didn't seem to know anything about it. During the sheriff's interrogation, it was all a total surprise to Kosankis. And, I don't think he was putting on a show of dumbing down, he's even too dumb to pull that off. He said that Philip uses him to do the 'heavy lifting.' He really didn't know anything about the applet or any funds being transferred. When Curtis figured out that Bruce had made a disk with information about Curtis' personal deals, he employed Kosankis as muscle to recover the disk.

Michelle stopped in mid-chew to digest this information. "Whatever Curtis is up to, the information that Bruce got on the disk must be pretty incriminating for him to hire these two goons. What exactly is on the disk?"

"There's a list of receivables, and another list of payments made, and several different bank accounts with lots of deposit entries. That's what we saw when Bruce decoded the disk. But, Curtis coded all the transactions. I mean, we saw transactions, but not specific names of the individuals involved or the banks where accounts are held. Whatever, it's probably the type of information that the IRS and the FBI would just love to look at. The transactions are probably illegal, and the transfer of funds from one account to another may indicate money laundering."

Michelle used a slice of baguette to soak up some of the tapenade sauce left on her plate. She looked up at Joshua and said, "I'm sure the homeowners at the Cove would love to see these records, too. But, here's an even better question—why would Curtis be trying to broker a deal for Philip to buy PSM at the same time he's draining five million dollars from our clients' reserves?"

"I don't get your point."

"Okay. Look, we know that Curtis is driven by greed. He sees eight hundred thousand dollars in the Cove's reserves, and knows that PSM has access to over five million dollars, representing the reserves of all our clients. So, why…"

"Wait a second. How does Curtis know that you have over five mil in reserves?"

"I think I told him. When he was first elected president, he asked what the Cove's reserves were for. I told him we insist that all our clients have reserves."

"Sounds like you were boasting."

"No, I mentioned it to him so that he'd understand

why he should support having reserves. Anyway, as I was saying, why would Curtis want to broker a deal to buy PSM if its main attraction is suddenly gone? Curtis and his undisclosed principal see our reserves as an asset of the company, rather than funds we're holding in trust. That's why they made the contract contingent on us producing a list of reserves we're holding for each client. So, back to my question: Who wants a community management company that has just lost all its 'assets' through an undetected electronic transfer?"

Joshua listened carefully. "Of course, I see where you're going now. PSM may have a stable filled with rich clients, but as soon as they discover that their reserves have been transferred to some Swiss bank account or are lost in a black hole in cyberspace, these clients are going to rush out the door to another management company. Right?"

"Precisely, Joshua. At least, that's what I think. You know the kind of people who sit on the association boards. They'd be scared shitless and mad as hell if they heard that all of their reserves had been sucked into cyberspace. Don't you agree that their first impulse would be to drop PSM and get another company? They might even decide to be self-managed for a time, while they nurse their wounds and get things back under control. Even if we have full insurance coverage, it won't prevent a stampede of clients leaving PSM."

"I agree," Joshua lamented. "To make the scenario even worse, the boards are going to expect full relief. They're going to drop you like a hot potato, then sue you to recover the lost funds through PSM's fidelity bond."

Michelle asked, "Does our fidelity bond cover electronic theft?"

Joshua ignored the question and stopped to examine his fork. "But, I'm still not sure I understand about Curtis."

He paused to organize his thoughts. "Okay, let's assume your scenario is correct—PSM loses the reserve funds you're holding for your clients, and the clients flee. Then, to state your question a bit differently, if Curtis knows about the transfer of reserves out of PSM, why would he want to broker a deal to buy PSM? Does Curtis think he could arrange a sale of PSM—based on an inducement, the material fact that it has over five million dollars in reserves—and in the meantime transfer the funds to himself?"

"That's it, Joshua," Michelle exclaimed. "You nailed it. You just answered both questions. Curtis doesn't know about the missing funds," Michelle said rapidly. "If he knew about the funds being transferred, he'd be transferring them to himself. He wouldn't need to broker the sale of PSM. The two scenarios are mutually exclusive."

"So, he doesn't know about the applet. He couldn't have been involved in planting the applet, which is how the funds were transferred. So, where does that leave us?"

"This puzzle is missing at least one piece. And, I have a hunch who that might be." Michelle took a sip of wine, her eyebrows raised, eyes gazing at Joshua over the rim of her glass.

44

It was early Sunday morning. An exhausted Sean Eastgate opened the door to his loft apartment and dropped an overnight bag and notebook computer on the tattered couch, one of the few pieces of furniture in the tiny loft. He was feeling stressed, with PSM screaming the loudest for him to fix a problem in its computers. He owed Michelle a call, first thing next week. And there were other clients starting to complain bitterly about his services. It was beginning to feel like a repeat of his failure in California that he had solemnly vowed to avoid.

His desktop computer, monitor, and printer were stationed on an old wooden library table on the wall opposite the couch. He had purchased the table at an antique furniture store, and it was now overflowing with computer manuals, magazines, and an assortment of computer chips wrapped in plastic and miscellaneous other spare parts. That table also did double duty as Sean's kitchen table—when he bothered to eat.

Hot and sticky air had returned to St. Louis, and the apartment was stuffy and sultry. Sean didn't care. The only thing on his mind this morning was to work on his computer, and he figured the project would take several hours.

Sean had just completed his work on the desktop when he heard a knock at the door. *It could only be a neighbor*, he thought. He opened the door cautiously and was surprised to see Michelle and a tall, good-looking man standing in the hallway. "Well, hi there, girl," he said. "I couldn't imagine who would be knocking at my door on a Sunday morning. During church hours, that is." This last remark was accompanied by a sly wink and a grin.

"I hope we're not disturbing you, Sean." Michelle introduced Joshua, describing him as a "friend" who was "just taking me to breakfast." Joshua was more interested in peering over Sean's shoulder, into the apartment, while Michelle explained that she was in the neighborhood and wanted to talk to Sean.

This is not good. Sean strained to act normal, as if nothing unusual were on his mind.

"Aren't you going to invite us in?" Michelle inquired.

"Well…uh…why are you standing here? Come on in." He gestured, and Michelle and Joshua walked into his tiny, sweltering apartment.

Sean closed the door behind his guests then ran ahead to remove the bags he had just deposited on the couch. He nervously picked up several piles of computer magazines scattered on the couch and put everything on the floor. "Here, I just cleared a spot for you. Would you like to sit down?"

Michelle remained standing in the middle of the room. She carefully observed Sean for a long moment. His lanky body was stooped over and he looked tired. His eyes were red-rimmed. He hadn't shaved. His long blond hair, always neatly brushed, was disheveled. It wasn't the image of the slick Sean she had known for the last year. "This visit won't take but a few minutes," she began. "Perhaps you've forgotten, Sean, but you were supposed to come in and give all the PSM computers a thorough inspection to see if you could spot the problem we're having. You thought it was a gremlin, which may mean something to you, but means nothing to me."

"I'm sorry, Michelle, but I've been so busy lately. The note must have slipped off my desk," Sean said, his head nodding to the large table with his computer and stacks of manuals and magazines. Are you still having a problem?"

While Sean's attention was focused on his conversation with Michelle, Joshua slipped away, and began casually walking around the room, observing. He didn't have any idea of what he was looking for. Perhaps, like obscenity, he would know it when he saw it.

Michelle, concerned about a direct confrontation, was subtle in her approach. "Sean," she began, very matter-of-factly, "Mac and I were doing a routine review of some of the reserve accounts, and we found that one account was missing some funds. It's possible that the initial entry put the funds in the wrong account, but it might be an unauthorized withdrawal. Anyway, it's a large amount of money, so I wondered if this might be somehow connected to this 'gremlin' problem you found the other day?"

Sean shifted his weight, uncertain how to respond. He turned away from Michelle nervously and was startled to notice that account ledgers were still open on the monitor. "Well, it could be a type of virus program that's infected your software," he said, easing over to the computer, where he clicked to close the program before Michelle could see the monitor. "Of course, computer technology is evolving so rapidly, you have to run hard just to stay in place."

Joshua followed their conversation as he casually strolled around the living room. He sensed Sean's nervous manner, evasiveness, and attempts to avoid discussion. Joshua approached the couch and the items that Sean had cleared away and put on the floor at the end of the couch.

Sean continued, speaking more rapidly now, "In fact, technology is moving so fast, that just the other day…"

Michelle interrupted impatiently. "Sean, have you heard of a virus called an applet?"

"Well, I haven't actually seen any professional analysis of an applet. I haven't heard any cases where such a virus had attacked…"

She cut him off again. "Is it possible that we could have an applet in our system?"

"I don't see how. We installed a state-of-the-art web security system at PSM. You couldn't catch a virus like an applet. The web security system is designed to block any virus that may be circulating through the Internet from infecting…"

Michelle became more persistent. "But, Sean, isn't there a way to circumvent the web security system by planting a virus directly into the computer system?"

"Well, nothing's bulletproof, if that's what you mean."

Joshua stopped at the end of the couch and picked up a black leather case. He turned the case over, examining it carefully, fondling the supple leather. "Hey, Sean, this case looks brand new. Did you get a new laptop? I'd like to get a new one. Do you mind if I take a look at yours?" Without waiting for an answer, Joshua unzipped the case.

"Well, actually, it's a notebook computer…" Sean stammered and walked across the room, hand extended to retrieve the leather case with its portable computer.

But, before Sean could reach Joshua, Michelle put her hand on Sean's arm, deterring his movement, as she continued to corner him with questions. "Sean," she said, "We're concerned about what might have happened to our reserve funds. Is it possible that an applet could have been injected into our system inadvertently? Suppose we inserted a new software program that was already infected by that virus?"

"That's possible." Sean couldn't gracefully break away from Michelle's grip on his arm, and could only watch as Joshua removed the notebook computer from its case, opened the top, and began inspecting it. Sean fidgeted and shifted his weight, not knowing whether to rescue his notebook computer from further scrutiny by Joshua or try to respond to Michelle. *It's time for these two to leave.*

Michelle observed Sean carefully. "Suppose an applet were injected directly into our bookkeeping software program, completely evading the web security system?"

"A lot of possibilities could explain your problem," Sean snapped in response, his frustration rising to the surface. "For all you know, it could be operator error, with all the data that's in your system." At first, he'd thought Michelle was merely tiresome, but now she had become thoroughly irritating. His expression turned cold and his manner became curt. "Look, I can't answer all your questions without looking at your system again. I'll come over early next week. That's as soon as I can do it." He wrenched his arm free of Michelle's grip and walked briskly over to Joshua. "Are you quite done examining my new notebook?" He brusquely took the little computer from Joshua's hands and replaced it in the leather case.

"Well, then," Michelle said to Sean, "I'll see you first thing next week, and I hope you can fix our problem." Joshua and Michelle moved toward the door. Michelle stopped in the open doorway, hands on her hips, glaring at Sean. "We're missing a great deal of funds. We don't take that lightly, and we don't expect you to, either."

"It was sure nice of you to drop by," Sean answered.

JOSHUA AND MICHELLE WALKED down the street from Sean's building toward her Ford Explorer. As Joshua settled in behind the wheel, he observed, "Now, there's a man who has just given new meaning to the word, 'preoccupied.'"

"And nervous."

Joshua pulled away from the curb. "How about anxious?"

"That fits. So does panicky."

"Scared and frightened?"

"No doubt. And, in a hurry to get rid of us."

Joshua and Michelle had arisen early at the Riverway Lodge, after only a few hours sleep, and had driven back to St. Louis in a hurry, eager to question Sean Eastgate. "Now that we've talked to him directly," said Michelle, "what do you think? Did we learn anything?"

Joshua reflected for a minute, scratching at the sparse sandy-colored stubble that was barely visible on his chin. He began thoughtfully, "Well, I didn't expect Sean to offer anything right on the spot. You were pretty confrontational."

"Well, I was subtle when I started, but he became so defensive and evasive. I thought he should have shown more concern. He should have been more responsive."

"Sean's reaction was what I would expect if he's hiding something. If he has something to do with the applet, he wasn't about to tell you. While we didn't gain any specific information that would incriminate him, he didn't give the impression that he's totally innocent. When you mentioned the problem of missing funds, all he did was dance around."

"Look at it this way, Joshua. PSM, one of his best clients, tells him we've just discovered that a lot of money is missing from one of our accounts. What reaction would you expect? I'll tell you—I'd expect shock and surprise, and a genuine interest in finding out what happened." Michelle's voice drifted off as she answered her own question. "But, that's hardly what he showed."

"More than that. He's the expert who designed and installed your system, including your web security system. When you specifically mentioned the possibility of an applet, the expert suddenly turned evasive, unable to offer an explanation."

"Unwilling would be the operative word."

"Plus, he was totally lacking in sympathy. He just wanted to get rid of you. Now, that response doesn't indicate guilt, but it's strongly inconsistent with innocence." Joshua grew quiet as he concentrated on driving the narrow streets downtown. He released a sigh. "The bottom line is that he told us nothing that would incriminate him, but he acted suspiciously. Michelle, I'm starved. How about some brunch?"

"Okay, but you're buying."

"Excuse me," Joshua said, "I'm not trying to sound insensitive, but aren't we supposed to split the bill equally? Isn't that in keeping with our agreement?"

"No, this situation comes under an exception to the agreement," Michelle said.

"Oh, I get it. You think that since we slept together last night, the sanctity of a purely professional relationship has been destroyed. Now, I get to pay full freight."

"May I remind you, Joshua, that while we may have stayed in the same room last night, we slept in separate beds. So, don't start thinking that we slept together. At least, though, you were a good boy, except for that terrible snoring."

"You must admit I was on my best behavior. I didn't belch, fart, pee with the door open, leave the toilet seat up, or smoke a cigar. Or scratch like a baseball player."

"I still respect you."

"I hope so. And I still respect you. So, what's the exception?"

"The exception," Michelle said, "Is that we're going for brunch at Union Station. The hotel there rolls out an outrageous brunch, and I'm famished after all this hard work."

"And, it's my treat simply because you have a deliciously complex personality?"

"No, you're going to treat me because we handled the arrangements last night in the proper manner. Nothing inappropriate happened."

Michelle and Joshua walked through the huge entrance doors and stopped in the foyer of the turn-of-the-century train station. In its heyday, Union Station was one of the three busiest passenger rail centers in the country. The stained glass windows above the entrance had been painstakingly restored to reveal the three allegorical maidens of rail travel in their days of glory, the others being New York and San Francisco.

Joshua gestured for Michelle to walk over to the far end of the entrance foyer, and he went to the other. They stood close to the wall on opposite sides, in a recessed area only about two feet wide carved into the vast arch, which was over one hundred feet at its base. Joshua whispered, "Can you hear me? What do you want for brunch?"

"Incredible," Michelle whispered back. "Cantaloupe, honeydew, strawberries with real cream. Lots of food, I'm hungry."

They continued their conversation for several minutes, marveling at the mystery of the famous Whispering Wall of Union Station. Then they walked up the marble stairs and entered the main lobby of the old station. The lobby had been completely restored, the marble floor and pillars were shining, the art glass in the palatial ceiling was glowing with a thousand colors in the sunshine, and the frescoes had been repainted to their original brilliance.

The restaurant overlooked the enormous train shed, which had been converted to an eclectic blend of busy boutiques and specialty shops that catered to gaggles of tourists. Joshua and Michelle joined the buffet line. Three tables long, the buffet was overflowing with America's bounty, tempting the imprudent to over indulge merely because the harvest was so abundant, appealing, and available. Michelle concentrated on the fruits and vegetables table, sensibly selecting slices of melon and a serving of pasta salad. Joshua was held captive by "omelettes to your taste," where the chef cooked a three-egg feast containing whatever might be required to sate a patron's palate. He recruited a second plate, adding bacon, sausage, lox, scalloped potatoes, croissant and butter, to haul his meal back to the table.

Michelle evaluated Joshua's breakfast as he sat down. "Have you heard of cholesterol?"

"Isn't that the book about this town in New England where all the people start dying from too much chlorine in their water? Stephen King wrote it."

"Never mind. I guess we've never had breakfast together before. If that plate is any example of how you eat when you're on your own, I'll have to go over your diet with you."

"While you were playing Clarence Darrow with Sean, I took a look at his laptop—sorry, his notebook computer."

"So? What of it?"

"A couple of little nuggets may be of interest. First, the only helpful thing that Sean said may be one word—new. He mentioned that his notebook computer was new, and he was very protective of it. Why?"

Michelle looked puzzled. "What's the difference if his notebook computer is new?"

"That question leads to the second little nugget. The store's name and address are on a label on the back of the computer. It said 'Der Electronika,' with an address in Zurich."

"Zurich, as in Switzerland?"

"I suppose."

"Joshua, why didn't you mention the label earlier? Maybe Zurich looks like a little nugget to you, but it could be the big breakthrough we've been hunting for!"

"I don't get it. He could have bought that computer anywhere, including through the Internet or a mail order catalog."

"Joshua, I don't think so. That's a store label, and it could be telling us that Sean was in Switzerland, famous for its numbered bank accounts. We don't have any time to spare. Grab some bagels, we've gotta get going."

"And leave my breakfast sitting here? You better have a good reason."

They hurried out of the restaurant. "Did you get the address of that store?" Michelle asked.

"Not exactly," Joshua responded sheepishly. "But I think the name of the street begins with 'Bahn' or something like that. I think."

45

"Joshua and Michelle jogged out of Union Station, Joshua still chewing on a strip of bacon. The noon heat and oppressive humidity were suffocating and hit them like a blast furnace as they passed through the revolving door and onto the sidewalk. Michelle gasped, straining to catch her breath. She was grateful at least to be wearing her loose-fitting linen shorts.

Joshua started the Explorer and pulled away from the curb. "So, what's the deal?"

"We're going to follow Sean. Just in case he decides to get the money, we'll know it's him."

"Michelle, you're certifiably crazy."

"Got a better plan?"

"Sure. Go to the local FBI or the police."

"I'd love to, but we have a few small problems. One, what hard facts do we have? They'll just laugh at us. Two, it would take too much time, and if Sean's leaving town quickly, as I think he is, we'd lose him. Three, if we lose Sean we lose the money. Probably forever."

"Do you have any idea what you're getting into? Even trained investigators would see danger here, and we have no training or experience."

"Joshua, we're just going to follow him, see where he goes. My hunch is that he'll lead us to his bank, where he's moving the money."

"Well, just following him could still be very dangerous."

"Maybe, but not likely. Sean's a loner—he's operating on his own. And, he's not a violent sort of guy. Last, if he takes a plane, he's not going to have any weapons with him. So, it's not going to be dangerous."

"Jeez," moaned Joshua. "You are one determined woman, Michelle."

"You promised to help, remember?" Michelle said. "You better not wimp out on me now," she added, playfully poking Joshua's arm. "Here's my plan. Do you have your cell phone with you?"

"At all times. So?"

"Me, too. I always keep it here in my bag." Michelle confirmed the phone's location with a search of the oversized canvas tote that served as her overnight luggage, briefcase, purse, and shopping bag. "Okay, Joshua, keep your phone on standby. Sean was so fidgety and eager to get rid of us my guess is that he's going to do something today or tonight, so we don't have much time. We may have only a few hours. We may have missed him already. I'm counting on the fact that the only direct flights to Europe leave here early in the evening. But, he could take a flight to any connecting city, like New York, Washington, or Atlanta. Or Chicago, which has flights on the hour. We'll need to split up. Stop at your place to pack a few things then go to his place and watch. I'll run home and pack quickly. Also, we'll need a few things from a shop I know about."

"You know what else? We've got to catch Angela on her cell phone."

"Maybe we'll have time to try later. But right now, we need to hustle."

Joshua stopped the Explorer in front of his house, double parked on the crowded street, and jumped out while Michelle slid behind the wheel. He said, "Pack comfortable clothes, and make sure they're conservative, functional, and as plain vanilla as possible. We're not going to a fashion show. First thing you pack should be your little blue book. Meet me back at his place as soon as you can."

Michelle drove away and Joshua ran into his house. He found a black duffel bag and stuffed it with slacks, jeans, shirts, underwear, and sneakers. Adding his shaving kit, he zipped the bag closed. He put on a dark blue blazer, which he thought worked well with his faded jeans, and scrambled through his drawers until he found his passport, which he thrust into the inside pocket of his blazer. He ran down the basement steps and filled Amourette's food and water dishes and stopped long enough to give her a quick belly rub. Good thing she could come and go through the dog door. He set the alarm, locked up the house, and ran down the walkway to trusty Old Blue. After three attempts, it finally cranked over. Joshua checked his watch and roared down the street in second gear. In just over ten minutes, he was parked down the street from Sean's loft building. He shut off the engine and reached for his cell phone again.

Michelle answered her phone on the second ring. "Hi, Michelle," Joshua said. "Where are you?"

"I went to the store. They had everything we need. I can't decide which color to wear first. I'm back at the condo, starting to pack."

"What kind of stuff did you have to buy, anyway? Never mind, you've really got to hurry. I just got here, and I'm parked down the block from his building, across the street, with a clear view of the front door and the driveway.

The problem is, I just realized that I can't tell whether he's still inside his apartment or if he's gone already. I'm not going to knock on his door again. Do you know what type of car he drives? I'll check the parking lot."

"No, I don't think I've ever seen his car. Do you want me to call Jenni? Maybe she knows."

"Never mind. He's walking out the front door right now. He's getting into an old Saab, faded red and rusting." Joshua switched his cell phone to the hands-free mode, started Old Blue, and ground the gears until it slipped into first. "Michelle, you've got to move. Stop packing and go. Get out to your car right away and head into town on Highway 40. Stay on the phone, and I'll tell you where to go. I'm starting to follow him—right now."

"But, Joshua, I haven't finished packing yet. I can't go this way."

"This is no time to worry about your clothes. You've got to get going. Right now."

"WHERE ARE YOU NOW, MICHELLE?"

"Just turned east on Highway 40. I'm at least thirty minutes from his apartment." She concentrated on her driving, pushed the Explorer to seventy-five, and moved into the carpool lane to pass the slower vehicles. "And where are you?"

"You won't be going to Sean's apartment. He drove south to the Forest Park Parkway, and...hold on...he's now turning west. That may be a break for us. I bet he'll go to the Inner Belt and then go north. That's the most direct way to the airport. We'll soon know—the exit to the Inner Belt is only about ten minutes from where Sean is now."

"I'm about twenty minutes from the exit for the Inner Belt."

"Did you remember your little blue book?"

Michelle didn't answer right away. "Um, what if I told you I forgot it? You interrupted my packing, remember?"

"You'd have to do a U-turn on the highway and run back to get it. And I'd be worried that the whole plan would have crumbled before we got started."

"Okay, so don't worry. I was just kidding."

"You may be missing your wits, but you didn't forget your humor."

"And you just wanted an excuse to leave without me."

"Okay, Michelle, we're getting near the Inner Belt. There he goes—he's turning north. Now I'm sure he's going to the airport."

"He might be driving to Chicago. You're about ten minutes ahead of me."

"Sean's really speeding up now. He's going seventy. But, at least he's not hard to follow. The old Saab is burning oil, leaving a long black trail."

Joshua followed the Saab another five miles and then exited to Lambert International Airport. "Michelle, he just drove past the short-term parking garage…now it looks like he's going past the intermediate-term parking lot. You know what that means."

"Um, let me guess. He's going to the long-term parking lot?"

"Gosh, you're smart. Yeah, but what it means is that he'll have to take the shuttle from there to the terminal. The shuttle is small—it's nothing more than a large van."

"You can't go in the same shuttle. He'll recognize you."

"But if I wait for the next shuttle, he'll have a ten minute lead, and we'll lose him in the terminal."

"Why don't you go back to short-term parking and leave your car there. Find a place to watch the shuttles come in. That way, you could keep track of him as he enters the terminal."

"Splendid idea."

The tires on Old Blue squealed as Joshua downshifted to second gear and made a tight turn to circle the terminal and find the garage entrance. A few minutes later, he was inside the terminal, standing on the upper level, watching through a window as the shuttle vans dropped off their passengers in the airport driveway. He told Michelle of his location as she scouted a vacant parking space in the short-term garage.

"Joshua, I'm on the lower deck of the garage."

"That's okay. Go into the terminal on that level, then find the closest escalator. Here comes another shuttle, the usual motley troupe of travelers are getting off. Wait—there's our guy. He's getting off right now, wearing jeans and a green polo shirt, and he's carrying a black suit bag, a small dark shoulder bag, and his laptop." Joshua placed the cell phone in the pocket of his blue blazer.

From his vantage point inside the huge windows, Joshua had a clear view of Sean entering the east end of the terminal, less than a hundred feet from where he stood. Joshua moved several feet until he was hidden in a group of waiting passengers. Michelle, meanwhile, inched her way up the escalator at the west end of the terminal. Joshua whispered into his cell phone, "Michelle, he just got in a long line at the ticket counter. He'll probably be there for a few minutes. I'll meet you halfway."

Joshua found Michelle near the newsstand. They hugged briefly, as if they always greeted each other with a touch. "Well, so far, so good," Michelle said. "I guess we can give our phones a rest now. You know, when you called me at the condo, I thought I'd never catch up to you."

They started toward the ticket counters. "How much did you manage to pack?" Joshua asked as they walked, glancing at Michelle's small carry on bag.

"I really have no idea. You interrupted me in the underwear drawer."

"That should give me something to think about."

"That's your problem."

"What's my problem?"

"That's all you seem to think about. Did you get a chance to see the departure schedule?"

"Yeah. A flight to Kennedy leaves in thirty minutes. After that, a direct flight to Paris in three hours, then one to London Gatwick about fifteen minutes later."

Michelle could see Sean at the ticket counter now. She put her hand on Joshua's arm and said, "Let's go to another counter."

"But, that counter isn't open—they're not selling tickets."

Michelle spoke to the woman at the ticket counter. "Hi, Julie," Michelle said. "How're you doing?"

"Hey, Michelle, going somewhere on our wonderful airlines?"

"I hope so. See that man over there, in the green polo shirt?" Michelle nodded in the direction of Sean, who was just getting his ticket at the counter about fifty feet away. Sean's head was jerking around, glancing in all directions. "We need two tickets on the same flight as his."

Julie looked at Michelle with an expression of puzzlement mixed with humor. "It's none of my business, but your trip sounds like a lot more fun than I'm having. Hold on, Michelle, let me see what I can do." Julie walked down to the next counter, whispered something to the clerk, and returned. "Michelle," she said, turning to her computer, "You're going to Kennedy in New York. The man over there asked for either the flight to Paris or the one to London, but both were booked. So, he got a ticket on Flight 721 to Kennedy, seat 23-D, which boards in twenty minutes, then he changes planes for…" Julie paused while she clicked more keys on her computer… "Frankfurt. Let's see what the availability is on the flight to Kennedy and the connecting flight to Frankfurt." Julie worked on the computer for a minute. "You're in luck, there are still a few seats available on both flights. By the way, the tickets he purchased are only one-way."

"Where does he fly after Frankfurt?"

"That's it," said Julie. "He terminates there."

Michelle looked over at Joshua, who swallowed noticeably and shrugged his shoulders. "Let's go for it," he said, as he pulled out his blue AAdvantage credit card. "Might as well earn some frequent flyer miles."

"Okay, Julie. We'll take two of everything that guy is getting. Oh, meet my…uh…friend, Joshua."

Michelle and Joshua walked briskly out of the ticketing area of the terminal, took the escalator down to the concourse level, and went through the baggage search and frisking that were now standard practice. Michelle stopped at the restrooms, reached into her all-purpose canvas bag, and said, "Here, take this one," handing Joshua a small package wrapped in plastic.

Joshua inspected the contents of the plastic bag and said, "What the hell is this?"

"Just what it looks like. Quick, go put it on."

When Joshua emerged from the men's room he looked around the bustling concourse for Michelle, but didn't see her. He put his duffle bag down, crossed his arms, and tapped his foot nervously. *Why do women take forever in the restroom?*

Suddenly, a woman walked up to him and said, "What took you so long? We better run—we can't miss this flight."

"Wow, it's incredible how much your appearance is changed by having long red hair. You fooled me, and I looked at you twice when I came out of the men's room."

"You, too. You sure look different with long hair and a mustache. The floppy fishing hat is definitely a fashion statement."

They got on the people mover and walked briskly by other passengers. "So, do I look more provocative and alluring?" Joshua asked hopefully, stroking his new mustache. "Perhaps a bit more handsome? More masculine? Sexier?"

"No. Just different."

"Thanks a lot." Joshua caught a glimpse of Sean ahead, clutching his boarding pass and laptop, entering the jet way to the plane. Sean stopped and looked around nervously before he disappeared in the gangway. Turning to Michelle, Joshua said, "You know, this stuff with Sean has all happened so fast. We haven't taken any time to think about what we're getting into. Trying to follow him to Europe may be risky and dangerous. Are you sure you're ready?"

"The stakes are high, Joshua. It's not just the five million dollars, although God knows that's a helluva lot of money. The critical point is that it's our clients' funds that they entrusted to me. The future of the little company that Mac and I started is on the line. My entire professional reputation and my career are at stake." Michelle straightened her shoulders and approached the jet way.

They handed over their boarding passes and started down the jet way to the plane. Joshua stopped outside the door of the plane and hugged Michelle.

"I'm thinking of a quote from Shakespeare, 'Courage mounteth with occasion,' " Michelle whispered in Joshua's ear.

46

"He's sitting only three rows ahead of us," Joshua said under his breath. "We'll need to keep our voices down."

"That shouldn't be too hard. I'm going to take a nap, and you're not going to stop me." Michelle put a pillow on Joshua's shoulder for her head and tried to find a comfortable position for the rest of her body.

Joshua watched out the window as the Boeing 737 gathered speed down the runway. "Michelle, look at that Boeing sign. It's longer than the first flight of the Wright brothers." But, Michelle was already fast asleep. Joshua pulled his hat down low over his forehead and attempted to read a magazine. But, he couldn't keep his eyes open and without realizing it, he, too, was soon asleep.

An hour later, Sean Eastgate got out of his seat to stretch his legs. He walked slowly toward the rear of the plane, his eyes working from side to side across the aisle, examining the faces of the passengers. He paused at the row where Michelle and Joshua slumbered and looked at them carefully, a puzzled expression coming over his face for an instant. But, he couldn't see their faces, and he moved on.

The plane bounced on the runway at Kennedy with a jolt that awakened Michelle and Joshua. Joshua searched for Michelle's hand and held it tightly as the plane taxied to the gate. They remained seated while other passengers deplaned, allowing Sean to stay far ahead. The connecting flight to Frankfurt wouldn't leave for an hour, so they had plenty of time. Indeed, they were concerned that the layover was too long. It increased the risk that Sean might spot them.

They followed Sean at a distance. He stopped at the men's restroom and then got a shoeshine. He bought a copy of Peter Mayle's *Encore Provence* and a green Michelin tourist guide to France in a bookstore. He worked his way to the international terminal and passed through security.

Joshua and Michelle exchanged wide-eyed glances as they noticed that passengers entering the international terminal were required to show their passports. Michelle whispered in Joshua's ear, "Guess what? We don't match our passport photos." They retreated from the security inspection area back to the restrooms. Joshua admired his new look as he passed the mirrors. He found an empty stall, removed his wig and mustache, and gently placed them in his shoulder bag. He returned to the concourse and waited near the door to the women's restroom. Michelle soon appeared, also sans wig.

They walked cautiously toward security and passed the inspection without incident. Since they would need to show their passports again before boarding, they would have to risk going without disguises for a few minutes. "Michelle," Joshua said as they approached the gate for the Frankfurt flight, "We have a few minutes before we need to board. Let's try to call Angela."

"What time would it be in Venice? I can never keep track."

"It's about seven hours ahead. Give or take an hour

or two." He glanced at his watch. "It's seven now, so it's about one or two in the morning wherever she is."

They found a waiting area that was quiet and largely unoccupied. Joshua found the slip of paper in his pocket containing the international code and Angela's hotel number and entered them into the cell phone.

The call was answered on the first ring. "Philip? Where are you?" Joshua could tell it was Angela's voice.

"Angela, it's me, Joshua. Where's Philip?"

"That's what I'd like to know. Last night, he said he was going downstairs to the lobby for an English newspaper, and he never came back to the room. He didn't call or anything. He just disappeared."

"Where are you?"

"The Hotel Flora in beautiful downtown Venice. It's on a canal. Everything here is on a lousy canal."

"But, I thought you loved Venice."

"I did."

"Did he take his bags?"

"No. They're all here. That's why I thought he was coming back." Angela started to rummage through Philips bags and the chest of drawers as she talked. "He may have taken his laptop and his cell phone. I don't see them."

"Angela, don't you think it's curious that he took his laptop and cell phone with him when he stepped out to get a newspaper?"

"Well, I should tell you more."

"Angela, Michelle and I are at the airport about to catch a plane to Frankfurt. What else should you be telling us?" Joshua put his head next to Michelle's with the phone between them allowing her to hear Angela's half of the conversation.

"Okay, but just the retelling is embarrassing. About an hour after I realized he hadn't returned, I walked down to the lobby and asked the clerk if he had seen Philip. The clerk said that Phil left with an Italian woman who had a rose tattoo just above her left breast. The clerk was very specific about that. And he kept saying, "*que bella, que bella*." So, I asked the clerk if the woman was a prostitute. He said he didn't think she was a prostitute, at least not one of the regulars, but that she worked in a men's clothing store off the Piazza San Marco."

"Angela, I'm sorry."

"Wait, there's more. Since you asked." She continued, sniffling, "When I got back to our room, I found a note he left in the bathroom. It says, 'My dear Angela, Three things I must say to you.' Joshua, are you ready for this? He's got three numbered points—he's trying to kill me with my favorite poison. I'll read them: '1. It's been fabulous traveling Europe with you. 2. I have a higher calling. 3. All you need to be happy is an occasional pity-fuck. Ciao, baby.' Can you believe it? Is that all I am, just a pity-fuck?"

Michelle took the phone. "Angela, remember that things usually turn out for the best."

"You sound like my mother, Michelle. Oh God, I can't think clearly. What do you make of his goodbye note, especially the part about having a 'higher calling'?"

"Bottom line? He left you, permanently," Michelle said. "Now, it's up to you not to fall apart."

Angela started sobbing. "If Venice is supposed to be this fabulous place for lovers, why am I having such a miserable time here?" Michelle had a shocked expression on her face, her eyebrows raised, and her jaw lowered.

Joshua retrieved the phone from Michelle. "Pull yourself together, Angela," he said as calmly as possible. "Here's what I want you to do." Joshua explained Michelle's plan. "Got it Angela? Stop crying, sit down, and make a list of things you'll need to do to get there. Give me a call on the cell phone as soon as you arrive. If there's any change in our destination in the meantime, we'll call you. We'll also call you when we have a better idea when we'll get there." He paused for a minute, listening. "Yeah, *ciao* to you, too."

Joshua hung up and leaned over to Michelle. "That was a good idea you had, having Angela meet us there."

"I usually have good ideas. We can use all the help we can get. And, maybe it will force her to be active, involved, so she'll think about something other than Philip leaving her for another woman."

The flight to Frankfurt was long and dark. The plane was a huge wide body, an L-1011. Joshua and Michelle were near the rear, almost a football field's length from Sean, who was in the front third of coach. After being seated, Joshua put on a salt and pepper wig with a short ponytail and topped it with a herringbone snap-bill cap. Michelle became a blonde with a black beret. They were concerned that he would deplane quickly, and they would lose him in the Frankfurt terminal. They would worry about that later. For now, they each needed to catch up on some much-needed sleep. Michelle was dozing before the plane took off.

They were awakened by the sounds of passengers raising the window shades and lowering the seatback trays. A clatter of plastic accompanied the flight attendants as they served the continental breakfasts. The aroma of fresh coffee, even though it was airplane coffee, energized Joshua. He looked forward to his first trip to Europe since his summer backpack tour in college.

"Are we there, yet?" Michelle mumbled, her face buried in Joshua's chest. He liked the way she woke up. Slowly, limb by limb, one eye at a time, and a little disoriented. This trip was also Michelle's second to Europe, her first being the semester she spent in France as part of a student exchange program at Mizzou.

"We're crossing the English Channel. It won't be long now."

They were both hungry, and finished their melon, croissants, and cheese quickly. Joshua went to the galley to beg for seconds.

AFTER THE PLANE TAXIED to the gate, it took an agonizing ten minutes for all the passengers to file off the plane. When Joshua and Michelle entered the terminal, Sean was gone. They followed the other passengers, who were being herded to customs where long lines had already formed at the several inspection stations. Joshua spotted Sean in the middle of the express lane at the far end. He'd been delayed because he had to claim the baggage he had shipped in cargo.

"Thank God for customs," Michelle said. "It allowed us to catch up."

"One small matter we forgot about." Joshua pointed to his wig. He nodded toward the rear of huge customs area, and they casually walked away from the crowded lines. Joshua held up his shoulder bag while Michelle removed her wig behind it. Then, it was Joshua's turn. When they once again matched their passport photos, they joined the express lane. They were far behind Sean, who was just now having his passport stamped and was clearing customs. He disappeared down a corridor to the right.

Most of the passengers were tourists, and the German customs inspectors waved them through. Even so, the express lane took a long time—just like at the supermarket. Finally, Michelle approached the customs inspector and placed her passport on the counter. Joshua came up and stood at her elbow, his passport already open. The inspector, seeing the American passports, looked at Michelle and inquired in English as to the purpose and length of their visit. "Tourism and pleasure. We'll be here about a week," she said, smiling in Joshua's direction.

The inspector smiled at Michelle, stamped their passports, and bid them a good journey. They passed through the gates, turned to the right, and raced into the corridor. "Wait, we almost forgot again," she said, pointing to her hair. They came to a halt in the middle of the corridor.

"We don't have time, Michelle. Let's just switch right here." Quickly, Joshua was transformed into a blonde with a black beret, and Michelle sported a salt-and-pepper wig with a ponytail, covered by the gray herringbone snap-bill cap. She opted not to wear the beard. "How many changes did you get?" Joshua asked.

"We have one more set," she answered, digging in her bag, "So I hope these can be used for a while, unless we find a place to buy another set." She swapped the snap-bill cap for a blue baseball cap with a cardinal perched on the front.

They ran down the corridor again, glancing ahead to see if they could spot Sean. Joshua held on to his Nordic wig and beret to keep it from flying off. "I need your baseball cap to keep this thing on."

They slowed as they approached the main terminal. Huge signs pointed in different directions.

DOMESTIC FLIGHTS. TRAINS. UNDERGROUND.

They looked at each other exasperated. "If you were Sean, what would you take to wherever you were going? If I'm Sean, I'm in a hurry. I take a plane. Therefore, we go left."

Michelle took longer to decide. "Let's see. If I'm Sean, the trip must be as confusing as possible. Haven't you noticed the way he's constantly looking around at all the passengers? No, if I'm Sean, I take the train. We go right."

"But, there's probably a lot of flights out of Frankfurt to Zurich. More than trains."

"You're right, but they'd be leaving the international terminal, not domestic flights."

"Oh," Joshua said, with a look of surprise. "I thought, with the European Union and all, that travel to nearby countries would be considered domestic. Let's check the flights first."

In the main terminal they found the schedule of arriving and departing flights. The next flight to Zurich was in two hours. They ran two city blocks to the train station. The next train to Zurich left in ten minutes.

"Come on, Joshua, we'll miss the train." They sprinted in the direction of the ticket windows, Joshua's blonde hair bouncing on his head and Michelle's shoulder bag banging against her side.

47

Seating in first class on the train hadn't been available, and Joshua and Michelle settled for a crowded compartment in a second-class car. Four people were already occupying the narrow cabin. On either side of the compartment, nearest the door, a couple in their late teens, huddled over a CD player in the aisle. It was as big as Joshua's duffel bag, and it blared German rap music.

An elderly couple had taken the window seats on each side of the aisle. Joshua placed Michelle's bag in the overhead luggage rack and followed it with his duffel bag. The kids ignored the newcomers and concentrated on the pounding beat. Michelle nodded to the elderly couple and offered "good morning" in English.

The woman returned the greeting with a tepid smile, but the man appeared enthused to have company. "Hello," he said with a British accent, "are you on holiday?"

"Oh, yes. We're tourists, from the States, just taking a little vacation," Michelle said, trying not to look too obvious while she adjusted her wig under the blue baseball cap. "We're going to Zurich. And you?"

The woman elected to avoid conversation, preferring to entertain herself with the German countryside racing by outside the window. Her companion was more gregarious. He wore a weathered wool tweed jacket with leather elbow patches and a wool slouch hat. "The Mrs. and I are retired now for several years," he shouted to be heard over the music, "but we like to get out of London for a bit of holiday, visit the Continent, see how the chaps over here are doing, you know." The old man suddenly stood up, approached the teens, and spoke sternly in German. The girl lowered the volume and flipped off the old man behind his back as he recovered his seat.

Joshua thought, *Teens. They're the same everywhere.* "Personally, I can't tolerate rap music," he said, "but it may have more cultural value than meets the ear. In fact, it's quite a unifying cultural element because it sounds the same from one country to the next. There's been some interesting research into this notion. Quite fascinating stuff, really. It seems that a team of music historians and cultural anthropologists did an extensive study, and they concluded that rap music has bounced back and forth across the pond a few times. The European rap picks up on the American model, which is a direct descendant of square dance music from our period of western expansion, which in turn traces its roots back to German folk dance music, going back several centuries."

"That sounds like something you just made up," Michelle said, patting her wig in place.

Without turning her head, the Mrs. spoke into the window, "Wherever it came from, it's absolutely *ruining* Trafalgar Square." She paused, leaned across the aisle and put a hand on her husband's knee. "Dear old Harry failed to mention that actually, we're going to the French Riviera. Harry would just die if he couldn't see all that terribly gorgeous young flesh once a year. As if the Brighton beach isn't enough for this coot's old muscle. But, I suppose it wouldn't hurt. God knows he can't do anything about it. That's right eh, m'love?"

"Now, Martha," he answered sheepishly, "a bit of a stout one never killed any man. At least, not that I've heard." Harry stopped, as if to ponder the accuracy of his statement. "Although at my age, one can't be too careful." He removed his slouch hat and scratched a bald dome that still boasted a few wisps of white gauze.

Michelle smiled at the elderly gentleman. A moment of quiet embarrassment passed, and Michelle said, "You must be looking forward to a warm, sunny climate."

Hands on his knees, he looked earnestly at Michelle. "Shame about your President. How wonderfully *dreadful*, all that mess. Quite."

Joshua came to full attention. "What about the President? What *now?*"

The Mrs. suddenly came to life and abandoned the German countryside to leap mouth first into the conversation. "Well, all that *womanizing*, my dear. Another tortured sex scandal, just broadcast this morning, full of characters right out of one of those soap operas you see on the telly. I say, Harry," she said with one eyebrow cocked at her husband, "how *does* the man have any time to do all his Presidential duties with some poor, defenseless wench in his lap all the time? I dare say."

"Now, Martha, that isn't the problem at all. The real problem is rather that the American media make such fuss, such a world-class to-do over a simple dalliance, a mere frolic. If this happened at No. 10 Downing Street, our PM would simply—and quite properly, I might add—give us a nod and a wink and move on. The tabloids and the cartoonists would have a jolly good time for a few days, trying to embarrass him and pad their outrageous profits." Harry was now twisting his hat, like wringing out a wet towel. "But the Americans, my *God!* They screw each other *all* the time, pardon my French, then wring their hands and revert to hypocritical Puritans when it suits their convenience. *Silly*, that's what it is. While you Americans are having your Thanksgiving holiday, we Brits give thanks that the Puritans left."

"But, Martha has a good point," Michelle responded. "What kind of a role model is the President for how women should be treated if he has one affair after another. And in the White House, of all places. He's a husband, a father, and a world leader. The President should control his libido," she added with a sidelong glance at Joshua, as if some hidden meaning, like a healthy vegetable, was being tossed in his direction for thoughtful consumption.

"No, on balance, Harry has the better argument," Joshua said, his arms outstretched, symbolically weighing the two sides. "The President didn't have an affair, at least not an *affaire* as it's come to us from the French. He just works off stress with cute, young bimbos. Actually, some of them are less than cute, but they have other ah… *attributes*. Those affairs mean nothing. They're not relevant. No harm, no foul. Let the poor man get on with the job we elected him to do which, I suggest, he's been doing in an excellent manner, including significant advances in gender equality. Just look at all the women he has appointed to cabinet-level positions. Besides, the President should be judged for what he accomplishes on Main Street, not what he does on the couch."

"Precisely, old chap. A trained tongue, I can tell. A barrister, that's what you must be. I shan't say we'll resolve this debate with our women, so if I may suggest, before the women sentence us to a good lashing or we have our brains pounded senseless by that rap music," he said, nodding in the direction of the CD player, "that we pop over to the dining car and see if there's a decent cuppa tea on this train. What say you two?"

"We two would enjoy that, wouldn't we, Michelle?" Joshua extended his hand to help her out of her seat.

Martha clutched her purse and straightened her dress. Harry tried to restore the shape of his hat. Joshua slid the door open, and the four of them stepped over the CD player and squeezed through the narrow opening of their compartment. They had to balance themselves in the aisle of the speeding train while they walked to the dining car.

Martha turned to Michelle and said in a voice loud enough for all to hear, "I've been admiring your wig, my dear. It makes you look much older, but ponytails are so cute."

Joshua checked his cell phone to see if Angela left any messages, but there was none. He wondered how she was doing.

THE VAPORETTO CHURNED THROUGH Venice's Grand Canal, reversed its engine, and bumped heavily against the old pier with a thud that shook the entire boat. Angela gathered her bags and started the long climb up the granite steps to the train station at Santa Lucia. Her wheeled carry-on bag clunked behind her with each step. Battering the defenseless luggage was approximately what she felt like doing to Philip. On the plaza high above the Grand Canal she paused for a final glimpse of the panorama of Venice. The canal water now looked green, and the pastel buildings glowed with warm tones in the early morning sun. *I'll be back, dear Venice, in happier days.*

Late yesterday afternoon, she had taken several rolls of her film for one-hour processing. Now, as she approached the ticket window at Santa Lucia, she pulled one of the photographs from her bag. It was a close-up of Philip and her with the Eiffel Tower looming against the sky in the background. After she purchased a one-way ticket to Zurich, with a change of trains in Milan, she placed the photograph on the counter for the clerk to see and hoped he spoke some English. "Have you seen this man, either yesterday or today?"

The aging clerk was dressed in a black suit and vest that must have been as old as he was. The cuffs on the clerk's jacket were threadbare and tattered. The collar on his white shirt, a full size too large, was frayed. The narrow black tie showed vestiges of various encounters with espresso and grappa. Tufts of snow white hair sprayed in all directions from under his cap, but his mustache was full. Angela considered that this was probably the poor man's only suit, and admired that he wore it with pride and dignity.

His craggy face studied the picture and he stroked his mustache for a minute. He lit an unfiltered cigarette with a wooden match, which he extinguished by a nervous and vigorous twitching of his wrist. He pondered the photograph some more. Angela thought he was either deep in thought or taking a quick nap. Yet a third possibility occurred to her. "Perhaps this will help your memory," she said, reaching in the security pouch she kept under her blouse and placing a new five-euro note on the counter. *It would be worth four and a half bucks.*

"Si, si." The clerk immediately came to life, his memory refreshed. His eyes lit up and a broad smile revealed brown teeth. "I remember him well."

"Was he alone?" Angela asked slowly, not really wanting to hear the answer.

"He bought *two* tickets, I remember," the clerk said, holding up two fingers and inhaling deeply on his cigarette. "There was a lovely girl with him, a Venetian girl, I could tell." The clerk studied the picture again, tapping

Philip's face with a stained forefinger. Another stroke of his mustache. "Ah! I remember now. She had a rose."

"A rose?"

"*Si*, right here," he said and reached across the narrow counter and touched Angela's breast. She retreated involuntarily, and he looked disappointed. He withdrew his hand and placed it over his heart. "*Que bella!*"

A tattoo of a rose. Angela ran her hand nervously through her hair. "What train did they take?"

The clerk stared blankly into space for a long moment, trying to focus through the feigned uncertainty. "My mind is not a computer anymore, I do not remember things well."

Angela showed him another note for five euros.

"*Si*, now I remember," he came to life again, plucking the money off the counter. "I think it was the train to Milano, the same as you are taking, but yesterday." More stroking of the mustache, then the gloom of hopeless uncertainty overcoming his face once again. "Or was it Roma? *Si*, it was Roma. No, could it have been Pisa?"

Angela's expression turned to disappointment. She brusquely replaced her security pouch beneath her blouse. "*Gracie, signor. Buonjorno.*" She turned and waved.

The clerk slipped the euros into a pocket in his vest. "*Buon fortuna.*"

Angela hurried down the platform, angrily threw her bags through the open door, and climbed the steps into the train. She settled into her compartment for the long train ride.

WHILE ANGELA SAT SILENTLY by the window and watched the Italian Alps come into view, her train sped west toward Milano. At the same time, Joshua and Michelle were enjoying their new travel companions as their train sped south.

"Before I retired," Harry was saying, "I worked for thirty years in the archives section of Parliament. Summers, I taught comparative literature at Oxford, mostly English and American literature."

Joshua was curious. "That seems like an interesting combination of work."

"Quite so. Actually, the bridge between the two is not as wide as one might think. The relationship between history and good fiction is a narrow one. For example, look at these titillating little scandals that keep coming out of your White House."

"But, our President is a survivor," said Joshua. "Nothing seems to stick on him."

"Precisely, old chum," beamed Harry, "reminds me of the famous quotation from Britain's most famous statesman, 'Nothing in life is so exhilarating as to be shot at without result.' The President would do well to read Sir Winston—his history of the Second World War."

Martha sat her tea down, loudly interrupting her husband. "Harry," she began in a scolding tone, "you'll soon put these nice young people to sleep with Churchill's history of World War Two. The problem with the President is that he prefers Mark Twain. 'In statesmanship, get the formalities right, never mind about the moralities.' "

"And that's the greatest disappointment for women," said Michelle. "He wasn't honest with the public in the previous scandals. It makes us think he's lying because he's forever deflecting questions about his affairs. Wasn't it also Mark Twain who said, 'I was gratified to be able to answer promptly, and I did. I said I didn't know.' "

Joshua held up both hands in mock surrender. "I can't keep up with today's topic, famous quotations. All I can think of is a quote from Tennessee Williams, which should not be recounted in polite company. But, look, Michelle,"

Special Assessment

Joshua pleaded. "The public would just as soon see this whole thing go away, like the other scandals, and let him do his job."

Joshua suddenly elbowed Michelle. He lowered his head and said, under his breath, "Don't look now, but look who's coming up the aisle."

Michelle pulled her cap further down her forehead. Sean Eastgate, wearing dark sunglasses, was walking slowly up the aisle of the dining car, steadying himself at each step, his head nervously twitching from table to table as he glanced anxiously into the faces of the passengers.

48

Angela walked around the Hauptbahnof, browsing through the newspapers at the bookstore, dawdling in the gift shop, nursing a latte in the coffee shop. She had checked the schedule and saw that it would be another hour before the train from Frankfurt was due in Zurich. Joshua had instructed her to be on the platform when the train arrived, to find a place where she could see but not be seen.

She walked out of the Zurich train station onto the Bahnhofplatz where the late afternoon sun was casting long shadows across the tree-lined plaza. The air was clear and cool. The trams were full of commuters. It felt good to stretch her legs, so Angela walked briskly around the plaza, her battered luggage in tow.

With five minutes to spare, she was standing nervously at the end of the long platform where the train from Frankfurt would arrive. She found a baggage cart loaded with shipping boxes and stood next to it, holding the newspaper in front of her face, pretending to read. *All I need is a trench coat.*

The train pulled slowly up to the platform and finally came to a complete stop. All doors opened, and waves of passengers began scurrying past Angela's station at the baggage cart. She held the top of the newspaper just below her eyes and watched the faces intently as they walked by. After almost all of the passengers had left the train, she noticed a young man motioning to her, a man with blond hair and a beret. *Jeez, it's Joshua! And there's Michelle next to him, wearing a silly looking gray wig with a ponytail and a Cardinals' baseball cap.* Angela followed Joshua's gesture and fell in alongside them on the platform.

"Okay guys, let me see if I've got this right." Angela spoke loudly so as to be heard over the noise on the crowded platform. "You've followed this Sean character some five thousand miles. You wind up here in Zurich, Switzerland. You think he has a numbered Swiss bank account here. You hope to see him going into a bank. You hope the bank is where he stashed the money. You hope to catch him with the money. You suppose that you'll get the money back. No facts, just a bunch of hopes, suppositions, and what ifs. Is that about it, or have I missed something?"

"Angela, you've got to keep your voice down," Joshua whispered. "Where did Sean go? Did you see him?"

"I don't think so," Angela said. "Do you guys have any idea of what you're doing?"

"We know he was on the train," Michelle spoke softly as she looked around behind her, "but we don't know which car. Hopefully, he's still behind us."

Angela had to jog to keep up with Joshua and Michelle as they walked down the long platform toward the entrance to the train station. "Tell me," she said, "what are you going to do if you see him withdraw a briefcase full of cash? Are you going to find a policeman, tell him about all your hopes and suppositions, and expect him to arrest Sean?"

Ignoring Angela's last question, Michelle scanned the platform. "Great," she said, her voice full of exasperation. "Just great. Now we've lost him."

"Why don't you call that sheriff you were telling me about?" Angela asked. "The guy who retired from the FBI. You said he even worked cases with Interpol."

"Angela," Michelle said, "I can assure you, this trip is not risky. We're just going to follow Sean to the bank. Besides, what could Sheriff Cooper possibly do? He's in Missouri."

Angela glanced at Joshua for support. Joshua shrugged and said, "Really, Angela, you always worry too much."

"Well, at least, give me Cooper's card."

"I don't know what good it's going to do," Joshua said, "But here it is." He handed the sheriff's business card to Angela.

Michelle was growing more impatient as they neared the end of the platform with no sign of Sean. "First," she said, "We need to find Sean before he leaves here. Let's figure out a place in the station where we can watch the rest of the passengers as they come through."

The three of them hurried to the entrance of the train station, taking up separate posts inside the main gate where passengers were streaming in. Joshua in his blond hairpiece was milling around a kiosk of magazines. Angela with the *International Herald* held over her nose was ostensibly occupied looking at postcards. Michelle with her gray wig and blue baseball cap was sitting on a bench pretending to read a map of Zurich. They studied the faces of each of the passengers, frequently exchanging glances at each other accompanied by slight shrugs to acknowledge no sightings of Sean.

The stream of passengers soon dwindled to a trickle, and still no glimpse of Sean. Joshua walked slowly past Michelle and whispered, "I'll take a look in the room marked '*Herren.*' Perhaps he's in there, tending to business." After a few minutes, Joshua returned, carrying three lattes on a tray and a disappointed look on his face.

Angela joined Michelle and Joshua. Michelle spoke first. "We've been tailing him for a full twenty-four hours, following him across two continents. How could we lose him now?"

"We have five basic scenarios," Angela said, starting another numbered analysis. "One, he never got off the train because he's en route to a further destination. Two, he got off the train at a previous stop, but you guys missed it. Three, he has a very clever disguise, perhaps dressed as a woman or a soldier, or he left the train with a woman while we were looking for a single man. Four, he crossed over to another platform and used a different entrance to come into the train station, totally bypassing our strategically placed stakeout. Five, he walked past me on the platform, but I didn't recognize him because I have no idea what he looks like."

Joshua groaned. "You don't know what he looks like? Now you tell us."

The three of them lingered in the middle of the Bahnhofplatz, a fog of frustration hanging over them. The station's public address system announced the departure of a train to Vienna. Throngs of passengers were jostling past them, luggage carts and shopping bags banging into knees. Each of the trio was nervously glancing over the shoulder of the other, hoping to announce a sighting. It resembled a Washington cocktail party, each political phony not wanting to miss "the ultimate encounter," loosely defined as "the need to talk to anyone else who was more important than the person you were talking to."

Joshua paced in front of the statue of Alfred Escher. "Damn," he snarled in disgust and grabbed his hairpiece and flung it onto the cobblestones of the plaza.

Michelle scooped up the blond wig and fixed it back on Joshua's head. "You're just tired," she said, showing considerable empathy. "So am I, but we've got to keep going." She stepped back to judge the mop on Joshua's head. "Look, based on what we saw in Sean's apartment," she said, "I think that Zurich was his destination and that he got off the train here. Perhaps he did have some clever disguise. More likely, Angela didn't know who to look for, and he just slipped past her."

"Let's focus on what we know for sure," Angela said. "It's already after four o'clock in the afternoon, so the banks are probably closed and won't be open until tomorrow morning. Assuming Sean is here in Zurich to make a withdrawal, he can't do it until tomorrow, say, nine o'clock at the earliest. So, we've got time to work out a plan. Maybe we should use this time to find out where he's staying."

"Hey, what about that computer store?" Michelle asked. "The place where Sean bought his laptop? It's probably still open. Maybe one of the people at the store remembers something about Sean. Maybe someone will know where he stayed the last time he was here. Joshua, give me the street address, and I'll find out how to get there."

"I didn't write down the street number," Joshua said, "but I remember the name of the street started with Bah." He looked up at the street signs and pointed confidently. "That's it. The Bahnhofstrasse."

"Let's see how far it goes," Michelle said. The three of them ran over to a map of the city displayed on a kiosk. Michelle pointed, "Look, we're here, at the Bahnhofplatz." Her finger moved to the corner of the plaza. "Here's the Bahnhofstrasse. See, it runs from where we are, right here, a long way. Many blocks."

Angela looked away from the map, across the plaza. "It's a pedestrian street. We could take the tram or walk. It doesn't look like taxis are allowed." Angela spotted a street vendor and said "I'm starved." She headed for a cart decorated with enormous pretzels on the other side of the plaza.

Joshua turned to Michelle. "Angela appears a little skeptical of our adventure. But, she'll get into the flow of things. Thanks to you, we have the beginnings of a plan, and that sure beats hanging around all these pigeons. Speaking of which, do pigeons prefer blondes? Are they going to be attracted to my beautiful blond hair and start a nest? Is there any pigeon crap in it?" Joshua said, as he bent his head forward for examination.

Michelle looked, but kept her distance, just in case. "No, but the wig makes you look like a Nordic hippie."

"Well, at least my hair is on straight, which is more than you can say."

Angela returned, chewing on a huge, steaming pretzel, about the size of a Frisbee. "I asked the pretzel man about the computer store," she said as she broke off pieces of pretzel for Michelle and Joshua. "He said, at least I think he said, there's a store about three blocks down the pedestrian mall, the Bahnhofstrasse," Angela explained, pointing. "He said it's on the right side. We should be able to walk it easily, except for lugging our bags."

Observing Angela's battered roll-on, Joshua said, "Now we know why they call it luggage."

"And we would have a chance to check out any banks near the store," Michelle said, ignoring Joshua's comments. "If we're really lucky, maybe we'll see a hotel in the vicinity. Sean's hotel."

The walk down the Bahnhofstrasse took about fifteen minutes, and they found Der Electronika crowded with well-dressed businessmen and women who were shopping after work. Michelle, Angela, and Joshua were impressed as they glanced at the high-tech computer gadgets and the wide variety of software available in foreign languages. As they looked around for a sales assistant, a young woman in a black business suit greeted them. Her badge indicated that her name was Gretchen.

"*Spreichen zie English?*" Michelle asked.

"Yes, of course," Gretchen answered. "Are you looking for a computer?"

It was Joshua's turn. "Not exactly. We're looking for a man who purchased an expensive notebook computer here recently. Maybe within the past week. Not quite my height," Joshua held his hand to his face at eye level. "With long blond hair."

"Is he American, also?"

"Yes." The mere question raised their hopes.

"Are you friends of his?" Gretchen inquired.

"No, I wouldn't say that," Michelle said. "Do you remember him?"

Gretchen pursed her lips and replied, "Such a man was here recently. I remember, because it was a slow day, and he was the only customer." Gretchen turned to look around the store. "Another clerk helped him make his purchase, but she no longer works here."

"Well, perhaps you remember something about him," Michelle said. "He purchased an expensive laptop here a few days ago. His name is Sean Eastgate, although he could have used something different here in Zurich. We found the name of your store on the label fastened on his laptop. He's…well, he's in trouble, and we need to find him. So, we decided to come here, in the hope that someone might remember something about him, anything, that could help us."

"Yes, I remember him well," Gretchen said warily, "How could I forget? He bought one of our best notebook computers, about four thousand dollars, U.S., and paid cash. He also purchased one of our new watches, called the 'smart watch.'"

"Do you happen to remember if he said anything about what bank he used?" Michelle continued the questioning.

"No, but of course, many banks are near here. After all, you are in the center of Zurich."

"Did he mention where he was staying, the name of a hotel, maybe?"

Gretchen paused, an index finger going to the corner of her mouth, as she considered the question. "Yes, but you can't let him know that you talked to me. You see the other sales clerk went out with him that night. She called me the next day and told me what happened. When he was in the store, looking at equipment, he began flirting with her, and maybe she was flirting with him. He asked her to dinner. Foolish girl, she decided to go. Afterward, they went back to his hotel for a drink. She told me that he was mean to her, that he tried to make her do...things to him." Gretchen stopped, her eyes now cast downward. "You know, sex things. She is just a simple girl from a small village in the countryside. It was not good. She said it was very offensive. She was lucky to get away from him. That is why you cannot tell him that you saw me."

"What was the hotel?"

"The Hotel Baur Au Lac."

"Where is this hotel?"

"Not far. Several blocks that way," she pointed across the street. "It is next to the lake."

"Could we use your phone to call the hotel? They could tell us if he's staying there."

"If it will help, I can call the hotel for you now, for the sake of my friend." Gretchen slipped behind the counter, found the number in the directory, and dialed. After a brief exchange in German, she hung up, a look of disappointment on her face. "The hotel says he is not registered. That's all they would say. But, it's still early."

"*Danke*." Michelle shook Gretchen's hand. "Thank you. You've been very helpful, and you can be sure that we'll not mention that we talked to you."

Michelle, Angela, and Joshua left the computer store and walked down the Bahnhofstrasse, Angela's bag bumping on the cobblestones. "I'm hungry." Michelle sounded weary. "Let's try one of those things," she said, pointing to a cart of knishes across the way. She handed the street vendor a twenty-dollar bill and asked, "Is this enough for three of these?" The man wiped his hands on his apron and took the twenty with a perceptible sigh, and using a pocket calculator, computed the exchange rate and the amount of change in Swiss francs.

The trio found a nearby bench and wearily plopped down, pondering their next move, disappointed that their only lead had evaporated so rapidly.

"We really need to find a currency exchange," Angela said. "I always feel better using the local currency. It makes me feel less touristy, you know? It's amazing how many currency exchange places you find in European cities, compared to none in the States. You know, the banks have the lowest exchange rates."

Neither Michelle nor Joshua responded.

Michelle looked around while she ate her knish. "Speaking of banks, I see four between here and the corner. Suppose Sean used one of them. He probably walked out of the bank and right into the computer store, like a huge magnet attracted him. It may be a long shot but, if no one has a better idea, I propose that tomorrow morning, we come right here, spread out so we can cover each of these banks, and wait for our good buddy Sean to show up."

"It's not a very specific plan," Angela said around a mouthful of knish. "Built around another supposition. However, I can't offer anything better at the moment. But, like I asked you guys before, then what? Let's say that we're lucky enough to spot him walking into one of these banks. What are we supposed to do then? That's the question."

Michelle studied the last morsel of her knish. "Yes, Angela, you've said that many times already. Let's discuss it tonight, when we're settled into a place. What I'd really like is a nice hotel room, a hot bath, and some rest. First, though, I need to purchase some necessaries, a toothbrush, and stuff like that. Is it true that some European women don't shave? Anyway, I was in such a rush to leave, I didn't have a chance to pack a razor, deodorant, or anything else. That shop across the street looks like a drugstore. Maybe it has a vending machine where I can buy some pantyhose. And, I need some underwear."

Michelle and Angela stepped inside the door of the drugstore, but Joshua decided to wait outside. He said, "I don't think I need any 'necessaries' today, so I'll just play sentry out here while you ladies do your shopping and engage in whatever girl talk the occasion may inspire."

Michelle and Angela roamed around the store for a few minutes. They located a display of razors, where Michelle selected a packet of women's disposables.

"What about hotel room arrangements for tonight?" Angela asked. "I don't want to pry, but it's not hard to notice that Joshua and you might want to be together."

"Oh, that." A look of embarrassment flashed across Michelle's face. "Well, maybe he wants to but, for me, the timing isn't right. Yeah, maybe I like him, maybe not. It's stayed at a professional distance so far, and I'm not rushing into anything, particularly under these circumstances. And, you shouldn't feel like the odd man out. Or, the odd woman, I guess. So, why don't we…" Michelle stopped in mid-sentence as she noticed the stunned expression on Angela's face. "Angela, what is it?"

Angela was crouching to hide behind a rack of pantyhose. She edged sideways down the aisle, peeking between cans of hair spray at someone in the next aisle. "See that dark-haired woman over there?"

"What, Angela? Why on earth are you gawking at that woman?"

"Well, let's walk by her and see if that thing on her front is what I think it is. See it?"

"A tattoo of a rose. On her left boob."

49

Angela hurried out of the store and found Joshua sitting on a bicycle rack. "Well, did you guys get everything you need? We're just going on a sleepover. Your humble sentry has observed a number of beautiful women saunter past his lonely post, but, unfortunately, has nothing to report about our subject. Sean hasn't walked past here since you guys went into the drugstore."

"Michelle is finishing getting her things, and should be out in a minute. You won't believe it, but I just saw a woman in the store with a rose tattoo on the same part of her anatomy as the woman Philip picked up in Venice."

"And you think she's the same woman?"

"I don't know, but she sure fits the description. Two men, in different instances, saw her in Venice, and they both kept saying '*que bella, que bella*,' as they pointed to their chests with mournful sighs. They were practically weeping." Angela's hand went over her heart. "This was the testimony of two men who had witnessed great beauty. If this is the same woman, I'd say she's overrated."

"So? Don't get your hopes up that you'll find Philip around here. Anyway, there could be thousands of European women with rose tattoos on their breasts, and you happened to hear about one of them and you saw another. I better go into the store and see for myself."

Just then, the dark-haired woman with the rose tattoo came out of the pharmacy, turned left, and walked down the street. Constricted by her short, tight leather skirt, she walked with quick, small steps.

"You won't need to go in, Joshua. She just came out, and there she goes," Angela said, nodding in her direction. Joshua's eyes followed Angela's gaze and quickly focused on a pair of hips jiggling against the tight skin of thin leather.

Michelle came out of the store seconds later. "Humor me for a bit, guys," said Angela. "I think we should follow Ms. Rose Tattoo and hope she leads us to something interesting. Like Philip, so I can kill him." Angela walked behind the tattoo lady, mimicking her tiny steps and swiveling hips.

Joshua and Michelle exchanged weary shrugs and followed a few yards behind. Joshua leaned over close to Michelle's ear. "Why are we encouraging Angela's fit of jealousy, when we should be finding out where Sean is staying? And getting a hotel for ourselves?"

Michelle's gaze was fixed on Angela ahead of her. She said to Joshua, "You should have seen the expression on Angela's face when she spotted Ms. Rose Tattoo in the drugstore! It was pretty incredible. Angela is convinced that this is the same woman who stole Philip away. And, she's determined to find out."

Joshua was also watching Angela, about ten yards ahead. "Like I just told Angela, there's probably a lot of women around here with tattoos. It doesn't mean that Philip is here. Just out of curiosity, did you notice what Ms. Tattoo bought in the drugstore?"

"Yes. She bought a tube of lubricant."

"Really? Old Blue has the same problem."

Michelle and Joshua had walked less than a block

down the Bahnhofstrasse when they noticed Angela had stopped in the middle of the mall and parked her bag. She just stood there, arms folded across her chest, while Michelle and Joshua approached. "So, where's Ms. Tattoo?"

Angela nodded with her head toward the blinking lights of the entrance to a disco nightclub. "Ms. Tattoo just walked into that place. Shall we go in and have a look?"

"She might work there, Angela," Joshua said.

"She looks the type," Michelle added. "Like a call girl, or a dancer. Maybe a hostess."

"Or, a stripper," Joshua said. "I agree with Angela, we should check it out."

Joshua felt Michelle's icy stare on the side of his face. "I don't think so," Michelle said firmly, but with a weary voice. "Look, Angela, Ms. Tattoo could be in there for hours, whether she's partying or working there. It will be dark soon. We need to find a hotel, get some rest, and we need time to develop some kind of plan for what we're doing. Tomorrow is a big day. And I'm jet-lagged and pooped from all this running around."

ANGELA, JOSHUA, AND MICHELLE found a room at the Hotel Limmat, which was on a street named In Gassen across from the Paradeplatz. The Limmat was only a two-star hotel, with tiny rooms and no amenities, but it was able to command high rates due to its location near the historic Fraumunster Church. The lobby carpet was threadbare, and the elevators belonged in a museum.

The trio squeezed themselves and their luggage into the tiny elevator for a trip to their room on the fifth floor. Joshua closed the metal gate of the elevator and, as their elevator lurched upward, the other elevator descended to the lobby. Its doors opened, and a man wearing sunglasses and a forest green Tyrolean hat walked out.

Sean strode over to the hotel concierge and asked the man to recommend a good restaurant nearby. The concierge suggested the Borse Halle, located off the Paradeplatz, past the huge Geschaftsstellen des Schweizerischen Bankvereins, near the Borse Stock Exchange. "*Danke*," Sean said, as he handed the concierge two Swiss francs and stepped onto In Gassen. Dusk was giving way to darkness, and a foggy mist shrouded the street.

Meanwhile, in their tiny room on the fifth floor, the travel-weary trio was sorting out the sleeping arrangements. They stood and stared for a minute at the two narrow beds, like American twin beds, only smaller. Even if the hotel had an extra rollaway bed, the room had no space for it. Two people could barely pass between the furniture as it was.

"Perhaps I should be a gentleman and offer to sleep on the floor," Joshua said.

"We object to the first part about you being a gentleman, but we accept your offer to sleep on the floor," Angela said. "I'll take this one." She flopped herself on the bed near the door.

Michelle surveyed the premises, contemplating the cramped quarters. "You're elected, Joshua, you get to sleep on the floor."

"On the other hand, if the two of you don't mind sleeping together, I'd take the other bed." Joshua threw his duffel bag on the remaining bed.

"I don't think so," Michelle said firmly. She placed his duffel on the floor in the corner of the tiny room, replaced it with her own, and headed to the bathroom. "I'm taking a short 'baawth,' if you guys don't mind." The door to the baawthroom closed all but two inches, and over the sound of trickling water she announced, "Angela, just knock if you need to use the toilet. Joshua, you'll just have to hold it." Then she closed the door, got into the tub, and adjusted the fickle stream of water coming from the hand-held showerhead at the end of a flex hose.

Joshua retreated to a corner and rummaged through his duffel bag for fresh clothes.

Angela was lying on her bed, hands behind her head, staring at the ceiling. "Be honest with me, Joshua," she said, "are you serious about Michelle?" But, before Joshua could respond, Angela was asleep, breathing softly.

AN HOUR LATER, MICHELLE and Joshua, refreshed and wearing clean clothes for the first time in two days, walked out of the Hotel Limmat into the mist. "It's just as well that we left Angela back in the hotel room," Michelle said as they headed down In Gassen. "She must be exhausted. Maybe we can bring back some hot food for her."

They had asked the concierge for his recommendation of a restaurant and received directions to the Borse Halle.

"I just want something light, how about you?" Joshua asked.

Michelle nodded in agreement as they walked along the north side of the Paradeplatz. Observing the fog and mist, she said, "I guess we won't be dining at a sidewalk café tonight."

On the south side of the Paradeplatz, obscured from view by the trees and darkness, a solitary figure wearing a Tyrolean hat and sunglasses walked alone, strolling slowly through the growing fog, heading in the opposite direction, back to the Hotel Limmat.

50

Michelle sipped her latte. "Do you think Angela will be okay? I mean, sleeping alone in the hotel room?"

"She obviously needs the sleep. The maids won't disturb her. That dump doesn't provide maid service." Joshua was busy with a mouthful of Swiss pastry. "This is really good," he said, holding the pastry for Michelle to admire.

Joshua and Michelle had awakened before eight o'clock that morning, dressed, and bought coffee and marvelous Swiss breakfast pastries. They were sitting on one of the wooden benches on the narrow island of green space in the center of the Paradeplatz. Michelle was now wearing the blond hairpiece, and Joshua had taken the gray wig. He cut the ponytail off, but attached the matching beard. They tried hard to appear casual, but their eyes were feverously scanning the entrances to the four banks visible from their bench. It was just before ten o'clock, and the morning air was cool and clear.

"Hey, Joshua, look what's coming down the sidewalk, on your right," Michelle whispered.

A woman with raven-dark hair was heading toward their bench, taking tiny steps in a tight silk skirt and spike heels. The other benches were already filled. "Hello, may I join you?" The woman had an Italian accent.

Michelle scooted over on the bench, closer to Joshua, to make more room for their unexpected visitor. Michelle felt conspicuous in her cheap wig and casually glanced at the woman, noticing the outline of a rose tattoo on her left breast, just above the low-cut neckline of her silk blouse. *People don't get tattoos in order to hide them, and this woman certainly doesn't try to hide hers.*

"Do you live here in Zurich?" Michelle ventured to the woman.

Ms. Rose Tattoo answered slowly, carefully searching for the correct words in English. "No, I am traveling." The scent of her perfume, abundantly applied, filled the air. "It is so wonderful here. The mountains are beautiful. The lakes are so clear and blue. Not like the dirty canals of Venice."

Joshua hadn't stopped searching the bank entrances, but he turned to the woman briefly and asked, "We're on vacation. What do you think of the shops here?"

"Oh, my boyfriend won't let me go shopping yet. He's an American. He told me that a rich uncle died and left him a great deal of money. He's collecting it right now in that bank over there." She pointed in the direction of the Zuricher Zentral Banque.

"Your boyfriend is an American, like us?" Michelle said.

"*Si*, Filipo is American. But he acts worse than an Italiano. He's a good lover, but he's mean to me. It doesn't bother me because he's going to be rich. We're going to be rich. How do you say in America? Filthy rich?"

Michelle and Joshua exchanged glances with raised eyebrows, and swung their gaze toward the Zuricher bank doors. Michelle turned back to the woman. "So, you must be excited. What do you and Filipo plan to do with… uh…his inheritance?"

"I say we should buy a wonderful villa in Amalfi,

where we could see the ocean from our bedroom and make love every morning and go on shopping trips to Roma. But he wants to go to Chile. Why South America, when you could live in beautiful Italy?"

Just then, Joshua's head jerked as he saw two men stepping into the bright sunshine from the Zuricher bank. Both were dressed in suits, and the briefcases they carried looked like they were loaded with bricks. One of the men was putting on his sunglasses, and Joshua immediately recognized Sean. Joshua stood up and said, "Okay, Michelle, let's go. It's *show time*."

Ms. Rose Tattoo was first off the bench, leaping with anticipation, clapping her hands joyfully. "Oh, there's Filipo. I hope he got the money. Have fun on your vacation." She turned to wave goodbye to Michelle and Joshua. Despite her tiny steps, she moved quickly across the grass, her buttocks jostling. *Allegro animato*, Michelle observed.

Joshua removed his disguise and tossed it in a nearby trashcan, but Michelle still wore her wig. They followed Ms. Rose Tattoo across the grass. As they approached Sean and the other man, who they assumed must be Philip, they could hear Philip yelling sharply at the woman, "Get lost, you cheap whore! Here's some money, take a train back to Venice. You're outta my life."

Ms. Rose Tattoo stood frozen, shocked, her mouth gaping open. She began weeping uncontrollably. Her sporadic breathing made the rose expand—blooming in fast-forward. Philip forced a thousand-dollar bill into the top of her blouse.

Sean grabbed Philip's shoulder and shouted, "Come on, we're wasting time. Let's get the hell out of here." They started walking briskly down the sidewalk, brushing Ms. Tattoo aside as they strode past her.

Joshua took Michelle's hand, and the two of them intercepted Sean and Philip, blocking the sidewalk. "What a small world," Joshua said, his arms outstretched in a mocking, exaggerated gesture. "Sean, imagine bumping into you in Zurich, of all places. The city of numbered bank accounts. And you must be Philip," he added. "I'm Joshua, Angela's law partner. You remember Angela, the woman you left behind in Venice?"

"And, I'm Michelle, the owner of PSM. You remember PSM, the company with the reserve accounts?"

As she spoke, Michelle stepped bravely in front of Philip, hands on her hips.

"Yes, how curious and amusing this encounter must be," Sean said. Turning to Michelle, he added, "Really, dear, that wig you wore on the train didn't do you justice. This one is so much more flattering. I missed you at the train station, too bad. Unfortunately, we really don't have time to chitchat right now. So, why don't you be good tourists and get lost?"

"Let's cut the crap, Sean," Joshua said calmly. "We know you guys have something that belongs to Michelle's company. It's time for show-and-tell. What's in the briefcases?"

"Just some consulting proposals." Sean tried to flash his bullshit smile, but it didn't stay put for long.

Philip, however, had no patience for such tactics. "Forget it, Sean, your finesse is not going to work with this jerk." Suddenly, a shiny black snub-nosed pistol appeared in Philip's hand. He pointed it at Michelle.

"Whoops," Michelle squeaked, her voice barely audible, her arms involuntarily folded across her chest. "You weren't supposed to have a gun."

ANGELA WAS CROSSING THE small park toward the Zuricher when she saw Michelle and Joshua. She was upset with herself for oversleeping, and she had dressed hurriedly to meet her friends. Even at a distance, she could tell that the two men talking to Michelle and Joshua were Sean and Philip. The conversation didn't appear to be cordial. Angela moved behind some bushes and reached for her cell phone.

"Christ, Philip," Joshua managed, his eyes fixed on the gun. "What are you going to do? Shoot us right here on the sidewalk, in broad daylight?"

"You're partly right, counselor," Philip said. "Yes, we're going to have to do something with you because you have a loud mouth and you know too much. But, it won't be here. Turn around and start walking, slowly, like nothing unusual is happening. We'll tell you where to go."

Joshua and Michelle exchanged worried glances, turned, and started walking slowly. Joshua remembered the funeral march in the second movement of Beethoven's Third Symphony. Michelle took his hand and squeezed hard. Philip and Sean were a step behind, their leather heels clicking loudly on the brick sidewalk.

"Turn right at the corner," Philip instructed. The foursome marched in close formation, turning into a narrow side street with cars parked on both sides. They walked in silence for half a block, when Philip barked another order. "Okay, stop here."

Joshua glanced around him at the small shops and cafés crowding the sidewalk. Low budget pensiones and apartments occupied the upper levels of the commercial buildings. He wondered if Philip and Sean had rented a room here. He wondered if the end would come, suddenly and unceremoniously, in one of these nameless buildings on a nameless street in Zurich. He looked over at Michelle, who was biting her lower lip, and leaned close to her face and whispered in her ear, "Whatever you do, don't mention that you-know-who is back at the hotel."

He felt the metal barrel of Philip's pistol poking at his left kidney. Joshua held his breath.

Sean stepped into the street and unlocked the doors of a small beige VW Golf. "Get in the back," Philip ordered, pushing the pistol harder into Joshua's kidney. The briefcases were deposited in the trunk.

Sean drove while Philip sat in the passenger seat. Philip turned to face the backseat, his pistol barely visible over the top of the seat, but clearly aimed at Joshua's chest. "Don't forget to buckle up girls and boys," Philip said, waving his pistol at his silent captives, "We wouldn't want you to get hurt right now, would we?" His eyes were hidden behind dark sunglasses.

Crouching behind a row of cars, Angela watched as the VW Golf drove away from the curb and headed down the street.

Sean guided the Golf over the narrow, congested bridge spanning the river. The deep blue of Zurich See was on the right, on the left church spires poked the skyline of the city like Gothic spikes. After jerking and lurching through heavy traffic, the car was soon traversing a winding country road, with dense forests and a purple range of the Alps looming ahead.

"So, tell me," Sean said, "How did you guys figure it out?"

Michelle responded, more angry now than frightened. "We found your little friend in our computer," she said.

"You mean my darling applet. She's my Special Assessment. Isn't she a clever girl? Or would you call her malicious? Clever or malicious? I still can't decide," Sean chuckled and turned around to see the expression on Michelle's face. "PSM was my pilot project, but it was so successful that I'm going to stay here in Europe and market the hell out of the applet. But, how did you trace her to me?"

"You certainly had knowledge of our computer and how to penetrate the great web security system you installed for us. Somehow, you got the code to the alarm system and let yourself in," Michelle said tensely. "But, you forgot to reset the alarm, which was our first clue that someone had broken in."

"Damn. I just knew I forgot something."

Michelle continued. "It wasn't until Joshua saw the new laptop in your apartment that we knew for sure that it was you who planted the applet. Your laptop has a sticker on the back, with the name of the store in Zurich where you bought it."

"Thanks for telling me—I'll be more careful in the future. Anyway, none of that makes any difference now. I've got two and a half million bucks telling me to start a new life somewhere in Europe. I'm not about to go back to the States. And you two can't be a nuisance and stand in the way of my plans."

"One thing I'd like to know, Sean," Joshua said. "How did you and Philip connect in the first place? And, why should you split all five million with Philip? You were the brains. You did all the work. You took all the risks. It doesn't sound like Philip did anything."

"Of course, it was my brains, because I created the applet," Sean said. "But Phil was the mastermind and planner. We first met six months ago in the exhibitor's hall at the national conference. He came up with the scheme to…"

"Shut up, Sean," shouted Philip, waving the gun angrily. Staring at Michelle with eyes ablaze, he suddenly yanked the wig from her head. "This thing really bugs me." Joshua quickly clutched Philip's arm and launched a fist at Philip's head. The blow momentarily stunned Philip, and Joshua swung again, but Philip slipped the punch and wheeled sharply around in the seat and brought his pistol down on Joshua's right temple with the dull thunk. Joshua slumped in his seat, unconscious, his head sliding down onto Michelle's shoulder, blood streaming down his cheek.

Michelle screamed in horror, momentarily terrorized. She cradled Joshua's face and pressed her hand on his forehead, trying to stop the bleeding. She ripped the bottom of her shirt, wadded the material, and held it to his temple. "You killed him, you bastard." She groped for a pulse in his neck. It felt strong.

Philip scowled at Michelle. "You're finally getting the idea. And if you don't shut your face, lady, I'll do the same thing to you."

"There's no need to hurt them," Sean said. "Let's just drop them off somewhere deep in the woods. By the time they get back to town, we'll be long gone."

"Sean," Philip said angrily, "You are such a wimp. These two are the only witnesses who can identify us. We've got to make sure they don't." He turned to look ahead through the windshield and pointed to his right. "See that dirt road up there? Turn onto that road and drive toward those trees up the hill."

In the few seconds while Philip looked forward, Michelle released her seat belt and reached over the top of the front seat, grabbing his face and digging her fingernails deeply into his eyes. Philip howled and dropped the pistol on the floor of the car. He gripped Michelle's wrists tightly and tore them away from his face. He turned in the front seat, got on his knees, and began beating Michelle on the face. She screamed and tried to fend off the blows, but she was no match for his size and strength.

Sean slowed the Golf and turned onto the dirt road. "Phil, stop already. You don't need to beat her like that." He steered the car into a grove of thick trees at the edge of a dense forest. Realizing Philip was serious about murdering them both, Sean made one last attempt to dissuade him. "Using a computer to steal some money is one thing, but murder is way beyond anything I'm willing to do," he told Philip. The car came to a stop, and Sean turned off the engine. "Philip! Let's just leave them here. It'll take hours for them to get back to Zurich. We'll be out of the country by then."

Philip ignored the conversation. He was quickly out of the car, opening Michelle's door and yanking her onto the damp ground. Her face was beaten and bruised, a black eye forming above her left cheek, and she appeared groggy. Both rear doors were open now, and Philip struggled to pull Joshua's limp body out of the back seat while Sean stood and watched, his arms across his chest. "Hey, don't bother to help, Sean." Philip said. Together, they pulled Joshua, feet first, out of the back seat and onto the ground.

While Philip and Sean were preoccupied with Joshua, Michelle edged over to the front passenger door and disappeared below the front seat. Suddenly, realizing she was in the car, Philip ran to the driver's door. He peered into the car just in time to stare into the barrel of his own pistol pointing up at him. Michelle held the gun with both hands, trembling and shaking. Philip was leaning into the car through the driver's door, and Michelle was kneeling on the passenger's seat, barely two feet away. "Back off, slime-ball," she yelled. "I'm not afraid to let you have one between the eyes. But I think I'll practice first with one between your legs. Step away from the car."

His arms resting on the sill of the driver's window, Philip turned his hands up in surrender, and said, "Okay, okay. Don't get jumpy with that thing." He appeared to be stepping back from the car, when suddenly he lunged, grabbed Michelle's wrists, and thrust the gun upward. It blew a hole in the roof of the little Golf with a thunderous blast. Surprised, shocked, and physically overwhelmed, Michelle struggled with Phillip, but he twisted the gun away, ripping her shirt open in the process.

Philip raced around the car to the passenger's side, and pointed the gun at Michelle. "Now, you get out of the car. Walk over there." He pointed with the gun. "To those big trees. Move it."

Michelle started walking, moving slowly to have time to think of a way to save herself.

Suddenly, without the warning of sirens or emergency lights, two white vans marked "Polizei" pulled onto the dirt road. "Halt!" a man's voice with a German accent boomed over a loudspeaker from the police van. "Stop immediately! Drop your weapon, right now!" Soon, police officers had Philip and Sean in handcuffs and secured in the back of the first van.

Angela ran from the van to embrace Michelle. "Thank God we got here in time," Angela said. Michelle was trembling as she hugged Angela.

Philip shouted through the open doors of the van, "Angela, wait! I can explain."

"Believe it or not, Philip," she hissed, "I have only two things I want to say. First, for you, prison may be your higher calling. Which leads to my second point, you're about to gain a whole new appreciation for the meaning of 'pity-fuck.'"

While a pair of uniformed policemen took inventory of the money in the briefcases, the officer in charge approached Michelle. He held out his hands in introduction and apology, "I am Chief Inspector Gelt, and you must be Michelle. It's so good to meet you," he said in slow but precise English. "I regret we could not get to you sooner, *Fraulein*, but it took awhile to locate the car and catch up with you."

Michelle stared blankly at Chief Inspector Gelt for a few seconds before she realized the ordeal was over. Unmindful of her torn shirt, she wrapped her arms tightly around Gelt. "You got here soon enough, that's all that matters," she said into his shoulder. "But, how did you know we were in trouble?"

"We would not have known at all, but your friend here, Angela, called Sheriff Jack Cooper," Gelt said, holding Michelle's shoulders. "Cooper called me immediately on the hot line and asked for our assistance. He is an old friend—we worked together on many big cases when he was with your FBI. Oh, did we have fun together, he and I, but that's another story." Gelt chuckled, reflecting an instance of nostalgia. "So, I said to Coop, 'Of course, how can we help?' He gave me Angela's cell phone number and we called her immediately. Fortunately, Angela knew the make of the car and the license plate number, and we were able to put out a bulletin right away. Then, we picked her up outside the bank and started tracking your car as it crossed the river." The Chief Inspector paused to scratch a spot on his chin. "You and your boyfriend are very lucky. If Angela had not acted so quickly, surely, both of you would be dead."

"You are my lifesaver," Michelle said, giving Gelt another hug. And, turning to Angela, said, "You—you are my hero."

Angela put her arm around Michelle as the two women went to check on Joshua.

"By the way," Gelt said, "Coop sends his best regards. And he told me to let you know that next time you decide to play cops and robbers, he'd like to be informed sooner."

51

Joshua clinked a fork loudly on an empty wine bottle until he had the attention of everyone seated at the table. He picked up his goblet of merlot and stood. "I propose a toast." Joshua waited for the sidebars of chatter to subside. "I want you all to know," he said loudly so that everyone around the table could hear, "That Michelle deserves all the credit for solving this case. Without her insight and dogged determination, two cunning criminal minds would have pulled off an electronic heist of more than five million dollars. The perfect crime—almost."

He was interrupted by noisy clapping. He had let his hair grow longer to cover the scar on his temple.

Continuing, he said, "When we were boarding the plane in St. Louis, I asked Michelle if she was aware of the personal danger that she was getting herself into. She said that the trust of her clients was at stake. She said that her professional reputation was at stake. And then, this woman, who must have ice water in her veins, quoted Shakespeare: 'Courage mounteth with occasion,' she said. Well, I was with her every minute of that occasion, and I can tell you that this woman has an abundance of courage. To Michelle." Joshua raised his glass and chugged half of the glass of wine. All the guests stood at once, raised their glasses and roared with approval. They drank and applauded noisily.

Michelle beamed and blushed as everyone around the table started clapping in rhythm, soon followed by a series of cheerful hoots. The group was seated at a huge table in the private dining room of the Riverway Restaurant—Bruce and Ronnie, Michelle and Joshua, Angela, Ham, Mac and Jenni, Sheriff Cooper and his wife, Emma, even Tank and Bruiser. It was a boisterous celebration.

Michelle stood and held her wine high. Her left eye still had signs of the shiner she got in Zurich. "Thank you, thank you all very much," she said. "Joshua mentioned the word, 'courage.' In my case, courage is simply not knowing when you shouldn't do something. Everyone deserves credit for this team effort. With special affection, I want to thank Angela, whose cool thinking under pressure saved Joshua and me from a rather disastrous ending."

The group applauded as Angela stood and held her arms high in acknowledgment. "Thank you, Michelle, for those kind words," Angela began. "I have five points to make in response," she said, and everyone around the table groaned. "Number one…"

"Angela," Michelle interrupted, "We love you dearly, but please spare us, just this once, from another multi-point presentation." Everyone clapped loudly in appreciation.

"Well, maybe just this once, or twice," Angela smiled.

"Next," Michelle continued, "Joshua gets the award for being unconscious through all the excitement on both occasions. First, here at the Riverway, when we rescued Bruce. And, second, in Zurich. So, tell us, Joshua, how did you manage it?"

Joshua raised his hands for quiet. "I've been accused by a lot of opposing counsel for being hard-headed. Now they know I'm serious about my reputation." There was laughter and more applause around the table. Joshua continued, "A special thanks to our great local Sheriff Jack Cooper, who not only understood the magnitude of the crime that was underway, but makes a great cup of cappuccino. Maybe he'll tell us about his political plans. How about it, Jack?"

Sheriff Cooper stood and acknowledged the applause. "I haven't had as much fun since we captured the Bixby gang in Chicago ten years ago. As far as my own political plans, there are some rumors that I'm being considered for statewide office—attorney general or even governor. But, my dear friends, I want you to know that I have no plans to run. Nor do I have any plan to make plans. My home is right here in Calvin's Creek." More applause, then the clapping gave way to chanting, "Four more years. Four more years!"

Ronnie stood up. "Sheriff, before you sit down, I want you to have this token of our appreciation. This work was made from a fantastic photograph that Michelle took the night you captured the black-suit bad guys." Ronnie handed Cooper a large package wrapped in heavy brown paper. The sheriff carefully removed the paper, revealing an oil painting of himself standing in the doorway of the kitchen, beaming and waving to the crowd of cheering patrons.

Sheriff Cooper stood and admired the painting for a long time, then he turned it around for all to see. "This painting is wonderful, Ronnie. I'm deeply touched and honored." Cooper's eyes were moist. "But, I was just doing my job. I'd like this painting to hang in the foyer of the restaurant, as long as Bruce will have it."

Michelle turned to the sheriff and said, "What do you think will happen to Philip and Sean?"

"Oh, they're being extradited to the States for trial by the district attorney. They broke a few federal laws in their little escapade."

"What exactly was Philip's role?" Ham asked.

"Both Philip and Sean had their eyes on PSM's reserves," Michelle explained, "But with separate schemes at the beginning. Philip was the real mastermind. He wanted to take over key management companies that had strong client portfolios and were strategically situated in growth markets. His problem was that he didn't want to spend any money through acquisitions or mergers. So, at first, he tried to move into the market by wooing particular associations that were upscale, like the Cove, and had plenty of reserve funds.

"Meanwhile," Michelle continued, "Sean had developed the applet and came up with this scheme of electronic transfers of funds. The problem facing Sean was that the virus wasn't capable of intercepting and transferring funds into another account that he could safely access. Once Sean figured out how to program the applet to solve that problem, he had a very powerful virus. Philip and Sean had met, believe it or not, at one of our national conferences last year. They shared their plans, then decided to help each other. Philip figured out the numbered Swiss account and told Sean how to set it up. That's when they became partners. But, actually, Sean did all the work and took all the risks. Philip stayed in the background until the electronic transfers were complete and money could be withdrawn."

"What's going to happen to King Curtis?" Jenni wanted to know.

Joshua paused to sip some wine. "The county prosecuting attorney has completed her investigation, thanks to the disk that Bruce got, and I'm confident a grand jury will investigate Curtis' complex web of bribes, kickbacks, and extortion. They'll trace all his illegal transactions and track where all the money went. And, if our suspicion is correct that Curtis moved money outside the U.S. and back, the Feds will probably get a crack at him for money laundering."

Michelle jabbed her finger in the air, mimicking Curtis with a cigar, and leaned into Joshua's face. Her eyes blazing, and in a raspy stage whisper, she said, "The people of the Cove elected me president, and I intend to serve out my full term. After all, the buck starts here." Then she began drumming her fingers on her stomach. The group celebrated her performance with laughter and more applause.

"It didn't take long for the owners at the Cove to topple King Curtis from his throne," Bruce said. "They held a special election to remove him last week, and ninety-five percent of the owners turned out. Many of them even stood in line for an hour to cast their votes. The result was that the entire board was tossed out, and a new group of reformers was elected. The first act by the new board was to offer my old job back as concierge, which I've declined in order to stay here. Also, the auditors are already reviewing the books."

"I've saved the best part for last," Joshua announced. "I have two envelopes, and I'd like Bruce and Michelle to join me here for the presentation." Bruce and Michelle stood and joined Joshua at the head of the table, puzzlement on both their faces. Joshua handed each of them an envelope, and continued, "PSM's insurer was enormously grateful that they recovered almost all of the stolen funds, with the exception of some seventy thousand dollars stolen in turn by a devious woman named Anna, who was sly enough to disappear. The insurer has agreed to pay a reward of ten percent of the amount recovered, which will be divided equally between Bruce and Michelle."

Everybody rose and applauded boisterously. When they finally stopped, Michelle said, "This is wonderful! I can tell you two things I'd like to do with this check that will solve big problems in my life. First, we'll buy an entire new computer system for PSM. Second, I'm going to sell my condo. I'm finished with condo living." Everyone laughed and cheered.

It was Bruce's turn. Ronnie joined him, and he hugged her for a moment. "Like Michelle, I will put these funds to good use also, first, by buying a token of my love and appreciation for a great friend and accomplished artist, Veronica Pulaski. An engagement ring." Ronnie jumped into Bruce's arms as the women cried and everyone applauded.

"And, second," Bruce yelled over the noise, "The Riverway will soon be under new ownership." More applause erupted, louder yet, and everyone stood and cheered for Bruce.

When finally the cheering had stopped and all were seated, Joshua stood up. He was hoarse. "Enjoy your dinner and wine, everybody. And all our thanks to Bruce and Ronnie for this wonderful banquet and for the complimentary rooms they provided for us tonight."

The food and wine were exquisite and plentiful. It was an odd assembly of people, bound together by the bullying shadow of Curtis the King of the Cove and the bizarre Case of the Special Assessment. Was the little applet clever or malicious?

They ate and drank long into the night, revisiting highlights of the case, swapping horror stories, and embellishing their individual roles. When everyone was too exhausted to continue, they hugged, and slowly drifted back to their rooms.

Michelle and Joshua left the restaurant and strolled down the path to the creek. They walked out on a gravel bar and watched the moonlight dancing on the ripples.

Joshua broke the silence. "You know, I think that tonight constitutes a date."

"Does not," Michelle said, a twinkle in her eye.

The lights of the lodge soon beckoned them back up the hill.

MARVIN J. NODIFF is a Missouri attorney, concentrating his practice in community association law. He is also an Adjunct Professor of Law at St. Louis University. Prior to law practice, Nodiff participated in several statewide and local political campaigns and worked in state government for eight years.

Growing up in Arizona, he earned a Bachelor's Degree at Arizona State University, followed by a Master's Degree at the University of Missouri—Columbia in history and political science. His juris doctor degree is from St. Louis University School of Law.

Nodiff, an amateur gourmet cook and photographer, lives in St. Louis with his wife, stepdaughter, and two Golden Retrievers.

Special Assessment is his first novel.